THEY LIVED AND LOVED
THE AMERICAN DREAM

BESSIE—She rose from the stage of the Yiddish theater to play hostess to New York's political and social elite. S̶h̶e̶ ... led many hearts, but ...

RYAN—The ... gentle touch ... violence prot ... lives of her th ...

NICK—His was a world of gambling, beautiful women, and constant danger. He owed Ryan his life—and hated him for owning his sister's soul.

JAKE—The lush sensuality of Key West lured him south, yet still he lived within Ryan's far-reaching empire. Bootlegging and the jaded passions of the rich were his secret prison.

MAX—He would become the golden cowboy of Hollywood, symbol of impossible success, trapped in a harsh marriage to a movie legend, longing for an impossible love.

BUT THEY WOULD PAY THE
PRICE FOR GLORY!

THE
WINE
AND THE
MUSIC

David A. Kaufelt

A DELL BOOK

Published by
Dell Publishing Co., Inc.
1 Dag Hammarskjold Plaza
New York, New York 10017

Dell ® TM 681510, Dell Publishing Co., Inc.

ISBN: 0-440-19376-1

Reprinted by arrangement with Delacorte Press
Printed in the United States of America
First Dell printing—August 1982

PROLOGUE

"Happy birthday, Bessie."

Hannah took her sleepy-eyed child from the crude bed and held her tightly.

"Why are you crying, Mama?" Bessie asked.

"Because I'm so happy, my darling."

Bessie hadn't really had to ask. Instinctively she knew why her mother's happy tears were filling her somber, dark blue eyes. They were going "home" for the day, back to the shtetl where Bessie's mother had been born, where Bessie's mother felt the comfort, the luxury, of being among her own kind.

As the sun began to fill the one-room farmhouse with its golden summer light, the young mother carefully dressed her child in a skirt and a blouse that had been made from the same rough material as her own. Though it promised to be an especially hot day, Hannah tied a babushka around her daughter's irrepressibly curly hair.

Bessie's hair was bright red, the color of poppies in full bloom. Hannah was of two minds about it. She didn't know whether to be proud of that extraordinary head of red curls or embarrassed by it. It always caused so much attention.

After a moment she wiped the tears from her eyes, kissed Bessie, held her firm little body tightly against her own, and then, together, they walked out of the farmhouse to the horse-drawn cart where her husband was waiting.

Hannah handed Bessie up to him as if the child were a precious, breakable, one-of-a-kind object, and he received her in kind. Abraham kissed Bessie roughly, his dark beard tickling her chin.

"*Mazel tov,* Bessie," he said as Hannah got up onto the cart.

"Speak Polish," his wife told him.

"It's a beautiful day for a birthday," Abraham continued in Yiddish. He didn't care what the neighbors thought, not on such a holiday of a day.

Bessie lay her curly head against her father's strong arm and placed her chubby hand into her mother's thin, tense one. Today, it had been made clear—in fact, promised for months—was to be her day. She had already received the doll which she privately despised. Its blond hair was so thin and straight. But she was looking forward to the celebration.

Living in western Poland in a Christian village, there were, by necessity, few celebrations. The villagers were not unkind. The tortures that Hannah's family had predicted—as a result of their own experiences in the "outside" world—had never materialized. They had been stories, Hannah concluded, meant to frighten her, meant to keep her inside the shtetl gates.

But not unlike the Jews in the shtetl, the Christians in the village distrusted the unfamiliar. Abraham, when he and Hannah moved to the village, decided that there was no need to emphasize his peoples' differences. The observance of religious holidays was conducted quietly behind the closed doors of their farmhouse or spent twenty miles away in the shtetl where he and Hannah had been born.

Life in the shtetl was more exciting than life in the sleepy village, Bessie thought. She was always happy to go to the shtetl, to pass through its enormous wooden gates onto the narrow main street. It was always so noisy. People were laughing and shouting and crying and fighting. Animals and children and vendors selling goods of every description were all mixed up together in a great conflagration of life.

By her mother's choice and her happy concurrence they were celebrating her fifth birthday in the shtetl, with the bewildering number of relatives her mother missed so terribly.

By a lucky chance Bessie's birthday fell on a shtetl holiday. There was to be feasting and dancing all through the day and, most wonderful, a unique event: a group of traveling singers, proud Jews from across the German border, were to give a concert in the afternoon.

From the moment they passed through the wooden gates, while her father was seeing to his cart and horse, Bessie was passed from one admiring relative to another. "That hair," Hannah's mother, a large woman who smelled of cloves and onion, kept saying. "Did you ever see such hair?"

"The face," her other grandmother, birdlike in a sateen dress, sang out in her small voice. "Such a face. A face for the angels."

Even the men, who gathered together around the

rough, outdoor table situated close to the well, took time from their religious and political arguments to notice Bessie. Pushing their skullcaps to the back of their heads, they wished her happy birthday and good luck as they caressed her roughly, their beards scratching her face. "We know where she got her blue eyes, Abraham," Bessie's grandfather teased as the wives brought food—challah and whitefish and red wine—to the table. "But from whence cometh those red curls?"

All through the day, while she sat on her grandfather's lap at the long table, while she played with her younger cousins, while her grandmothers fussed over her, she was aware of the stranger.

He and the other singers had arrived shortly after Bessie and her parents. She was shocked to see that he was smooth-shaven, that neither he nor his friends wore skullcaps or long black coats, that they stayed by themselves under the old oak tree on the far side of the well. To her elders the young singers from Germany seemed—if not contemptuous of the shtetl and its people—certainly superior and removed.

To Bessie the young men from Germany were like the angels in her father's only book, an illustrated Bible. Out of the corner of her eye she watched them as they lay on the grass, smoking thin cigars, eating little, laughing among themselves. They were so much younger than the men from the shtetl; so much freer.

And there was that one among them whose every move Bessie followed. He had sand-colored hair and eyebrows and lashes so light he appeared not to have any. Accustomed to the hirsute faces of her father and her male relatives, Bessie felt that this young singer from Germany had the cleanest, most open face she had ever seen.

In later years one special moment was to stand out clearly from that dim but cherished day. It occurred when they had all gathered in the basement of the oldest building in the shtetl, the wooden synagogue, and had grown suddenly quiet. The lead singer—the beautiful man with the sand-colored hair—stood up to sing by himself.

He walked among them as he sang in his clear, sweet voice a song Bessie already knew. It was her mother's favorite, *"Rozhinkes Mit Mandlen,"* "Raisins and Almonds." He was standing in front of the bench where Bessie and her mother sat when he reached the final chorus. Encouraging everyone in the basement to sing with him, he bent down and took Bessie up in his strong arms. He hoisted her up on his shoulders and marched around the room, singing. Everyone stood up to watch them, to sing, to experience the particular joy the singer had brought with him. Even more than his voice it was his presence which cut through the fetid atmosphere in that makeshift auditorium, promising everyone there a fresh and full future.

At the end of the song he set Bessie down and looked at her. "Why are you crying, little mama?" he asked, putting his hands on her shoulders, kissing her cheek.

"Because I'm so happy, my darling," Bessie answered, just as she had heard her mother answer her that morning. He laughed, kissed her again, and gave her his beautiful white handkerchief to wipe her tears.

Immediately after, Bessie's father gathered her and her mother up and rushed them to the cart. The shtetl gates were closing at dusk and wouldn't be opened until the following morning.

On the long way home both Abraham and Bessie could feel Hannah's sadness. She hated to leave her home. Abraham put his arm around his wife and held her, telling her again that if they had stayed in the shtetl, if they had not taken the chance, the risk of leaving, they would have had a terrible life. "In the village, at least, we have our own house; we eat well, we have privacy and cleanliness."

She agreed but he knew she already missed her family. She was twenty-one, a girl herself. To take her mind from the shtetl, he asked her if she had enjoyed the singing. She replied that she had. "Especially the lead singer, the one who took Bessie up in his arms. Such a handsome man."

"A beautiful voice," Abraham admitted. "Like Cantor Habbastatter."

"He looked," Hannah said, "like a Yankee."

It was not the first time Bessie had heard the word "Yankee." Cousins and friends of cousins often turned up at the farmhouse, passing through on their way to Germany and then to that promised land, America, where the Yankees lived.

As they rode home in their cart, Bessie resolved to grow up to be a singer, to marry her Yankee, to live with him in America.

* * *

A month after that memorable fifth birthday, during the harvest when Abraham was especially busy, supplying horses for the villagers, another cousin arrived.

"Why do we have so many cousins?" Bessie asked her mother as she watched the newcomer unpack her traveling bag, usurp Bessie's bed.

"All Jews are cousins," Hannah said.

"Yes, and all men are brothers," Mildred Meyerwitz returned dryly. She was a fifty-year-old spinster who had earned her living working as a seamstress for a rich Jewish family in Krakow. Having saved all of her earnings, she was on her way to America.

"I'm a little old to start a new life in a new country," she admitted. "But God knows, it can't be any worse there."

After a day and a night under her cousin's roof, as she watched Bessie sweep the dirt floor of the single room and then carefully spread red sand across it to make it suitable for her father's last meal of the day, Mildred cleared her throat and spat delicately into a lace handkerchief.

She had important news, she announced when Abraham sat down at the small table where Hannah had placed the heavy, aromatic stew she had made. "I wanted to spare you, believe me; but in my heart I knew I would have to tell you. For your own sake."

The Cossacks, she said, were riding across Poland, pressing into service Jewish children for yet another of the tsar's wars.

"The Cossacks would never come this far," Abraham said, pushing his plate away, looking up at his wife. "Never!"

"That's what you'd like to think," Mildred said, "but I'm telling you different." Once again she spat into her finely embroidered handkerchief. Then she gave Abraham and Hannah a long account, filled with graphic details, of Bessie's future if the Cossacks were to get hold of her.

"And there's no doubt that they will," she said. "Your villagers may not be so anti-Semitic now, while you're selling them horses. But wait. They're gentiles, aren't they? They're Polish, aren't they? Do you think they'd risk the wrath of the Cossacks by denying them one small Jewish child?"

Early the following morning, while it was still dark, Bessie's mother once again dressed her in the skirt and blouse that had been made from the same material as her own. Again she fussed with the child's babushka. But instead of securing it over the red curls, she pulled it away and buried her head in the child's sweet-smelling hair, sobbing uncontrollably.

Though she didn't know why, Bessie, too, began to cry. Her father came into the house with a strange new expression on his face. He took Bessie from her mother and carried her to the cart where Mildred and her lace handkerchief were waiting.

As the cart drove off, Bessie's mother came to the door of the little house and cried out, "No, wait, Abraham. Wait!" She ran after them for some way, for once not caring what the gentile neighbors thought. But the horses were young and strong, and she was soon left behind.

Long after Hannah was lost from sight, Bessie was still looking back. She wondered why her mother had acted so strangely, why she had made Bessie wear her special-occasion clothes, why she felt so frightened. She looked up at Mildred who wore a tight smile on her pale face. And then she looked up at her silent father who held the reins of the horses with a too firm grip.

He took Bessie and Mildred Meyerwitz across the border and into Germany where the train would pick them up and carry them to Antwerp where a ship was waiting to take them to America. He explained this carefully to the child.

"And you and Mama?" Bessie asked.

He pulled her to him so that his beard rubbed against her face and then he kissed her several times. He didn't leave the cart. He sat in it as Bessie and Mildred boarded the train. From his seat he was on a level with them. Through the train's window he watched Mildred remove the babushka from Bessie's head, exposing that mass of red curly hair. Mildred folded the square of cloth and placed it carefully in her traveling bag without returning his gaze.

The train began to move, the horses shied backward. Bessie's last view of her father was another clear memory she was to carry with her and periodically take out and examine for the rest of her life. He had had tears in his eyes. Up until that moment Bessie hadn't known that men could cry.

BOOK ONE

DAWN

CHAPTER 1

Mildred Meyerwitz's greatest fear was that she wouldn't pass the physical examination given all immigrants at Ellis Island, that she would be sent back to Europe, to Poland, to more years of drudgery. Holding her head high, she willed herself not to cough as the doctor thumped her chest and her back and nodded, going on to the next woman in line. After that ordeal, after an Irish official shortened her last name to Meyer, she found herself on the crowded, terrible-smelling streets of New York's Lower East Side, Bessie's hand in hers, following the broad back of yet another cousin, Mookie Goldstein.

Mookie, a short, impatient man, took them to a room on the fifth floor of a yellow brick tenement where several mattresses lay rolled up in a corner. Three other women, recent arrivals, slept there, too. Mildred coughed. She couldn't help it. The terrible odor in that room. Mookie looked at Mildred and then at her handkerchief.

"One sure thing," he said. "You ain't working in my restaurant. That's all I need, a lunger in my kitchen." He owned Goldstein's Vegetarian Kosher Dairy Restaurant, located on the corner of East

Broadway and Clinton Street. It catered to those newly arrived immigrants who could afford to dine out and to the new aristocracy of the immigrant community, the members of the Yiddish theater. It had been understood, when he agreed to sponsor her, that Mildred would work there.

"You sew, right?" Mookie asked, and Mildred, frightened and ill, said yes, she sewed.

"That's all right then. You rest today. Tomorrow you ask somebody to tell you where this is and you ask for Mr. Schneeweiss." He handed her a note with an address and a name on it. "This guy's got a heart. He'll employ anybody."

"And the child?" Mildred asked.

"Bring her around in a couple of years. Right now I can't use her."

"What does she do when I'm at work?"

"What do I know? Let her sit here. She's got a roof over her head, don't she?"

For the first four days Bessie stayed in the evil-smelling room and waited for Mildred to come home from the factory, carrying tins of cabbage soup she had bought en route, along with the round onion bread they sold at the bakery on Rivington Street. Bessie scarcely knew who the women who slept in the room with them were. They got up so early in the morning and returned so late at night, she wasn't certain she would recognize any of them if they met in the daytime.

On the fifth day, intolerably bored and not a little cold—it was unseasonably cool for early October—Bessie opened the door which led to the passageway and the dark, awful bathroom and looked down the iron steps. There was a small black cat at the bottom of the steps. Carefully she made her way down to it. The cat darted away as soon as she approached, going out through the open doors onto the street. Bessie followed.

The cat waited on the curb, maliciously. As Bessie reached for him, he ran into the street. Again she followed just as a red ice van was turning into Essex Street. Its rear wheel struck her and sent her flying up against the curb. Before she lost consciousness, she saw a woman in a blue and white nurse's uniform bend down to help her.

"The child can't stay in a room all day waiting for you to come home, Miss Meyer. It's true she wasn't hurt this time but . . ." The woman was large and handsome and, though she spoke Yiddish, she wasn't like any other woman Bessie had ever seen before.

Mildred stood in the corner of the paneled room and wrung her handkerchief, trying not to cough.

"And you, my dear, should be under a doctor's care."

"There's nothing wrong with me," Mildred snapped.

"There is but I shan't pursue it. I want you to bring the child here to the Settlement early each morning on your way to work. I'll see to it that she gets some sort of schooling and keeps out of the way of ice vans. You can pick her up each evening after work. She'll have three healthful meals a day and she'll be able to play in our little yard with other neighborhood children. Lord knows what will happen to her if left to her own devices all day long.

Good evening, Miss Meyer. I expect to see you here
bright and early in the morning."

For the next three years, as Mildred's handker-
chiefs became increasingly threadbare, continually
dotted with blood, Bessie spent six days a week at the
Henry Street Settlement, with Lillian Wald and the
other members of the Visiting Nurse Service that Miss
Wald had founded. She learned to speak English; she
learned about the comradely love that existed between Miss Wald and her neighbors and her staff;
and she learned to make herself useful around the
Settlement House, taking messages, running errands.

Not long after her eighth birthday, when it was
deemed time for Bessie to enroll in public school, her
English finally sufficient, Bessie woke up one day to
find that the other three women had left for their
jobs, leaving their rolled mattresses behind, but that
Mildred was still in bed.

Bessie gingerly approached Mildred. She was still a
little frightened of her. She wasn't at all certain why.
She didn't see very much of Mildred during the week
and on Sundays, when it wasn't too cold and Mildred
wasn't too tired, they would go down to Battery Park
and watch the boats. She would hold on to Bessie
with one hand and her handkerchief with the other.

On that morning in August, when it was already
over eighty degrees in that room, Mildred's hand felt
as cold as a piece of ice. There was blood on the
front of the thin cotton nightgown Mildred had worn
no matter what the season and her skin was as gray as
a winter's sky.

Bessie sat on the edge of the bed, holding Mildred's

cold hand until Miss Wald, worried about her little redheaded friend, came into the room and found her there. She took the child in her arms, and, putting a sheet over Mildred, carried Bessie from the room.

"It was a judgment," Mookie Goldstein said as Mildred's coffin was being lowered into the ground of the B'nai Israel Cemetery in Long Island City. He was paying for what he called "the whole shebang." He had a strong sense, he said, of family. He had agreed to take the redheaded kid to live with him. Miss Wald had attempted to get him to promise to allow Bessie to go to school, but charity, as even she knew, had to end someplace and it was enough that he was taking the kid in. She was going to have to work just like everyone else.

"Why a judgment?" his dim wife, Rifka, asked as soon as the little rabbi finished the Mourner's Kaddish.

"Because," Mookie said, pulling at his short, thick nose impatiently, looking down at Bessie who stood next to him, her curls an audacious defiance of the cemetery's dark atmosphere, "there were no Cossacks riding across Poland. Mildred wanted a kid and she saw Bessie and she concocted that story to get her."

"How do you know so much, big shot?" Rifka asked.

"Because at Pesach, when Mildred had an extra glass of wine . . ."

". . . she wasn't the only one . . ."

". . . she told me the whole story, the *gonsah magillah*. Abraham and Hannah believed her. It was a terrible thing to do but Mildred didn't get much joy from it. Poor bitch."

"So now," Rifka said, looking impatiently at Bessie who was standing over the open grave, her red curls blowing in the wind, "you can tell Abraham and Hannah in the twice yearly letter you get Schwartz to write for you that they can have their kid back."

"Yeah? And who's going to pay her fare? You and your brother, Morris?"

There were two storage closets in the long, narrow apartment over the restaurant in which the Goldsteins lived. Bessie slept on a mattress crammed into one of them. "Not so many people in this country have their own room," Mookie Goldstein told her when he showed it to her. "You should be thankful."

Moishe Katz, still another Goldstein connection who worked as the restaurant cashier, was assigned the other closet.

In the outer room Mookie and Rifka slept and noisily made love.

There was to be no further talk of school, no afternoons spent in the little yard behind the Settlement House on Henry Street. Bessie worked fifteen-hour days, beginning at five in the morning with the making of the oatmeal, ending at eight in the evening with the preparation of the following day's "strictly fresh" vegetable salads.

But she liked the restaurant. Not the kitchen where she worked but the dining rooms where she wasn't allowed. There were two. One was narrow with a long, chrome cafeteria and a glass case behind which sat Moishe Katz and his cash register. The second dining room was far more grand, with a hand-painted mural of an Anglicized, blond-haired Christopher Columbus discovering America. As often as she could, Bessie would stand by the swinging doors, peering through the round windows at the "swells" who dined in the waitered, chandeliered splendor of the main dining room. The cook, a fat, friendly man, would occasionally stand with her, pointing out celebrities from the Jewish theater.

And one Sunday night Moishe Katz was handed two tickets to the theater by one of those celebrities. He asked Mookie if he might not take Bessie with him and Mookie said yes, go already.

Seven years after Bessie arrived in America, she made her first excursion to Second Avenue where the Yiddish theater presented operettas in five acts and nine tableaux and musical dramas based on the classics.

Awed by the grandeur of the Roumania Opera House, Bessie silently followed Moishe up the marble stairs to the fifth balcony where, enthralled, she watched Boris Thomashefsky play a Yiddish Hamlet. In the middle of his soliloquy he managed to work in the song: *"A Brevele der Mama,"* "A Letter from Mama." Along with everyone else in the theater Bessie broke into tears as she listened to the poignant words of that song as sung by that handsome Yiddish Hamlet.

All the way home Bessie was uncharacteristically silent. "What's the matter with you?" Moishe Katz wanted to know.

"Shut up," she told him. She was savoring every moment of the evening and she wasn't going to allow Moishe Katz, with his filthy jokes, to ruin it for her.

From that moment on she saved every penny she could get her hands on and twice a month she would manage to get to either the Roumania or the Oriental. As for so many other newly arrived Americans, the Yiddish theater was the only unalloyed joy in her life.

Her favorite actress was Jenny Kohen because no matter what part she played, she invariably broke Bessie's heart. Thomashefsky, of course, was her favorite actor. Whether he was a grand duke or a low rabbi, he always managed to get in *"A Brevele der Mama."* It never failed to make her cry.

When Bessie was thirteen and Rifka Goldstein was upstairs being delivered of her long-awaited first child, Mookie handed Bessie a stack of menus and told her she was the hostess for the night. "Until Rifka gets on her feet again. Then you go back to the kitchen."

The hostess's job was to escort those guests who chose to bypass the cafeteria counter and introduce them to the regular dining room, seating them at one of the round, tablecloth-covered tables, placing a menu in the hands of each.

"Do I get a raise?" Bessie found herself asking.

"You get what you always get," Mookie told her. "Food and a roof over your head."

"I don't have a dress good enough to wear," she told him, holding out the soiled skirt she wore. All of her clothes, plain pinafores and blouses, came second-hand from the Settlement.

"Go put on one of Rifka's dresses already and stop bothering me." He placed his wide, thick hand firmly on her behind and left it there for a moment. It occurred to Mookie, and not for the first time, that little Bessie's body would more than fill his wife's dresses.

While Rifka lay sleeping, Bessie quietly went to the wardrobe and removed the one dress of Rifka's she had long coveted. It was a thick brocade, almost the exact shade of red of her hair. She took it down to the kitchen and put it on, tucking the bodice under, touching her curls and pinching her cheeks as she tried to catch her reflection in the bottom of one of the huge copper pans hanging above her.

Then she forced herself to walk through the swinging kitchen doors into the restaurant where she tried, as nonchalantly as possible, to assume her part at the door. Moishe Katz, a green visor on his forehead, his fingers on the cash register, turned pale and then pink.

"You look like an actress," he said, awed. But Bessie had already turned to greet her first guests.

After one week as the hostess she asked Mookie how she was doing. "You talk too much," he told her. After two weeks, when Rifka allowed as how she was ready to "get back into harness," Mookie looked away and said maybe she had better stay upstairs and take care of baby Esther.

"You let her take my best dress and she looks like something off the street," Rifka complained. "And I'm not even saying which street."

"The men like her, Rifka."

"And you don't, Mookie Goldstein?"

That night Bessie heard the door of her closet open. She knew who it was. Mookie had been especially attentive all evening, coming back to the restaurant after an evening of drinking schnapps at the Knights of Pythias lodge. He had patted her behind with increasing ardor, forcing himself up against her whenever they happened to be passing one another in the narrow aisles of the restaurant.

She was frightened. She knew that she had to be especially careful, that if Rifka woke, she would be blamed, forced out of the apartment, and out of her job. She desperately didn't want to have to work at a cigarette factory on Union Square. She liked being the hostess at Goldstein's Vegetarian Kosher Dairy Restaurant. When she was in her red brocaded dress, the orange menus under her arm, leading patrons to their tables, she felt as if she were on stage.

The door closed, Mookie lay down next to her and took her in his short thick arms. He smelled of whiskey and sour cream. As he reached for her breast, she jerked her knee up into his crotch. He pulled back and opened his mouth to shout but she put her hand over it and held it there until the pain subsided. After what seemed a long time, he managed to stand up and get himself out of the storage closet.

Bessie lay back on the mattress. She was still frightened. Frightened that Mookie might come back; frightened that in the morning he would fire her. I won't sleep with him, she said to herself. I won't. I'm waiting for my Yankee.

Mookie ignored her in the morning and was curt with her for several days but he wasn't a malicious man. He told himself he couldn't fire a genuine asset to this business because of one well-placed knee.

On a cold evening in the early fall three stars from

the Oriental Theater entered the restaurant with their stage manager, a short, intense man named Rudolph Zuckerman.

"Is that *the* Jenny Kohen?" Bessie asked him after the actors were seated and Zuckerman was on his way downstairs to the washroom.

"Yeah."

"I love her with all my heart and soul."

"If you love her so much, go give the waiter a nudge. She's waiting for her herring salad."

On the way back to his table, Zuckerman stopped and looked into Bessie's dark blue eyes and then down into her throbbing bosom. He handed her a ticket to *Dos Yidishe Harts* which was then playing at the Oriental. It starred, along with Jenny Kohen, David Kessler and Malvina Lobel. "So maybe you'll come backstage afterward, Red, and I'll introduce you around."

The following evening, having talked Moishe Katz into taking her place, she went to the Oriental, still wearing the red brocade dress. After the performance, her eyes filled with tears from the poignancy of Jenny Kohen's performance, she fought her way backstage. Zuckerman was standing just inside the stage door, balancing himself on his heels, his hands on his hips, his hat far back on the top of his head.

"Nice to see you, Red, but I got too many headaches not to mention heartburn to kibitz tonight. We'r opening Thursday with *Der Yidisher General* and I still need six singer-dancers for the chorus."

"I sing and dance," Bessie lied.

"In Yiddish?"

"In Yiddish."

"Yeah?"

"Yeah."

"How old are you, Red?"

"Eighteen."

"No, you're not." He looked at her for a moment. "But I'm going to buy it, heaven help me."

After her first tryout it was clear to Zuckerman that the red-headed kid might, with coaching, get away with a song but it was going to take more than three days to turn her into a dancer.

She begged him to let her stay. "Even way far back in the chorus."

He put her in the final tableaux. The entire cast was in it, costumed in red, white, and blue Uncle Sam suits. At a signal from Zuckerman the band vamped a few bars, the trap door in the center of the stage opened, and Bessie rose out of it. Sick and scared, and, at the same time, her heart bursting with pride, she continued to rise as the band went into "The Star-Spangled Banner" and the audience stood up and sang along with the cast. Wearing the august robes of the Statue of Liberty, a tiara with sixteen burning candles encircling her flame-red hair, Bessie stopped rising some sixteen feet above the stage, looked down at the cast and then out at the audience singing, and promptly burst into tears. She was happy. The audience sang louder.

By the time she was sixteen, she had graduated to "supporting soubrette" and was featured on the posters as Madam Bessie Meyer. She was most successful in the innocent pieces of Goldfaden and Gordin, playing the ingenue with such actors as Jacob Adler

and David Kessler, Bertha Kalisch and Kenni Lip-
stzen. Occasionally she earned fifty dollars a month,
more often forty-five.

She had left the Goldsteins' apartment and restaurant and was living in a room in the Essex, a hotel on
Second Avenue near Fourteenth Street where many
of the Yiddish theater actors boarded. It was a dark
room, furnished with heavy mahogany pieces, and the
bathroom was at the far end of the hall. It cost fifteen
dollars a month. But it was the first room with a window Bessie had ever had to herself and she would
spend hours in it, for the sole purpose of enjoying the
luxury of being alone.

Moishe Katz made it a point to see every play in
which she appeared. Occasionally she would go
downtown with him after a performance to have a
late dinner with Mookie and Rifka and their child,
Esther. Twice a year Mookie received a letter, painstakingly written in Yiddish, from her parents. Her
mother had had three more children, brothers she
would never see. At the end of each letter there was
always a reminder to send love and regards to Bessie.
It was clear she had become as vague to them as they
had become to her.

"You ever going to marry me?" Moishe asked as he
walked her back uptown after one such dinner and
letter reading at the restaurant.

"I'm never even going to get engaged to you."

"Don't tell me you're not lonesome, Bessie."

"I have a feeling I'd be more lonesome married to
you."

"So go ahead, stay a prisoner all your life. Save
yourself to be a great actress."

"I'll never be great, Moishe. I haven't got it in me. I can sing loud and I can dance hard but I'm no actress. Not like Jenny. She can wring their hearts with a word. I can't get a tear with a fifteen-minute soliloquy. I wish to hell I could. I'm just not tragic enough."

"So marry me."

"Say that one more time, fat boy, and I'll knock your block off." She put her arm through his to soften the words but her blue eyes were looking straight ahead, uptown. "I'm fighting tooth and nail to get myself out of the Lower East Side, Moishe—not to sign a lifetime contract with it."

CHAPTER 2

She ran up Second Avenue as fast as she could, forcing her way through the pre-theater crowds, the strollers, the street entrepreneurs selling hot sweet potatoes and jellied apples. Many stopped and followed the girl with their eyes, her red hair and supple body making them feel young again, if just for the moment.

Bessie ignored the sidewalk johnnies and their whistles. She was late. Lateness was the one sin Zuckerman never forgave. She was appearing as the second soubrette in that Goldfaden war-horse, *The Sorceress,* at the Grand, and Zuckerman, she knew, was perfectly capable of docking her pay for a week.

But she had a very good excuse. It was her birthday, her seventeenth birthday. She had celebrated it by spending the afternoon at the Henry Street Settlement with Miss Wald—though she never did get to tell Miss Wald that it was her birthday.

She had meant to but the moment she had stepped into the old, beautiful brick house, she found Miss Wald examining an eight-year-old boy whose arms and legs were covered with hideous bruises.

"Bessie, you couldn't have come at a better time.

Take Senator Lewis on a tour of the neighborhood. He wants to make a report in Washington. Agnes, you and Mary take care of the boy." She put on her bonnet and blue cape and marched off to confront the child's parents. The two nurses took the child upstairs to the infirmary and Bessie was left alone with the narrow-shouldered, bespectacled young man who seemed more like a teacher than a senator. "And take him on the A route," Miss Wald, putting her head back in the door, shouted.

The A route was reserved, usually, for young ladies of good families who came downtown to volunteer their services in helping the poor. If they returned after being taken on a tour of the A route, Miss Wald would allow them to work at the Settlement. Most of them never came back.

Bessie dutifully led the young senator up filthy flights of urine-smelling tenement stairs where it wasn't odd to find three families living in one room with the only toilet backed up. The rats and other vermin didn't bother to move out of their way. She led him down into steaming basements where girls sewed under single lightbulbs and into factory lofts where the windows were black with grime and young boys with old faces rolled cigarettes for twelve hours on end. She took him to a brothel where young women with bad teeth and filthy dresses offered him their services. She took him down to the concrete banks of the East River where the paper boys lived without family or shelter or any sort of human warmth except for what they could get from one another. She took him through filthy soup kitchens and long, narrow saloons where out-of-work men sat at tables holding on to empty beer glasses, their eyes staring off into space.

She had given him the A route.

"You've been very kind," the young senator said when she had brought him back to 265 Henry Street where Miss Wald was waiting for him in the Settlement's dining room. "Though I doubt very much if I shall be able to eat my dinner."

"You might tell them all in Washington what you've seen," Bessie said. "And then all the senators can contribute the price of their dinners to the Settlement."

"Perhaps you should come to Washington," Senator Lewis said, "and tell them yourself."

And then Miss Wald had opened the door and Bessie had looked behind her to the big clock and realized how very late she was. She said good-bye to Miss Wald and to the senator and then started to run.

It had been an odd but somehow satisfactory way to spend her birthday. She always felt at home at Henry Street, with Miss Wald, and the senator had been such a nice, polite man. She wished she hadn't been quite so outspoken.

She turned up the dark alley which led to the stage door, knowing Zuckerman would be waiting for her, tapping his tiny black patent leather shoe, and then she lost her balance and stumbled, nearly falling. She looked down. In the late evening summer light she found that she had tripped over a body. It was a young man, dressed expensively but conservatively in a black suit and tie, and a white shirt with a stiff collar.

"My Yankee," Bessie said aloud and then, because

he groaned, tried to put the idea away. But he had sand-colored hair and eyebrows and lashes so light they appeared not to exist. Her thoughts returned to the dim memory of the German Jew who had taken her up in his arms on her fifth birthday, who had sung *"Rozhinkes Mit Mandlen"* to her.

He groaned again and she ran up the iron stage door steps to call Rudolph Zuckerman for help. She hoped that the man stretched out in the alley wasn't dead.

He wasn't. Zuckerman helped Bessie get him up and into her tiny dressing room.

"Why don't you leave it alone, Red?" Zuckerman asked, pausing for breath.

"Because I have a heart, you selfish bastard, and I wouldn't leave a man to die in an alley, that's why, you rotten son of a . . ." Anger had made her brave with Zuckerman.

"You'd better get your *tuchas* out on that stage, Red, or *you'll* be out in the alley."

"Get him a doctor."

"All right already."

By the end of the second act Ryan was sitting up. By the end of the fourth act, there being no doctor available, he was drinking a whiskey Zuckerman had secured for him. By the end of the fifth and final act he was able to answer questions.

Bessie changed behind a screen while she questioned him. He told her his name, that he was a New Yorker, born and bred, that he had been brought up in the Catholic religion but did not practice same, that he was not in the theater or in business or in any of the professions.

"So you're a gentleman."

"Oh, no," he laughed, and Bessie couldn't help but notice that he had very nice teeth. "I'm a politician." He explained that he had had a "discussion" with four other politicians which ended in the Grand Theater's side alley.

"You were talking politics?" Bessie asked, coming around the screen, wishing she were wearing her black dress which was a touch more ladylike than the red one she had on.

"Actually," he said, looking up at her, "we were talking numbers. Those gentlemen were attempting to convince me to stick to my side of town."

"And did they?"

"Not for a moment." He laughed his attractive laugh again and said, "You're going to find out, my dear, that I'm a very stubborn man."

"Since I do not include among my acquaintance either racketeers or politicians, I doubt very much if I shall have that opportunity," Bessie said, using a high-toned accent she had cribbed from the German-Yiddish actress Bertha Kalisch.

He insisted on having the horse-drawn hack take her to her hotel first and then insisted on escorting her into the lobby. "I want to thank you for what you did for me tonight," Ryan said, taking her hand in his. "You're not only incredibly beautiful, you're marvelously kind." He kissed her hand and Bessie watched him limp back to the hack, wondering what had hit her. She felt not a little dazed and, for no reason she was going to allow herself to come up with, jubilantly happy.

She held the kissed hand a little away from her

body as she walked up the Essex's carpeted stairs, as if that hand had been blessed and become a sacred object.

"Fency delency," old lady Greenberg, who ran the hotel for her son and was sitting behind the desk, a witness to the scene, called after her. "Just don't let me catch you with that *shagitz* in your room, miss, or you'll be looking for a new hotel."

Bessie didn't hear a word. She hummed *"Rozhinkes Mit Mandlen"* to herself and tried to remember exactly how it felt when Ryan's lips touched her hand.

Ryan was born in the section of Manhattan known as Hell's Kitchen. His father, an immigrant Irishman, had deserted his mother a month before he was born. Kathleen Ryan, a lean, determined woman, turned to her brother for financial support and the church for spiritual comfort. She received a minimum of both.

She had two obsessions: Ryan and the numbers. "It's a sucker game," Ryan—when he was old enough—would tell her.

"The day my number comes up," Kathleen said, "I'm going to take a hansom down to your uncle's fine office and spit in his fat, red face."

During the winter months Ryan attended Jesuit schools, the tuition for which was paid for by his eccentric bachelor uncle, Tim Ryan. Big Timmy, as he was called, had amassed a great deal of power in the back rooms of Tammany and a large fortune when he established one of the early numbers rackets in New York. In his way Big Timmy was as much obsessed by numbers as his sister. Only he played them from the other side.

He shared another interest with his sister and that was an almost fanatical concern with his nephew. Ryan was to be his substitute son. Ryan was to assume his mantle.

During the summers, when Big Timmy decamped to his mistress and his house in Saratoga, Ryan lived with his mother in her cramped, gray, antiseptic apartment, filled with lace antimacassars carefully placed on green upholstered furniture. He took his meals with her but the rest of the time he ran with the Hudson Dusters, a young lower Tenth Avenue gang whose principal activity—before Ryan joined them—was to pillage the wharves and warehouses on the Hudson River. Ryan introduced them to the money to be made collecting for his uncle's numbers games.

"In the winter," Ryan was to tell Bessie, "I was being groomed to be one of the more influential power brokers in this country, sitting next to the sons of the richest Catholic families in New York. In the summer I was dodging police up and down Tenth Avenue, eating cold beef and drinking tepid tea at my mother's table."

Kathleen Ryan's number never did come up. She died, comfortably poor, with her last combination on her lips. Relieved—he had never liked the austere life his mother led—Ryan went to live with his uncle in his mansion in Brooklyn Heights.

Though he didn't miss the Dusters, he had managed to, as he put it, "cement several friendships" with them. These were to stand him in good stead in later years. Joseph "Bumps" Bogan was a Duster with whom he never lost contact.

There was, however, to be a long separation. He went to Yale and later to Columbia Law School. After he received his degree, making the Law Review, and still under Big Timmy's tutelage, he went first into the wards where he served as councilman for two years. And then, when Big Timmy died, unmourned, unloved, unforgiven, Ryan left politics as an active participant and began to promote his own candidates from behind the lines. Long after it had become a political liability, long after he had no use for the money it brought in, Ryan continued to run the numbers racket.

He hadn't liked his mother but he had loved her more than he had ever been prepared to admit. His admittedly sentimental attachment to the numbers was his own way of observing that austere woman's memory. "Who knows," he said to Bumps Bogan, "maybe through the numbers I'll make some poor widow rich."

"Sure," Bumps said. He had grown into a thin, dangerous man and was Ryan's deputy in charge of the numbers.

To the world Ryan was a respected lawyer, a power in New York to be courted. Before Big Timmy died, he had arranged for Ryan to marry the ex-governor's daughter, Grace. She gave Ryan "family" in the guise of two daughters, born three and five years, respectively, after the marriage. But Grace also gave him respectability, opening doors to old New York houses that had been closed to him before.

He certainly didn't love her. They both knew that. But he didn't entirely dislike her, either. She was a bit like his mother, obsessive about cleanliness (she had a brigade of uniformed maids in each day to clean their Brooklyn mansion) and the church.

Both before and during his marriage Ryan had had a variety of sexual episodes, but few long-term affairs. By the time he met Bessie, he had come to the decision that a man in his position needed an official mistress.

Bessie was young and beautiful and in the theater. She was a Jewess, exotic and appealing and she had, he thought, exactly the right note of required flamboyance.

Also she had a spirit, a hard and wonderful flame of life burning inside her that ignited a sexual response in himself he hadn't thought he possessed. Ryan wanted Bessie Meyer from the moment he saw her. And, in his own deliberate way, he set about getting her.

CHAPTER 3

For two weeks Ryan sat first-row center at every eve-ning performance of *The Sorceress*. His controlled, aristocratic face seemed totally out of place in that sea of ruddy, emotional men and women. It was as if—as Zuckerman said—the tsar had joined the peasant's revolt.

For two weeks, after every performance, there were a dozen red roses waiting for her.

"You'd better be careful, Red," Zuckerman, work-ing a toothpick around his mouth, told her. "This one means business."

"I can take care of myself, thank you very much, Mr. Zuckerman. And I would be happy, if in the fu-ture, you would mind your business."

"He's waiting in your dressing room."

She told herself she was a fool but her heart seemed to be beating so loudly she was sure he could hear it when she opened the dressing room door and found him seated on the only chair, his legs crossed, his hands casually folded in his lap.

"What're you doing here, fat boy?" Bessie asked, going directly behind the screen, not trusting herself to face him. Dear God, she asked herself, what am I so nervous about?

"I've come to tell you how much I've enjoyed these past two weeks."

"You don't understand one single word of Yiddish. How could you sit through that mishmash every evening?"

"I'm learning," Ryan said, standing up, coming round the screen. She stood there, perfectly still, in the thin slip she had worn under her costume. "Listen to this," he said, putting his fine, smooth hands on her shoulders. *"Oy, vey* and *vey ezh mehr."* He pulled her to him and kissed her. His tongue went into her mouth as his free hand went under the slip and moved slowly over her round, firm buttocks and then up in between her legs and then slowly, his two fingers began to go into her. After a moment he stopped and pulled away. She felt as if her breathing supply had suddenly been cut off.

"You've never made love before?" he asked her.

"No," she said. And then, "But I want to." She had looked down at his face, over the footlights, all through those two weeks and the most awful thoughts had been in her mind. Twice she had forgotten her words and Zuckerman had had to shout them to her over the music, giving her his most baleful look from backstage.

Ryan pulled her to him again and once again he kissed her, his tongue going inside her mouth, meeting hers while his free hand went under the slip. This time he didn't try to penetrate her. Instead he caressed her breasts and then allowed his hand to move down to that secret place between her legs.

There was a knock on the door. "We're closing the theater in five minutes, Miss Meyer," Zuckerman shouted. "The management's not running an all-night hotel for its players."

Ryan took her to the suite of rooms he kept at the Claridge. She hardly noticed the paneled walls, the prints of hunting scenes, the honey-colored leather sofas.

They hadn't said a word in the carriage or even as they walked through the Claridge's opulent, deserted lobby. He led her into the bedroom, turning up the gas lamps so the room was illumined with a soft, golden light.

He helped her out of her clothes and kissed her again. She thought she might faint if she weren't so excited. Of course she knew what men and women did in bed. Everyone in the theater had at least one lover and some of the women were quite graphic about their experiences.

But what surprised her most was this feeling she couldn't describe, she couldn't name. It left her both weak and aroused at the same time; it was disturbing, yet gratifying.

Ryan kissed her nipples, running his tongue around them so that they stood up hard and straight and then sucking them so that she pulled his head closer and thrust up her pelvis. He moved his head down, his tongue tracing a line between her breasts and her vagina. He pushed her legs apart and began kissing her there and then she almost screamed as his tongue reached in and sought out her most sensitive spot. Again she grasped his head and pulled him down upon her. And then, just as she thought she couldn't stand it any longer, he stood up and pulled away.

"Please," she said.

"Just one moment, my darling." He took off his shirt and then his trousers. He was broad in the shoulders, narrow in the waist, with muscular legs and a flat, well-defined chest. He took her hand and placed it on his penis. It was hard and thick. He pressed it against her mouth but all she could do was kiss it. It seemed much too big to take into her mouth.

He moved to the back of the bed and then squatted over her so that she could see his round, thick balls and then his penis was once again pushing against her mouth as his head went down between her legs and his tongue pressed into her. She found herself opening her mouth and his penis going in and she thought she would choke but suddenly she was aware of his tongue down between her legs and then she was sucking on him greedily. He pulled away after a very short time and she was sorry that he did.

"Have I done something wrong?" she asked.

"No, God, no. I have to wait for a moment," he said, sitting on the edge of the bed, his hand still between her legs, stroking her. Then he stood up and pushed her legs apart and slowly he lowered himself into her and Bessie felt the most exquisite pain in the world as he broke through and she wrapped her legs around his thin waist and her arms around his neck. He rode her, pushing himself in and out, and she met him, thrust for thrust, and suddenly it was over in one huge explosion.

"I love you," she said to him.

Later, after she had bathed, after he had taken the bloody sheets and bundled them up and threw them into a corner, she asked him what the maid was going to think.

"We'll tell her that we had a little accident." He lay down next to her and she put her hands on his penis and watched it again become erect.

"I don't suppose," she said, "you'd like to have another little accident?"

Though he was gentle and caring as he went into her, she was sore and it was painful for her. Still, she thought, it's the best pain I ever felt in my entire life.

She saw him three, four, sometimes five nights a week all through the fall and the winter and on into the spring, when she had gone into Horowitz's *Mishka and Mashka*.

"What does your wife think?" she asked him when he had come to her at the Claridge late on Christmas Day.

"Oh, Grace doesn't think," he had said, kissing her. "Grace prays."

He had asked her if he shouldn't take precautions, use a "safety." "You wouldn't want to get pregnant, would you?"

"By you I would," she had answered. "Then I'd never lose me."

"You're never going to lose me, my dear. That thought needn't concern you."

She still didn't want him to wear a safety. She loved the touch of his skin, the feeling of him entering into her. Their lovemaking, impossible as it seemed, became progressively more satisfying, more exciting.

He wanted her to move into the Claridge but she refused; she would meet him there any night he chose, but she liked her room at the Essex. "I'm a free woman, fat boy. This way I can come and go as I choose."

"Why do you call me fat boy?"

"Because only people like you, who live off the fat of the land, can afford to be so trim."

"You've been talking to the socialists again."

"Thomashefsky won't let them near the theater."

"How would you like to leave the theater?"

"For what? A suite at the Claridge where you'll drop in twice a week and the rest of the time I'll go crazy playing solitaire?"

It was early in the spring. He got out of the bed and went to the window and pushed the heavy green curtains aside so the thin sunlight streamed in. He moved back to the bed and looked down at Bessie and ran his hands over her body. "You're the most beautiful woman I've ever known," he told her. She tried to pull him down but he resisted. "No, I just want to look at you. It's not every fellow that owns a live Rubens."

"You don't own me, Ryan."

"I want to."

And then he lowered himself down onto the bed and they made love and after, while he lay in her arms—it was the one way he ever got a good night's sleep, he claimed, when she held him—he told her his plan.

"I'm going to open a restaurant near City Hall. The building's already bought. It's been furnished and staffed. All very high toned. It's going to be a place where the most powerful politicians in New York can come and feel free to be indiscreet. All it's waiting for is you to make it live. I want you to manage it for me."

"Listen, Ryan," she said, cupping her hand on his chin and turning his face to her, "I got news for you: I already ran away from one restaurant."

"This one comes with a house, a maid, and me."

"Three times a week."

"I'll try to make it five."

She moved away from him and turned toward the window. "If you had met me before Grace, would you have married me, Ryan?"

He looked over at her, amused. "Never in a million years, my dear. As my mistress, you're a wonderful asset. As my wife, well, that would have been another story."

"Ryan," she said, getting out of bed, putting on the thin silk wrapper he had bought her, "next time I ask that question, do me a favor: lie a little."

"Where are you going?" he asked.

"To get dressed. If I'm going to be running a restaurant, I'd better see what it looks like, don't you think?"

The main dining room had green velvet walls and two dozen crystal chandeliers and a special table, right in the center of the room, where she learned to sit and hold court. On the nights when Ryan couldn't be with her, she stayed on at her table, amused by the men who tried to win favor with Ryan by courting her.

Senator Lewis, the man she had given the A tour to

on her seventeenth birthday at Henry Street, became a regular when he was in New York. "Did you get all those fat guys down in D.C. to give up a meal?" she asked him.

"No," he admitted, polishing his glasses, "but I did try. They need to take the A tour in person."

"You send them up to New York and I'll personally give it to them."

She did what she could for the Lower East Side people, learning to trade favors with the most skilled politicians. "You get Miss Wald the money she needs for the new playgrounds and I'll put in a good word with Ryan," she told more than one councilman.

"You're my most powerful lobby," Lillian Wald told Bessie when Bessie would visit the Settlement. "And don't blush. It doesn't become you. Now come upstairs. There's a young runaway up there I think you can talk some sense to."

In the two years Bessie had been managing B's Gardens, Ryan had solidified his political position in New York. No candidate stood a chance without his backing; no legislation was passed without consulting him.

He spent several nights a week with his wife and daughters in the estate he had built for them in Oyster Bay, Long Island. Grace never questioned him as to his whereabouts during the rest of the week, telling her friends that his work often kept him in the city. He was always on call for the occasional dinner parties she would give, with usually at least an archbishop in attendance. He always spent Sundays and holidays with Grace and the children. She had very little to complain about.

"Did you go to church?" Bessie liked to ask him on Monday mornings when he would return to Manhattan.

"Yes, my dear, I went to church. Grace has had her own chapel built. I suspect that my immortal soul is safe."

Bessie lived in a small brownstone, a hundred-year-old house, behind B's Gardens on Lower Broadway. Next to B's Gardens and on the far side of her house was another structure, a green-painted clapboard building where there was gambling on the first floor, women on the second.

Bessie resolutely refused to know anything about the Green House, as it was called, and what went on inside. She barred Bumps Bogan from her restaurant.

"Tammany is one thing," Bessie told Ryan. "Hoodlums are another." Ryan agreed to keep Bumps and the activities of which Bumps was in charge out of Bessie's sight.

It was only when Ryan's personal candidate became mayor of New York and an invitation to his inaugural party arrived addressed to Miss Bessie Meyer did she realize how important she had become in her own right.

"You don't seriously intend to go, do you, my dear?" Ryan asked, amused at how pleased she was.

"Why not?" Bessie was sitting at her dressing table, preparing to go to the restaurant, wishing her red hair was a shade paler, wondering what on earth she was supposed to wear to an inaugural party.

Ryan waited a moment and then said, "Grace will be there."

Bessie looked in the mirror at him sitting so poised,

his legs crossed, his face half in the shadows. "So she will," Bessie said, returning to her hair. "I'd almost forgotten, fat boy, that you had a wife."

He stood up and went to her, placing his hands on her bare shoulders. She shivered. If only, she thought, she didn't feel that way *every* time he touched her. "I won't go. It's a ridiculous idea. The mayor's only being polite." She stood up and moved away from him. "What would he want with a greenhorn like me at his party?"

Ryan laughed. "Bessie, our new mayor thinks you're the smartest woman in this city, the only one who has any idea about the realities of the poor and the Lower East Side. He's said more than once that you've got more sense in your exquisite little finger than ninety percent of the men in Albany and that includes our dear but dumb governor." He walked across the room and took her in his arms. "You're not only smart, Bessie: you're legit. Most everyone else in politics is twisted, somewhere along the line."

"And you, fat boy?"

"Oh, you've made an honest man of me, my dear."

"Oh, yeah? What about the numbers? What about the Green House with the gambling and the girls?"

"The numbers, the games, and the ladies are strictly on the up and up, I'm pleased to inform you. No one gets cheated; no one gets robbed when they take their pants down. That wasn't always so." He kissed her.

"So now I'm Little Bessie Meyer, the Yiddish Reformer." She returned his kiss. All the fight was out of her, and she was ready to be whatever Ryan wanted her to be.

*　　*　　*

The mayor's inaugural party was held at the Astor in the grand ballroom. There were two orchestras, sixteen courses, and a small army of waiters. The Astors, the Rockefellers, the Fish family were all well represented. As were the O'Malleys, the Goldbergs, and the Antonuccis.

In the end Bessie had agreed to go with Senator Lewis who asked her, shyly, to call him Edward. She said she would try. She wore a ball gown made of green satin and one piece of jewelry, a fourteen-carat emerald Ryan had given her for her twenty-second birthday.

"You look magnificent," Edward Lewis said to her.

"I don't feel magnificent, Edward."

She couldn't eat but she did dance and she did manage to talk and laugh with the others seated at her table. And every once in a while, she would look up at the dais and see Ryan and the woman next to him, Grace. She had a wide face and a thickish nose. Her dress was dark gray and made her look as if she had a body shaped like a potato. But she had that hauteur, that commanding poise, Bessie always associated with the very rich.

After the cherries jubilee, after the mayor had made his speech and had come to her table and kissed her cheek, she asked Edward Lewis if he wouldn't take her home.

"The night is still young, Bessie," he said, somewhat recklessly for him. "We could go on to the New York Roof."

"The night feels very old to me," she said as he helped her on with the cape made of the same material as her gown. As they walked out of the ball-room, she looked up at the dais once more. Ryan was looking at her. She tried to smile but she couldn't. He nodded and then went back to the conversation he was having with the man on his right. But Grace Ryan had been staring, too. Grace did manage a smile, and in that moment Bessie knew that Grace Ryan was perfectly aware Bessie was her husband's mistress. And she—Grace—didn't care. What Grace Ryan cared about was sitting on the dais.

Bessie spent a sleepless night during which she made several resolutions that all disappeared the next morning when Ryan slipped into her bed and gave her the sort of comfort it seemed she couldn't live without.

CHAPTER 4

"Some swanky place," Mookie Goldstein said for the fifth time. Sundays were Bessie's loneliest days and she occasionally invited the Goldsteins, along with Moishe Katz, for Sunday dinner at B's Gardens. Rifka didn't say a word; she ate her food very quickly and then spent her time attending to her child's wants. Baby Esther, Bessie reflected as she watched Rifka fuss over her, was going to be a beauty. She had black hair and huge eyes and the kind of chubby cheeks that portended a flawless complexion.

"You ever want to put a little money into the Lower East Side," Mookie said, sucking his teeth, "I wouldn't mind branching out."

"I already put a little money into the Lower East Side," Bessie said, but Mookie wasn't listening. He was watching an elegant family of Yankees being led to their table. The money she put into the Lower East Side went to the Henry Street Settlement. It was tit for tat, she told herself. Ryan's numbers took money out of the poor households; his restaurant put it back in.

As bored as she was with the Goldsteins, she knew enough about herself to realize she envied them. Especially on Sundays. They were a family. In fact they and Miss Wald were the closest to a family she could claim. She wished, more than ever, that she could have Ryan's child.

"Want to come back to the house and play a little pinochle?" Moishe Katz asked her.

"Yeah, don't be such a hoity-toity," Mookie, who was growing fat with minor affluence, said. "Come on. I'll treat you to a glass of tea."

She thanked them but she said no, she had to close the restaurant, she had business to attend to.

They kissed her; they thanked her but she knew they left B's Gardens with a sense of relief. It had been an ordeal to get dressed up, to watch their table manners, to feel so out of place amidst the opulence of B's Gardens.

She went to her office, which Ryan had caused to be shirred in a dark red silk, and sat at the narrow mahogany desk and looked at the books, at the numbers the accountant had so painstakingly inked into the lined columns. B's Gardens was very profitable. But not nearly so profitable as the dark green building, the Green House, next door. Despite the shirred walls she fancied she could hear the gamblers. Sunday was a good day for the casino and for the girls upstairs. It was the day when lonesome men tried to fill up the gap.

I must stop being so unhappy, she told herself, standing up, catching sight of a letter from Edward Lewis she had left on her desk. He regretted asking her to marry him and hoped that her refusal would not cause a rift in their friendship.

"He'd regret it a hell of a lot more," she said

aloud, "if I had accepted." In his own way Edward was the consummate Yankee, much more of an American than Ryan. His family had come over on the Mayflower which explained, he said, why it would be perfectly right for him to marry her. "We need some strong new blood pumped into our veins," he said.

"I wouldn't exactly be a political asset."

"I'm not married to politics. There are other ways a man can spend his life."

"Then there's Ryan."

"I'm willing to forget him if you can, Bessie."

"Ah, but that's the rub, Edward. I never can."

For a moment she had played with the idea of marrying Edward Wharton Sloan Lewis, fantasizing living in his Fifth Avenue mansion, receiving guests at his residence in Washington. And she laughed, telling herself that even her imagination couldn't stretch that far.

She stood up and made a resolve to write him the following day, to tell him that of course their friendship would continue. She liked him so very much and, at the same time, respected everything he stood for and tried to do.

Ryan, she knew, was not a man whose ideals she was ever going to respect. If only his smile didn't turn her insides to jelly and his touch didn't drive all decent thoughts from her mind. She let herself out through the seldom-used side door that led to a narrow alley which, in turn, led to Broadway. She hadn't wanted to face the waiters cleaning up, the Italian major domo, Antonio, with his air of implicit sympathy. They all, she reflected as she locked the door after her, felt sorry for her.

Though God knows why anyone should feel sorry for me, she thought as she walked up the alley toward Broadway. I own a restaurant that's making tons of money—Ryan had put B's Gardens in her name only the week before—I have beautiful clothes, valuable jewels, and I am loved. Whatever else I may think about Ryan, he does love me. I should be counting my blessings instead of . . .

And then she heard a noise from the opposite end of the alley, the end which led to Green House. It was a piteous noise. At first Bessie thought it had been made by an animal, some dog or cat in pain. She turned and went in its direction and, when she heard it again, realized it was a human cry.

She turned the far corner at the end of the alley which led to a door in the dark Green House. Three men stood there. One was holding a young man's arms behind him. The third was Bumps Bogan. In the moonlight she could see that he held a long and sharp knife in his hand as if it were a pen.

"Please don't do it again, Mr. Bogan," the young man who was being held said. "Please." He looked up and Bessie held her breath. One of his eyes was filled with blood. "I'll get the money, Mr. Bogan."

"It don't matter anymore, kid," Bogan said and carefully placed the tip of his knife a quarter of an inch into the boy's unbloodied eye. Bessie screamed and Bogan turned around.

"Evening, Miss Meyer. You lost or something?" He started to walk toward her and she fled, running up the alley, the sound of the blinded boy's cries following her.

She was quite clearheaded by the time she reached

her house. She took her old suitcase and packed it
with only what she thought she would need. She left
everything else behind: her jewelry, her elaborate
gowns, the emerald Ryan had given her. She hesitated at the door, thinking that she must write a note
and then decided that it would take too long, that
there was too much to say.

"You going away, Miss Meyer?" her maid, Minnie,
a woman who had become her friend, asked, coming
from her room wearing a flannel nightgown.

"Yes. Tell Mr. Ryan exactly that. I went away."

"Do you want me to tell him where, ma'am?"

"No. Just tell him I left, Minnie, will you?"

And then she stepped out into the night.

It took him a month to find her. At first he thought
she had gone to Edward Lewis in Washington. When
he found she hadn't, he learned that Zuckerman was
taking a Yiddish theater troop to South America; but
it turned out Bessie hadn't gone there, either. A
woman at the Oriental said Bessie had been seen in
Coney Island and someone at Coney Island thought
she had signed up with a theater in Atlantic City.

It was only when he went to Goldstein's Vegetarian
Kosher Dairy Restaurant and cornered Moishe Katz
("I haven't seen her, Mr. Ryan, I swear to it") that it
suddenly occurred to him where she must have gone.

A young woman at the desk said she would have to
see, she wasn't sure, and then Lillian Wald herself
came out into the reception area. "She's upstairs in
her room, number three. I know all about you, Mr.
Ryan," she said, looking at him with a stern eye. "I
don't like you. But keeping you away from Bessie

isn't going to help the situation, I know that. She has to face you out someday and it might as well be right now. Go on up."

Ryan executed a half-ironic, half-serious bow and went up the staircase the Settlement's founder indicated. He knocked on the door of room number three and heard Bessie tell him to come in. She didn't seem to be surprised.

"You look wonderful, my dear," he said, smiling at her. "Bleeding hearts seem to agree with you."

"Don't come any closer, fat boy. I have something to say to you."

"I'm not going to attack you, Bessie, darling."

"No, I suppose you would leave that up to Bogan."

"You won't see him again. He has orders never to come near B's Gardens, never to come near you."

She stood up and moved away from him, retreating to a window seat that overlooked the playground. "You're so very certain I'm coming back, aren't you, fat boy?"

"If I had been so certain, my dear, I wouldn't have come for you, myself. On bended knee, as it were."

She looked at him. His easy smile was gone and his pale eyes, seemingly lashless, seemed devoid of the usual irony she had always found there. She realized he was pleading with her, in the only way he knew how.

"I will come back," she said but held up her hand to keep him from coming closer. She didn't want him to kiss her, not yet. "But there are conditions. I'm not going to ask you to give up your business. That's what I intend to call what you do: business.

"I know you won't give it up. I don't think you

can. And I don't want lies, not now. What I do want is to never hear of it again. If I have to be with you—and I know I do have to be with you—I never want to be mixed up with your numbers and your girls and your games. I never want it to touch my life. I'll never stop seeing that boy in the alley and your henchman sticking his knife into his eye. Never.

"I feel as if it were I who held the knife, Ryan. I feel dirty and criminal and unsound." She began to cry and this time she didn't stop him from walking across the room and taking her in his arms.

"Will it ever stop, Ryan?" she asked him. "Will you ever stop?"

He didn't answer her. He pulled her to him, his fingers grasping her arms, and kissed her. "I knew you'd come back," he said when he let her go.

"I think I would have found the strength not to," she said, moving away, picking up the suitcase that stood by the door, "if not for one little minor miracle."

"What was that?" he asked, taking the suitcase from her.

"I'm going to have a baby."

She miscarried one month later.

Ryan blamed himself, uncharacteristically. He had insisted they make love the night before she hemorrhaged. Minnie said it was her fault, letting Bessie go out for a walk when she should have made her lie down. The doctor said it was no one's fault, that it was a natural selection process used by Mother Nature.

Only Bessie said nothing. She knew, in her heart,

that by going back to Ryan, pregnant or not, she had condoned his lawless use of violence. She didn't go to a synagogue but she knew her Old Testament. An eye for an eye, she thought. She was being punished.

The doctor told her she would never have another child.

She was being punished but good.

For her twenty-third birthday, to help her forget that disastrous past year, Ryan gave her a necklace of cabochon rubies and a party at B's Gardens. Representatives from Tammany, Albany, and Fifth Avenue attended. John McCormack had been engaged to serenade her with "My Buddy" and "Dear Old Pal of Mine."

"What does he think I am, a dog?" Bessie asked with something like her old spirit. Ryan was worried about her. She smiled just as often but she never seemed to cry anymore.

As McCormack concluded his second chorus of "Dear Old Pal of Mine," Moishe Katz appeared in the entrance. Bessie signaled the headwaiter that he was to be allowed in and he made his way to her table. He whispered that he had a letter from the Old Country.

"A fine time to be delivering letters," Bessie said.

He shrugged his rounded shoulders. "Mookie said it was important."

She excused herself and led Moishe to her office where she examined the envelope, staring at the heavy, European writing, weighing it in her hand. The last time she had been to see Mookie, he had wondered why her parents hadn't written in almost a year. This letter was obviously the answer.

"You going to open it?" Moishe asked.

"Eventually." She didn't like it. It had taken a long time to find her and she distrusted anything that inexorable. When she opened it and had Moishe read it to her (she had never learned to read Yiddish well enough to get through an entire letter), she knew her instincts, as usual, had been right.

Hannah and Abraham were dead, victims of the influenza. There were the three children, Bessie's brothers, they had written about in their letters over the years. They were now, respectfully, fifteen, thirteen, and twelve years of age. What is to be done with them, the letter writer, one more relative whose name Bessie had never heard of, wanted to know.

Bessie sat for a moment, looking at the letter in Moishe's hands. Then she stood up and went to the safe, removed two thousand dollars from it, and gave the money to Moishe Katz. She told him to go get himself a money belt, to go to Poland, to get her brothers, and bring them back to her.

There was no doubt in her mind that Moishe would do what she told him. He always had and now, with her new glamor and the protection of Ryan, he was more her slave than ever.

She returned to her birthday party and was surprised when Ryan handed her his silk handkerchief.

"It's nice to see you crying again," he said. "You always cry when you're happy, my dear. And I like to see you happy. Makes my life that much easier."

She took his handkerchief, dabbed at her eyes, and didn't correct him. Somewhere deep inside her she mourned her mother and father and again, still, the child she didn't have. At the same time she felt that she had been forgiven. She was going to have a family, after all.

CHAPTER 5

Ryan stood in the overfurnished central hall of the brick town house he had bought for Bessie on Eighteenth Street, fixing his tie in the gold-framed convex mirror. He was not, he knew, a handsome man. His seemingly lashless eyes gave his face a sinister look which he had thought, as he was growing up, would displease most women. It hadn't worked that way, he reflected, thinking of Bessie asleep upstairs in her gilded bedroom and of Grace, presumably at her prayers in her chapel on Long Island.

It was early in the morning but he was late. He had to see Bumps Bogan. It had come to his attention that a certain numbers runner was holding out on them. That would never do. Then Ryan was scheduled to have breakfast with the mayor at his mansion. The newspapers were publishing their periodic exposé of police corruption and a new police chief had to be chosen. Ryan looked at himself in the mirror once more and headed toward the front door just as there was a cautious rap on it.

Moishe Katz stood on the white marble steps, looking green and unhealthy in the clean June morning light. He wore a brown and greasy chesterfield and held a matching derby in his hands. Behind him stood three boys disguised as old men. They wore top hats over skullcaps, long black coats over tieless and collarless and once white shirts. They had long and curling sideburns and the eldest had the hint of a blond beard. The three of them stood very still, their hands behind their backs, their eyes wary, as if they were waiting for some elaborate trick to be played upon them.

"Bessie's boys," Moishe said, somewhat unnecessarily. "Boys," he said, switching to Yiddish, "meet Mr. Ryan."

The boys swept off their hats, reminding Ryan of one of the choruses he had seen in a Yiddish musical during his days of courting Bessie.

"Bessie is sleeping," Ryan said. "Then she has to go down to the Henry Street Settlement. Miss Wald wants to buy a new building and Bessie's going to help her get the money. What I think you should do, Moishe," Ryan said, handing him two ten-dollar bills, "is take the boys down to the Allen Street Baths. Get them scrubbed down, deliced. Buy them new clothes, get their hair cut. Bring them back here around noon. Just make certain they're a little more"—he searched for a word—"presentable."

Moishe led the three brothers into the Allen Street Baths, got them washed, and made them promise to sit still until he returned. He took their clothes, told the attendant to give them to someone who deserved them, left the bathhouse, and returned an hour later with three large boxes under his arm. Before he allowed them to put on the new "Yankee" clothes, he had them go to the barber in the basement who took off their sideburns and a good deal of their hair.

The new suits were chocolate brown with wide, white chalk stripes and made the three brothers seem even more theatrical, like a vaudeville act, the sort that did somersaults in midair. But they were proud and pleased with their new "American" appearance.

"I'm a regular Yankee," Nick, the youngest, said in English. "A regular goddamned Yankee." He had been practicing with Moishe on the boat.

His two older brothers, Jake and Max, cuffed him good-naturedly. "Yeah, sure," Jake said.

"Cut that out," Moishe said, pushing them out the door. "Come. We've got some time, we'll walk a little. We'll save Mr. Ryan a few pennies and I'll start your American education with a view of the greatest metropolis that ever was and that's ever going to be."

"Who's Mr. Ryan?" Nick asked as they walked up Second Avenue, passing the restaurants and cafés and hotels and extravagant food stores.

"A very important person," Moishe answered, pointing to the Oriental Theater, telling them their sister had appeared there, becoming "a world-famous actress of the very top class."

Adjacent to the Oriental was a narrow storefront with black curtains in its windows. Half a dozen people were standing in front of it, waiting for the store to open.

"What are they waiting for?" Max, the eldest and the biggest, asked in Yiddish. Max rarely spoke. Moishe could count on his fingers the times Max had asked him a direct question.

"That," Moishe answered, "is what is known as a

moving picture palace, but one of the smaller variety." He took his pocket watch from his vest, studied it, and then examined the small, printed place card in the store's window. "Okay. We'll go in. It will help with your education." Moishe had missed the motion pictures while he was in Poland.

He pushed the boys in ahead of him and handed the shirt-sleeved man at the door, the proprietor, twenty cents. The proprietor closed the door after them and they took their seats at the front of the long, narrow room, on a wooden bench.

A fat woman moved up and down the aisles, handing each of the patrons a glass of soda pop and a "schmear" of ice cream on a paper plate. Once everyone was served, she sat down at a small, upright piano located under the screen and began to play. The lights went off, the whir of the projector fought with the piano music, and Tim Bronco appeared on the screen, riding a huge black horse.

Nick clutched his older brother's arm. "Is it going to kill us?" he asked and was loudly shushed by the other members of the audience. Jake took his hand. Nick, surprisingly, let him hold it.

Twenty minutes later they emerged into the sunshine. Jake and Nick had been as much impressed by the soda and the ice cream as by the moving pictures. But Max hadn't eaten the food.

"So what do you think?" Moishe asked him, touched by the boy's expression.

"What do I think? I think it's a miracle."

"That's good because now we have to go face another miracle: your sister, Bessie."

* * *

The boys had been put in the large wallpapered, wainscotted drawing room. Moishe and Bessie were in the central hall, Bessie darting glances at the drawing room's closed doors. "I'm scared to death, Moishe," Bessie said. "What do I know from boys? I've never felt so frightened in my life. I'm so afraid I'm going to do the wrong thing. Maybe I already have. Maybe I shouldn't have brought them here." She sat down on the marble bench that no one had ever sat on. "I wish to God Ryan were here. He would be good in this situation." She stood up again and looked at the drawing room doors. "Moishe, I feel like I felt the first time I appeared on the stage as the Statue of Liberty. Sick and scared."

"You were a big hit then, Bessie. Believe me, you're going to be one now."

With an effort she pushed aside the doors and went in to the drawing room. The boys were sitting together on a black horsehair sofa, facing the fireplace. Nick was in the middle, sitting close to Jake. The three of them had their hands folded and resting in their laps.

Bessie stood against the mantel, below the painting Ryan had commissioned Kotuk to do of her. She looked as lovely in life as she did in the painting and almost as awesome.

She had no idea where to begin. She studied each of the boys' faces as they avoided her eyes. It was quiet in the room, the heavy draperies and Oriental carpets muffling what little sound there was on Eighteenth Street or in the other parts of the house.

She longed for some accident, some commotion to break the atmosphere. What do they expect? she won-

dered. The two older ones are too big and too fair to
be Jews. So help me, she thought, they could be
Yankees. Especially Max. What Jewish boy besides
Thomashefsky ever had such shoulders, such stature?

The middle one, Jake, already I can see he's too
charming. He wouldn't work on the stage; his smile's
lopsided but in a roomful of women, I know who
would be the center of attention. With dimples, yet.

But the little one, Nick, he at least looks like father. The exact shade of blue-black hair, those same
dark blue eyes. Well, we all have blue eyes but his are
special.

Max, the eldest, is a man already. Sixteen. That
means Jake is fourteen and that little one—God, how
he looks like father—must be thirteen. I hope he's
been bar mitzvahed already; I couldn't go through
that.

She stopped thinking and sat down in the outsized,
old-fashioned green leather chair Ryan had insisted
upon and now she was glad that he had. The boys
looked uncomfortable on that horsehair sofa. She
wished they would unfold their hands or sit back or
stop stealing glances at her as if she was Moses on the
Mount.

"I am your sister," she said, somewhat unnecessarily, and the three boys looked at her and then
away again. "I've brought you to America to help
you, to try to give you a better life. And I brought
you here because you are my family. I want you to
know I'm prepared to love you, to do everything I
can to help you succeed. It's very important in this
country that you become a success.

"To start with, you're going to learn to speak English. You haven't got a chance here until you can read and write and, most important, speak the language. Me, even when I was here five years, I only spoke Yiddish. Your friend, Moishe Katz, still has an accent you can cut with a paper knife. But you, you're going to be letter perfect. Right?"

She waited for one of them to say something but they couldn't. Not in that palatial room. Not under the gaze of those remorseless blue eyes, in the presence of this beautiful red-haired sister, so rich, so strong she even gave orders to Moishe.

"Dear God up in heaven," she said aloud. "I got three *schlemazels* on my hands and not one of them can open his mouth. Talk. Somebody please say something. Anything."

The youngest, the bravest, Nick, raised his hand.

"What are you doing?" Bessie asked the boy, so reminiscent of her father. "I'm not your teacher. I'm your sister. Talk. And put that hand down."

"Sister," Nick said, getting up from the horsehair sofa.

"Yes?"

"Sister . . ."

"Say it already."

"Sister, I have to go *pishen*."

"Oh, God, what did I do to deserve this? Don't tell me. I already know." She took Nick's hand and led him out into the hall where the gas lamps were being turned up by the maid, and then down a shorter hallway which ended in the most up-to-date, most expensive W.C. she could buy. She looked at him for a moment, touched his shoulder, and turned to leave.

"Sister," Nick said, calling her back as she realized

Max and Jake had followed them and were standing in the doorway, watching.

"Yes?"

Nick was staring at the gleaming white apparatus that rose above the toilet and disappeared into a box attached to the ceiling. "Sister, how does the machine work?"

He stood there, looking up at her, his two hands held out in a gesture so characteristic of her father that she felt he might be in the room and suddenly she pulled the boy to her and began to cry as she kissed him. Max and Jake came into the bathroom, wondering what was wrong. She looked at them and pulled them to her, crushing Nick between them, kissing each of their faces and crying.

And suddenly they were all kissing and crying and hugging one another. "My poor brothers," Bessie said, hugging them. "Poor things. To be left alone like that and then dragged to a country where you don't know the language or the ways and I've done nothing but shout at you from the moment I saw you. Don't worry," she said, the tears cascading down her cheeks. "I'm your sister and I'm going to take care of you."

"Sister," Nick said, getting himself out of her embrace. "Sister!"

"Yes?"

"I have to go *pishen*."

Bessie wiped her tears and laughed, showed Nick how the toilet worked, and took Jake and Max out into the hall. "Nothing," she said, "should disturb the little Polish prince and his *pishen*."

* * *

In the morning, around the table in the breakfast room, while Minnie was bringing stacks of hot cakes from the kitchen, Bessie was answering questions, giving an abbreviated version of her life after she left Poland. By the time the sweet cakes were served, and she had instructed Jake not to dip his roll into his coffee, she knew she had reached the point where she had to introduce, conversationally, Ryan.

"The man you met yesterday, when you first arrived, Ryan, is my friend."

She looked at her three brothers in their absurd suits and waited for some reaction. There was none. They continued to eat. "He lives here some of the time," she continued.

"Is he your husband?" Jake asked, putting strawberry jam on his roll.

"We live together," Bessie said, pushing her plate away, "as husband and wife. Ryan is not my husband. He has another wife." She had made up her mind that morning that she was going to make her relationship as clear as she could. If they didn't approve, if they had problems, she wanted to face them at the onset.

The three boys continued to eat. It was not their place, they reasoned, to question their magnificent sister's way of life. It was only several days later, when they had met Ryan and had shared two or three breakfasts with him, that Nick stopped her on the stairway. He was on his way to the attic which had been converted into a classroom. Bessie was on her way downstairs to meet Edward Lewis. They were going to give the junior senator from Maryland the A tour of the Lower East Side.

"Sister," Nick said to her, putting his hand on her arm, "am I your friend, like Ryan?"

"No," she said, pulling him to her, embracing him. "You're my brother. That involves being a friend and much more."

She watched him go on up the stairs, unsatisfied with the answer she had given him, to the makeshift schoolroom where Master Felix Feinswog held forth, teaching the boys English six hours a day, six days a week.

"You're working them too hard, Bessie," Ryan told her. "They'll end by hating school."

"I had to go to work when I was eight years old. What I would have given to go to school."

She insisted they speak English at all times. When they spoke to her in Yiddish, she would pretend she didn't understand. She saw them but one evening a week and that was on Sunday when they shared dinner together. Bessie had decided to close B's Gardens on Sundays when Ryan was in Oyster Bay. More often than not the four of them would eat Sunday dinner in the breakfast room.

"Sister, you're always so sad on Sundays," Nick said to her on one such evening as they played a complicated card game he had introduced her to. Max and Jake had gone to the movies to see Tim Bronco and the servants had been given the night off.

"I am not," Bessie said, putting her cards down. "Well, I am maybe a little. Sundays are the days most people share with the people they love."

"And you don't love us so much?" Nick asked, matter-of-factly, gathering up the cards.

She wanted to reach for him, to embrace him, but

she knew he didn't like being touched so she folded her hands and watched him start a solitaire game. "I love you all very much. But I'm like other women. I should like to have my husband here with me."

"I don't like Ryan, Sister."

"Why? It's because of him we can live like this."

"He makes you unhappy."

Ryan kept a respectful but friendly distance from the three boys. He said he was giving them time to get used to him, to America. He said he liked them, that they were smarter and in most ways better than he had expected.

"The truth is, my dear, that I'm a bit frightened of them. Especially young Nick. He's so direct in his wants, in saying how he feels. I'm used to a more Anglo-Saxon sensibility, I'm afraid, in which no one says what he means."

"Perhaps you'll learn something from the Meyers, Ryan."

He cupped her breast and leaned down to kiss it. "I already have, my dear."

He insisted the brothers attend her twenty-fourth birthday dinner. It fell on a Sunday and he was going to hold the party in B's Gardens. "They'll learn that I'm not so terrible after all."

"I wanted to keep them away from the restaurant," she said. "I don't want to corrupt them so fast. There's plenty of time to learn about restaurants."

"My dear, you make B's Gardens sound like an opium den."

"And you don't think, fat boy, that opium's never been smoked there?"

Finally she agreed. After all, Ryan was staying in

New York for her birthday, so she would compromise, too. "They can come, but only for the dinner. Afterwards they go straight home to bed. And if I catch any of them—especially Jake—going near the Green House, all I can say is watch out and don't say I didn't warn you."

He laughed. "Why especially Jake?"

"He stands at the bottom of the stairs and waits for the maids to go up and down so he can look under their dresses. And little Minnie is suddenly running up and down the stairs an awful lot."

"He'll have to learn sometime, Bessie," Ryan began but seeing the look in her eyes, he began talking about the arrangements for the party.

She bought them black suits and new stiff-collared white shirts, gentleman's boots. Ryan had gone down to the restaurant early, to supervise the preparations. Bessie and the boys arrived promptly at eight.

They had never seen her dressed formally before. She wore a pale green gown which was cut a trifle lower than she would have liked—she didn't want the boys to think she was a *koorvah*—and Ryan's emerald around her neck and his ruby on her finger. Minnie had brushed her curls high up on top of her head and though the August evening was warm, she wore an ermine shrug on her shoulders.

"You're very beautiful, Sister," Max told her, and she knew that he had not said it as a compliment but as a statement of fact. She felt very flattered.

Two doormen held the etched glass doors for them and as they walked in, three hundred people in formal dress stood up and sang "Happy Birthday to

Bessie." The three brothers walked behind her as she
went to her table, the center table, greeting friends,
introducing Max and Jake and Nick.

"I'm so proud of them," she said when they were
all seated. "I'm so happy, Ryan. I have a family."

He pressed his knee up against hers. And on this
one Sunday night she had Ryan.

Amelita Galli-Curci stood up and prepared to sing
and Bessie took Ryan's handkerchief from his pocket
and dabbed at her eyes. "I don't suppose," Bessie
said, "she knows *'Rozhinkes Mit Mandlen'*?"

Late that night Ryan was trying to prolong his second orgasm. He had turned the gas lights up and
propped her legs against his shoulders, inserted the
thick head of his penis just inside her. "Please," she
said, "please put it in."

As slowly as he could, he began to fully enter her
when the door to their bedroom burst open and Nick
came running in. Ryan pulled out of her and
shouted, "Get out of here, you little bastard. What do
you think you're doing . . ."

"I thought you didn't sleep here on Sunday night,"
Nick said, his face pale, his body trembling. "I
thought . . ."

"Get out!"

Nick dropped the present he had brought to his sister on a table and ran out of the room. Bessie stood
up, reaching for her wrapper. "And where do you
think you're going?" Ryan asked, pulling her back
onto the bed, pushing her facedown as she tried to
struggle, entering her as savagely as he could from behind.

CHAPTER 6

The Pierce Arrow drove down Second Avenue causing even the most jaded to stop for a moment and stare. It was twice as long as any ordinary automobile and painted a deep caramel color. The driver's cabin was open and the chauffeur who sat in it, oblivious to the weather, wore caramel-colored livery.

"Why can't I have a plain black Ford?" Bessie had asked Ryan.

"Because," he had answered, "I have a plain black Ford." There were times, when he was "cementing relations," that he didn't want to be recognized. "You, my dear, are my great luxury. Don't deny me."

She rested her head against the upholstery and thought about Ryan and, of course, about Nick. She had gone to the boy the following morning and tried to explain. "That's the way we show our love for one another."

"Yeah," Nick said. "That's not what they call it in the Old Country."

"I want you to apologize to Ryan, Nick."

"For what?" he asked, sitting up in his bed, pushing his blue-black hair out of his eyes.

"For bursting into our room without knocking."

"It's your room, Sister."

"Oh, no. Don't make that mistake, Nicky. I share that room with Ryan." She put her hand out and touched his forehead, just as their mother used to do. "If you don't apologize, Nick, I don't think you're going to be able to live with me anymore." He stared at her with black eyes. "Ryan's very angry and the truth is, he has what to be angry about. He talked about sending you away to school. I want you to stay here with me, Nick. I don't want you to be sent away. I couldn't go with you. But all you have to do, for me, is apologize. It's a very little thing for me to ask of you, isn't it?"

"Where is he?" Nick said, pushing the blanket aside, getting into his robe, looking like a little general, full of resolve. He strode down to the breakfast room where Ryan, having been introduced to the delights of lox and eggs, was dining on them.

"I apologize," Nick said, standing in front of him and, after a moment, offering his hand.

Ryan put down his fork and studied the boy who was treating him as a peer. Then he smiled. "Apology accepted," he said, offering his hand.

"Thank you," Nick said and left the room.

Only Bessie, seeing her younger brother's face as he went to his room, knew what that apology had cost him. Since that morning Nick and Ryan had avoided each other as much as possible and, when not possible, had been scrupulously polite with one another. It made her head ache when she thought of the two of them and, as she rode down Second Avenue in that ridiculously opulent car, she wondered not for the first time if she could ever give Ryan up. But even when she disliked him most, the thought of his body—long and clean limbed—made her go a little weak inside. There must be something wrong with me, she thought, to always be thinking of getting into bed with him. Nice women, she knew, never had such thoughts. Of course they never had such a delirious, delicious time in bed, either.

The Pierce Arrow pulled up to the curb at Tenth Street and the chauffeur got out and opened the rear door for her. Half a dozen people stopped to watch Bessie with her red curls and her silver-blue stone martens get out of the limousine and walk into the narrow shop without one wasted gesture.

Once inside she stopped, loosened the furs around her neck, taking a moment to adjust her vision to the dark auditorium. Then she moved up and down the makeshift aisles, paying no attention to the half-hearted objections of the audience.

It took her only a moment to find him. He was sitting in the first row, the tallest, broadest-shouldered member of the daytime moving picture watchers. All of his attention was focused on the small screen where a granular Tim Bronco in leather chaps was rolling a cigarette while the man behind him, the villain, was getting ready to draw.

Bessie put her hand on Max's earlobe and gave it a pull which woke him up to the reality around him. "Come with me, fat boy," she said, getting him off the wooden bench. "And I'm warning you right now: I don't want to hear one word, not one, solitary word."

"Bessie, let me stay till the end. Please. Only five more minutes."

She turned and went back up the aisle. Max followed, his head continually turning back to the screen where a white title on a black background read: "The villain prepares to shoot."

"Not one word," Bessie repeated as they got into the limousine. "Not one single, solitary word. I have enough trouble on my hands without this."

Max watched Bessie from the corner of his eye as the car drove back up Second Avenue; she looked dangerous. The car deposited them in front of the house on Eighteenth Street.

She led the way into the library, draped her furs on the sofa, and sat down, smoothing her fashionably tight skirt. Max began to put himself into the leather chair.

"Don't get comfortable," Bessie told him. "You may not be staying."

"Bessie . . ."

"Not one word." She turned her face to the windows and stared at the heavy, ball-fringed draperies she had had installed after she had seen a similar window treatment in Mrs. Astor's drawing room. She waited a full minute and a half before she turned to Max who was standing by the door, his hands behind his back, looking up at the ceiling.

"How did you get so big?" Bessie asked him. "No, don't tell me. I don't want to know. What I want to know is where you get the goddamned nerve to miss your English lessons? Not once. Not twice. But consistently for the past two weeks.

"Feinswog only confessed this morning. You think I'm paying him for my benefit? Your two brothers are up there, learning to be somebody. And you, what are you doing? You're sitting in the nickelodeon, watching grown-up men play cowboy.

"Is that what you want, Max? Is that why you came to America? So I could support you while you waste your time? Aren't you ashamed? If you're not, I am. If you don't want to be a success, *I* want you to be a success. *I* want you to be somebody. *I* want to be proud of you."

She turned away because she didn't want him to see her crying. She wished that for once she could get emotional without tears. Max crossed the room with two strides and, sitting next to her, put his arm around her shoulders. "I like them horses, Sister. When I was a kid, I used to help Pa get the horses. We'd go over to Germany, get them horses, and bring them back and sell them to the *goyim*. Pa taught me a trick when we were trading in Germany. We had to pay for them horses by how tall they were. So I'd get on one side of the horse, kneel down and feed him sugar while Pa and the dealer measured his height on the other side of a fence. The horse's head was down by me, eating sugar, so we used to pay less."

Bessie looked up at him. His blue eyes—lighter than hers—shining, and he had that innocent, manly smile on his face and she didn't know whether she wanted to slap him or kiss him.

"He likes 'them' horses," she said, compromising and taking his hand. "He used to help 'Pa.' You're learning English from the movie titles and you're talking like a ranch hand. So what're you going to be when you grow up?"

"I want to be a cowboy in the movies, Bessie."

She dropped his hand and stood up and walked to

the mantel and looked up at the Kotuk portrait without seeing it. It's a moment like this, she thought, when I need a man to help me. She thought of Ryan and then she thought of Edward Lewis. He would be helpful. But Edward Lewis, she thought, didn't have Ryan's smile or his touch and he had told her that he was marrying a distant cousin of his, a plain-faced but determined Bostonian, as dedicated to public service as he.

She made her mind up, quickly as usual. "All right. Mookie Goldstein has a relative in California who makes moving pictures. Do you want to go out there and work for him?"

"More than anything, Sister."

He walked across the room and kissed her. "You're very good to me, Bessie." She was going to miss him, she knew. He never said much, in English or Yiddish, but he had a quiet strength and a power that in some ways she had come to depend upon.

"Promise me that if you don't like it, you'll come right back."

"I promise," he said solemnly. "And I'll go to school and I'll be a doctor."

"A horse doctor, if I know you."

It took some months for letters to be written, for assurances to be gained, for the day of departure to be set.

Finally, one year after he had arrived in New York, Max left it on a rainy and unseasonably cold June day. He had five hundred dollars in a money belt around his waist, a letter of introduction in the breast pocket of his best black suit, a passing knowledge of English, and an intense desire to be a moving-picture cowboy. Giving in to the tears, Bessie kissed him good-bye and then watched the train chug itself out of Grand Central Station.

"He's going to be all right," Nick said to her, putting his hand on hers.

"He's going to be more than all right," she said, taking her hand back, reaching over and pulling Jake's handkerchief from his pocket. "He's going to be," she said, wiping her eyes, "America's first Yiddish cowboy."

CHAPTER 7

In December, 1916, when the newspapers were filled with Europe's Great War, Jakey Meyer turned seventeen. He had graduated, with honors, from Mr. Felix Feinswog's English classes and he was bored.

He was bored without his older brother, Max, to give him direction and he was bored with his younger brother, Nicky, shadowing him. He was bored with the overfurnished house he lived in. He was bored with going to bed every night at ten. He was bored with his sister, Bessie, schlepping him down to the Lower East Side three times a week to inspect filthy tenements.

Most of all Jake was bored with the erection in the crotch of his tweed trousers that arose at all hours of the day and night, that was as persistent as Nicky, as relentless as Bessie. Twice he had trapped Bessie's saucy little maid, Minnie, upstairs but both times she had wriggled and fought and moved her body against his so that he had come before he could even get her skirt off.

When his sister asked him what he wanted for his seventeenth birthday, he was tempted to tell her. They were sitting in Goldstein's Vegetarian Kosher

Dairy Restaurant after what seemed a pointless visit to the Settlement, eating pirogen and sour cream. Bessie was concerned about Nick, because he wouldn't eat, and Jake was concerned with Mookie's daughter, Esther, whose dark hair and decidedly voluptuous figure gave him an immediate but not surprising erection. Most every woman under the age of fifty did.

"So what do you want for your birthday?" Bessie repeated. Watching Esther artfully move her full backside around the tables as she handed out menus, he told Bessie he wanted to go to England to join the war. He loved his sister but he wanted to get away from her all-seeing eyes so that the could spend his days and nights making love to ravishing women.

"Out of the question, fat boy," Bessie told him. "In January you're going to enroll in the Levi-Cole Preparatory School for Pre-College Students. I spoke to Charlie Levi myself and he says in maybe a year you'll be ready."

"For what?"

"For college. You're going to be a lawyer."

"I don't want to be a lawyer."

"That doesn't enter into it."

An early dinner was held at the house on Eighteenth Street on Jake's birthday night. As a concession to Jake's assumedly emerging manhood, Esther Goldstein had been invited. The evening was to end with Jake taking Nick and Esther to the million-dollar Strand Theater on Broadway where they would see Mary Pickford in her latest film, hear the great organ and the thirty-man orchestra, and sit in comfort on the second tier of what was being described as "that new eighth wonder of the world."

Bessie and Ryan attended a fund-raising ball for New York's governor at the Hotel Astor. Bessie sat with Edward Lewis and his pale, homely, endearing wife, Alma. As usual Ryan was on the dais with Grace, spreading charm and affability among New York's power brokers.

"I wonder if part of my need for him," Bessie said to Edward as Alma danced with the governor's aide, "doesn't stem from the fact that I can never really have him."

She watched him being attentive to the governor's wife and she watched his wife, Grace, darting little glances at Bessie, at Ryan, at the man sitting by her side.

As always Ryan danced the next to the last dance with Bessie. Grace, in a pale pink gown that didn't help her complexion, continued to talk to her neighbor but didn't miss a step as Ryan and Bessie, with perfectly matched poise, waltzed around the ballroom.

"You're looking extremely lovely tonight, Bessie."

"As are you, fat boy." She pressed up against him for a moment and then moved back again. "I haven't seen much of you this week."

"The exigencies of the state and the church"—he glanced at Grace—"have been keeping me busy. I shall be in residence on Eighteenth Street in the next day or so."

"How I wish I weren't going to be there, waiting for you."

"You might wish it, my dear, but you'll be there.

Just as I will. We love each other too much to give up what we have."

"You could give Grace up."

"I could but I shan't. If I did, I wouldn't be who I am and then you might find you don't like what you've wound up with."

"You and your Jesuit logic." She pressed up against him again.

"If you do that one more time, my dear, I'm going to embarrass myself."

The dance ended, he escorted Bessie back to her table, executed a half bow and turned and went back to his wife and his governor.

Jake and his young lady friend, Esther Goldstein, were in a hotel on Second Avenue. He was sitting in a chair, fully clothed, while Esther walked around the room, naked.

"Don't make a move, Jake," Esther said. "Don't come near me. You promised you wouldn't. This was the birthday present you asked for and here it is. If you come near me, I'll scream."

"Esther," he said, having difficulty speaking. He had never seen anything so beautiful as this nude girl with her round ass and her full breasts and the patches of black hair under her arms, between her legs. "Esther, please, just let me touch you. I promise I won't do anything else. All I want to do is touch you."

Esther was getting chilly, the room not as well heated as it might have been, and the idea of parading around nude in front of Bessie Meyer's brother had lost its charm. He looked harmless enough, sit-

ting in that shabby chair, his big hands folded in his
lap, his blue eyes so entreating.

"All right," she said, lying down on the bed which
looked none too clean. "You can use one hand and
you can touch me for five minutes. The minute both
hands touch me, I get dressed and go home."

"You want to see me without clothes, too, Esther?"

She looked up at him standing by the bed. His face
was so white she was afraid he was going to be ill.
But he had nice broad shoulders and looked solid
and thick and she did rather want to see what he
looked like nude. "All right," she said grudgingly.
"It's only fair."

He nearly ripped his shirt off and he did have a
nice chest, muscular and hairless and wonderfully
white. Then he turned his back and took off his shoes
and his socks and, still turned away, his trousers and
his long underwear. She wanted to reach out and
touch his *tuchas* but then he turned around and she
gasped. "I never thought it was going to be so big,"
she said, looking at his rock hard cock.

"It's not so big," he said, sitting on the bed, putting
one trembling hand on her breast, bending down to
kiss her. She forgot all about her one-hand rule as she
tasted his sweet breath, as his tongue met hers and
her hands reached for him, grabbing his cock.

"Don't," he said, pushing her hands away.

"Why not?"

"Just wait a few minutes." He kissed her again and
she felt his hands moving all over her, reaching down
between her legs, his fingers massaging her pussy.
Without thinking she reached again for his cock and
began massaging it and suddenly her hand was wet as

Jake groaned and held her so tight she thought she was going to break in two.

"I came," he said and lay back on the bed. She looked down at him and saw the thick, white liquid. He looked even more helpless now, lying on the bed, his eyes closed. She liked him better this way. She put her hand on his cock and began to massage it. She wanted to see if she could make it hard again. He wasn't responding. She rolled over on top of him and kissed him, putting her tongue in his mouth as he had done to her.

He was almost hard again and it was nice to feel his cock against her body. Still kissing, his strong, big hands on her breasts, he rolled her over again so that he was on top of her, his cock massaging her pussy, going up and down, up and down, so that her legs moved apart, as if by their own volition, and Jake suddenly had her legs in the air. He was kissing her and it felt so nice, the head of his cock now fully hard, moving up and down against her. She couldn't stop him. And then he moved his hands down so they were cradling her ass and his cock was going into her and she tried to stop him but there was this terrible, wonderful pain as he ruptured her and he came simultaneously.

"I thought there'd be more blood," Esther said as she looked at the sheet.

"You're so beautiful," Jake said, taking her in his arms, looking down at her wonderful curves, at her soft, miraculous flesh. "I knew it was going to be like this. I knew it was going to be just like this."

"Jake," Esther said after a moment, pushing him

away. "I have to tell you something: it wasn't so wonderful for me. You hurt me real bad."

"I promise you, Esther," he said, pulling her back into his arms, "it will be much better the next time."

"Yeah? And when's that going to be?"

"In about three minutes," he said, rubbing his cock, once again rock hard, up against her.

Three weeks after the New Year, as Jake came in from a long, terrible day at the Levi-Cole Preparatory School, Minnie, Bessie's little maid, told him that his sister wanted to see him in the drawing room. "And she don't mean maybe, honey."

Bessie was standing in front of the mantel, the fire behind her, the portrait of her illuminated by the soft glow of the gas lamps. She was wearing a dark red dress and if Jake hadn't known her, he would have sworn she was one of the great American-born, genuine Yankee ladies who rode up and down Fifth Avenue in their long, black cars.

She walked across the room, after he had closed the doors behind him, and slapped him across the face. "You sit down, fat boy, and you listen to me. You're the kind of lady-*gayer* who gets ruined quick and fast. One look at your face and anyone with half a brain can see you're a sucker for the women, the wrong kind, the ones who'll never love you back."

"Sort of like you and Ryan in reverse, huh?" Jake said and immediately wished he hadn't but that slap had hurt and he wished to hell he knew what she was talking about.

"We're not talking about me, *Yonkle*: we're talking about you. You got a dark blue suit, don't you?"

"Yes, why?"

"Because next Sunday afternoon, instead of taking little Esther Goldstein to that fleabag hotel on Second Avenue, you're going to the shul on Rutgers Street and marrying her."

"But, Sister, I don't . . ."

"She's pregnant, you dummy. Didn't anyone ever tell you about safeties?"

"I don't want to marry Esther Goldstein."

"You should have thought of that in December. Now it's too late. Don't look so sad," she said, putting her arm around him. "It could be a lot worse. She's a nice enough Jewish girl. Your age. She'll make you a good wife. But I want to warn you, Jake, right now: you be a good husband to her or I wash my hands of you. No fooling around, you understand?"

"I understand," Jake said. He saw all the women in the world he wanted to make love to disappear from his mind. Only Esther, who had to be coaxed and coddled and blackmailed into bed, remained.

"The day after the wedding, you're leaving New York. Mookie and Rifka insisted. They don't want everyone on the Lower East Side to know that their daughter had to get married."

"Where am I going?" Jake asked.

"To Florida. Mookie has a cousin who's willing to employ you. Maybe in a year or two, you'll come back, with your wife and your baby, and you can start over again." She kissed him. "You're going to like Key West, Florida. I swear it, Jake."

CHAPTER 8

"I don't want to be at B's Gardens anymore," Bessie said to Ryan as they lay in the huge bed on a Saturday morning.

"Her ladyship is bored?"

"No," she said, stretching her arms over her head, then letting them drop slowly. "Yes. I miss Max and I worry about Jake and I'm tired of glad-handing second-rate politicians." She put her arms around him, kissing his chest. "I need something new in my life."

"You could work at Miss Wald's Settlement full time. Nursing the poor, feeding the sick. Or is it the other way around?"

"You never have understood my attachment to Henry Street, have you, Ryan? You wouldn't. Anyway I couldn't do that all of the time. You've corrupted me. I need a bigger gaiety."

He laughed. "We were meant for each other, my dear. I've been thinking along those very lines myself. As soon as I let you out of this bed, I want to take you uptown. I have a little surprise for you."

After they made love, Minnie helped Bessie to dress, and Bessie roused Nicky from his bed. ("He studies too hard," she explained to Ryan.) Ryan had the chauffeur bring the Pierce Arrow around and told the driver to go up Broadway.

The car stopped in front of a large, limestone facade. Workmen were, at that moment, putting letters on a twenty-foot-high sign which read: B's Other Place.

Ryan escorted her through the thick glass doors, Nick following. They descended a palatial set of marble steps and went through a mirrored dining room and up onto a mirrored dance floor.

"You like it?" he asked, stopping her in the middle of the dance floor.

"You know I do. It's exactly my brand of *schmaltz*: tons of mirrors and a fortune in gold-leaf columns. What did it cost? A quarter of a million?" He nodded. "You keep cementing those relationships, don't you, Ryan?" She looked at their reflections in the mirrors. "And there's an upstairs for the girls, I suppose. And a downstairs for the games?"

"No, my dear. You underestimate cabarets. They make enough money on their own. Here, we'll keep the girls on the stage and the gamblers can go downtown."

She looked up into those seemingly lashless eyes. "Can I trust you, Ryan?"

"You don't have to, my dear. I'm giving you fifty-one percent interest in this place. You'll run it as you wish. I'll be a quiet, very silent, minor partner. Come, I want to show you your office. The lawyers are there, waiting."

He took her to an office one flight up which overlooked the dance floor. While the lawyers were shuffling papers, readying them for her to sign, she went to the interior window and looked down. Nick was standing at the edge of the dance floor, watching the Society Dance Team work their way through the Castle walk, the maxixe, and the Argentine tango. The woman's hands were clasped around her partner's coat collar while he held his around the base of her neck.

"Nick should be up here with me," Bessie said. "He should see how the lawyers work."

"I think," Ryan said, joining her at the window, "Nick's more interested in how the dancers work."

The lawyers offered her the papers which she took a half hour to read and then, pen in hand, looked up at Ryan. "You promise me this joint's going to be on the up and up?"

"I promise, Bessie."

She signed her name half a dozen times, stood up, and went back to the window. Nick had taken the male dancer's place and was leading his partner around the floor to the Castle walk.

"That boy is dance crazy. Whenever I want him, he's running to the tango palaces."

"That's not all he's running," Ryan said, but Bessie was already halfway down the stairs. She wanted to inspect the kitchen of her new and wildly extravagant cabaret.

If Bessie noticed that Nick had a new gold watch, remarkably similar to the one Ryan kept in the waist pocket of his vest, she didn't comment on it. Nor she she attach any undue significance to the fact that Nick had several new suits, a collection of natty ties, and what seemed to be a good deal of spending money. His report cards from Levi-Cole were glowing testaments to the quickness of his mind and in the back of her own mind she thought that perhaps Ryan was giving the boy money, that though they seemed as distant as ever, they had made a separate peace and that one of her favorite fantasies—Ryan seeing Nick as the son he never had, the one he had lost—was about to come true.

Nick missed dinner the night before Vernon and Irene Castle, at thirty thousand dollars a week, were to open B's Other Place. "Thomashefsky doesn't earn thirty thousand a year," Bessie had complained but Ryan had insisted. He wanted, he said, the best.

She ate alone—Ryan was in Oyster Bay celebrating his eldest girl's birthday—in the breakfast room, angry with Nick, anxious about him. He had been quieter, more remote than usual lately and suddenly the thoughts of the gold watch, his new clothes, were disquieting.

She left half her dinner and went into the drawing room and sat down and read a letter from Max again and then she picked up a report Miss Wald had asked her to read, a recommendation for the establishment of a vocational counseling service for the young and poor of the Lower East Side. She couldn't concentrate. She looked at her lapel watch and realized it was close to eleven. Nick never stayed out that late; not that she knew of, at any rate.

At eleven thirty she told Minnie to call the chauffeur down. She wanted to go round to the tango palaces on Third Avenue where she thought Nick might be. He might be ill, she thought. Or drugged. Or God knew in what condition.

And then there was a hard knock on the front door and Bessie, putting a restraining hand on Minnie's shoulder, went to open it herself. At first she thought no one was there, and then she heard a noise and looked down. Nick was there, at her feet, his knees up to his chest, his arms tied behind his back. A long car had just pulled away from the curb.

Bessie screamed just once. Then she got down to business. She and Minnie got him inside and though there was blood all over his face and it was obvious that he had been stabbed several times, he was still alive.

She refused to think. She sent Minnie for Dr. Deehl with orders not to come back without him and had the chauffeur carry him up to his room. She got a washcloth and bathed his face and was relieved to see that the bleeding there had already stopped; that his eyes, while already black and blue, had not been damaged.

"Sister," he managed to say as she gently tried to get him out of his suit.

"Quiet," she ordered. She gave up trying to get his jacket off and finally cut him out of it with a large pair of sewing shears.

She almost screamed again when she saw, after she sponged the blood away, that his entire body was covered with tiny stab wounds. His underclothes, which had stuck to the wounds, had to be peeled away and though he was conscious now and aware of the pain, Nick didn't say anything until she was finished.

"Sister," he said, "put a sheet over me."

"I can't. It would stick to the wounds and we'd

never get it off you. Where the hell is that goddamned doctor?"

He arrived some twenty minutes later, covered
Nick's body with antiseptic and gauze where it was
necessary, and constructed a tentlike affair so that the
sheets and blankets wouldn't touch his skin. He gave
Nick a sedative and took Bessie outside to the landing.

"It's not serious," he said. "A boy like that will
heal quickly enough. What I want to know is what
maniac did that to him? He must have some forty-odd
tiny knife wounds all over him. It must have hurt
like the dickens. Afraid I'm going to have to report
this, Miss Meyer."

It was more of a question than a statement and it
didn't take her long to convince the doctor that it was
his duty not to report the incident, that it was merely
a case of boys being boys and she would take care of
the culprit.

Of course she knew who it was. She had seen the
knife that inflicted Nicky's wounds blind a young
man in the alley next to the Green House. She
thanked God that it hadn't blinded Nick as she
cursed Ryan's man, Bogan.

Ryan strode in the next morning while Dr. Deehl
was with Nick. He found Bessie in the drawing room
and he shut the doors after him. They sat down on
the black horsehair sofa and looked at each other.

"Bogan didn't know who Nick was. Not until the
end when one of the men recognized him. That's why
Nick isn't blind. That's why he's not lying in an alley
in Chinatown."

"My brother . . ." Bessie began.

"Your brother is a numbers runner for Owney Madden who's trying to encroach on my territory. Your brother isn't only doing the tango at those cheap dives he goes to every night. He's making collections. He's doing the paying out. For Owney 'Killer' Madden. Turns out Nick has a very good head for numbers, for combinations. What happened to him is standard Bumps Bogan operating procedure for any runner moving into my territory. They all know it; they all run the risk."

"Nicky's going to be a lawyer."

"Oh no, he's not, my dear. He hasn't been to Charlie Levi's school since the first week. You keep paying Charlie, Charlie keeps issuing glowing report cards. Your brother's already up to his neck in the rackets. Working for Owney Madden, I'll tell you something: he hasn't got a chance."

"Ryan," Bessie said, after a moment, "what am I going to do?"

He took her in his arms and he told her.

She waited a week, until the wounds had begun to heal, until he was able to get out of bed. He sat in the maple chair in his room, she stood at the window looking out on Eighteenth Street.

"I've lost two brothers right after I found them," Bessie said. "I don't want to lose you."

"You're not going to lose me, Sister."

"Yes, I am. I'm going to lose you forever if you keep on being a runner for Owney Madden. Next time they find you, they'll kill you. Or they'll blind you. Or they'll castrate you. This time," she said, turning and looking at his pale, still bruised face, "you were lucky."

"So what do you want me to do? I want to make money. I want to buy my own clothes, pay for my own food. You want me to be Bessie Meyer's little brother all my life."

"No. But I want you to live. And I want you to be whole. And I want you to be with me. I love you, Nicky."

"So what do you want me to do?"

"I want you to work for Ryan."

"Ryan?"

"Listen to me, fat boy: you quit Owney Madden now and you'll be dead in a week. No one retires from Owney's employ."

"How do you know so much?"

"I'm a quick study, just like you, Nick. If you go to work for Ryan, you get automatic protection. Madden won't touch anyone working for Ryan. It's a fact, an ugly one, but there it is."

"Who do I have to kill?"

"No one. He says he'll groom you to take over the business side of his dealings. In the beginning you'll drive for him. You'll go wherever he goes. You'll learn."

"I hate his guts."

"You'll be safe," she said, going to him, taking his hand. "Ryan promises me that. And you'll be with me."

"Bessie . . ."

"I need you, Nicky."

He looked up at her. "Who's going to teach me how to drive? Bumps Bogan?"

BOOK TWO

MORNING

CHAPTER 1

Max walked out of the railroad station into downtown Los Angeles and felt an overwhelming sense of freedom. The buildings were low enough and spaced far enough apart so he could see the sky which was a clear and perfect blue, not unlike the sky on certain summer mornings in Poland. Everything in New York had been either too large or too small for him. The claustrophobia he felt in New York, that sensation of being boxed in—indoors and out—had disappeared almost from the moment his train had crossed the Hudson.

But he saw the same enlistment posters he had seen in Chicago and in South Dakota and in Los Angeles as in New York. The most affecting, the one that worked hardest on Max's nature, showed a woman and a child in rags, a huge vista of carnage behind them, and the message, "Don't Let It Happen Here" in black type underneath.

He saw the poster as he left the railroad station but he didn't stop to study it as he had during train stops in railroad stations across the country. He wanted to survey this new and amiable landscape; he wanted to walk for miles, to work the kinks out of his muscles, to fill his lungs with the clean, warm air.

As he walked, he noticed that there were few people about, another consolation. He decided he was going to like Los Angeles. He approached a mild-looking policeman who was almost as tall as he and who seemed a decade too young for his job. Max asked the way to Hollywood.

The policeman, looking at and listening to Max, wondered how anyone who "spoke so foreign" could appear so American. After a moment he put his thought into words. Max explained that he had been born in Poland, that he was Jewish.

"Jewish?" the policeman, Joe Rakin, said slowly. "I guess that explains it. You just hit town, huh?"

"Yes."

"Come all that way by yourself?"

"From New York."

Joe Rakin was impressed. "Weren't you afraid?" he asked. "I hear there's a lot of slick men on those trains."

"I got nothing to lose," Max said.

Joe Rakin put Max aboard the trolley that would take him to Hollywood after arranging to meet Max later when he would introduce Max to his landlady. He was sure she had a room for Max.

The trolley stopped directly in front of the main entrances to Great Western Moving Pictures, Inc. It covered over two hundred acres and boasted its own police force, fire department, street cleaners. It had libraries, greenhouses, schools, a hospital, mills, shops, forges, and an enormous reservoir.

Barns, corrals, huge indoor and outdoor stages,

dressing rooms, and prop departments took up a quarter of the acreage. Outdoor sets included New York Street and "Rue de la Paix," where occasional comedies and romances would be filmed.

Behind those streets were miles of open country where the majority of Great Western's films were shot, where herds of horses, mules, sheep, and cattle grazed for the sole purpose of providing Great Western motion pictures with authenticity.

Great Western had a structured social order as rigid and as complex as any feudal state, complete with knights and crusaders (cowboys turned movie heroes), serfs, blacksmiths, couriers, benevolent tyrant. This last was Uncle Joe Goldstein. Starting life as a tailor's apprentice in Warsaw, he became a full-fledged tailor in New York, invested his money in nickelodeons, and almost immediately became a financial success.

When his suppliers couldn't give him the sort of films he wanted to show, Uncle Joe put his clothing business behind him and went west to establish his own motion picture company. Great Western was the name and the goal of his new venture.

Max arrived at its thick iron gates, took in the two twenty-foot-high lead horses standing on their hind legs in front of the entrance, and stepped up to the guard. He presented the letter, cautiously kept in the pocket of his dark blue suit jacket during his trip, which identified him as a Goldstein relative.

The guard, Patsy, a fat man with ungenerous instincts, scanned the letter, holding it in his right hand and hitting it a few times with his left, attempting to decide whether or not it was counterfeit.

After a few minutes of deep concentration he handed the letter to the young Oriental girl Max had been studying with equal concentration. She had been sitting on an overturned soapbox next to the gatehouse, painstakingly using watercolors to paint the lead horses.

She was sixteen, though she looked younger. Her name was Mitsuko, which she refused to allow to be shortened or Anglified and she was the only child of Uncle Joe Goldstein's chauffeur. Mr. Tanaka was a man who had come down in the world the moment he set foot on American soil. In Japan he had been a respected member of the samurai class but marriage to a woman of the merchant class had caused him to emigrate. She had died on giving birth to Mitsuko, leaving her husband alone in a strange world.

An acquaintance told him chauffeurs were in great demand so he took his money and invested it in learning a marketable skill. His goal in life was to buy land up the coast, to become what would have been unthinkable for him in Japan, a farmer.

It was only after several years, when he had saved the necessary money, that he learned it was illegal for anyone born in Japan to own property in California. He was waiting for his daughter to reach the age of eighteen and then she would buy the land for him, using his savings.

In the meantime Mitsuko went to American schools, which was thought an affectation in the Japanese community. During her summer holidays she accompanied her father to the studio.

Though he had seen Chinese men in New York, Max had never seen an Oriental woman before and certainly not a Japanese one. He didn't care if the guard took all day to read his letter; he couldn't take his eyes from the girl's face. He thought she looked wonderfully rare, like a beautiful porcelain figure Ryan had once given to Bessie. She had the same fragile, lovely features.

"Sure I will, Patsy," she answered in perfect American English to the guard's request, thus shattering Max's illusion that she spoke some exotic, musical language. She put aside her paint box and jabbed her brush in a glass of water. Taking one last look at the huge blond boy standing by the gate, his satchel in his hand, she took the letter and ran through the gates toward the adobe building known as Headquarters.

As she ran, she whistled a song popular just then and one which her father found particularly offensive, "Don't Wake Me Up, I'm Dreaming." As she climbed the staircase which led to Uncle Joe's office, she thought that the person at the gate whose "fate she held in her hands" (she had been reading *Ivanhoe* before school ended), was quite simply the most beautiful man she had ever seen. She could hardly wait until the evening to tell her best friend, Sharon Yamanaka, about him. She wondered how he managed to shave the deep cleft in his chin and whether he was still growing because she certainly knew she was. She was going to be a tall Japanese lady, she had decided.

"Mitsuko, sweetie, you've got paint all over this thing," Townie, Uncle Joe's Number Two Assistant complained. The Number One Assistant had been an early hostage to the war, one of the first men drafted under the first Selective Service Act which had been passed some months before in the early spring of 1917.

All men between the ages of twenty-one and thirty were being drafted. Townie, born Charles Harrison Townsend, Jr. to a Waterloo, Iowa, Episcopalian minister and his wife, was twenty-two; but he had asthma and other disabilities.

"Not another cousin," Townie said to Mitsuko as he took the letter, wiped the envelope carefully with a cloth, and proceeded to read. "I suppose he's five feet high, weighs two hundred pounds, soaking wet, and has left a long and successful career as a master tailor behind him in high middle Slavakia."

He turned from her without waiting for an answer and knocked on Uncle Joe's door. There was a muffled noise, a sort of bark, and Townie entered the office, reemerging a few moments later. "Have him come back tomorrow at ten, would you, Mitsuko? And if there's any polite way to tell him to bathe, please do so."

Mitsuko ran down the stairs and stopped in the small chauffeur's office where her father waited for Uncle Joe, studying produce manuals. She threw her arms around him. He looked up somewhat startled and patted her hand and smiled at his American child. She left her father and ran back to the front gate with the message.

"Thank you," Max said.

"You're very welcome." She sat down once more on the soapbox, taking her brush from the glass of water. "And Townie says to take a bath."

Though he would have liked to have asked who

Townie was, to have stepped through the gates and looked around the grounds, the girl's self-possession and the guard's disinterest were too daunting.

He took the trolley back to Los Angeles, found Joe Rakin waiting for him, and was taken to the Sierra Arms where Joe fixed him up with a room for fifty cents a night, breakfast and dinner included.

He spent half the night walking around Los Angeles, listening to Joe, who had unfairly been given extra duty on the night shift. "Here's what I'm planning, Max," Joe said, finding it easier to talk to his new friend than to anyone he had met in Los Angeles since he moved there. "I'm saving up my money for one big, helluva night in New York City. Soon as I spend all my money, I'm going to go to the nearest enlistment station and sign up."

Max digested this for a moment and then said, "Why?"

"Why? I want to see New York. I hear it's . . ."

"No. Why are you going to enlist?"

"You see that poster?" Joe asked, pointing to yet another print of the mother-daughter scene that had haunted Max from New York. "That's part of it. But more, I believe in this country. I believe we have to protect it. This country's been mighty good to me. I'm willing to lay down my life for it."

"But, Joe," Max said, putting his hand on the young, earnest policeman's shoulder, "no one's threatening America."

"Not yet. But if we don't stop those Huns now, they're going to be here. You wait and see. They got submarines up and down the East Coast right this minute." Joe Rakin was thoroughly versed in the propaganda spewed forth from Britain. He believed every word of it.

Max didn't—he knew about too many European territorial wars—but the poster continued to pop up in his mind every once in a while and he wondered what would happen if the Germans defeated England and France.

He said good night to Joe and went on up to his room. He wasn't surprised when the landlady's thirty-year-old spinster daughter opened her door to him. When he had been barely thirteen, delivering milk to the gentile houses in Poland, he found that he was called upon to service certain local housewives in other ways. Unknown to his brothers he had had several sexual adventures on the ship coming to America, many more in New York. It seemed quite natural to him that this uncompromising older woman would want him to make love to her.

As he lay in her sagging bed, his arms behind his head, her firm, dark body crowding him up against the wall, he wondered why he wasn't homesick. He discounted the woman next to him. Sex wasn't a panacea for Max; it was a natural function. But he was so far away from everything he had known, from Bessie, from his brothers, from everyone he cared for. Still he felt comfortable, even happy.

I suppose, he told himself, I'll get lonesome later on. And then he fell deeply, dreamlessly asleep.

He was early for his appointment, his blond and wavy hair still damp from the bath and the shampoo he had insisted upon. His landlady's daughter had obligingly filled the tub and stayed on to wash his hair, scrub his back. She liked, she said, a clean man.

Joe Rakin had had breakfast with him and walked him to the trolley, wishing Max luck.

Mitsuko met him at the gates. She was wearing Oriental clothes, a dark silk kimono, and as she stood under the huge lead horses that were Great Western's trademark, waiting for him, Max thought he had never seen a more perfect or exotic sight.

"This is an historic moment," Mitsuko said as they stood for a moment under the horses and stared at the cowboys and the makeup men and the costumers and the cameramen, crisscrossing one another across the front lot, each intent on his business. "You should savor it."

Max looked down at her and smiled. "I am."

She took his huge hand in her fragile one and led him through the gates, onto the Great Western lot, guiding him around the old stagecoach that was being trundled out to the valley and through the maze of industrious extras to Headquarters.

Townie got out of his chair and looked at Max with a sideward glance. "Dear me, you're a big one." He studied the blond hair and the blue eyes and the big shoulders. "You're about as likely to be related to Uncle Joe as Lillian Russell. But not to worry. Uncle Joe's not going to ask for a blood test. He needs men."

Townie knocked on the mahogany paneled door, a somewhat suitable anachronism in the adobe wall, and opened it, ushering Max into a dark room, some sixty feet square, filled with what passed for antiques.

"How old are you, kid?" Uncle Joe, short and ro-

tund like the cigar he was puffing, asked, looking
Max up and down, mentally taking his measurements.

"Seventeen years of age."

"Where'd you learn to speak English, Perth Am-
boy? Never mind. Sit down. You going to run and
join the army, kid?"

"For what?"

"That's what I'm sitting here trying to figure out.
For what? For some *cockamaimie* war over in the Old
Country that's got about as much to do with us Americans as chopped liver." Uncle Joe stood up and
moved around to the front of the desk, which his
dealer claimed once belonged to Marie Antoinette.

"Stand up, kid." Max did so. "How tall are you?"

"Six feet, three inches."

"Who'd ever thought Mookie Goldstein had you in
him?" Max was being passed off as Mookie's son. "So
what kind of a job are you looking for, if you don't
mind my asking? And you can sit down again before
answering."

"I want to be a cowboy in the moving pictures."

"Oh, yeah? So does everyone in this country between the ages of eight and eighty-eight. You can't be
a cowboy, kid. One, you're too young; and two, you're
a Yiddle and take it from someone who knows, kid:
there's no such thing as a Yiddish cowboy.

"But before you go away mad, I got another proposition for you: you know how to drive a wagon with a
horse?"

Max said that he did.

"Good. I got tourists fighting all day long to get in
here at two bits a head. All they want to do is watch

us make the western movies. Don't ask why. They do, that's all. Your job is to pick these hayseeds up at the front gates in a buckwagon. Then you drive them out to Western Street, let them watch ten minutes, and then you schlepp them back to the front gate, and pick up the next load.

"For this I'm going to give you twenty bucks a week. A lot of money for a nice and simple job, no? Well, let me tell you something, kid. It ain't so simple or so nice.

"I got a bunch of *mishugah* cowboys here. They could turn President Wilson into a Republican. For some reason beknownst only to themselves, they don't want the tourists. Why? Don't ask me. And for God's sake, don't ask them. They just don't want them and that's that.

"You think I haven't tried to talk to those bastards? I go down and I tell them, nicely, look, the tourists pay your salaries when your lousy two reelers don't make a dime. They tell me, politely, because this is my studio, to go stick my thumb up my ass.

"So what your real job is going to be, your major job, is not driving the buckboard. It's going to be keeping the tourists quiet. No mumbling, no yapping, no little hysterical ladies making a whole commotion when one of the boys gets splattered with tomato ketchup. You keep the ladies calm and quiet and you keep your job.

"And whatever you do, kid, you don't let no cowboy talk to no tourist. That can never happen. They got mouthpieces on them, them cowboys, they could make Fatty Arbuckle blush.

"So you want to start now or you want to think it over?"

"Right away, Mr. Goldstein."

"Uncle Joe to you, kid. We're relatives, ain't we? Another time we'll get together, you come meet my missus, my darling daughter, we'll play a couple of hands of gin rummy. Meanwhile you got a place to live? You got money in your pocket? Good. I'm going to turn you over to my Number Two Assistant, a little *fagele* named Townie. Don't worry about him. He's peculiar but his heart's in the right place. Now be a good boy, kid. Don't get into trouble with the dollies. Don't go to war."

Townie took Max to the costume department located in a barnlike building behind the commissary. "Everything at Great Western—or Great Goldstein, as we who know call it—has a number," he told Max. "Uncle Joe's Number One, natch. I'm his Number Two Assistant. You're his Number Three Guide. Now I want you to prepare yourself, darling, for his Number One Queen, a second-rate wardrobe mistress named Ronnie Magador. If he makes a pass, don't look menacing or threaten to beat him up. That sort of thing only encourages Ronnie."

An hour later Townie led a transformed Max out into the sunshine and toward the blacksmith shop where the buckboards were kept. Max had been dressed by Ronnie Magador in Great Western's Number Five Western Garb. It consisted of a flannel shirt, brass studded wrist guards, fringed gauntlets, a red and yellow bandanna, worn full in front, Levi jeans, tooled black and white Texas boots, and silver spurs.

"I look like a genuine cowboy?" Max asked, pleased.

"You look like a marzipan pretzel," Jenny Moore said, putting her own fringed and gauntleted hand to her copper-colored hair. "Don't let those oaters see you or they'll eat you alive." Her hair curled in an engaging way. She had gray eyes. Her flannel shirt had been retailored to give maximum emphasis to already prominent breasts.

"Try to curtail your natural bitchiness, darling," Townie told her. "You two are going to be buckboard mates."

She snorted and turned her back on them. Jenny Moore was seventeen, she said; a runaway heiress from a Pittsburgh mining fortune, she said. She wanted, more than anything else, to be an actress in moving pictures. While waiting to be discovered, she rode the buckboard with a megaphone in her hand, repeating the memorized script for the tourists with a deadpan delivery that never failed to amuse Townie. "There, on your right, the Tim Bronco Company in the last throes of battle with the Comanche chief, Tomahattan, and his bloodthirsty band of . . ."

For the first few days Townie sat up front on the buckboard with Max, giving him pointers on how to deal with the openly hostile cowboys ("Ignore them, darling.") and with the credulous, adoring female tourists. "Smile, Max. They think you're a movie star."

After a week it was clear that Max could handle his assignment on his own and Townie went reluctantly back to his desk in front of Uncle Joe's office.

Max and Jenny met every morning, except Sun-

day, at the blacksmith's shop though they said little
more than good morning. Or at least Max said good
morning. Jenny Moore was saving her voice for the
buckboard and for the occasional run-in she managed
with the studio directors.

They would spend the day hauling wagonloads of
tourists past the barns and corrals on the back lot, cir-
cling round and ending up on Western Street where
members of what was known as the Hollywood
Posse—genuine cowboys who had reached the final
frontier—would be grinding out strenuous two and
three reelers.

Max and Townie and occasionally Jenny would
lunch together at a table reserved for what Townie
described as "the upper-echelon service types" in the
commissary. The Hollywood Posse's table, headed by
Tim Bronco, was at the far end of the huge, window-
less space. More than anything Max wanted to sit
with the cowboys.

"You couldn't look like that and be as simple as
you seem, could you?" Jenny asked when he voiced
this desire. She wiped her face with the paper napkin
Great Western supplied with the box lunch, stood up,
and walked deliberately by the Directors' Table
where she dropped the cardboard box. None of the
men at the table missed a beat in their conversation.
More than one woman had dropped a box by their
table and though Jenny was undeniably more attractive than most, Uncle Joe took a vehement stand
against fornication with the help. "Don't shit where
you eat," was one of his favorite homilies.

"Most of the time," Max said, watching Jenny

pick up the fallen debris of her lunch, "I don't know what she's talking about."

"I may be wrong, my dear, but I do think our Jenny is trying to provoke you into making a pass," Townie said.

"She hates me."

"That doesn't signify."

"I don't think I even like her."

"She is not," Townie allowed, "the most popular woman on the payroll."

"I like you a lot, though. You've been a great friend, Townie. I want to thank you."

"Dear God, just what I was looking for: a friend. Listen, Max, you'd better move out of your landlady's daughter's bed in L.A. and take a place here in Hollywood. There's a one-room apartment below mine which has two virtues: it's on Cahuenga so you won't have to trolley out here every morning at the crack of; and I can keep an eye on you. We don't want you waking up some morning married to your landlady's daughter. Oh, don't worry. I shan't try anything. I haven't the faintest idea of what I'd do if you said yes."

"Drop to your knobby knees," Jenny—who had returned to the table—said, "close your eyes, and open your delicate, rosebud mouth."

Two days later, after a dry-eyed farewell with his landlady's daughter, Marie, Max moved out of the Sierra Arms in Los Angeles and into the Monte Excelsior Hotel and Apartment House on Cahuenga Boulevard in Hollywood.

He tried to persuade Joe Rakin to come with him.

120

"Naw," Joe said. "I don't trust all them actors, movie people. My dad used to say they were heathens, just like the Chinese. I'd better stay put. I'm close to getting my money together and then I'm going to go to New York, have my night, and enlist."

"Marie's going to be lonesome, when I'm gone," Max said, putting his arm around his friend's shoulder, watching his freckled face go red. "I told her you would come and keep her company some night."

"What'd she say?" Joe asked.

"She said that would be just fine, she'd been trying to get you in bed since you got here, but you were such a little Baptist. Go on in tonight, Joe. Just lay there. Marie will do all the work."

"I will," Joe said. But he didn't. He sat in his room all night, trying to work up the courage to go knock on Marie's door but she had been right: he was a little Baptist even if he stood six one in his stocking feet. He was also, at nineteen, still a virgin, but he figured that when he got to New York, he'd change all that.

After Max moved out, they met each other once a week for spaghetti dinner at Baronne's on Third Street. Joe would talk about the war and Max would listen but he wouldn't say anything.

"Don't you want to fight for this country?" Joe would ask, trying to goad his friend into taking some stand on the war.

"Not yet," Max would say, drinking the Chianti Baronne served for a nickel a glass, avoiding the war posters that peppered the walls. "Not yet."

Max spent his days driving the buckboard around Great Western, being as cordial as he could to the lady tourists who filled it, more or less ignoring Jenny Moore.

When he wasn't riding the buckboard, he sat at the gates with Mitsuko, answering questions about his life, fascinated by her remarkable facility to paint exactly what she saw.

"I'll be really good," she told him, "when I can paint what I can't see." For no reason he could come up with, this remark made a good deal of sense to Max.

Occasionally he'd spend an evening in bed with one of the secretaries or script girls he met at Great Western, Uncle Joe's dictum concerning only his upper-echelon employees. More often than not, he'd end up in Townie's tiny living room, eating omelettes, listening to Townie discourse on the five years he had spent in Hollywood, on the movies, on life.

Townie explained that he liked men. Max said that he did, too.

"You are an idiot, Max. Listen: I like to go to bed with men. I like to make love to them. I like to have sex with men. I am what is known as a homosexual. You do understand my drift?"

Max put down his fork and gave Townie the special smile he reserved for him. "Sure," he said.

"No, you don't. You couldn't and still have that endearing, dumb smile on your gorgeous, chiseled face. Let me try again: Max, I like to take off all my clothes and get another man to take off all of his clothes and then we get into a bed and rub nasties together and, if all goes well, we both have orgasms."

"So what?" Max asked, digging his fork into the tomato surprise Townie had made.

Sometimes Jenny Moore joined them for dinner. Max treated her in much the same way he treated Townie: with good humor but less affection.

"He's so goddamned frustrating," she complained to Townie. "His idea of a hot time is to sit around and watch the Jap chauffeur's daughter smear paint around."

"She's marvelously elegant, don't you think? That fragile way she holds herself . . ."

"That kid's as fragile as Joe Goldstein and every bit as dangerous. If you think, for one solitary moment, that she doesn't know Max is standing there, watching her every move, you're a bigger dope than he is."

"Darling, she's only sixteen."

"So was Cleopatra."

Jenny finally decided that if anyone was going to make a move, it was going to have to be her. One evening in early September, during a sudden and exhausting heat wave, when Townie had been invited to a drag ball at Ronnie Magador's, and the last load of tourists didn't leave the lot until after seven, Jenny offered to fix Max a meal.

"That'd be great," he told her. "I got nothing else to do."

She took him to her "studio" apartment which was a room in a clapboard house on La Cienega with a chorus-girl kitchen and a shared bath.

"You a pansy?" she asked him, handing him a glass of the tepid beer she had bought in a pail at the corner saloon. "You don't look like one but I learned long ago you can't judge a fruit by his cover and you and Townie . . ."

"You mind if I take off my shirt, Jenny? It's terribly hot in here."

"No, go ahead."

"What about my trousers?"

She watched him strip. Sweat was pouring down his body. He walked across the room, nude and erect, and pulled the Murphy bed out of its hiding place on the wall. She thought she had never seen a more beautiful man. She took off her dress and went to him. He assured her, in the Murphy bed, that he was heterosexual.

"It took a long time for you to get around to making love to me," she said later.

"I don't like you all that much."

"Thanks."

"Out of bed, that is," he said, reaching for her once more.

He disliked the Murphy bed, too, so he began taking her back to the apartment on Cahuenga three, four times a week, directly after work. They'd make love and then go up to Townie's for dinner.

"I'm beginning to feel like somebody's mother-in-law," Townie complained. He and Jenny were having lunch at the commissary. Max was with Mitsuko at the gates. He looked at Jenny and took a bite of his hard-boiled egg. "What's it like?"

"Enormous."

"I wasn't asking for measurements. He's remarkably free about scampering around in the buff. I've seen his penis. Enough to make one faint with desire. What I'm trying to get at, darling, is the essential experience."

She hesitated for a moment, uncharacteristically.

"He's the most gentle lover I've ever had," she said after a time. "Not too much in the way of foreplay. A certain amount of kissing, petting, and pitching woo but not so that it gets tedious. He knows what he's after and pretty soon he's going into me like a thick knife slipping through butter.

"Don't ever let anyone tell you, Townie, that it's just as good small as it is big. He slides that salami into me and we fit together like a brand-new jigsaw puzzle. I don't do much. I more or less lay there and he moves me around. He has incredible timing. He knows exactly when to do what, when to move it here, when to shift it there. For a kid from the middle of nowhere, Europe, he knows more positions, more ways of twisting it and me around than any illustrated manual I've ever come across. Jesus, I get hot just thinking about how he . . ."

"Stop, Jenny, I'm begging you. I'll pass out if you don't."

"I'm telling you, Townie: if that guy would once let me sleep with him overnight, I'd marry him and give up my career in a minute."

"Darling, I hate to burst your bubble but it seems patently clear that Max doesn't want to marry you, nothing could be further from his mind; and, not to mince words, riding a buckboard with a megaphone in your hand would not be much of a career to sacrifice if he did."

By the end of the following spring Uncle Joe Goldstein had lost forty percent of his men between the ages of twenty-one and thirty-five to the Selective Service. He was pursuing his own policy of appeasement, hoping that the eligible males left wouldn't suddenly desert Great Western for the Great War.

Most of his cowboy stars were over thirty-five, but still he wanted to keep them happy. Up to a point. He was not, he said, giving way on the controversial and still steaming Tourists-On-the-Set issue.

The cowboys, Tim Bronco in the lead, continued to lobby to bar the tourists, angry with Uncle Joe for inflicting semihysterical women on them while they were executing the difficult and often dangerous stunts that made up the bulk of their films.

It was early in that summer of 1918, while Europe was doing its best to kill off its young men, and soon after Max turned twenty, that he drove the buckboard onto Western Street where Tim Bronco was filming one of his early full-length features.

Max felt something was wrong but he wasn't certain what it was. Jenny, unconcerned, was going through her speech with her usual deadpan delivery. The women in the buckboard, in their blue cotton dresses, with their expectant faces, were prepared for a minor thrill. They held each other's hands, readying themselves for their first sight of Tim Bronco in person.

Bronco, an original member of the Hollywood Posse, toughened by years on the ranch and rodeo circuit, was turning out dozens of "Bronco Tim" films a year, making more money than any Western star outside of Tom Mix. He was known for his temper, for his prejudice toward Indians, and for his slant-eyed, snubbed-nosed profile.

When Max pulled the buckboard up to the ramp where the ladies were to disembark to watch the filming, Bronco was standing in the middle of Western Street. The ladies gasped. He stood in a typical stance, a Bronco trademark: his feet wide apart, both hands on the silver pistols he wore in black-leather holsters around his waist.

It was a dry, hot California day. Dust exploded in small clouds each time someone moved. To the ladies Western Street seemed especially real, the façades of the saloon and the hotel needing paint, the stable at the far end looking as if it were about to cave in.

Tim Bronco waited until the ladies were lined up on the ramp and had become silent. He never looked in their direction, not once. He simply began to shout, as if they had interrupted him but now he could go on.

Now even Jenny realized something was off. Bronco barely spoke at the best of times. He never said a word when he was on the set.

"You goddamned cocksucking bastard. You wet-backed, fish-eyed chili dipper. Get your ass out here. I'm going to show you a few gringo tricks."

The ladies, sweating lightly in the midafternoon sun, closed their ears to the language. "So authentic, isn't it, Margaret," one said to the other, clasping her white-gloved hands.

Max thought it was too authentic. He was about to get his charges back aboard the wagon when the saloon doors flew open. Concho, a Mexican Indian who usually appeared as the villain in Bronco westerns, flew out with a knife in his right hand. He tackled Bronco around the neck with his left arm, pulled him down to the dirt street, and, raising the knife over Bronco's chest, stabbed him. He pulled the

knife out and blood, thick and red, spurted everywhere.

The woman who had stood closest to the street
turned to Max and began to scream. Bronco's blood
ran down her face. The other ladies stood back, some
of them screaming; but Max had lost interest in
them.

Bronco had somehow thrown Concho off of him
and was slithering backward in the dust of the street,
pulling his .45 out of his holster, trying to stop the
blood with his free hand. Concho began to move back
toward the saloon but Bronco began firing. Blood immediately soaked the Mexican's shirt as he fell to the
ground.

Two Indians, with short, fat knives in their hands,
came racing out of the crowd of extras and crew that
had been watching from the folding reflectors at the
opposite end of Western Street. Half a dozen cowboys, seeing them, came out of the falling-down
stables, guns in their hands. Concho and Tim Bronco
lay in the middle of Western Street, covered with dust
and blood.

Before the cowboys and the Indians could come together, Max leaped over the ramp barricade and
jumped between them.

"Get the fuck out of the way," one of the cowboys,
a man with a wide, thick face told him. Max hit him
on the flat underside of his jaw. He went down immediately. Suddenly everyone on the set was fighting,
but with their hands. Twenty minutes later only Max
was standing and just.

The lady tourists had long since vanished in the

direction of the main gates, their screams and shouts boomeranging around the front lot.

Max looked down at Tim Bronco and thought, for a moment, that he saw a leg move. Then he was sure of it. "Get Doc Moody over here right away," he shouted at Jenny who was still standing on the ramp. Then he saw one of Bronco's slanted eyes open, followed a few seconds later by the other.

"Who in goddamned hell are you?" Bronco asked, getting himself off the ground.

"Yeah," Concho said, sitting up taking careful aim, throwing his knife at Max as Bronco shot him with his silver pistol. The one was rubber, the other filled with blanks.

"We kinda thought," Bronco said, replacing his pistol in its holster, "that we'd give them tourists a real show."

"Well," Max said, looking around at the knocked-out cowboys and Indians, "you kinda did."

"Say, you know how to ride a hoss, fella?" Bronco asked.

Max had bit parts in Bronco's next few short films and was the villain in Bronco's second full-length feature. "Poor Tim," Townie said, after he viewed the finished product. "He doesn't have much sense of self-preservation, does he? Max makes him look as if someone sat on him. Someone big."

Even to Uncle Joe, who liked to protect his established stars, Bronco seemed shorter and stubbier than before. Max, with a stock villain's sneer on his face throughout, managed to look heroic and homespun.

The audiences came out rooting for the villain.

It was Townie's job to report on the fan mail, to keep Uncle Joe abreast of what his audiences were saying. "So what are they saying?" he asked Townie.

"They're saying Max Meyer, if they only knew his name." It was Uncle Joe's policy to credit but one star per film.

"Get that kid up here, right away."

After the preliminaries, after the inquiries about Mookie and one more recapitulation of the Bronco-Concho incident, Uncle Joe sat back in his chair which had once, he had been assured, graced a sixteenth-century papal chamber. "So, kid," he said, "I got a little proposition for you."

"You'd better talk to my agent, Uncle Joe."

"An agent? Already he's got himself an agent. *Pupick,* you've shown your face in maybe two and a half movies and already you've got an agent?" Uncle Joe sighed heavily. "So who is he, this agent?"

Max pointed his thick index finger toward the window seat behind Uncle Joe. Uncle Joe swiveled his chair around. He stared at Townie. Then he swiveled back to stare at Max.

"It was as if," Townie was to later tell Jenny, "Jesus was deciding whom to accuse first: Pontius Pilate or Judas Priest. In the end he buried his bald head in his hairy hands and went into This-Is-the-Thanks-I-Get which he cut short by some ten minutes, aware that I had already heard it on at least half a dozen occasions."

Uncle Joe finally stood up and turned to Townie. "Tell your star that I'm offering him, on a silver platter, a plum of a part every actor on this lot would cut off his right ball for: the starring role in the full-length Joseph Goldstein/Great Western feature production of *The All-American Cowboy*."

"I'll take it," Max said, standing up. "You two work out the details." He left Headquarters and ambled over to the front gates to watch Mitsuko, now involved in a detailed painting of Patsy, the guard. Townie took his seat and, before Uncle Joe could say anything, began negotiations by saying how much Max would receive *if* he took the role.

The All-American Cowboy, produced in the last three weeks of June, 1918, was released in the first two weeks of the following month. It was the poster, almost everyone concerned agreed, that made it the success it was.

The idea was conceived the night Townie had invited Max, Jenny, and Carleton LeMay, the line producer assigned to the project, to his apartment for "pasta à la Townsend." Carleton LeMay was the only college graduate at Great Western, a handsome blond man in his early twenties.

He came into the kitchen where Townie was tossing the pasta and poured himself a glass of wine. "What's that?" he asked, pointing at a framed illustration hanging on the wall next to the sink.

The film that had launched Maurice Costello at Vitagraph had been prompted with a poster; Vitagraph's public relations director, an especial friend of Townie's, had given him a reduced version of it.

"If it worked for Costello," Carleton LeMay said, "it may work for Max."

The subsequent poster revealed Max sitting on a white horse, two smoking pistols in his hands, a bruise over one eye. He was shirtless, a pose Townie insisted upon. "Listen, darling," he told Carleton Le-May. "Up until now cowboys have been more buttoned up than your Aunt Nell. Put that physique in front of the Altoona Alhambra on a Saturday night and you'll have lines running round the block."

"Sure," Carleton said, looking at Max dubiously.

From virtually the moment the poster was placed in its frame in front of San Francisco's Silver Palace Moving Picture Theater, where *The All-American Cowboy* premiered, every cowboy star had to have well-developed biceps, triceps, and pectoral muscles. For the first time in Great Western history, women outnumbered the men in the audience.

"Listen, Uncle Joe," Townie said when it came time to negotiate Max's next film. "When he gets off that horse and looks into the camera's eyes, smiling that ridiculously earnest smile of his, females all over America start to breathe heavy."

"I don't care if they wet their pants," Uncle Joe said, closing negotiations for the day. "Not one single solitary nickel more."

The All-American Cowboy was scheduled to open on Broadway in early August, close to the day when Bessie's birthday was to be celebrated. Her party, she wrote Max, was a command performance. "You be here, fat boy," she told him. "And for once, we can all go to the movies together. I've finally heard of a film I wouldn't mind seeing."

"How much money you got saved up?" Max asked Joe Rakin over their last spaghetti dinner at Baronne's.

"Nearly three hundred bucks. I'm just about ready to go." The newspaper that morning had carried a description of a battle in northern France in which four hundred Englishmen were killed. It had been one of the worst catastrophes of the war. "How much you think a fancy hotel in New York would cost, Max?"

"Nothing. You're going to stay with me at my sister's house. It's about as fancy as you can get. I'll give you a night on Broadway and it won't cost you a penny. As of now you're officially invited to Bessie Meyer's birthday party."

The day after they arrived, Bessie insisted on taking everyone to see *The All-American Cowboy* on Broadway. Joe Rakin, who blushed each time she looked at him, was to sit next to her, as the guest of honor.

Jake, who had left his wife in Key West because she hated to travel, sat on one side of Max, Nick on the other. Before the film began, Jake told Max that he liked living in Florida and no, he didn't miss New York.

"Not one little iota?" Bessie asked, turning her head around, her red curls flying.

"Only the family," Jake said, kissing her.

Sitting in the Paramount, watching himself on the screen, reminded Max of his first taste of moving pictures, when he and his two brothers and Moishe watched Tim Bronco in the nickelodeon on Second Avenue.

After the film Bessie stood up and started clapping. And suddenly everyone in the Paramount began clapping, too. Bessie put her arm through Max's and led him up the aisle and out onto Broadway while everyone in the audience stood up, still applauding.

"You!" Bessie said, pulling him to her, kissing him under the Paramount's marquee. "You! Who would have thought a person could be so triply blessed: handsome, talented, and Bessie Meyer's brother to the bargain. I'm so proud, Max, I'm bursting."

She gave up trying to hide her tears and her eyes glistened as she hugged and kissed him once more. "I was never all that good at acting. But you, you're going to be better than Thomashefsky. You wait and see."

Bessie's birthday party that year was Ryan's idea of an Indian progressive supper, one held in Manhattan. One hundred guests, including Joe Rakin, in white tie and tails, met at Murray's for champagne cocktails. They went on to the Claridge for soup and fish. The main course—pheasant under glass—was served under the New York Roof: dessert, baked Alaska flambé, was presented at Rector's. Dancing and entertainment began at midnight at B's Other Place.

"Breakfast," the newspapers and tabloids reported, "was served amidst the potted palms of the 400 Club." But neither Max nor Joe Rakin made it to breakfast. Instead they were upstairs at the Green House next door to B's Gardens down on Lower Broadway. Max was making certain that Joe Rakin did not leave New York a virgin.

After his visit to the Green House and several hours spent in the all-inclusive embrace of that establishment's warmest siren, Joe Rakin's face was red

for days. His night in New York had been more spec-
tacular than he had ever supposed.

Before he and Max went back to Bessie's, he insisted on stopping off at the enlistment center on Broadway. "In the morning I may not have the nerve."

He went in by himself, leaving Max to study the
posters on the outside of the square brick building.
There was an old one hanging there, one dating back
to when Max first went to California. It was the
woman and child in rags, an endless vista of carnage behind them, with the message, "Don't Let It
Happen Here."

"Goddamn it," Max said, ripping the poster from
the wall.

"So, *nu?*" Uncle Joe Goldstein asked Townie, prod-
ding him in the shoulder with his small, hairy fist.
"When's he coming back. He's been in New York
long enough. What's he got, a dolly there? I'm ready
to talk turkey. About a very hot property."

The Return of the All-American Cowboy was the
hot property but Townie told Uncle Joe Max wasn't
interested.

"If you're trying to hold me up for more money,
you little *chazer . . .*"

"He's not coming back, Uncle Joe."

On August 25, almost a month before the third Selective Service Act was officially passed, calling for all
able-bodied men between eighteen and forty-eight to
join the war effort, Bessie entered the room where
Max was sleeping.

"You don't knock?" he asked, happy to see her. Her hair was as red as he remembered it and she seemed slimmer and more beautiful than ever.

"Not in my own house," she said, sitting on the edge of his bed, touching his forehead to see if he had a fever, that trick of hers which seemed somehow to have been passed onto her by their mother. "I just want to tell you that you have nothing to worry about."

"I never did."

"I'm talking about the new Selective Service Act. Edward Lewis tells me it's only a matter of weeks before it's officially passed. Ryan's fixing everything."

"No, he's not," Max said, taking her hand.

"And why not, may I ask?" Somehow she felt closer to Max now than when he had lived with her. He had become not only a star in the moving pictures, but an adult, too. "And why not?" she repeated.

"Because I've already enlisted, Sister."

Despite Bessie's protests, despite Uncle Joe's telegrams, Max and Joe Rakin sailed for Europe on October 8, 1918. They had spent nearly a month in Trenton, New Jersey, learning which end of a rifle was which, how to salute an officer, how to answer a Hun if captured. On weekends they went to New York where Bessie fed them at B's Other Place and society girls taught them the Argentine tango.

It was the happiest time in Joe Rakin's life and he said so on the troop ship he and Max were being shipped out on. Max didn't say anything. He watched the Statue of Liberty disappear in the distance and then he and Joe went down to find their bunks. He wasn't at all certain how he had ended up joining the army and he couldn't understand how Bessie had once played the Statue of Liberty. She didn't look a bit like her.

CHAPTER 2

It was a freezing Saturday afternoon in December, 1918, when Kay was first introduced to B's Other Place. She had started out, that morning, with good intentions. She and her husband, Dickie Hull, were going Christmas shopping. But the crowds and the weather and Dickie's easy charm persuaded her to put it off.

"Let's have a drink first and warm ourselves up," Dickie said.

They wound up getting "fairly stinking," in Dickie's phrase, first at the Palais Royale and later at Healey's Golden Glades where they had run into the Robinsons.

When Dickie suggested moving on to B's Other Place, Bill Robinson objected, saying it cost a fortune to step into the place. "The party's on me," Dickie told him and Maisie Robinson stood up and said, "Okay, dearie. You twisted my arm."

Dickie Hull's father had made a fortune manufacturing army uniforms and, upon his early death, had left several million dollars to his son. "I shall spend it well, if not wisely," Dickie vowed.

There weren't many people at B's; Saturday afternoon was the time when only inner-circle drinkers congregated there. A society dance team made up to look like Mae Murray and Clifton Webb were practicing for the evening show which starred the Dolly Sisters.

"Let's get ginny," Dickie said, ordering pink ladies all around. "We've got to stay ahead of Prohibition."

"You're so far ahead," Maisie Robinson told him, "it will never catch up."

Wartime Prohibition, in effect for several months in an effort to conserve grains, had been lifted as had the one A.M. curfew, immediately after the Armistice. But twenty-two states had already voted dry. New York, as Dickie Hull knew it—Rector's, Resienweber's, Ciro's, and Jack's—was almost over and Dickie was aware of it. He told his wife he was only waiting "for them to clean up Paris and then we'll go and live and drink there."

Kay said that was a perfectly marvelous idea. She had married Dickie that fall mostly because her father, an Old New York Wall Street lawyer, had so vehemently disapproved of him.

She was nineteen and looked younger in the modish furs and gowns Dickie had introduced her to. She still mourned her mother, a frail, delightful woman, who had died during the 1916 influenza epidemic. She blamed her mother's death on her father's disinterest, on his stoic, Protestant-ethic way of life. When Dickie, rich, six foot four, and an ex-Princeton football player, had boozily told her he loved her, that he wanted to marry her, she immediately took him up on it.

B's Other Place, Kay thought as a headwaiter led

them to a table in the front tier overlooking the
dance floor, was exactly the sort of establishment her
father would have had shut down and her mother
would have adored. Though B's was more than adequately heated, she shivered, attempting to put the
memory of her parents aside by sipping at her gin
and concentrating on the dance floor.

A boy who seemed to Kay to be about her age was
leaning against the chromed railing, watching the
Webb-Murray look-alikes go round the floor. He had
the darkest blue eyes she had ever seen and the thickest, blackest lashes. Staring at him from thirty feet
across the dance floor, she was fascinated by the trick
he had of looking up and through his lashes, of keeping his eyes on the dancers' feet, seemingly memo-
rizing their every step.

His black hair was slicked back and he wore a dark
suit of some thin material that emphasized his wide
shoulders and narrow hips.

"He looks like a dansant gigolo, doesn't he?"
Maisie Robinson asked in her attractive, throaty
voice.

"That waiter interest you, Kay?" Dickie asked.

"I don't think he's a waiter, dearie," Maisie said.

He had high, romantic cheekbones. He had a kind
of style Kay hadn't seen before. And he leaned
against the railing with the sort of insolence she associated with the depraved men who appeared in the
novels she had read after lights-out at boarding school,
men who performed "unspeakable acts." She laughed
and pushed her gin glass away but found herself looking up, again, at the boy-man across the dance floor.

He sensed her attention and stared back, taking in

the table at a glance, dismissing them, and turning again to the dancers.

"I believe my bride has grown weary of me," Dickie said, putting his head on Maisie Robinson's ample shoulder.

At that moment Bessie came into the room, stopping to say hello to Dickie, allowing him to introduce her to the Robinsons and his wife. "You're far too pretty for Dickie Hull," Bessie said to Kay, and Dickie laughed, pleased. Bessie had become famous for insulting her customers, and indeed it had become a mark of special attention.

Kay watched as Bessie, in a blue dress the color of her eyes, walked over to the boy watching the dancers, her red curls bouncing all the way. Bessie placed her hand against his forehead, as if testing his temperature. He looked up, irritably, and suddenly, through his smile, his face was transformed. He was no longer a sullen dance hall gigolo but a charming, even a beautiful boy on the verge of manhood.

"He couldn't be her husband," Kay said, "or her son."

"No, dearie," Maisie told her. "He's her brother and he's going to be a killer when he grows up."

The boy, laughing at something Bessie was saying, suddenly grabbed her hand and tugged her onto the dance floor. The orchestra was playing a ragtime song called "Hot Mustard," and he led her into one of the many variations of the Castle walk. Bessie, in her blue gown and her red hair, and her brother, with his dark sleekness, made the professional dance team seem gauche and heavy-footed in comparison. Even the waiters stopped moving about and watched as they moved around the dance floor, the boy absorbed in the intricacies of the steps he was executing, Bessie absorbed in his delight.

When the dance ended, the boy spinning Bessie around in a final flourish, everyone in the cabaret clapped. Even the man standing in the doorway which led to the offices. He caught Bessie's eye, smiled, and nodded and went into the office area.

"One more dance, Bessie," the boy pleaded.

"Not now, Nicky," she said, kissing his cheek, disengaging herself, following the sandy-haired man through the doorway.

"When Ryan calls, Bessie Meyer jumps," Maisie said, upending her glass.

"Anyone ever tell you, Maisie," Bill Robinson said, "that you know too much?"

"Not recently, dearie. Do you think I can have another drink?"

The orchestra was playing a slow fox-trot, "Give Me the Moonlight, Give Me the Girl," when Kay felt a hand on her shoulder. She looked up to find Bessie's younger brother staring down at her. "Dance?"

"Go ahead," Dickie told her. "Teach the boy a new step or two."

Kay allowed herself to be led onto the dance floor. He held her tightly as he danced her around the floor with his professional expertise. She could see Dickie and the Robinsons watching as he put his mouth next to her ear. "I got a hard-on for you the second you walked into this joint."

She tried to push him away but his hand on the small of her back forced her closer. "Meet me Monday at the Claridge. In the afternoon. Tell him you got to go shopping."

"How old are you?" she asked because she felt she had to say something, to break the mood. She felt as if she were a scrap of iron, caught up by a powerful magnet.

"Twenty. I'll be in the lobby. Three P.M. sharp." He broke away as the music ended and, putting his hand on her arm, led her back to the table.

Dickie was much amused. He stood up to help Kay into her seat as Nick nodded and walked away.

"You've got yourself an admirer," Dickie said and Bill Robinson laughed. Maisie, however, looked at Kay speculatively. Kay asked for another pink lady.

She went to the Claridge on Monday afternoon, she told herself, to talk to Nick Meyer. He was too young to be so corrupt. She was going to help him.

Instead he helped her. "Right into bed," she said later, laughing at the memory. It wasn't until much later that she found out he was only sixteen years old, that she wasn't his first woman or even his tenth. He had introduced himself, shortly after his arrival in America, to the girls upstairs at the Green House.

Kay Hull had never been to bed with anyone but her husband. It had never occurred to her—before that afternoon at the Claridge—that love didn't have to take thirty-five seconds, that the man didn't have to do all the work to receive all the pleasure.

That afternoon at the Claridge, Kay Hull had her first orgasm and her first intimation that her marriage was not going to last. The boy she was in bed with, the boy who had been so revelatory, broke another convention that until then she was certain was a basic rule between men and women who had had sexual intercourse: he was not going to profess eternal or any other kind of love to her.

"What do I know from society dames?" he asked, his blue eyes staring up at the intricate molding on the Claridge ceiling, a thin, black cigar in his mouth. "I wanted you. I had you. And maybe I'll see you around sometime. Maybe I won't."

"You bastard," she said, starting to get out of the bed.

He grabbed her wrist, pulling her back. "Okay. What're you doing tomorrow afternoon about this time?"

She began to see Nick Meyer, four, sometimes five times a week. She found herself wanting to be with him all the time. I am clearly insane, she told herself, but, still, there it was. She knew so little about him, and what little she did know, she had had to drag out of him.

He spent his days driving cars for Ryan, accompanying him on his various trips. Sometimes to Albany, sometimes to Brooklyn, Jersey, Long Island. "He's good at 'cementing relations,'" Nick said when she asked about Ryan.

"What's your ambition?" she asked, changing the subject; there was something about the way he talked when he spoke of Ryan that scared her.

"To fuck, dance, and gamble, more or less in that order."

"Those aren't ambitions. They're pastimes."

"Excuse me, teacher. My ambition in life is to be the toughest and best fucker, dancer, and gambler in the city of New York."

She saw him for almost a year. Always in the same suite, always the same routine, always the same indelible pleasure.

But on October 29, 1919, the day after the National Prohibition Act passed President Wilson's veto, Dickie announced that they were leaving for Paris within the month.

"I don't suppose you'd marry me," she said to Nick that afternoon.

"Nope."

"Why not?"

"For starters, you ain't Jewish. For closers, I just turned seventeen. Bessie would never let me."

She saw him once before she departed for Paris. He had left a message with her maid and she went to meet him at the Claridge. She told herself she wasn't going to make love with a seventeen-year-old boy again but once she was in the suite, in the bed, with his arms around here, his age didn't seem to matter.

Afterward he told her that maybe someday they could marry.

"It's never been as good with anyone else," he said as if he had twenty-year's experience behind him. "It's never going to be."

"How do you know?"

"I know and you know. Don't you, Kay?"

"Yes, goddamn it."

"Maybe next year I'll get a little cabaret of my own going."

"Next year? Next year there won't be carbarets. People aren't going to pay a two-dollar cover to drink grape juice."

Nick smiled that smile which transformed his face

and gave her one of his rare, affectionate kisses. "You're such a dumb Dora, Kay."

He went home to dinner with Bessie and she went home to supervise the packing, though Dickie said it wouldn't be necessary. "You can get all new things in Paris," he told her.

CHAPTER 3

No one had told them that Key West was in a tropical zone. It had taken a week to reach that island city, the last day spent on Henry Flagler's fifty-million-dollar folly, the Florida East Coast Railroad.

Their train had arrived four hours later and they were the only passengers to disembark. Jake and Moishe, wearing their blue serge suits, sweated copiously and continually as they stood in front of the depot in the full heat of the February sun, looking up and down the deserted street.

Esther, wearing her black tweed traveling suit, a cream-colored double-ply satin blouse hand embroidered by her mother, and various weighty undergarments, sat on an overturned cardboard suitcase, fanning herself with her hand.

One of the last of Key West's mule-drawn trolleys pulled up and stopped, the driver looking expectantly at Jake. "Maybe we should get on the trolley, Moishe," he said.

"And go where? And do what? No, no, *Yonkle*. We have to wait for Mr. Shuster."

Jake looked at Moishe and then at his bride who was in that state of semihypnosis she seemed able to put herself into at will and watched the trolley move on. He took off his jacket.

"You'd better put that jacket on, Jake," Moishe said to him. "Mr. Shuster has the reputation of being a very proper man."

"If he's so proper, he'd be at the station to meet us."

"We're four hours late."

"Maybe he thinks we missed the train."

"Where are you going, Jake?" Esther called out, seeing her husband walk off.

"To find out where this guy lives."

"Just don't get lost, Jake," Moishe shouted after him. Moishe had been put in charge of the little expedition by Bessie and he didn't want anyone to find fault with the way he carried out his duties.

Jake went up to a small, dark man, leaning against an unpainted wooden cottage, smoking a cigar. He was a Cuban who liked to say he was a Mexican and was named Luis San Obispo.

"You know where Leon Shuster lives?" Jake asked him.

Luis San Obispo took the cigar from his mouth and spat onto the street. Then he replaced the cigar in his mouth and closed his eyes.

"Thanks a lot," Jake said. "For the information."

Luis San Obispo let him walk away a few steps before asking him if he wanted to try a good cigar. Jake allowed as how he would and took the brown panatela that had suddenly appeared in Luis Obispo's hand. Luis watched as Jake lit the cigar and waited while Jake puffed on it.

"Best damned cigar I ever smoked," Jake said, smiling.

"No shit," Luis said. "I rolled it."

At that moment Leon Shuster pulled up in his new Ford.

"The train was hours late," Moishe said to Leon in Yiddish as Leon drove them to the north end of the island where he had his dry goods emporium.

"We don't speak that language here," Leon said. "And," he went on, turning to look at Jake in the back seat, "we don't stand around street corners talking to Cubans. Not on this island."

Leon Shuster was proud of the fact that he was one of the only Jews to be born on Key West, a genuine Conch, as the native sons called themselves. His father had arrived as one of a band of Jewish peddlers in the eighties, selling goods at discounted prices. When the Key West Merchants' Protective Association was formed and passed a law requiring all peddlers to pay a thousand-dollar license fee, Leon's father was the only one who didn't leave for Miami. He had prospered through the Spanish-American War and he had held his own during the periodic slumps.

Shuster's Store was the largest dry goods store in the Florida keys. It stood at the corner of Flemming and Grinell, a long and narrow white clapboard building with high ceilings and rows of glass display cases.

Leon, his wife, and five children lived in one of the old waterfront houses on Front Street, surrounded by palm trees, frangipani, hibiscus, and bougainvillea.

His wife, an import from Atlanta, welcomed the newcomers with a traditional kosher meal. "Though we consider ourselves native Conchs, we have never forgotten the fact that we are Jews," Leon said over dinner. Esther and Moishe applauded this sentiment while the eldest of the Shuster children, a pretty dark-haired girl of fourteen, told Jake that meat from the conch shell—a local delicacy—was about as kosher as salt pork.

Jake laughed and was rewarded with a grim look from Leon Shuster.

In the morning, over breakfast, Leon informed Moishe that he would in the future be addressed as Murray. Afterward he took the three northerners to Shuster's Store where he had them outfitted in clothing more suited to the climate. Payment, it was understood, would come out of Jake's and Moishe's monthly checks.

Esther, three months pregnant, looked especially beautiful in the white dresses she acquired. They emphasized the glow of her olive skin and the sheen of her black hair which she wore *en bouffant*. Leon presented her with a palmetto fan and she was never, from that moment, to be without one.

From the very beginning Moishe was smitten. He was a man who habitually attached himself to strong Jewish women. Finding himself at the southernmost tip of America, where there was a premium on strong Jewish women, he found himself longing for Esther. He was always fetching bits of ice for her, wrapping them in a handkerchief so she could press them against her forehead. "I suffer so terribly from the heat," she liked to say, "you should never know."

The three of them lived in a small clapboard house behind Shuster's Store on Flemming Street. It was owned by Leon Shuster and payment of its rent was also taken out of Jake's and Moishe's paychecks. It had a front porch with two columns and barely enough space for two wicker chairs; a tiny living room with a sofa and two rattan chairs; a dining room just large enough for a table and chairs; and two upstairs bedrooms in what had once been the attic. It had a pressed tin roof upon which the tropical sun beat down and too few shade trees to protect it. The kitchen and the outhouse stood on either side of the cistern which collected their water in back of the house.

On a Friday evening a month after they arrived, when Jake and Moishe returned from Shuster's Store, they found Esther at the foot of the stairs, unconscious. Moishe ran to Leon Shuster's house and Leon himself went for the doctor who closeted himself with Esther in the tiny master bedroom for well over an hour.

"She's going to be fine," the doctor told Moishe, mistaking him for Esther's husband. There was a moment of silence in which no one corrected him. "The baby, of course, is dead."

She had tripped, she explained, going up the stairs. It had been so hot, she had had an attack of dizziness, and fell.

"I thought you said you tripped," Jake said, sitting next to her on the bed, holding her hand.

"I tripped. I fell. What's the difference? Now," she said, looking up at him, "we can go home, Jake."

"You can go home any time you like, Esther," he said, dropping her hand on the starched white sheet. "Me, I like it here."

Though she had grown up in her father's restau-

rant, she knew little about cooking and was disin-
clined to learn. After the miscarriage a black woman
with the unlikely name of Blondell was hired to
"help" with the cooking. She was very young, somewhere in her mid-teens, and claimed her father had
been an African king, kidnapped by the slave traders
when he was a child. She was short and fat and after
listening to Esther's somewhat incoherent explanation
of Jewish dietary laws, continued to cook as her
mother had taught her.

Jake, Esther, and Moishe suddenly found themselves eating such forbidden foods as pork, rock
shrimp, and conch meat in the form of fried fritters.
Blondell specialized in varieties of fish none of them
had ever heard of.

"What kind of fish is this, Blondell?" Jake asked
one evening several months after they had arrived in
Key West, pointing to a piece of delicately fried and
beautifully flavored fillet.

"That there is what we call Jew fish," Blondell
said, setting down a platter of fried plantains on the
table. "You shouldn't take no offense."

Moishe put his fork down, looked at Jake, then at
Esther and finally at Blondell who, it was obvious,
was perfectly serious. He jumped up from the table
and ran to the backyard. They could hear him
throwing up in the backyard.

"That man certainly has a sensitive stomach,"
Blondell said, snatching one of the plantains, pop-
ping it into her mouth and going back to her kitchen.
Jake and Esther continued to eat.

Jake, in his white suit and shoes, with his fair hair

and broad shoulders, was a model clerk in the flourishing emporium; only Leon didn't approve. The naval installation, which had been allowed to go to seed after the Spanish-American War, was being infused with new life. By July it was operating with a full staff, daily rumors of German submarines off the coast having some basis in reality. Leon Shuster's contract with the navy was solid and lucrative.

Jake, with his easy ways and his patience, his willingness to spend time with customers, was soon asked for by name by the navel stewards as well as by the local housekeepers and the few members of the Cuban community who traded at Shuster's.

Leon would stand at the far end of the store by the cash register, a thumb hooked in his waistcoat, watching Jake sell Louise Askin's housekeeper an extra bolt or two of cotton. "I don't like his methods," Leon objected to his wife over Sunday dinner, the time set aside for conversation. "I don't approve of that boy. Too easy with the ladies. And I see too much of him. Wherever I look, he's there. Now Murray's a perfect clerk. Never seen, barely heard."

Jake and Moishe walked the few yards to the store each morning at seven, had their coffee and sweet cakes with the other clerks in the back room, and were on the floor by eight. The store was closed between twelve and one when Jake and Moishe would go back to the house for luncheon with Esther, cooked by Blondell. After her miscarriage Esther never seemed to move from the upholstered sofa in the living room, the palmetto fan in her hand always working. Lunch finished, Jake and Moishe would return to the store for another five hours.

After work Moishe would go to the back of the house to soak his feet and Jake would walk over to Jack's on Simonton Street, the most proper saloon in Key West. Beer was a nickel a glass but each customer was allowed no more than three glasses, Jack not wanting anyone to overdo.

After his three beers Jake would go back to the house, have a bath out in the tub behind the cistern, providing Moishe hadn't used all the water for his aching feet, and then go in and eat Blondell's food.

Moishe, tired after the long day, remained silent during the meal. Esther only spoke to complain about the heat. They could hear Blondell out in the yard, talking to the neighbor's girl, and the rooster down the street courting the chickens. The heat, especially during that first summer, was as solid and intrusive as another human presence.

Jake waited a month and then decided to resume sexual relations with his wife. She objected, said it was too soon, that she was still sore "down there," that perhaps in September she would be all right. Jake told her it was going to be all right now. He promised to be gentle.

"I don't want another baby, Jake."

"You won't have one," he said, showing her the safety he had bought at Shuster's Store.

At nine o'clock every evening, when it cooled down a bit, Jake would take an unwilling Esther by the hand and they would go upstairs to their little oven of a room and he would get out the cumbersome safety and put it on and then work out his frustrations by making love to her. Moishe would sit in the dining room, his elbows on the table, his eyes on the ceiling, listening.

After a while Jake stopped wearing the safeties and Esther stopped complaining about being sore when they had sex, but for all intents and purposes whatever love their marriage had contained had dissolved when Esther had her miscarriage.

Occasionally Jake would walk over to Duval Street and stand in front of one of the saloons called the Bucket of Blood. There were half a dozen of them, all independently owned, all sharing the sailors and seafarers and adventurers and local boys out to have a good time.

Jake would look in through the open doors and watch the girls and the young sharks, drinking beer, dancing to the Negro bands' up-tempo jazz. He especially liked the smell of those saloons, coming at him in small, sharp doses each time the doors swung open. It was a composite smell, made up of sweat and sawdust and alcohol and cheap, seductive perfume.

It was all he could do to keep from going in. But he had promised Bessie that he was going to be a *mensch* and who knew what would happen if he strolled in to one of the Buckets of Blood and had a few beers and got to talking to one of the women standing at the bar. If he had listened to Bessie in the first place, he reasoned, turning away, he wouldn't be married to Esther.

He'd been more disappointed by the miscarriage than he had expected. He had looked forward to the consolation of a child, a little girl (he had secretly hoped) he would be able to spoil and love.

He would come back from his walks to Duval Street frustrated and unhappy and sit on the front porch, smoking Luis San Obispo's hand-rolled cigars while Esther slept upstairs and Moishe lay awake in the room next to theirs.

In March, 1917, one of the most stalwart supporters of America's entry into what was then being called the "European" war was Florida's own Senator Devon.

Like Claude Wheeler, his prospective son-in-law, the senator was a native Key Wester, a Conch who could trace his roots back to the eighteenth-century pirates who waited off Key West's shore for likely booty.

Whereas all traces of lusty high-seas crime had been obliterated from Claude's person, there was still something of the pirate about Senator Devon. He was a big man, scrupulously polite, who had worked his way through his father's money on the way to becoming senator and was now intent on amassing a fortune of his own.

He had been known to receive certain visitors in his big house on Whitehead Street where his frail wife, Elizabeth, had died giving birth to his daughter, Virginia, who seemed to be made of the same strong, sturdy material as he.

It was said that the visitors who came to Devon House, where the senator seemed to spend a great deal of time for a man who was supposed to be in Washington, gave him presents—usually in the form of cash—in the hope that the senator would vote one way or the other on such matters as government appropriations, wartime contracts, et cetera.

The senator had two public weaknesses. One was his daughter and the other was Claude Wheeler who lived in a small house on the other side of Whitehead and was the sort of lad, the senator said, he would have liked to have had for a son. That he was to have him for a son-in-law seemed just one more layer of icing on the senator's very rich cake.

The senator had known—indeed he had grown up with—both of Claude's parents who had died in their early middle age after unexpectedly producing Claude. He was charming and charmed, a golden boy, handsome as an Arrow shirt model, with perfect poise and a devout respect for what he considered the basic pleasures of life: women and liquor.

His duties as the officer in charge of supplies for the naval installation often brought him to Shuster's Store. Shuster supplied the naval station with its produce, grown on various Florida keys, and with its coal which was brought to the station in barges from the North and stored there in oversized sheds. While arranging for and directing these deliveries, Claude became acquainted with his mercantile counterpart, Jake Meyer.

He immediately took to Jake because he seemed as easygoing and affable as himself; and because he was so unlike Claude's unimaginative fellow officers, domestic chaps who shuddered at the thought of active service, who couldn't wait to run home to their pale wives and clinging kiddies.

Claude was often required to travel to other ports to purchase those supplies for the naval base which

Leon Shuster couldn't acquire through normal commerce.

War gave the naval steward certain powers. Claude was able to commandeer one of the ferries from the Havana-Key West run, though he more than adequately compensated the P&O Line for the loss of their ship. With a submarine escort Claude would sail to Havana, to New Orleans, and occasionally to Mexico, and stay a few days sampling the wine and the women.

Claude, bored with the company of the aforementioned fellow officers and not deigning to mix with the enlisted men, suggested to Senator Devon, who had great influence at the naval installation, that it might be well if a civilian versed in dry goods barter accompanied him on his trips to foreign ports. Claude didn't want the navy to be cheated because of his inexperience with trade.

The senator had a word with the admiral and then another with Leon Shuster and in a matter of hours Jake Meyer was at Lieutenant Wheeler's disposal.

Their first trip was to Cuba for fruit, beef, and rum. When the ferry docked in Havana harbor, Claude gave instructions to the man immediately below him in rank, saying that he and Mr. Meyer would return in two days time. He expected the ferry to be fully and properly loaded. Then he led Jake into the city of Havana where they spent the following two days and nights at the home of Madam Sucre's. There wasn't a girl at Madam Sucre's who was over nineteen, white, or unhappy in any way. They had all been rescued by Madam Sucre from far worse situations and each of them had been trained in the art of pleasing a man.

The girl Madam Sucre called her daughter would stand behind a screen in the main salon and watch the other girls attired in white camisoles circulate around the room until one was chosen. The daughter would look longingly as the girls climbed the stairs to the bedrooms, followed by the beautiful sporting men of Havana.

The daughter, Nancy, had her favorites, but when Jake appeared, with his lean, dark blond good looks, so foreign from any man she had ever seen, she begged her mother to allow her to sit in the main salon. "Just to sit, Mama. I just want to talk."

Madam Sucre locked Nancy in another part of the mansion, provided Jake with an African woman of astonishing proportions, and immediately made plans to send her daughter to the convent school on the far side of the island. She had known the day would come when she would have to send Nancy away, but she had hoped it would not be so soon. Nancy was going to marry a physician's son; the contract had already been paid for and signed.

"What did you think of Madam Sucre?" Claude asked Jake as they returned to the ferry, both a bit the worse for wear. "Best-looking black woman I've ever seen. Can't get near her, though. Made it crystal clear the first time I saw her that she only provides the goods, not the services."

"I liked the little girl," Jake said.

"There were a lot of little girls, Jake."

"Her little girl, the light-colored one with the huge eyes who kept staring at us from behind the screen."

"Oh, Madam's brat. Forget her. Madam has her heart set on Nancy marrying a doctor's kid from Haiti."

During the following months they often returned to Madam Sucre's and visited similar establishments in New Orleans, Puerto Rico, and the Yucatán, while on supply-acquiring missions.

"Your wife mind you being away so often?" Claude asked Jake.

"No, she's relieved, I think. Esther understands the importance of our work."

Claude laughed and threw his arm around Jake. "Next week we're going to Savannah. But you'll have to behave, my friend. I'm introducing you to a different sort of society and a very different sort of house. I can hardly wait to see what you'll all make of each other."

It was a Southern evening designed to appeal to her lowest tastes, Frances Ellington thought. The red-hot sun, backlighting a row of Georgia yellow pines, was just beginning to set. The air was thick and sweet with the scent of lilacs. Her aunt's plantation house, Rokeby, looked exactly as it had the day it was built in 1801, the Civil War somehow having passed it by. All we need are the darkies singing, Frances thought.

She didn't like the South and she didn't like Rokeby but it had seemed, at the time, an appropriate place to go for six months, to hide for a bit.

Frances Ellington was thirty-two years old and was often and sincerely described as handsome in the South where her particular brand of Anglo-Saxon beauty—dark and full—was not especially understood or appreciated.

She came from an Old New York family. Her mother had been one of the few wives imported from the South who had survived the New York social scene.

Frances was in a state of disgrace. She was divorced, from a boyhood friend who, it had turned out, preferred his valet to her in bed. She had left New York after two years of difficult legal involvements during which she managed to shed her husband.

She was the first member of her family to sunder a marriage. And it was so definitely her doing. Her husband would have been content to linger on in that odd union forever. "Austen, his valet, and me," Frances told her mother, who was, admittedly, a little at sea when it came to the subject of homosexuality.

Immediately after the divorce Frances was sent to her Aunt Liza's plantation near Savannah, supposedly to recover. Rokeby was very beautiful with horses and magnolias and hoards of black servants who seemed to never have heard of the Emancipation. But Frances, after all, felt she had little to recover from. Aunt Liza was sweet but she led a retiring, horsey sort of life and after two months of that Frances took herself to New Orleans where she promised her mother (her father had given up on her) that she would live quietly with distant relatives in the old quarters, engaging in water painting and floral arranging.

But it was hot, the flowers drooped; she really wasn't much good at water painting; she decided what she needed most was a man. She hadn't been in New Orleans quite three weeks before she fell in love.

He was married and had Edgar Allen Poe eyes and a suitably romantic disease, consumption. He was also unconventional enough to leave his wife and to live with Frances for seven years before the disease killed him.

Devastated, she didn't know what to do or where to go. She hadn't really liked New Orleans but she had been in love there and now that he was dead, it seemed an impossible place to be. She wondered if she shouldn't die, too, when an invitation from Aunt Liza came, asking her to come and stay at Rokeby for as long as she liked. Frances knew that Aunt Liza had been provoked into issuing the invitation by her mother but she went anyway. She had to get away from New Orleans. Rokeby had been an effective way station in her life once before. Perhaps it would prove so again.

She had thought that she would be alone at Rokeby with Aunt Liza, called upon only to be polite at the evening meal. She had had no idea that Virginia Devon, a distant cousin, was there, too, spending one year at Miss Annabelle Doyle's School for Young Gentle Ladies in nearby Savannah.

Not that she saw a great deal of Virginia who seemed much too spoiled, too self-involved to share her grief with. Frances spent her days on the north porch, reading her lover's poetry, realizing she was indulging in the most wearisome sort of behavior—the kind she would never have been able to abide in anyone else—but nonetheless unable to get herself out of it.

Not even Virginia's contempt ("Aunt Liza, I don't know why you put up with her," Frances once overheard Virginia saying to her aunt. "Why she's not only been divorced, she's a notorious woman.") moved her. Months after she had arrived at Rokeby, she was still able to see people only in the evening. My days, she told herself, are devoted to my ghost lover.

Each evening she and Virginia would dress and come down the huge mahogany central staircase just before dinner, seating themselves at opposite ends of the huge wicker sofa Aunt Liza had the house servants place on the front veranda every day at six P.M.

That evening fruit punches had been served and Aunt Liza had left her two relatives alone so that she could ready herself for the gentlemen callers.

"What gentlemen callers?" Frances asked Virginia in one of the few direct questions she had ever posed to that young woman.

"My fiancé," Virginia allowed, keeping her eyes set on the far horizon, "and a friend of his." The sun sank lower in the sky and behind the wicker sofa where the cousins sat, in the house, through the open, arched doorways, wooden fans revolved and the servants giggled, lighting the evening candles.

Just as the sun finally set, like a magician appearing on the stage at the appropriate moment, Claude Wheeler materialized, his yellow hair making him look like an American Apollo. He ran up the wooden steps that led to the columned veranda and took Virginia Devon's proffered hand.

"Claude," she said in a voice much older than her seventeen years, "I thought you were never coming."

If Claude Wheeler was Apollo, Virginia Devon was Diana, fresh from the hunt. A nineteenth century Di-

ana who should have been dressed in sixteen crinolines, with iron-curled hair and white gloves. As it
was, she managed to give the impression that she was
the daughter of the plantation, welcoming her young,
brave Confederate lieutenant home from Gettysburg.
She was so blond, her hair was almost white and her
thin, even-featured face could have served as a model
of classic beauty but for the eyes. They were dark
green and secretive and seemed to forever be concen-
trated inward.

Virginia stood there for a moment in the soft light
from the kerosene lamps and the candles, holding
Claude's hand as if it were a precious but still negoti-
able possession.

"And I do hope you're going to introduce your
friend, Claude," she said reproachfully.

Claude stepped down into the darkness and reap-
peared a moment later with Jake, who seemed too
large for the low-ceilinged veranda, too contemporary
for the anachronistic night. It was as if, Frances
thought, watching Claude introduce Jake to Virginia,
a modern soldier was being presented to an antebel-
lum belle.

"And this is my distant connection," Virginia said,
bringing the two men to where Frances was sitting,
for the first time in a long time interested in a man
who wasn't dead. "Mrs. Frances Wellington. From
New York."

Frances held out her hand and Jake took it but he
wasn't looking at her. He couldn't take his eyes from
Virginia.

"I think you two had better go upstairs and dress.

Amos will show you to your rooms," Virginia said. "You've kept us waiting quite long enough."

Dinner was a formal, difficult event. Aunt Liza, more vague than usual, talked exclusively about local affairs, leaving Jake—and to some extent, everyone else—out of the conversation.

Claude kept holding his glass up for the servant to fill it while Jake's eyes continued to return to Virginia who steadfastly ignored his attentions. She had taken his measure and she decided she didn't like what she saw.

"Claude, please pass me those milk biscuits. I adore them so," she said, and Jake reached across the table with his long, muscular arm, swooped them up, and handed them to her. "Thank you, Mr. Meyer," she said, taking a biscuit and putting it on her plate, "but I distinctly remember asking Claude to pass me the milk biscuits. There was no need to exert yourself like that. Claude, honey, do right that salt cellar your friend turned over. You know how superstitious I am."

After that there was very little conversation with the exception of Aunt Liza wondering what young Bromley Spear was going to do with the forty acres he owned on the far side of the new highway.

Later Frances found herself alone with Jake Meyer on the veranda. He stood leaning against one of the mammoth Doric columns, smoking a cigar, staring inside into the small parlor where Claude and Virginia were dancing to "Dardenella" on the wind-up Victrola.

"That sort of behavior is not calculated to make a

woman feel overly desirable," Frances, shocked, heard herself saying.

"I didn't get what you said," Jake told her, forcing his attention away from Virginia and Claude.

"She is very beautiful," Frances admitted. "Do you mind if I smoke, too?" She took a small silver case from her purse and lit a thin, brown cigar.

Jake laughed and sat down on the wicker sofa next to her. He watched her smoke. "You're very quiet," she said to him.

"Not all that much to say."

"Tell me where you come from."

He turned so he could watch Claude fox-trotting Virginia round the small parlor. And then he began to tell her about himself. His fair hair combed straight back, his profile with its strong nose and lop-sided half smile lit by the lanterns strung across the porch, made him appear to Frances as if he were on the alert, waiting for something to happen.

Later, after he and Claude went into the library for what was to be a last drink while Virginia and Frances went upstairs to their rooms, Claude asked him what he had thought of his fiancée.

"She's the most beautiful woman I've ever seen, Claude. When I was a kid in Poland and they used to tell us about the women in America, I thought they all looked exactly like Virginia."

"Glad you approve. I don't exactly see her like that, 'cause I've known her damn near all my life. We're getting married in December. The senator, that old bastard, finally gave his approval."

"Lucky," Jake said, finishing his brandy.

"I guess so," Claude said, filling both their glasses

once more. "I get to live in Devon House which is just about the nicest damn house in Key West and the senator's already promised us a whooping allowance but you know something, Jake? I'm sure as hell going to miss Madam Sucre's." He put on his white jacket and stood up. " 'Course there ain't no law that says I can never go back. No enforceable law, that is." He told the servant waiting in the central hall that he could put out the candles and he and Jake went up the stairs.

Frances was waiting in Jake's bed. She had decided, once again, that what she needed was a man.

For the next hour or two she forgot about her ghost and her sorrow and Jake forgot about the girl with the white-blond hair and the dark green eyes.

On the day Claude and Jake were to leave Rokeby, Virginia asked Claude if they could have a few moments alone after the long and elaborate breakfast Aunt Liza had insisted upon. She took Claude into the morning room, an octangularly shaped space with French doors set in each of its eight walls.

"I always feel as if we're in a birdcage in here," Claude complained. "What did you want to talk about? You haven't been exactly polite to either Frances or Jake." He sat down in an upholstered chair and tilted his head so he could look up at her.

"I never intended to be polite to Frances. I can't imagine what Aunt Liza was thinking about when she invited that woman here. As for your friend, I want to make it clear, Claude, that the next time you come here, you won't bring him. You must see you can't bring someone like him into a house where I'm living."

"What's wrong with him?" Claude asked, looking away.

"You know very well what's wrong with him. He's foreign, to begin with. He's a Jew to end with. And in between he's no gentleman. I don't like the way he looks at me and I should think that you wouldn't, either. Besides," she said, and it was her turn to stare out through the French doors, "every servant in the house down to little Amos knows that your friend Mr. Meyer and Frances have been sleeping together from the night he arrived."

"Why that proves he's a gentleman," Claude said, jumping up and putting his arms around Virginia. "He never said a word to me about it."

"Oh, Claude," she said, pushing him away.

"And he couldn't be planning to ravish you, Virginia, if he's otherwise occupied. That's not the way it works."

"Claude, I don't want to know him."

"But it's all right if I do?"

She looked perplexed for a moment. "But why do you want to, Claude?"

"I like the man, honey. More important, as soon as this war's over, he and I may very well turn out to be business partners."

After another long meal, this one at midday, Virginia bade Claude and Jake a formal good-bye, just touching the latter's hand. Frances, saying she had a headache, had said good-bye before luncheon.

Virginia stood on the veranda and watched the two young men, both laughing about something Claude was saying, get into the cart. Still laughing, they were driven off by Amos who had gotten the big old bay out for the trip to the port. As the cart was about to pass through the Rokeby gates, she saw Jake turn and look back at her.

"He's half her age," she said to herself as she turned and went into the house.

In the following months Claude made several trips to Savannah, to Rokeby, alone. But when he went to New Orleans or Mexico, or especially Cuba, on the P&O commandeered ferry, he would ask Jake to accompany him.

It was early in December, 1918, while Normandy villages were being torn to pieces, straffed by the opposing armies, that Claude and Jake made their last trip to Havana, to Madam Sucre's house.

"I see she's got her brat back," Claude said as they were about to leave, Madam's daughter standing on the far side of the silk screen, peering intently at Jake.

"What's your name?" Jake asked her.

"Nancy Sugar. I know yours. It's Jake Meyer and your Señor Claude's Jewboy friend."

At that Madam Sucre's black hand whisked the girl out of sight, leaving Jake and Claude much amused.

What with a last drink at a café, a faulty engine, a missing crew member, they didn't arrive at Key West until two A.M. Sunday morning.

"You want to go fishing on Monday?" Jake asked, as they were about to part. "Leon Shuster's been giving me Mondays off, seeing how hard I'm working on Sundays with you on these important buying trips."

"Can't, Jake," Claude said and paused. "Virginia's coming to Key West. Fact of the matter is, I been waiting to tell you this all weekend. The senator's giving us a big engagement party up at Devon House this afternoon. I want you to come by and have a drink."

"I'm not going to do that, Claude."

"I guess you're right, Jake," Claude said after a moment. "You usually are." He put his arm around Jake for a moment and saying, "I'll be seeing you, pal," was gone.

Jake walked home, pausing on Caroline Street to study the demented Ficus tree that grew there with its aerial roots all twisted up in the air. He wasn't tired. He wasn't desperately unhappy. He knew he didn't want to go to Devon House to toast Claude's and Virginia's engagement.

He didn't much want to see Virginia ever again, he told himself. It was too hard wanting her so badly and not liking her all that much. And it was too obvious what she thought of him. Fact of the matter is, he thought, I never want to be in the same room with her again.

He turned up the path which led to his house, went round to the back, and washed his face with water from the cistern. He entered through the back door, hoping he wouldn't wake up his wife.

Esther wasn't expecting him home until Sunday night, and if she was roused, she would feel obliged to ask him about his trip and he would feel obliged to lie about it. They hadn't made love in months.

The thought of Esther with her thick, white skin and her permanently sleepy eyes revolted him. A memory of Virginia shot into his mind. She had been on a black horse, racing Claude who had chosen a white mare, across a field on the north side of Rokeby. She had been dead serious about beating Claude. One could see in her green eyes, in the tautness of her face. Her white-blond hair had come undone and was streaming behind her, making her seem oddly ethereal and alien.

He pushed the memory from his mind. The wide floor beams of the house creaked with each step he took. He thought of sleeping on the porch but he knew from past attempts that the mosquitoes wouldn't cooperate. He forced himself up the stairs to the bedroom he shared with Esther.

He opened the door as quietly as he could and stepped inside. The house seems very quiet, he thought. He wondered why Moishe wasn't snoring as he took off his clothes, pulled aside the mosquito netting Esther insisted upon, and eased himself into the bed.

It was the smell, he realized, that was all wrong. Esther smelled sweet and sour, like stuffed cabbage. The smell he was smelling was more bitter, older, less spicy.

He reached out to touch Esther and found his hand grasping a hairy thigh. At that precise moment Jake suddenly realized that the only sound in the entire house was his breathing. He got out of the bed, let the mosquito net drop, and lit the kerosene lamp.

Burrowed under the netting, crushed up against the far side of the bed, were Esther and Moishe. She was red in the face, presumably from the effort of holding her breath; he was green. Moishe was the first to move. He jumped out of the bed and got down on his knees. "Don't kill me, Jake," he whispered in Yiddish. "I beg of you, don't kill me, Jake."

Jake looked down at the thin, quivering man at his feet and then at Esther, fatter than he remembered her, shivering in the bed under the mosquito netting. He felt overwhelmingly sorry for the both of them. "I ain't going to kill you, Moishe," Jake said.

"No, Jake?"

"No. I got something much worse for you than that."

"What are you going to do, Jake?"

"I'm going to make you marry the bitch, Moishe."

He arrived in Manhattan on a cold day in mid-December. He was admitted to the house on Eighteenth Street by Bessie's little maid, Minnie, who didn't recognize him for a moment.

"Jesus, Jakey," Minnie said, standing back, looking him over, "you've grown. You're looking better than ever. This time if you chased me up the stairs, I might let you catch me. Come on, Bessie's in the drawing room."

"What are you doing here?" Bessie wanted to know, after she had kissed him half a dozen times. "Trouble?" Her blue eyes showed concern.

"Not exactly," Jake said, giving her his lopsided smile.

"The last time you looked at me like that, Jakey Meyer, I had to get you married."

"Well, Sister," Jake said, sitting down, "this time I want you to get me unmarried."

*   *   *

That evening, after dinner with Nick and Bessie, Jake was taken into the drawing room where Ryan sat in his green leather chair, waiting for him. Bessie closed the sliding doors and looked at Jake. "Tell him everything. Don't leave out one single detail. Go ahead. Talk."

Jake told his story as Bessie stood in front of the Kotuk portrait, at the mantel, the fire reflecting the fine gold threads in her black dress, highlighting the incredible intensity of her red hair. She was still as slim and as lovely as she had been when he first saw her.

Ryan listened, his lashless eyes staring at Jake without expression, his fingers held together, making a church.

When Jake finished, Bessie went to him and put her arms around him. There were tears in her eyes. "It's my fault," she said. "I should never have pushed you into that marriage. Sending you away like that, just a boy . . . God knows what I was thinking about. You'll have to forgive me, Jake."

He hadn't felt sorry for himself until that moment. He had only felt relief. But Bessie's tears and comfort made him feel sad, made him feel somehow regretful.

Ryan coughed and crossed his elegant legs. "The divorce is no problem. Though I think it might be best if we went for an annulment. Not so easy in New York but we can get your friend Lewis to talk to his wife"—Alma Lewis had been made a New York Supreme Court Judge—"and go *in camera*. We can claim they were both too young, that there have been no marital relations . . ."

"Esther's pregnant again," Jake said.

"By that bum, Moishe Katz?" Bessie wanted to know.

"No. By me. They both swore that they had only been in bed that one time and knowing Esther and Moishe, I'd believe it. Typical of them to get caught their first time out. No, the kid's mine. I want him to have my name."

"And what makes you so sure it's going to be a boy?"

"I don't want Esther to have my daughter," Jake said as if that were enough. He turned back to Ryan. "Better get me a divorce, if you can."

Bessie looked at Ryan who nodded.

"Of course I'll pay you . . ." Jake began.

"This divorce is on me," Bessie said, getting out of the sofa. "I got you into this, I'm going to get you out." She opened the drawing room doors. "Don't move. I'll be back in fifteen minutes. We're going up to B's. I have a little surprise for you."

"What's the surprise?" Jake asked Ryan after she had left.

"Bessie is resuming her career tonight."

She had been bored and not a little depressed. She had worried about Max in France and Jake in Florida and Nick now firmly established in Ryan's organization. Running B's Gardens was too easy and trying to drum up money for the Henry Street Settlement too frustrating. During the war government funds had virtually dried up. Even Edward Lewis hadn't been supportive. "We need the money for the war effort, Bessie."

"What about the war on the Lower East Side?

What about feeding those hungry people? What's going to happen after the war when all those men come back and there aren't jobs for them or places, decent places, for them to live?"

"You really should come down to Washington and talk to some people, Bessie."

"I'm coming." She went and everyone had been very polite in their neat offices at the Senate and there had been a dinner at the White House but no one, not even the President, had wanted to hear what she had to say and consequently they didn't.

"You're too lovely to be concerned about all that, Miss Meyer," the President had said.

She had returned to New York furious with Edward Lewis even though he had tried, furious with herself. Nick only seemed happy when he was at B's, dancing or drinking, and Ryan was spending less time in New York and more time traveling, "cementing relationships."

"We're going to make a lot of money after this war, Bessie," he told her. "Prohibition is going to make us wonderfully rich."

"We already are," she objected. But she had realized early on that Ryan wasn't in it for the money.

"You need something new in your life," Lillian Wald had told her on one occasion when she was visiting the brick house on Henry Street. "You're much too young to be so frustrated. You've got so many options, Bessie."

"Yes?"

"You could start by breaking with Ryan." Lillian Wald was not a woman to be indirect.

"I've tried that. I need him."

"You could go back on the stage."

"I was never that good an actress."

"No. But you had a reasonable stage presence. I remember seeing you once, oh, several years ago, in a musical *Romeo and Juliet* at the Oriental. You played the nurse and you sang the funniest song."

" 'My Kinda *Mieskeit*.' "

"You had the audience crying and laughing at the same time. You gave everyone a lot of joy that evening, Bessie. It was as if a party had spontaneously happened."

"Only the guests had to pay to get in."

And it was that conversation which gave her the idea. B's Other Place was closed one night a week, Mondays. She would open it up on Monday evenings, charge an enormous cover, provide her own entertainment, and donate all the profits to the Settlement.

"Who's going to come?" Zuckerman—whom she had hired away from Second Avenue to book the acts, to run the shows—asked.

"Everyone," Ryan had answered. "Charity always makes for wonderful publicity. You'll see, Zuckerman. You'll have the Vanderbilts, the Roosevelts, the Astors, and the Rockefellers reserving tables months in advance. Make it a very dear cover, Bessie."

"And who's going to open, Red?" Zuckerman wanted to know after Ryan had left. He put his feet up on her desk and tilted his hat. "Who you going to get to open, without pay?"

"Me," she had said, pushing his feet off the desk.

Ryan had been right. New York society, tired of wartime austerity, had booked every place in the cabaret. They felt they could legally celebrate if the profits were going to a worthy cause.

"I'm a nervous wreck," Bessie told Ryan as Minnie tried to pin diamond clips to the red curls.

"No, you're not, my dear." He looked around the dressing room, at the blue mirrors Bessie had insisted upon, and smiled. "You're excited and happy and, I might add, exciting. This reminds me of our courting days. I'm falling in love with you all over again." He told Minnie to get out, he would help Miss Meyer finish dressing. Then he put his arms around Bessie and pressed himself up against her.

"Ryan, I'm going on in ten minutes."

"That's all it's going to take. I want you now, while you're all hot and nervous. I want to be inside you. I want to be exposed to some of that energy you're generating." He locked the door, unbuttoned his trousers and took off Bessie's dressing down. It was one of the fastest but possibly most satisfying sexual episodes of their life together.

Afterward, she asked him if she looked too cheap with all those diamonds in her hair and up and down her shapely arms.

"No, my dear, you look impossibly expensive; like a great painting, you don't have a price tag. It's what keeps me coming back. I think it always will."

"Tell me that in twenty years, Ryan. Now what dress should I wear? The red and silver for sex or the blue and gold for class?"

"The blue and gold, my dear. You've got enough sex as it is."

"So now you're telling me I need class, huh?" she

said, struggling into the red and silver dress, as Zuckerman's small fist knocked on the door.

"I'm nervous, Ryan. Hold me for a moment." He put his arms around her. "I haven't done this in such a long time. What if they all get up and walk out? What if it all boomerangs? What if. . . ?"

"Hey, Red, get your *tuchas* out on that stage," Zuckerman shouted through the door as if she were still in the chorus and he was still her boss.

She laughed and opened the door. "Go to the boys, Ryan. And tell them not to sit on their hands when everyone else starts with the rotten tomatoes. Excuse me. With this crowd, it'll be pomegranates."

She stepped out on the stage feeling nauseous and scared, but as soon as she launched into her *spiel*—"I want to sing you a song my mother used to sing to me when I was a child"—she felt that wonderful confidence that had gotten her through her experiences in the Yiddish theater. *"Rozhinkes Mit Mandlen"*—despite what Zuckerman had said about the *goyim* not understanding—brought a huge round of applause and her medley of war songs hadn't left a dry eye in the house. For her last song she stepped off the stage and moved around the tables, singing the ridiculous lyrics one of the boys in the orchestra had writen to an old and bawdy vaudeville standard after he had heard Bessie calling everyone in sight "fat boy."

As the spotlight followed her from table to table, her diamonds reflected the light and her slim body seemed to move with a kind of magic, like a figure from a moving picture. There wasn't a sound in the vast space except for Bessie's voice, singing the words

of that banal song which somehow affected the entire
audience.

> "Hey there, Fat Boy, where you been?
> Hey there, Fat Boy, move right in.
> I'm going to tell you a secret.
> that shouldn't be told:
> When your arms are around me
> I turn all hot and cold.
>
> "Hey there, Fat Boy, give me a kiss.
> Hey there, Fat Boy, you've been missed.
> If you'll be my lover, well,
> I won't run for cover . . .
> Hey there, Fat Boy, let's go."

Later, after the applause and the congratulations,
after the counting of the take, Bessie presented the
money to Lillian Wald who looked dowdy and aristocratic in a long red gown. Nick and Jake had gone to
the house on Eighteenth Street to sleep. She and
Ryan sat in the back of his black Ford when it pulled
up to the house. He kissed her. "I'll see you tomorrow night, my dear. You were wonderful this evening.
Just wonderful."

She slipped her arms out of her sable coat and put
them around him. "Stay with me tonight, Ryan."

"I can't, my dear. Grace . . ."

"I never ask you. Just this one night."

He held her for a moment. "I would like to, Bessie.
I simply cannot." He rapped on the window and the
driver, Bumps Bogan, got out of the Ford and went
around and held the door for her and walked her to

the door, waiting until Minnie let her in. Bessie turned and watched as the black Ford raced off to Oyster Bay.

The following day, as arranged, Jake met Ryan at the Eastern Club for lunch. The club, an enormous Venetian Stanford White palace located halfway between Wall Street and City Hall, was Ryan's favorite midday haunt. He'd sit in an enormous green leather club chair, smoking an occasional cigarette, charmed by the red plush and the gray marble, feeling large and important despite the fifty-foot ceilings and the crows of oversized portraits of generations of New York's oldest and richest and, quite possibly, homeliest men looking down on him.

There, politicians and statesmen, supreme court justices and stock exchange seat holders, corporate lawyers and Mid-Atlantic state governors would nod to him, would sometimes engage him in conversation. He knew they didn't like him, that they didn't approve of him. His uncle had never gotten near the Eastern Club. But Ryan had. It was a wonderful possession, power. He liked it much more than money though he wasn't even certain exactly how he had acquired it. He had backed certain men for office, he had granted certain favors, he had dissolved certain debts, forced payments on others and, after a time, he realized he had power. It was a heady experience. He wasn't going to let any of it go.

A manservant escorted Jake to where Ryan was sitting, but Jake seemed unimpressed by his surroundings. He was too intent on his errand.

Ryan refused to discuss anything more relevant

than Bessie's "comeback," than Prohibition, during luncheon in the oak-paneled dining room. It was later, over coffee for Jake, China tea for Ryan, that he allowed Jake to talk about what he had come for.

Fifteen minutes later, after Jake had waxed ecstatic about Flagler's railroad, about the tourist influx expected in Key West, Ryan interrupted him.

"As I understand it, you want me to lend you five thousand dollars to buy half of a ferry service between Key West and Cuba. I'll tell you what, Jake. I'll give you the money, interest free. If you don't show a profit within two years, say by this time in 1921, I will become a third partner in the enterprise. Then, if the ferries are a success with tourists going to Cuba and manufacturers' goods coming to the States, you'll give me my five thousand dollars back and we'll be quits. What do you say?"

Jake took Ryan's hand in his and pumped it enthusiastically, thanking him, beginning to go on again about the profits to be made in Key West—Havana transport when Ryan interrupted him. "I only wonder why you didn't go to your sister for money?"

"Oh," Jake said, lighting a Luis San Obispo cigar. "I want this to be strictly business."

A week later Jake was on his way back to Key West, a certificate of divorce in one pocket, Ryan's check for five thousand dollars in the other.

CHAPTER 4

When Max Meyer left Hollywood for New York and later, the Geat War, Jenny Moore left, too. "I'm going home," she told Townie. "To think. I'm doing something wrong and I want to find out what it is."

She never told him nor anyone else where her home was. Her accent was quintessentially American, accentless. She might have come from Des Moines or Philadelphia.

Actually she came from Buffalo, New York, where her father, a stout and exceedingly hale fellow, lived in a dark red early Victorian house surrounded by his collection of timepieces (from grandfather clocks to a thick gold watch said to have been owned by Disraeli) when he wasn't involved with his hugely successful bakery which supplied bread and rolls to the railroads.

He was a staunch member of the Buffalo Baptist Church, to which he tithed a tenth of his yearly income and was said to have mourned Jenny's mother, who died of pneumonia in her thirtieth year, far too much to take another wife. In reality he valued his privacy, his freedom to wind his clocks. He prided himself on the fact that he was a conservative man, a pillar of his church, an exemplary citizen of his city, state, and country.

When he saw Jenny standing on the steps of his bakery business, with her bobbed hair and kohled eyes, he wondered how he had ever been able to forget her existence. She seemed so much larger than life. Larger than his life, anyway.

She stayed with him for several weeks during which time she threatened the very fabric of that life, threatening to accompany him to church in her black dress with the beaded top, astounding her sister who acted as his housekeeper by appearing at midday wearing a Chinese robe, a cigarette holder firmly clamped between rouge-darkened lips.

Finally he gave her three thousand dollars with the proviso that she stop desecrating her mother's name— Jenny—when working in the motion pictures and that as long as she continued to lead such an obviously sordid life, never to return to Buffalo.

She was gone within the hour.

She turned up in Hollywood a week later with her new name—Araby—and a new, glamorous wardrobe. She took a page advertisement in *Variety* which featured her in a dress made of bugle beads and the headline: "Araby Moore Is Back In Hollywood." In a small body of type at the bottom of the page it was implied that Miss Moore was ready to consider her next starring vehicle.

What William Fox was doing for Theda Bara and Metro for Francis X. Bushman, Araby Moore was attempting to do for herself: create a star. She sat on the sofa in Townie's apartment and waited for ten days.

"Why the hell won't they bite?" she asked Townie over spaghetti on the final night of her vigil. "They need stars."

"This is true," Townie agreed.

Broadway stars, in those closing days of the war, were asking for a great deal of money to appear in motion pictures mostly because they were frightened of film. The established stars—Pickford, Fairbanks, and Chaplin—were asking for a percentage of the gross, making plans to form their own companies.

"I should be a natural," Araby complained.

"One ad in *Variety* does not a moving picture star make," Townie said, helping himself to salad. "Tomorrow you'd better come round to Great Western, get down on your hands and knees and plead with Uncle Joe for your buckboard job back again."

"Never."

The following day, as she prepared to take Townie's advice, a messenger appeared from Carleton LeMay. She put on the bugle bead dress and went to see him at his new office on the Pathé lot.

Carleton LeMay had left Great Western to become a junior producer at Pathé where he started out making a series of two reelers called "Mable and Mert."

"Jenny," Carleton said, kissing her hand. "I almost didn't recognize you."

"It's Araby now, Carleton. And I'm here to save your career."

She showed him a script that she said was to be the war film to end all war films and backed it up with a cable from the famous Parisian cameraman-director, René St. Clair. He had spent two weeks in Hollywood two years before, most of it in Jenny's—Araby's—bed and felt the cable was an easy way to pay her back, especially since she had wired him not only the words, but the money to pay for it. In it he agreed to shoot the film for her.

LeMay, impressed by St. Clair's endorsement, read the scenario, decided it was a long shot and that a long shot was what he needed to get his career moving.

"Troops will play troops," Araby promised him. "Red Cross nurses will play Red Cross nurses. We'll have them standing in line up and down Broadway, fighting to get in."

Carleton LeMay managed to get seven thousand dollars out of Pathé for the project, gave it to Araby, and wished her Godspeed. He thought the idea was a good one and if anyone could bring it off, it was René St. Clair.

Araby managed to get to Paris on a troop ship carrying nurses and soldiers for the final assault against Germany. Once there she found that René St. Clair had become a hopeless drunk and that there was no film to be had in any event. Even if there were, St. Clair told her, there was no way to process it because Germany had been the French movie industry's prime source of picture carbon.

Araby Moore prided herself on the fact that she was a woman who knew when to cut her losses. After three days in Paris she put her screenplay in her suitcase and her suitcase in the back bedroom of St. Clair's filthy apartment on rue du Bac. Then she went to the United States Army headquarters on the Quai d'Orsay and tried to locate Max.

The public information officer told her that he had

been attached to a battalion of gunners from Alabama and sent, with Joe Rakin, to the front.

Araby then asked about passage home and was told there was no available space for civilians for at least a month. She left a letter for Max, which the officer promised would get delivered, and went back to René St. Clair's apartment.

Max never did learn what part of France he had been stationed in. He only knew that it was freezing cold and the army-issue overcoat was warm enough but not big enough and he couldn't shoot a rifle with it on and he wanted to be able to shoot when he had to.

At night he tried to sleep while propped up against the side of the foxhole he shared with Joe Rakin, one hand on his rifle and one part of his mind alert to signs of attack, to the possibility of gas or a bomb or a German soldier gone crazy with hunger and fear, jumping into the foxhole and bayoneting him. It had happened.

At night he could hear the Germans singing. A few of the Alabama boys sang, too, but mostly it was the Germans.

After two weeks Max knew he wasn't a man anymore but the machine his drill sergeant had promised he would be: a fighting machine. The days were the roughest because there was always the fear the company commander would call for an attack. He had done so twice and each time the Alabama company of riflemen was halved. It was clear the Germans in the foxholes four hundred yards or so away couldn't attack but they could defend.

It was also clear, to Max, that he had to get Joe Rakin out of the foxholes. Joe Rakin had never gotten the hang of the gas masks and once, when gas came seeping across the lines and down into their foxhole, Max had had to forcibly hold the mask over his head while Joe sputtered and puked and nearly suffocated. Joe Rakin had also not learned to eat the food that was passed out once each day and which Max refused to think about. Max just ate it. Like a machine.

After Joe Rakin had stopped eating for two days, except for some brown, wormy apples that had appeared from God knows where, Max force-fed him once a day.

"Why are you trying to keep me alive?" Joe Rakin asked in the last conversation the two men had.

"It'll be over soon."

"I'm not going to want to live after this, Max. How can I live with myself? I can't even shoot a goddamned rifle without wetting myself. I'm not a man, Max. Not like I'm supposed to be."

Max started to say that no one was but it was then that a corporal named Chapman, casually performing his guard duty, was shot full of holes by a nervous Alabaman who thought he was a German. Chapman fell into the foxhole Max and Joe Rakin were shivering in and they stood there, watching everything ooze out of the corporal, helpless to help him or themselves.

Joe Rakin closed his eyes and began to retch. Max climbed out of the foxhole and went to find the sergeant from the medical detachment who was in a tent a mile behind the lines, playing dominoes. Max tried to convince him to send Joe Rakin back, anywhere out of the foxholes but the medico wasn't listening; he had heard it all before.

When Max got back to the foxhole, someone had gotten Chapman's body out and Joe Rakin was standing in one corner, without any clothes on, whimpering like a hurt dog. Max took off his too tight coat and threw it around Joe's shoulders and then he took Joe and held him in his arms. Joe let himself be held and stopped whimpering—for which Max thanked God—and started crying.

It was then that the gas alert was sounded. Max looked around for their gas masks and Joe screamed, shaking off the coat, and jumped out of the foxhole and ran, naked, toward the German lines.

Max crawled out of the hole and crept to the place where Joe's body lay, halfway between the two armies. The irony was, Max thought, that there had been no gas; another false alarm.

Joe wasn't dead though he was pretty well shot up. Max tried to pull him back toward the foxhole, but Joe, with the last of his strength, resisted, holding on, digging into the dirt with his fingers.

"I want to die here, Max," he said, suddenly sane. "I want to die in No Man's Land."

It was then that Max was shot. The rescue team found him an hour later and took him back to the medical unit. They left Joe Rakin's body where it lay.

Max had been wounded in the head but it was a superficial wound, the German bullet having grazed his scalp. He was sent to a hospital in Paris, given his accumulated mail, and a two-week leave after which he was to return to the front lines. Among his letters was the one from Araby.

He left the hospital and went directly to St. Clair's rue du Bac apartment where he found Araby, alone, in bed. That first time he didn't bother to take off his uniform.

They spent most of his leave in that bed in St. Clair's back bedroom. When they weren't bouncing up and down on what was left of St. Clair's back bedroom mattress, they were sitting in a tiny theater on the boul' Mich', watching early Tim Bronco films. Max refused to say a word about the war or the front lines or how he came to be wounded.

Araby thought he looked odd. It was not simply because some of his hair had been shaved off where the bullet had grazed his head. That was bandaged anyway and made him seem even more handsome. But there was a peculiar look in his eyes that made it appear as if he were staring directly through her, seeing some terrible private image of his own, one too ghastly to talk about.

Later she couldn't decide whether she was careless because it was obvious he was hurting so much inside and she wanted some way to break through to him; or because she was feeling lonesome and depressed and not a little isolated.

Max went back to the front after his two weeks but he returned after a day because of a brigade command snafu brought on by the phony peace and then they had another two weeks in bed and in the movies with Tim Bronco.

By the time there was a genuine cease-fire, Araby was genuinely pregnant and Max was acting more

like his old self though there were still nights when
he couldn't sleep and other nights when he could but
cried and screamed from the nightmares.

Araby cabled LeMay that the film had been made
but destroyed by the enemy, that she was coming
home with an even greater war story, and then she
made an appointment with the neighborhood abor-
tionist.

St. Clair introduced the two women. The abor-
tionist was an old woman who looked, Araby decided,
like Madame Defarge and smelled like a clove of raw
garlic.

The day before she was to face what she thought of
as "the knitting needles," she asked Max to take her
dancing.

They were standing in a once deluxe public room
in one of the small, private hotels on the rue St.
Honoré. Streamers had been fixed across the ormolu
ceiling and red, white, and blue balloons hung from
the chandelier, all in a foreign attempt to celebrate
the Armistice.

Araby and Max were the only Americans there, the
Yankee soldiers wanting a bigger gaiety and the
French, after all, not having much to celebrate.

They were dancing to one of those melancholy, patriotic songs Tin Pan Alley had been exporting
throughout the war—"Hello Broadway, Good-bye
France"—when Max suddenly kissed her on the lips.
She looked up at him, surprised. He rarely kissed her,
except in bed. He seemed to be seeing her for the first
time since he had returned from the front. He put his
arm around her and said, "Happy New Year, Jenny."

"This isn't New Year's," she told him.

"It's the Jewish New Year."

She hadn't planned to tell him but he looked so open and so human suddenly that she said, "Well, I got a little New Year's present for you, kid. As my father would say, there's a bun in the oven."

Max insisted they be married by a rabbi. But the rabbi's secretary insisted, in Yiddish (Max had to translate for Araby) that the rabbi couldn't marry them unless the young woman was Jewish.

And suddenly Araby remembered she was Jewish after all and they were married in a yellow stucco shul in the middle of the fourteenth arrondissement, Max in a *yarmulke*, Araby in a white satin gown she had managed to borrow from Foucard-Bromberg's costume department.

When they returned to New York, Araby found she had made herself an implacable enemy.

"She chased you there and she got herself pregnant and she twisted you into marrying her. I don't care if you were married by King David's rabbi. I don't want to know from her." Bessie was adamant.

"She won't see you," Max told Araby. "She says Jake and Esther were one case, they were just kids. You and I are another."

"I don't give a good goddamn. She's your sister, not mine. Anyway, I've already written to Townie that we're coming back to Hollywood."

On the tedious ride the West Coast, she continued to think, to plan. She was going to have to give Carleton LeMay something for his money if she were ever going to have a career in motion pictures and she didn't have much to give.

Max was content to let her think. His wound had totally healed, his bandages were off, and he looked very much like the same man who had gone East to join the army over a year before. He stared out at the countryside, seeming content to do nothing but be. He refused to talk about the future or the past. "You figure out what we're going to do," he said. "I'm leaving it all in your hands."

"And you, you're going to spend the rest of your life mourning that fifth-rate fag who got you into the war in the first place?"

He got up and went to the observation car. She hadn't meant to say what she had said but he was infuriating. Here she was, four months gone and they had maybe four thousand dollars to their name, thanks to Bessie's largess and what was left from Le-May's money. She thought of getting up and going after him but she didn't. He'll get over it, she thought. She still had a dilemma to solve.

Her first impulse had been to make a "splash," to enter Hollywood with as much publicity as their money could buy. But when she thought it through, she decided that a pregnant actress who had never appeared on stage or screen and a one-picture Polish cowboy star had better come in quietly.

It was true that *The All-American Cowboy* had been a huge success. But Araby read her *Variety* and knew there was a surplus of westerns on the market, that last year's socko was this year's egg.

Townie had left Uncle Joe's employ when Max had left Hollywood. He found that he enjoyed being an agent and had taken on three or four aging cowboys as clients. Surprisingly this proved profitable and he was able to rent a small house on Gower Street, a couple of blocks north of Hollywood Boulevard.

His new office-home was in walking distance of Century Studio, two acres on Sunset Boulevard of falling-down bungalows, ramshackle sets. It was there that the two and three and four and, occasionally, five reelers his clients appeared in were churned out in a matter of days and sometimes hours.

Living with Townie was a stunt man named Rodney Jones who extorted money from him and, on occasion, beat him up. "Nothing too severe," Townie told his intimates. "Black eyes as opposed to broken arms. I adore him."

Araby and Max Meyer arrived during one of their more violent disagreements. Max was bigger and Araby was louder and between them they had Rodney Jones out of Townie's house and life in under ten minutes.

"Thanks, I think," Townie said, nursing a bruised cheek.

Max wanted to go to a hotel but Townie offered and Araby insisted that they move into his second bedroom. "Now that it's empty," Townie said.

"He needs a keeper," Araby told Max, lying down on the bed, putting her shoes on Townie's new chenille bedspread. "If we're not here to protect him, he might get himself killed."

The day after they arrived, while Townie fixed their breakfast, he asked what their plans were.

Araby said she was thinking of exactly the right way to reapproach Carleton LeMay—who had made some headway at Pathé—but there wasn't much she could do until she had their child.

"You can be the godparent," she told Townie. "Don't waste money on bassinets and such. Try silver spoons and perfect porcelain baby plates."

Max laughed. "We'll buy own own silver spoons, Araby."

"With what?"

"I'm going to see Uncle Joe tomorrow. He'll give me a job."

"Of course he will. Holding a spear in some spaghetti opera or standing behind the bar in a saloon on Western Street. I'm not letting that happen, Max." She turned to him and her large, dark eyes were filled with anger. "I'm not starting all over again, Max."

There were a few moments of silence, broken by Townie, heaping pancakes on their plates. "Besides," he said, "Uncle Joe wouldn't see you anyway. Not now. His daughter's getting married on Sunday, at last."

"This year's wedding?" Araby asked innocently, her eyes suddenly going soft, her interest diverted.

"Everyone will be there except us," Townie assured her.

Uncle Joe Goldstein planned and executed his daughter's wedding to his accountant as if it were the most important production in Great Western's history. All of the reigning royalty of Hollywood were invited and accepted. A photograph of the celebrants, to be used as a publicity still, was taken the day before the actual wedding, to insure the photograph's success. Polly Moran, Norma Talmadge, Doris Kenyon, Creighton Hale, Madge Evans, Mae Murray,

Willian Farnum, and Buster Keaton were chauffeured out to Great Western and appeared in the first two rows of the photograph.

Charlie Chaplin, Mary Pickford, Tom Mix, Douglas Fairbanks, Wallace Reid, and Marion Davies sent their stand-ins who made up the back two rows of the photograph.

No one sent their stand-ins to the wedding which was held at Uncle Joe's Beverly Hills estate, Goldstein-Ville. A Spanish-Moorish hacienda-castle, it was filled with suits of armor from the prop room and overstuffed sofas from a downtown Los Angeles furniture store. Uncle Joe had caused a mechanical drawbridge to be installed over a moat filled with enormous goldfish. The latter caused John Gilbert to christen the house Goldfish-Ville.

It stood on three Sunset Boulevard acres, was surrounded by ten-foot-high wrought-iron gates, and was landscaped with palm trees, swimming pools, and tennis courts.

There were three entrances to Goldstein-Ville. The main entrance was flanked by stone portals crowned with stucco pineapples and featured a turreted guardhouse. The guard, outfitted in Goldstein livery (powder blue, pale yellow striping), stopped each limousine that sunny wedding morning, carefully inspecting each invitation.

The caterers' trucks were sent to the delivery gate which was located in the back of the house near the kitchens.

The third entrance was off Sunset, a discreet flight of tiled stairs which led to a narrow gate buried in a small copse of japonica and other shrubbery. On the far side of the gate was a path which led to a small, enclosed "folly" where Uncle Joe enlightened new starlets once or twice a month.

The path continued around the folly, through another thicket of shrubbery, and out into the sunshine where it widened considerably and led to the western side of the main house where the dining room was located, on the second floor, overlooking the grounds.

A pair of eighteenth-century French "castle" stairways, as conceived by Great Western's set designers and carpenters, led up to the dining room where the wedding guests were assembled at one large horseshoe-shaped table. There, two waiters—extras on the Great Western payroll—were assigned for every guest.

The huge windows which Uncle Joe had caused to be installed in the western façade were wide open so that the well-kept grounds of the estate could be seen by all of the guests at the table. More than one member of the party remarked on the beautiful weather—it was a sunny, January Sunday—as they found their places. The brighter the star, the closer he or she got to the bride and Uncle Joe.

By the time the first course was served, many of the guests were showing high spirits, due to the champagne they had drunk and, in several instances, the cocaine they had snorted. Cocaine was popular that year.

The Great Western Orchestra had been engaged to play love songs on the balcony behind the table. It normally played on movie sets, helping actors summon up appropriate emotions. The "William Tell

Overture" was a favorite for the kind of heroics Great Western stars were expected to display.

Behind the orchestra were cameramen, shooting the proceedings for the future and for the newsreels. Uncle Joe Goldstein was a firm believer in home movies and the publicity value of photographed private events.

Happy with what he personally considered "a class affair," Uncle Joe, wearing morning jacket and striped trousers, stood up at the appropriate moment—after the remains of the beef Wellington had been carted away—to make a toast, his eyes going misty at the emotions in his pigeon-shaped breast.

Looking out through the huge open space created by the opened windows, seeing his domain before him, he lifted his glass above his head. His guests grew silent and looked up at him. He began to speak when he suddenly stopped in mid-gesture, one hand with the glass still above his head, the other held out in a declamatory pose. His eyes, demisted, had assumed a rotund, wild look that caused his silent guests and frightened staff to turn from the contemplation of his visage to the vista before him.

There a familiar vision greeted them. A rider on a perfect white horse with a silver saddle and reins was galloping up the path, out of the shrubbery which hid the folly. The orchestra immediately went into the "Willian Tell Overture," while all assembled watched the rider's progress, transfixed.

Barbara La Marr took a pair of mother-of-pearl binoculars from her purse and reported that the rider was dressed in white satin cowboy clothes with silver studded wrist guards, silver fringed gauntlets, and a silver mask. Then she put the binoculars on the table, upended a glass of champagne, and signaled to one of her waiters for more.

Meanwhile two bodyguards had appeared and flung themselves at the horsed intruder. The music intensified to indicate danger. The rider dropped his silver reins and knocked both attackers aside. But not before they had torn his shirt from his body, completely exposing his chest.

It was a beautiful chest, muscular, with a thin line of hair running down its center, disappearing under the heavily studded silver belt buckle.

"My Lord," Barbara La Marr said, back at her binoculars.

The orchestra once again changed tempo, segueing into the "Saber Dance" as the rider and horse crashed through the first floor doors and trotted up one side of the eighteenth-century staircase. He cantered around the table and stopped in front of the bride, a youngish woman who looked like her father.

The masked rider leaned down, took the silver rose he had had clenched in his teeth, and handed it to the bride. Then, in a sudden burst of passion, he pulled the bewildered woman from her seat, kissed her squarely on her mouth, released her, and cantered off down the second staircase and out into the park and off into, as Wallace Reid would have it, "the Sunset Boulevard."

Olga Rastanovitch, a character lady who had always been eighty-four, stood up and fainted into the arms of her young and handsome waiter. "He was sveating," she shouted, before she closed her eyes and in her best tsarina accent. "Sveating."

*   *   *

For a week no one in Hollywood could speak of anything else. Prints of the home movies Uncle Joe had had made were pirated and shown in private screening rooms. Who, it was asked, was the masked man?

Some thought it was Wallace Reid and that his double had played the wedding. Others said that it was the girl's bereft lover; but no one quite believed that, the girl was so clearly loverless.

Though he wasn't renowned for his showmanship, it was also bandied about that Uncle Joe had gotten up the stunt as an entertainment, as a novel way in which to entertain his guests and, possibly, to introduce a new star.

Uncle Joe knew immediately who the masked man was but he screened *The All-American Cowboy* just to make certain. He waited a week before he sent the car. "It's the Dusenberg," Townie shouted from his post behind the living room curtains. "He must be serious."

Max got in front with Mr. Tanaka and talked with him all the way to the studio about his plans for buying a farm.

"It will be soon now," Mr. Tanaka told him.

"Now remember," Araby said to Townie as the car rolled through the gates, passing the rearing iron horses. "You're Max's agent but I'm going to handle the negotiations."

"I remember," Townie said.

"I'm better at dealing with men like Uncle Joe than you are," she said as Patsy, the guard, waved them through and Max asked Mr. Tanaka where Mitsuko was.

Before Mr. Tanaka could answer, the front door of the car was being opened, by Uncle Joe himself. "Long time no see," Uncle Joe said, studying Max. "So how was the war?" he asked, escorting Max up to his office, one hand on Max's arm, the other grasping a cigar. Araby and Townie followed, a few steps behind.

"So-so," Max answered, picking up Uncle Joe's Yiddish inflection.

"Where'd you get the nag?" Uncle Joe asked, sinking down into his papal desk chair. "Nice-looking horse. Maybe we can use her." He pressed down a lever, recently installed into his desk, which alerted his secretary that he wanted tea with three spoons of sugar and just a touch of milk.

"I went out to Mixville and borrowed the biggest white horse they had," Araby said, closing the door of Uncle Joe's office behind her, choosing the chair next to his desk. "I'm afraid she's under contract."

"I knew it was you," Uncle Joe said. "I knew in my heart this wasn't Max's kind of business."

Townie began to say something but there was a knock on the door and Uncle Joe's secretary came in with his tea. It took Max a moment to realize who the beautiful Japanese girl was.

"Mitsuko," he said, standing up.

With a dancer's poise she placed the lacquered tray on Uncle Joe's desk as that gentleman beamed up at her serious face. "You can't call her Mitsuko anymore, Max. She's now my Number One Executive Secretary, Miss Tanaka."

She turned to look at Max. "You have changed," she said. "You look older and bigger. You couldn't have possibly grown, could you?"

"What about your painting?" he wanted to know. "Your school?"

"Listen, children," Uncle Joe said, putting one hand on Mitsuko's arm, the other on Max's, escorting them both to the door. "You two go outside and have your little class reunion. If you don't mind. The adults will stay here and do a little business."

Max looked at Araby. "You don't care if I . . . ?"

"It will be best, darling," Araby said in her refined voice. "Townie and I will take care of everything."

Max followed Mitsuko out the door, closing it behind them. Without a word she led him down to her father's office and into a small back room the walls of which were covered with paintings of oversized fantasy flowers.

"They're wonderful," Max said after a moment. "I've never seen anything like them."

"You see," Mitsuko said, taking his big hand in her small, delicate one, "I've finally learned to paint what I can't see."

He stood looking down at her. She wore a pale blue blouse and a long dark skirt. Her thick, lustrous black hair had been pulled back and tied into a bun. She wore no jewelry, no makeup. She should have looked like she wanted to: a very efficient executive secretary.

"You're so beautiful," Max said. "I used to sit in the foxhole when Joe was going on and on about his father's farm and think about you. I used to wonder what had happened to you, what was going to happen to you. I used to picture you on *your* father's farm, in overalls and pigtails, milking cows. I thought he'd have that farm by now. I never thought you'd turn into a woman in such a short time."

She took his hand again and put it up to her cheek. "I never thought of you, Max, as anything else but a man."

He bent down, without knowing it, to kiss her when the outer door opened and Mr. Tanaka stepped into the room. "Mitsuko," he said, and his face was stern, "you must not bore Mr. Meyer with your paintings."

"Yes, *papasan*," Mitsuko said, letting go of Max's hand.

"Return to your office. I will escort Mr. Meyer on a tour of the new commissary building."

Max watched her leave and then he faced Mr. Tanaka. "She has grown up almost overnight," he said.

"She is a very young woman, still," Mr. Tanaka said, softening, leading the way to the new commissary.

Araby watched them from the turretlike window Uncle Joe's office.

"Sit down," Uncle Joe told her. "A woman in your condition shouldn't be standing."

"You're being very thoughtful, Uncle Joe."

"And do me a favor: don't call me Uncle Joe. Mr. Goldstein or plain Joe, if you want. But not Uncle Joe. I want to tell you something, girlie: I don't like what you did. That was a sacred occasion for me. You messed it up. My only daughter's only wedding. It was supposed to be a big event in my life. It wasn't supposed to be *schmaltz*."

"Uncle Joe," Townie began.

"No excuses. No more niceties. That was one wedding I can't reshoot. I'll tell you something else: I'm very good at forgiving but I never forget. Now let's hear your proposition."

By the time they left his office an hour later, Araby had Max under contract for two years with Great Western Moving Pictures, Inc. for five thousand dollars per week. His first film was to be entitled *The Masked Rider,* and Spring Stevenson—Uncle Joe's favorite writer—was to script it. Twenty thousand dollars, more than twice what he had spent on any other film, was to be put into publicity. Araby was barred from the set.

They told Max about the contract on the way home.

"I don't like it," Max said. "I don't like the way you got it."

"I got it the only way anyone ever gets anything in this town," Araby told him. "Now get off your high horse. You're not Tim Bronco and this isn't the America of the Golden West. You're in a tough business but right now, thanks to me and your wedding ride, you're in the catbird seat. If Joe Goldstein hadn't given you that contract, there were half a dozen men in this town who would have. Now listen to me, Max . . ."

"Shut up. I've listened to you long enough. I got a better deal to offer Uncle Joe." He looked down at Townie. "Come on, agent."

Araby shouted after them as they left the house and headed for the trolley but Max wouldn't look back. They found Uncle Joe on the set of a western Fred Thompson, the ex-minister, was making. No one looked happy.

"He wants to tear up the contract," Townie told Uncle Joe.

"What's the matter, it's not good enough?"

"Max wants to make one film for you. If it's a success, you give him five percent of the gross. If it flops, you give him one week's salary and we call it quits."

"Why?" Uncle Joe asked after a moment.

"I'm not out to cheat you, Uncle Joe," Max said, holding out his hand. "And you can't afford that kind of a contract now."

"How do you know?"

"My sister's friend, a guy named Ryan, told me."

"And how does he know?"

"Ryan knows an awful lot," Max said, still holding out his hand.

Uncle Joe finally took it. "You're a genuine *mensch*, Max, even if you look like you're one-hundred-percent American. And I'll tell you what: if *The Masked Rider* flops, I'll give you two weeks' salary."

When they got back to the house on Gower Street, the door on the second floor was locked. "Goddamn it, Araby, let me in," Max shouted.

"Go fuck yourself, you immigrant."

He used his body to break through the door. She was on the bed, her stomach in the air, a pad resting on it, a pencil in her hand. "What the hell do you think you're doing?"

"I'm writing my screenplay for Pathé," she said,

not looking up. "Someone better make it in this family."

He lay down next to her and put his arms around her. Araby let him hold her but she continued to write.

Two months later Carleton LeMay accepted her script in lieu of the seven thousand dollars he had given her to make *A Woman of the Trenches* and filed it in his wastepaper basket.

Max completed his first full-length feature under the name devised by Townie, Ram Page. *The Masked Rider* was the biggest hit Great Western had had in several years and put Great Western in the black again.

A month after its release, in the early spring of 1919, Araby gave birth to a six-pound girl with Max's eyes and coloring.

"You'd think I had nothing to do with her," Araby said, handing the baby over to the nurse.

They called her Anna because Araby said she "sure as hell wasn't going to call her Bessie."

Jake and Nick sent congratulatory telegrams, a doll designed for an eight-year-old, and a set of trains geared for ten-year-old boys. Bessie sent five telegrams, a basket of canned and kosher food, and threatened to come. As much as he would have liked to have seen her, Max told her to wait awhile, that Araby wasn't quite recovered. He didn't say recovered from what.

Uncle Joe Goldstein sent a silver spoon and asked Max to go on a publicity tour across the country but both Townie and Araby advised him not to. Max did not sound like Ram Page looked.

At Townie's suggestion, and with Max's vehement support, Mitsuko was hired away from Great Western and employed as Anna's nurse. Uncle Joe loudly disapproved. More quietly Mr. Tanaka made his objections known, and he and his daughter had the most serious disagreement of their lives.

But Mitsuko, as she herself said, knew what she wanted.

CHAPTER 5

It was spring of 1921 and it was Paris and all the insomniacs Kay knew were spending the early morning hours—after the bars and cafés had pulled down their shutters—at the all-night cinema on the rue Monsieur le Prince.

At nine in the morning, when Paris was at its most deceptively innocent, she would stroll over to the Flore and order what was being called the American breakfast: Pernod and croissants.

Dickie and Kay Hull were still nominally married, sharing the same shabby-grand apartment on the avenue Raspail. They hadn't made love together in almost a year. Dickie Hull was otherwise engaged. The Frenchwomen liked his open manner and his white, healthy teeth. All of his liaisons took place in the afternoon because, Kay surmised, his partners were married or had other plans for the evening.

They slept together, without touching, in the lumpy and ancient bed each night.

"Why not have some fun?" Dickie asked her, meaning, "Why not have sex with someone?"

She didn't know why she didn't. She told herself it was because she didn't like French men on any level, least of all sexual; and all the Americans she knew were filthy, not many having access to baths.

It was the mechanics of it that got her down: taking off one's clothes and not getting the zipper right; climbing into a stale bed, assuming absurd positions and emotions; getting out of the stale bed, taking a French bath with a tiny washcloth and a pan of suspect water and a great deal of eau de cologne; getting back into one's clothes; and that last, suffocating obligatory kiss; "*au revoir, chérie.*"

The Fitzgeralds were there and so were the Murphys and she thought them all fearful frauds, most likely, she told herself, because they didn't like her. They liked Dickie (why, she wondered, did everyone dote on Dickie?) and took him around to out of the way cabarets on occasion.

She continued to drink. After all, she reasoned, that's why we're in Paris. She went on picnics in the Bois. She sat around artists' studios but refused to model. "I'm not anxious," she would say, "to be preserved for posterity." She went to Spain by herself where its charm eluded her and she became sick from the food. She danced the shimmy to "Indianola" in a green cloche hat and Michael Arlen bought her a drink. She continued to sleep with Dickie in the flat on the avenue Raspail.

Once she persuaded a rich publisher's son—a thin man from San Francisco named Fatty Freeman—to take her to the Stein ménage where she was relegated to a back room to discuss rabbit stew recipes with the women. Miss Toklas took a shine to her.

"I can't imagine eating rabbit," Kay said to put her off.

"You're not a vegetarian, are you?" she asked. "There's nothing worse than a vegetarian, Mrs. Hull."

"Oh yes, there is," Kay told her, standing up, going to look for Fatty Freeman among the men and Miss Stein. "I'm kosher."

The next time she saw Miss Toklas was at a hot, smoky reception for a wasted poet at Sylvia Beech's bookstore. She came striding up to Kay and said, "I found a market where one can get kosher rabbit. Will you come and dine on Sunday?"

Kay said she would and did because she wanted to see the paintings in that famous dining room; but they were all hung too close together so that they looked like one immense Rorschach. Again the men were all huddled in one room around Miss Stein while Kay and Miss Toklas ate kosher rabbit.

Someone must have informed her that Kay wasn't Jewish, let alone keeping strict dietary observance, because the next time they met, Miss Toklas walked past her as if she didn't exist.

She thought of suicide, not because she was snubbed by Gertrude Stein's lover but because everything seemed pointless. She felt, in truth, that perhaps Miss Toklas was right, that she didn't exist. She bought some pills but at the last moment lost her nerve. She thought of going home and even wrote, but her father made it clear he didn't want to see her again and her thoughts went back to suicide.

Dickie was "sublimely" happy. That was a word he used often, one which never failed to irritate Kay. "In a year or two," he told her, "we'll go home and have two sublime children."

*   *   *

It was early in April and the all-night cinema was featuring Ram Page in *Son of the Masked Rider*. After the film she and Fatty Freeman walked over to the Flore where they ordered Pernods and sat smoking cheap Spanish cigarettes while the dappled Paris sunshine crept through the trees.

She was more than bored that morning; she was frightened. She thought about Dickie and she thought about the pills in the drawer of her dressing table. Fatty Freeman bought her another drink. He was very nice looking, she thought. A Harvard boy, all serious and full of detailed ethics. "Bad as all that?" he asked, looking at her.

"Infinitely worse."

"Want to come to my place and talk about it?"

"Not even a little," she said, putting her hand on his.

At three in the afternoon, she was still at the Flore, still at the large table on the far right, refusing offers to go to boxing matches and dansants and nickel bars and live sex shows in the suburbs. She was feeling no pain, she told herself, using one more of Dickie's odious refrains; and, at the same time, very sorry for herself.

"There is nothing worse than a Pernod drunk," she said.

"You can't sit here all day," Fatty Freeman said. "Let me take you home."

"This is my home, Fatty, darling."

Suddenly there was a hand on her shoulder and a voice was cutting through the Pernod fog. "How you doing, baby?"

She knew immediately that it was Nick. She hadn't seen him for two years and though he had changed in certain ways, he still was very much the same person she had known. At nineteen he seemed more mature, more complete, than any of the thirty-year-old men sitting around the Flore.

"Marvelous," she said, looking up at him, attempting the right note of nonchalance though she felt as if she had been electrocuted. "Want a drink?"

"Nope." He put his hand on her wrist. "Come on, let's get out of this joint."

"See here," Fatty Freeman began, standing up, "that's no way . . ."

"I'd *love* to get out of here," she said to Nick, standing up carefully, avoiding looking at Fatty.

"You're stewed, ain't you?" Nick asked, taking her arm, steering her along St.-Germain-des-Prés.

"Possibly a trifle steamed."

He looked at her disgustedly. "Last thing I'm going to put up with is a stewed tomato." She looked at him to see if he were kidding, if he were being intentionally funny, but his face held no expression.

He hailed a taxi and pushed her into it. He said something to the driver who didn't understand, then he put a printed card under the driver's nose. The driver either couldn't read the writing or he couldn't read. Nick retrieved the card and Kay translated.

"How did you find me?"

"What makes you think I was looking for you?" He reached into his jacket pocket and pulled out a folded magazine clipping. It was a photograph of Kay and some dubious Russian count dancing at a *bal masqué*. She had gone as Lilith and hadn't worn much. The accompanying article decribed the shame of America's youth wasting itself in the ultimate city of sin, Paris, France.

"Where'd this come from, the *Police Gazette*?"

"Shut up."

The taxi stopped in front of a large, marble-faced house in a section of Paris Kay wasn't familiar with. An old-fashioned servant opened the door. "Good afternoon, Mr. Meyer. Madam." He led them up the most beautifully proportioned staircase Kay had ever seen and into a room with a fire burning in the green marbled fireplace. The walls were shirred with green silk, the bed canopied in the same material. It stood at the far end of the room between a pair of leaded panel windows that overlooked a small, enclosed garden.

"Whose house is this?" Kay asked.

"It belongs to a friend of a friend of mine." He went to her and put his arms around her.

"I should bathe first," she said.

"You can take a bath later."

He pushed her up against the silk-covered wall and kissed her. At the same time he lifted her skirt, pulled down her panties and dropped his trousers all in what seemed like one movement. He kissed her again as he lifted her left leg and went into her. She had an orgasm almost immediately. He did a few seconds later.

Afterward, after they had bathed together in the huge pink marble tub, after they had made love together, she lay in the bed and watched him as he moved around the room with his choreographed strut. He was looking for one of the black Cuban cigars his brother sent him from Florida. He found one, clamped it between his teeth, and lay down next to her. She studied the darkness of his hair, the olive skin of his body in which every muscle was as clearly defined as a medical textbook's anatomical drawing.

"You should be a Roman," she said, tracing the profile of his face with one finger. "Not the emperor, perhaps; but certainly the captain of the imperial guard."

"I ain't no Roman," he said, taking her hand and placing it on his equipment. "I'm a one-hundred-per-cent American Jewboy." He smiled one of his rare smiles. They never reached his eyes, she thought. His eyes remained empty and silver blue like those of a winter fox.

"You make me feel very young, Nicky," she said, putting her head on his shoulder and, for no reason she could think of, began crying, great big little-girl sobs. He held her and kissed her.

Later, over a perfect French supper at Fouquet's which he wasn't at all certain he liked, she asked him if he owned his cabaret. He told her he didn't, that he was still working for Ryan. "Too much competition," he told her. "Besides I got my eyes set on something bigger than a speakeasy. But I need plenty of money to set it up."

The waiter poured her another glass of wine and she asked him what he was doing in Paris.

"Same thing you are. Lapping up the culture. Why don't you lay off that wine?"

"Try some. It's marvelous."

"I never touch booze, 'marvelous' or otherwise."

"How long shall you stay?"

"A couple of weeks. Ryan thought I needed a vacation. Plus the fact I have a little business to attend to, some relations to cement."

"What sort of business?"

"Listen to me, baby girl," he said, putting his hand on her chin, turning her face to his. "My business ain't your business. Your business is being nice to me. Getting into my bed when I'm in the mood. Making sure my buttons are on my shirt and my trousers are pressed and my food is on the table."

"Hey, wait a minute. We're not married."

"We will be," he said, signaling for the check, "soon as you divorce that lunkhead."

Nick went to see Dickie Hull the next morning. "If you hurt him," Kay told Nick, "I won't go through with it."

"Me? That big lunkhead is twice as big as me."

"That big lunkhead doesn't carry a gun."

"You think I'd use a gun on *him?*"

When she arrived at the apartment on the avenue Raspail, Dickie was there, waiting for her. He sat in the ultramodern chromed chair Sarah Murphy had gotten him to buy while Kay packed. "I don't understand," he said.

"I'm not at all certain I do, either, Dickie."

"He's a gangster, Kay. A common little racketeer."

"He's certainly not in your league, Dickie."

"He's a Jew."

"My God," she said, looking for a lace chemise she had spent too much money on. *"Quel horreur!"*

"I know I've fooled around. But so have you. Or at

least you had the opportunity. I never stopped you, did I?"

"Where the hell is that goddamned chemise?" She pulled out all the drawers in the chiffonier and found it under a pile of Dickie's broadcloth shirts.

"We could go home and start a life, Kay."

"Too late." She looked out the window, through the mass of curtains hanging over it, and saw Nick reach across the taxi driver and hit the horn twice with the heel of his hand. "I couldn't if I wanted to."

She snapped and strapped the suitcase, bent over and kissed Dickie on the forehead. He was crying. Six feet two, she thought, a former Princeton halfback, a man with a private income of fifty thousand per, and he was crying because the wife he hadn't slept with in over a year was leaving him for a short Jewish racketeer. Well, she supposed, that was something to cry about.

"Good-bye, Dickie," she said, hearing the horn blast again. She took a last look at that empty, overstuffed apartment, at the man who had been her husband, and left.

"What were you doing," Nick wanted to know, making room for her in the back of the taxi, "fucking him good-bye?"

Later she asked him if he had come to Paris only to find her and he admitted that that was at least one of the reasons. "I want you to tell me that you love me," she said.

"I do."

"I want you to tell me."

After a moment he finally strangled it out. "I love you, Kay."

She kissed him and told him that she loved him, too.

"Okay, already. Do me a favor and shut up and go to sleep." But she couldn't. She lay there on her side, her hands folded neatly under her head, Nick's tough arms around her and she felt, if not exactly reborn, suddenly and totally alive.

They left for Marseilles a week later and then sailed aboard a freighter carrying wine to Cuba. The crew were told they were honeymooners and kept out of their way. They made love in the mornings and sunned in the afternoons. Kay didn't have a drink and Nick didn't wear his gun until they pulled into the port of Havana two sleepy weeks later.

CHAPTER 6

It was five P.M., beer time in Key West. Jake Meyer and Frances Ellington were sitting on the balcony outside Jake's sitting room. He was smoking one of Luis San Obispo's cigars, looking out at the Atlantic where the entire fleet of the Meyer-Wheeler Ferry Line was docked at the foot of Simonton Street. Frances sipped her beer and watched the trolley move up and down Duval Street, like a machine out of a rotogravure cartoon.

They seemed—and, in truth, were—very comfortable with one another. That hadn't always been so. For the first two weeks after Frances had left Rokeby and had moved into the rooms above Jake's in Key West, they had slept together every night.

Then, one morning, Frances woke up and watched Jake shaving. "There's nothing sexier," she said, still in bed, looking at him in front of the washbasin and the brass-framed mirror in the adjoining room, "than a young man shaving. It's such a deliberate act." She stretched her body under the light cotton sheet and tried to remember what she had been like when she was nineteen. Absurdly prim, probably. She was glad she wasn't nineteen any longer but she also knew she wasn't ecstatic about being thirty-four.

"Jake," she called out, reaching for the cup of coffee he had left on the rickety bamboo table next to the bed. "Why do you sleep with me?"

"You're pretty damned good in bed, Frances," he said, moving the straight razor up the slope of his muscular neck, shaking the shaving soap from it, and proceeding to his chin. "And besides, I like you a lot."

"That's more or less what I thought, Jake." She closed her eyes for a moment, and then opened them and stared up at the revolving fan. "Listen, Jake; we're not going to sleep together anymore."

"Why the hell not?" he asked, putting the straight-edged razor down, washing his face with water from the bowl.

"Because liking me isn't a good enough reason to sleep with me. Not for a person like you, Jake. Maybe someday it will be but right now it's not. You're young and you're romantic and certainly you don't mind obliging a lady once or twice but for the long run, Jake Meyer, you have to be in love."

"Frances . . ."

"And stop feeling all responsible for me. I came to Key West of my own free will, not because you and your magnificent body were parked here. I came because it sounded like a good place in which to write and it is. And I came because I felt like being mean to dear cousin Virginia and I am. Each time I've seen her on the street, she's gone snow white and given me the directest cuts I've ever received. Coming to Key West and taking rooms in the Jefferson Hotel on

Duval Street was the surest way I knew of putting the final nail in the coffin of my social status.

"I didn't come here pursuing you, so you can take that grandiose notion out of your head, Jakey. I'm fifteen years older than you and I've enjoyed what we've had but let's end it now, while we can still like one another. We'll be better friends than we'll ever be lovers, Jake."

He put down the towel he had dried his face with and came over to the bed. "I was thinking, Frances, of asking you to marry me."

"You are a first-class idiot, Jakey Meyer. With charm, lots of charm. It's a good thing I'm going to hang around for a while to take care of you. Now what about the friendship? You want to shake on it?"

"Frances . . ."

"You want to shake on it, Jakey?"

He took her hand and kissed it and she patted him on the cheek. "You're such a sweet boy, Jakey. And so young." She got out of the bed, found her wrapper, and put it on. She took more more look at him as he stood watching her, a towel around his waist. "When you get older, Jake, don't ever let anyone denigrate the pleasures of young flesh. Take it from me, darling, there's nothing like it."

She let the louvered door shut after her and ran up to her rooms, averting her face so her maid, Evangeline, wouldn't see her tears. "I'm an old fool," she said to her mirror. "But not such a fool to try to keep him."

As they sat on the balcony, drinking their beers, Jake watched his two ferries—well, his and

Claude's—bob up and down on the waterline. They had no ballast, no manufacturers' goods to weigh them down. They were empty—Jake and Claude's ferry line was bust. "It never had much of a chance," Jake said, half aloud. The Conchs had their own ways of getting back and forth to Cuba and the river of tourists supposed to arrive in Key West via Flagler's railroad was, in reality, a trickle. What tourists there were traveled the established P&O Line.

What's more, it had turned out that when a manufacturer had to ship to Havana, there was no reason for him to put into Key West and transfer his goods to a ferry. The large Cuban sugar and fruit plantations, all American owned, had their own freighters going to New York or through the Panama Canal to the West Coast.

"Someday I'm going to stop dreaming," Jake said, this time loud enough for Frances to hear him. She put down the soda-pop bottle in which the beer was served and smiled at him.

"What happened on your last trip to Cuba? I thought you were going to speak to . . ."

"Trouble is, they wouldn't speak to me. P&O's got them all sewed up."

"You were there over a week. That was a very long silent dialogue."

"Why'd you have to go and have all your hair cut off?" Jake asked, pointedly changing the conversation.

"I'm a victim of fashion. Here's another." She looked down at the street where Claude Wheeler's car was pulling up at the curb. It was long and black, and impossibly expensive, one of the models postwar

Germany was already producing, a gift from his prospective father-in-law.

Claude ran up the steps with his usual enthusiasm but his expression was heavy and tired. His marriage to Virginia was but a week away and Frances thought that that young woman, now established at Devon House, was probably wearing him down. Claude Wheeler always made Frances think of vanilla ice cream. It was the white suits he wore, she decided. Somehow they looked more virile on Jake.

Claude had also changed his hairstyle, parting it in the middle and sporting a new, yellow moustache as if it were a not quite fresh boutonniere kept in a glass of water overnight.

Luis San Obispo, employed by the hotel at Jake's request, brought a chair and a whiskey in a soda-pop bottle without being asked.

"Everybody's talking about that piece of yours in the magazine, Frances," Claude said. Her first story had been published in *Harper's* that month.

"I've noticed. The respectable ladies of the town have begun saying hello to me."

"Takes time in a small town like this," Claude said, upending his pop bottle, "for folks to get to know you."

"Slow acceptance is too much like slow torture for me, Claude. I either want it to stop altogether or pick up speed and do its damnedest." She took her soda-pop bottle by the neck and stood up. "You mustn't mind me, Claude. I've had one beer too many. Good night. Good night, Jakey."

They watched as she made her way up to the third floor. "She's still a heck of a good-looking woman,"

Claude said, tilting his chair back against the balustrade. "Though I never do know what in the hell she's talking about."

The chair almost fell out from under him, Jake catching its back at the last moment, holding it upright. "Wedding nerves," Claude said, reseating himself. "You know, Jake, it's going to be a small wedding. Just family."

"I understand," Jake said, though he knew that five hundred people had been invited, that Claude and Virginia had had a well-publicized argument over whether or not Jake was to be issued an invitation.

"I want him to be the best man," Claude was reported to have said by the Devon cook, a cousin of Frances's maid, Evangeline, who promptly told Frances, who diplomatically informed Jake.

"Then you'd better find yourself another bride, Mr. Wheeler," Virginia had told him, turning on her heel and walking calmly into the sewing room where Evangeline's first cousin was working a manual fan. Claude waited five minutes before following.

That late afternoon, sitting at the wrought-iron table, Claude looked down at Duval Street and then up at the red and blue sky and then out at the ocean, carefully avoiding the ferries docked at the end of Simonton Street.

"You're the only decent person I know, Jake," he said. He waited for a moment, hoping Jake would say something but Jake continued to pull on his cigar. Jake knew what was coming, but for once he had no desire to make it easy for Claude.

"Virginia doesn't want me to be in the ferry business. Neither does her pa. They think it's not gentlemanly for me to be the co-owner of a ferry line."

"Especially one that's not making any money."

"There's that." Claude ordered another whiskey. "They're not against it if we show a profit. The senator says he'll give us six more months. If can start pulling some money in, then he'll let me keep my share."

"He'll *let* you?"

"As a silent partner. It's the best I could do, Jake. We're going to be living in his house. He's already footing all the bills. He says he can sell my ferry to a man up in Miami for what I paid for it."

"Don't worry about it, Claude," Jake said, standing up. "The money I borrowed for my half of the business is long overdue. We got a third partner. I'm going to meet him on Friday. He's going to solve all our problems."

Jake went into his sitting room, closing the door after him, leaving Claude and his whiskey out on the balcony. Even through his door Jake could hear the woman's-tongue tree on United Street making a terrible racket, its seed pods rattling in the wind.

In the beginning Esther and Moishe and the baby—Jake's son, David—would travel from their home in Miami to Key West once a month. But Esther, with her orthodox wig, and Moishe, in his shiny blue suit, climbing up the front steps of the Jefferson, sitting on the balcony, drinking genuine soda pop in the eighty-degree weather, was an experience that made all concerned uncomfortable.

Jake began going to Miami once a month, sometimes on the train, more often hitching a ride on a barge. Esther and Moishe had a small stucco house which somehow reminded Jake of Poland. They seemed prosperous enough. Moishe ran a small restaurant-speakeasy. Mookie, Esther's father, had supposedly lent him the money to open it.

During his visits they treated Jake as if he were the head rabbi, both Esther and Moishe fussing over him until he would ask to see the child. "I put him on my knee," Jake told Frances, "and he tries to grab my fingers with his thick, little hands. All the time the kid's laughing. I've never seen him cry once. And he's growing. I can't get over it how that kid's growing. Each visit I'm seeing a whole new kid."

Ryan was sitting in the green overstuffed sofa when Jake went up to Miami that late spring Friday. He was holding the child. "What your sister would give to see him," Ryan said, bouncing the boy on his knee. "Next time I come, I'm going to bring the dear girl along. This is a nephew she shouldn't miss."

Jake took David and kissed him. "Where's Esther and Moishe?"

"They wanted to give us an opportunity to talk. They're so discreet, Esther and Moishe, these days."

"What's there to talk about?" Jake asked, holding his son. "The ferries are a bust. I owe you five grand and I can probably sell my ferry for about three."

"Oh, dear boy, there's no need to talk of selling. Remember our agreement? I'm now your partner. Your very silent partner." Ryan crossed his legs and touched his fingertips together. "I think I may be able to help you turn your business into a profitable one. An extremely profitable one." Jake held onto the boy as Ryan talked.

Jake returned to Key West on an overcast Saturday in early June, the day before Claude and Virginia were to be married. As he carried his valise up the stairs of the Jefferson, his white suit wrinkled from traveling, he saw Virginia's father, Senator Devon, entering the suite of rooms he kept at the far end of the Jefferson's second floor.

"For reasons," the senator had announced, "of cognition and meditation. Damn it all," he said, once or twice too often, "a man can't think in a big house with half a dozen negras always underfoot. Damn it all, a man needs a little R and R where he won't be interrupted."

The senator's R and R was a tragically lovely Cuban girl, not quite sixteen. She was hustled up the back stairway to the senator's rooms by her father, the third and least of the town's morticians. Her face was always perfectly composed but her eyes, constantly on the move, gave her away.

Jake had Luis San Obispo prepare a bath, after which he changed into a clean white suit. He stood on the balcony for a moment but the muffled sounds coming from behind the senator's doors drove him down to the Jefferson's café where he ordered a plate of *arroz con pollo* and a bottle of beer-disguised-as-pop.

It was close to midnight and Jake was on his twentieth beer, when Claude's car pulled up. He said he was "a little worse for wear," the town's acceptable young bloods having given him a bachelor party.

"Nice to have you back," Claude said, dropping

into the empty chair at Jake's table. His tie was undone, his dinner jacket soiled. He asked Luis San Obispo to bring him a whiskey.

"You know we don't serve alcohol on these premises, señor."

"You can't protect the world," Jake told him. "The señor's as drunk as he's going to get. Another whiskey won't kill him."

Luis San Obispo, clucking in disapproval, brought Claude a pop bottle filled with whiskey. "Tonight, my dear old pal, is my last unmarried night, my last night of freedom. What say we visit Madam Fudge together and enjoy the pleasures she purveys? My treat."

"I'll have to say no, Claude," Jake said formally. He knew that after twenty beers, if he wasn't going to be formal, he was going to pass out. "I have an appointment in a few minutes." He took his silver pocket watch with the gold chain out of his vest pocket and studied it.

"Jake," Claude said, putting his arm around Jake's shoulder. "We're still friends, ain't we?"

Jake removed Claude's arm and set it on the table. "No. Now we're business associates. You're just one of my silent partners. I'm the only working one. From now on the Meyer Line—notice I've omitted the Wheeler—will leave passengers and freight to ships like the *Governor Cobb*.

"Beginning *mañana* the Meyer Line will be carting sugar from Havana harbor to Key West, transferring it to Florida's East Coast Railway at the Trumbo docks.

"We will be making two runs a week. Net profits to

the company will be, I am told by our silent partner in New York, somewhere in the neighborhood of ten thousand dollars a month. That should please you and the senator and the senator's daughter."

Jake managed to stand up. "But I think you should know, partner, that the sugar will be in the form of rum, whiskey, French wines, and whatever other illegal beverages our secret partner in New York manages to purchase. If this form of transporting sugar offends you and your new in-laws' sense of what is right, I am prepared to buy you out. I have the money. I am, officially and suddenly, a success." He turned in the direction of the Jefferson steps.

"Jake . . ."

"We never were friends, Claude. You don't know how to be a friend. Maybe I don't, either. We drank together and we screwed together and now we're going to be lousy bootleggers together but don't get confused, Claude. We're not friends."

Another long open car pulled up in front of the Jefferson. Virginia sat in the back, the Devon's driver, Poor Willy, at the wheel. The earlier, threatening clouds had passed and the moon glistened on Virginia's silver-blond hair which she had refused to bob. It had been piled high on her head, secured by tortoiseshell combs. She seemed impossibly expensive, completely out of reach, as she sat watching the two men, her cat-green eyes assessing the situation.

After a moment she stood in the car and opened the door without making the slightest movement to get out. "Mr. Meyer," she said. Jake bowed his head slightly. "Doing your best, I see, to spoil my wedding. I'm not going to allow that to happen. Get in the car,

Claude. Willy will take you home. I'll drive your car."

Claude stood up, just, while Poor Willy left the touring car and went to help him down the stairs. While this operation was taking place, Virginia left the back of the Packard in much the way a nineteenth-century queen might have left her carriage. She walked to where Jake was standing, propped up by the stairwell post.

"After tonight, Mr. Meyer," she said, looking at him directly, "I would very much appreciate it if you would have nothing more to do with Claude. He has promised me that he is going to sever all of his connections with you and I want to ask you to help him do that. You are turning him into a hopeless alcoholic and I am giving you the benefit of the doubt when I say that I am sure you have not been aware of that unpleasant fact.

"Please, Mr. Meyer, leave my future husband to the society in which he was raised. I think you and he will be happier. I know you want Claude to be healthy. Good night, Mr. Meyer. And good-bye."

She slid behind the wheel of Claude's car and effortlessly drove away.

The Honey Boys' sugary blues came at Jake from inside the café. He went in and ordered his twenty-first beer of the evening.

In the morning Virginia Devon was married to Claude Wheeler in what the Key West *Citizen* described as "the Wedding of the Decade." Jake was on his way to Cuba.

Jake had two errands to take care of in Havana.

One was personal, the other economic. He attended to business first, meeting his brother, Nick, on board a luxury yacht moored in Havana's harbor.

"You're looking good," Nick said, putting his feet up on the white leather banquette on which he was sitting. "Make yourself comfortable. We got a couple of dozen greasers to meet, each one more crooked than the next. You got any of those cigars?"

Jake tossed a box filled with Luis San Obispo's hand-rolled specials to his brother, looked up at the mural of Venus greeting Aphrodite on the salon's ceiling, and whistled. "Who's boat is this?"

"Belongs to a guy named Armando Galvez. He's already been squared away. You hungry or you want to get started?"

"How old are you, now, Nicky?" Jake asked, looking at his brother in his thin, dark suit.

"A hundred and twenty-six." He pulled a silk rope and a boy Nick's age brought in a tray of rums and another younger boy brought in a tray piled high with sliced turkeys, hams, and fruits. "Send the first one in," Nick told the younger boy.

They spent the next two days talking with Cubans either involved in the government or in what one gentleman called export-import. There was the minister of the sea and the master of the harbor and the customs inspector and the chief of police; and there were men without titles and men without names and men who talked too much and men who didn't say a word. But they all bowed, they all shook hands, they all received a white envelope filled with money from Nick.

"Is this what's known as cementing relations?" Jake asked after they had seen the last man on Nick's list.

"That's one way," Nick said. "Later we may have to resort to the other. But in the meantime everything is hunky-dory. From now on the only man you have to deal with is Galvez. He'll let you know when the booze arrives from Marseilles and when and where to pick it up. When Galvez gets bumped off— and he will, these guys always have a short term in office—then we go through this all over again with the new guys. That's what's called politics."

"You know too much, Nicky."

"Yeah? Well, Ryan's a good teacher, Brother."

They shook hands and Nick went on board the *President Tyler,* which was sailing for New York and Jake went to Madam Sucre's.

She received him in the drawing room in the section of the house her clientele were never allowed into. There was a white piano and peacock feathers in oversized turquoise vases and an intricate pattern of deep blue and gold tiles covering the floor.

Madam, in her black dress, with her black hair pulled into a difficult chignon, could have passed for an aging, dusky duchess in a Goya household painting. She stared at him with her uncompromising eyes for a full minute and then told him to sit down. "I don't approve of this transaction, señor," she finally said in a deep whisper. "She might have married the black doctor's son in Haiti and been respectable. But she wants you and I admit I trust you more than I trust the black doctor." She turned and looked at the paneled mahogany door and then back at Jake again. "I tell you something, Señor Jake.

Nancy is not my daughter. One of the girls, a careless
girl, had her and then died. There is no way on earth
to tell who the father is but he must have been
highborn if only from the cast of the girl's features."

"I don't care about all that, Madam Sucre."

"But I do." She turned away again and her hands,
heavily veined, clutched a fan of black feathers. "You
will be good to her, Señor Jake. If you don't want
her, after a while, bring her back here, you understand?"

"I understand," Jake said and there was a knock on
the door and Nancy, wearing a white dress, came in
and suddenly the heavy atmosphere in the room vanished. She went to Madam Sucre first and kissed her
and though that woman remained immobile, there
were tears in her eyes. Then she went to Jake and
put her hand in his.

As they left, Jake placed a white envelope—not dissimilar from the envelopes Nick had been dis-
pensing—on a chinoiserie table. Madam used the edge
of her dress to dry her eyes—the lace handkerchief
was for show—and picked up the envelope. "No good
will come of it," she said to herself. "I just know no
good will come of it." She stood staring at the closed
door and so forgot herself that it took her some ten
minutes before she turned her attention to the con-
tents of the white envelope.

The Conchs, the local Key Westers, firmly believed
that Jake Meyer had won Nancy Holliday from a
gambler who had brought her from France to
Havana. She was just seventeen, a light coffee color
with turquoise eyes and the sort of body, Frances El-

lington thought, that particularly affected men in the tropics. It was slim and lithe and might, in time, become rich and voluptuous but that wouldn't be for many years. In the tropics the bud was often more rare and appealing than the full bloom.

Not that Frances was jealous, she decided. Or as jealous as she might have been. She liked the girl and the ingenious way she told her version of how she and Jake had met: quite properly, in the parlor of her godmother's *ranchero*. "I fell in love with Jake immediately. We eloped that very same night. Now," Nancy said wistfully, "I can never go home again."

She was more accomplished than most Cuban girls, Frances admitted. She could read and she could speak English and Spanish and a sort of odd patois and she had a grace, a way of walking, that reminded Frances of young upper-class English girls and their mania for deportment.

"Perhaps," Frances said to her maid, "they did meet in her godmother's parlor." Evangeline laughed and shook her head.

Jake bought Nancy a tiny house at the end of Pinder Lane, reengaged Blondell as housekeeper-cook, and asked Frances to help Nancy furnish her new home.

She agreed though she was reluctant. "I may not be jealous," she told Evangeline, "but the idea of decorating my ex-lover's new mistress's home is a touch too Parisian, even for me." But Nancy was so sweet, so innately charming, Frances found herself spending her afternoons at Shuster's Store, choosing materials, studying wallpapers and paints.

Jake, it was understood, would continue to keep his

rooms at the Jefferson where, like Senator Devon, he would repair of an evening to meditate and cogitate. "Well," Jake said, "not exactly like the senator."

Virginia and Claude Wheeler returned from their European honeymoon in the middle of the steaming summer because Virginia was also anxious to redecorate. Her project was her father's home, Devon House, where she and her husband planned to reside.

The three women met on a very hot Wednesday afternoon in the cool recesses of Shuster's Store: Virginia, taking a cabbage rose chintz in her gloved hands to the light to inspect it for flaws; Nancy and Frances bouncing on a long, wicker davenport on the far side of the bolts of fabric where the furniture was kept, attempting to see if the cushions were comfortable enough for a man of Jake's size.

"It's your house," Frances pointed out. "If *you* like it . . ."

"No, it has to be right for Jake," the girl insisted.

At that moment Virginia, carrying the fabric, turned the corner and came face-to-face with her cousin and Jake Meyer's kept woman. There followed a long silence while the clerks and their customers watched to see what would happen next.

"It was better than a play," old lady Thirkell said to her companion, Julia Garronne. Everyone knew who everyone was. Certainly Virginia was aware of Nancy's identity. She hadn't been in town more than an hour before she had heard of Jake Meyer's "concubine."

The two of them, both so beautiful, in such opposite ways, studied one another with real interest. It was Virginia who turned away first. "Mr. Shuster," she said, handing the bolt of chintz to him, "would you send this over to Devon House this afternoon. I want to study it where there are no distractions."

Virginia was wearing a white suit she had bought in Paris. It had blue piping and nautical buttons and made her seem to be the only person in Key West who wasn't sweating on that sweltering afternoon.

Jake came up the stairs as Virginia was leaving. They stood facing one another in the doorway until Jake stepped back and Virginia went down to her car.

"How do you like the davenport?" Jake asked Nancy and Nancy replied that she didn't think she liked it at all.

Jake rarely saw Claude that summer. Claude had bought himself a speedboat and was busy organizing the Key West Athletic Club which fronted the southernmost beach. Only very occasionally could Claude be seen climbing the stairs of the old Jefferson Hotel for a late-night conference with his former friend and current business partner.

BOOK THREE

NOON

CHAPTER 1

In the early 1920s a series of sex-related scandals rocked Hollywood and caused a peculiar double-value system of morality to be established. Female stars—especially those of the vamp and siren variety—could engage in the most sordid activities on screen. But off the screen their lives had to be impeccable, free of any taint.

At the same time it was considered poor box office public relations for the leading stars of the day to be married. "Who," Uncle Joe Goldstein asked, "wants to go to the movies to see a married lady do the hootchy-kootch? You could stay home and watch your wife for free."

After William Desmond Taylor was killed and Fatty Arbuckle was accused of causing the death by rupture of Virginia Rappe, male stars also had to be discreet about their private lives. Though they, too, could take little public comfort from a happy, domestic homelife. "The little girlie from Puala, Washington, ain't going to the movies to see somebody else's husband, you know what I'm talking?" Uncle Joe asked.

This odd Hollywood standard—no sex and no

spouses—was the cause of some very convoluted arrangements, not the least of which was that between Max and Araby. Though they lived in the same house and were the parents of a child, elaborate precautions were taken to keep those facts from *Photoplay* and other fan magazines of the day. For the public Max lived by himself and exercised a great deal. Araby resided with a widowed mother and spent her nights reading the classics.

By the spring of 1922 the fan magazines were very much interested in both Max and Araby.

Araby Moore's career had taken longer to establish than her husband's. LeMay had switched from Pathé to Paramount and when Araby turned up two weeks after giving birth to Anna, he didn't bother to see her. The receptionist told her to leave her screenplay. "Mr. LeMay will get back to you, dear." He hadn't forgotten the money he had given Araby to make *A Woman of the Trenches* but he had more important matters on his mind.

He was looking for a new Theda Bara, then the biggest star in Hollywood, earning four thousand dollars a week. The project in which LeMay proposed to introduce his new, competitive siren was called *Cleopatra, Serpent of the Nile*.

He was again the only college-educated producer on the lot, one of the few non-Jews, and everyone was watching carefully to see if he would trip on an untied shoelace or an overbudgeted, under-grossing film.

Talent searches had been launched around the country but by the time Anna was a month old, LeMay still hadn't found his Cleopatra.

He had three possibilities but he knew none of them had the kind of magnetism that made and kept Theda Bara a star. The boys in the front office were putting pressure on him to start the film before the talent search publicity began to misfire and LeMay had to admit, if only to himself, that he was in trouble.

He was sitting in his office, getting his hair cut, surrounded by gofers, when his secretary told him two men were there with a delivery.

"What the hell," he said, waving the barber away. "I need a delivery. Send them on in."

Two men in overalls came in, carrying a large, rolled Oriental carpet on their shoulders. They put it down on the floor, gingerly. "You want us to unroll it, boss?" the bigger one asked. LeMay said he did and they proceeded to do so.

Lying in the middle of the carpet was Araby, wearing pearls on her breasts and a fringed, gold lamé G-string over her other private parts. Her copper hair had been dyed red with henna and had been threaded with pearls and aquamarines. Her eyes had been made up to reflect the aquamarines.

The barber dropped his scissors and the gofers stopped breathing as Araby stood up and went to LeMay, crossed scepters in her hands. "I am your Cleopatra, oh master, your Serpent of the Nile."

LeMay, laughing, returned to his chair, signaling the barber to begin cutting again. "Listen, Araby, honey," he told her, speaking over his shoulder. "I'm sorry you went to all this expense and trouble but we're not doing George Bernard Shaw's *Cleopatra*.

We're doing mine. Boys, you want to help Miss Moore into a taxicab?"

She stormed out as LeMay told the barber to cut a little more around the ears.

He waited for two days which, he decided, was as long as he could afford and then he called her. She insisted he send a limo so he went out to the little house on Gower and picked her up himself.

He took her back to his place and told her to get undressed. She did, slowly. He didn't bother taking off his trousers. He turned her around on her knees and entered her the back way. When he was finished, he pulled out and zipped up and said, "Now, Miss Moore, perhaps we can talk business."

Later he told Townie, "I figured if she could turn me on like that—and you know my usual preferences, dear Townie—she'll have them coming in the aisles."

By the spring of 1922 Max had completed six Ram Page films for Great Western, starring, producing, directing and, occasionally, increasingly, editing them.

"Ram Page is not only a world-famous actor," Uncle Joe said, barging into the editing room, pronouncing actor as if it began with an "h." "Now he's an editor to the bargain. Leave it to Gellis, Max," Uncle Joe said, pointing his finger at a small man looking over Max's shoulder at what everyone hoped was the final print of *Dead Man's Folly*. "What do you think I'm paying him for? Come on, Maxela, play a couple of hands of pinochle before lunch."

"Can't, Uncle Joe. Tim Bronco's waiting to see me."

"And that's another story without an end. He's drinking more and showing up less."

"What's that supposed to mean?" Max asked, looking up.

"That's supposed to mean that I want to get the little never-has-been off my payroll."

"You get rid of him, Uncle Joe, and I shut down work on *Oklahoma Kid*."

"Just what I need, a loyal actor and it's costing me five thousand a week," Uncle Joe said, capitulating.

"You can afford it." Max washed his hands at the sink and left the editing room. Uncle Joe stood still for a moment, looking discontentedly at Gellis. Max put his head back inside the room. "I'll be in your office at two P.M. sharp. But no pinochle. Gin rummy."

"Ten cents a point, quarter a box," Uncle Joe said, brightening visibly.

Tim Bronco, shorter and stubbier than ever, was waiting for Max in Max's dressing room, a weathered shack with a six-foot-square bathtub in its center. As Bronco waited, he paced around the bathtub, of which he disapproved, occasionally hawking and spitting tobacco juice into the spittoon Max had taken from one of the sets and installed in his dressing room for Tim Bronco's convenience.

Bronco had been playing sidekick to Max's All-American Cowboy in all of the Ram Page films despite Uncle Joe, despite Townie.

"We're paying him too much," the latter said on more than one occasion. "If you want to know the Truth."

"I don't want to know the Truth," Max said. "As you would say, Townie, all I want to hear are glori-

242 DAVID A. KAUFELT

ous lies." Townie had laughed but had not given up his position that Tim Bronco was too old, too short, and too drunk, most of the time, to play Max's shadow in the All-American oaters.

"He gave me my first chance."

"Yeah? And my mother's brother gave me my first delicious taste of sex," Townie countered. "I'm not supporting him, am I?"

When Max came into the dressing room, Bronco stopped pacing and leaned against the wall, spitting into the spittoon, hitching his jeans up on his nonexistent hips, rubbing his hand over his battered face.

"How are you, Bronco?" Max asked, removing his boots, putting his feet in the bathtub, running the water. "Laying off the sauce?"

"Nope."

There was a moment's silence and then Bronco said, "I come to say good-bye, Max."

"Where you going?"

"I figure it's time I got back to my wife, back to Texas."

The fact that Tim Bronco had a wife was a surprise but almost any voluntary piece of his biography would be. Max knew almost nothing about Bronco's past.

"What're you going to do about money?"

"I been saving some. I got fifteen thousand in the bank. That should see me."

"You don't have to go, Bronco," Max said, taking his feet out of the tub, drying them on a thick towel.

"It's time I went. I'll see you, Max."

Max watched as Bronco stepped out of the door and already missed the tough little man's presence.

Just then Townie came in after a perfunctory knock. Max told him he better start looking around for a new sidekick for the All-American Cowboy.

"Not a moment too soon. Don't look at me like that. Bronco was on his last legs and you know it. What's this?" Townie held up a sheaf of tightly furled papers Bronco had left behind. "A year's supply of rolling paper?"

Max took it from Townie and spread the papers out on his desk. It was evidently a scenario. The only words on the first page were: "Cowboy by Timothy Wainwright."

"That's Bronco's real name," Townie said. "Who would have thought he knew how to write?"

"Townie . . ."

"Okay, Ram. I'll take a walk and let you peruse *War and Peace* in silence."

Max sat down on the sofa and began to read.

Later, after Max's gin game with Uncle Joe, while he and Townie were driving home to Ram-A-Dies, that opulent limestone house Araby had caused to be built in "the style of the Taj Mahal," Townie asked about Bronco's script.

"I want you to read it, Townie," Max said, pulling into the circular driveway, stopping in front of the house.

"Max, the man could hardly speak the language much less . . ."

"Forget all that and do me a favor, will you? Read the goddamned script."

"Don't take out your anger with Araby on me, Max. I may be only a ten percenter . . ."

"Who says I'm angry with Araby?"

"Please. Every time I sit between you two at dinner, I get indigestion. It's like having bookends, Sitting Bull on one side, General Custer on the other. You two ever talk nice to each other anymore?"

"Araby hasn't got the time for nice. That's what she told me when I asked her the same thing." He put his big hand on the little man's shoulder. "Go read the script, Townie. I want to know what you think."

Avoiding the house, Max walked around it through Araby's English Garden to the pool—eight hundred square feet of imported mosaic tile and sky-blue water—where Mitsuko was sitting. She was in the shade offered by an oversized date palm wearing a shapeless white dress.

"Where's Anna?" Max asked, standing over her.

"Afternoon nap." She stood up. He didn't move away.

"How do you manage to look so beautiful all of the time?" he asked her.

"Max . . ." Her dark, almond-shaped eyes looked into his clear blue ones and for a moment they didn't speak.

"How long will Anna be napping?" he asked, taking Mitsuko's hand, leading her into the building that was used as a pool house.

"Max . . ." she said but she followed him.

Townie spent the next hour reading and rereading *Cowboy*, an original screenplay by Timothy Wainwright. He was living in one of the Ram-A-Dies turrets. "I have my own little bedroom, my own little studio, my own little bathroom, my own little private entrance. I feel as if I'm in Lilliput," he told his best friend, Ronnie Magador.

"I didn't think the Taj Mahal had turrets," Ronnie said.

"Araby improved on the original design."

"I can't imagine why you live there."

"It's a little bit like having a family, Ronnie."

"I wouldn't know, darling, from families," Ronnie said.

Townie finished the scenario for the last time and, putting it under his arm, ran down the marbelized central staircase, stopping at the table carved in the shape of an elephant where the servants left his mail. He put his two letters in his jacket pocket and the *Los Angeles Times* under his arm and continued through the central hall and out to the swimming pool. Anna, swathed in a towel, was on a white wrought-iron chaise longue, her eyes tightly closed.

"What are you doing, baby girl?" Townie asked her, kissing her forehead.

"Sunbathing," she said, not opening her eyes.

"Where's Daddy?"

"In the pool house, drying off."

Townie pushed his way through the swinging doors that made up the front entrance of the pool house—a miniature replica of the main house without the turrets—and, giving his perfunctory knock, walked into Max's room.

They hadn't heard him. They were laying on the chaise longue, having just made love. Max's strong arms were wrapped around Mitsuko's long, graceful body. Their eyes were closed. They looked, Townie thought, as if they were in what his father used to call a state of grace.

He closed the door and went out and sat at Anna's side. He knew himself well enough to realize that he was jealous; not for Max's body; certainly not for Mitsuko's, perfect as it was. He was jealous of the experience. He wanted to be able to make someone as happy, as ecstatic as those two were able to make each other.

He opened up the *Times* to the entertainment page which consisted of press releases printed, more or less verbatim as handed out by the studios. He read the banner-headlined article with at least as much interest as he had read Tim Bronco's scenario and with just as much surprise.

"Your mouth is open, Uncle Townie," Anna said, opening her eyes, finished with her nap. "You'll catch flies."

"Someone's going to catch someone, little princess Anna," Townie said, carefully folding the paper, putting it to one side, and then suddenly swooping down and scooping a delighted Anna up in his arms. "Now what am I going to do with this captive heir to the throne apparent?"

"Tickle her?"

"Yes. I think that just might be the punishment to fit the crime."

Anna giggled helplessly.

Later, while Mitsuko took Anna up to the main house for her supper, Townie sat on a swing Araby had had gilded while Max lay on the chaise longue next to it, watching the water in the pool. Each time

Townie moved, tiny flakes of gilt came off on his trousers.

"Had Araby strolled into the pool house, the resulting scene wouldn't have been remarkably pleasant," Townie said.

"I know," Max admitted.

"Had the child taken it into her head to see where Daddy and Auntie Mitsuko were, it certainly wouldn't . . ."

"I know, Townie. I know. We couldn't help ourselves. That's an excuse I'd never buy from anyone else but it's the Truth."

"As you once said to me, Max, I don't want the Truth; just give me glorious lies."

"I'm going to have to change the situation. What'd you think of the script?"

"I'm going to let you get away with changing the subject only because there's nothing else for me to say. As for *Cowboy*, it's a brilliant scenario, one of the great—in my estimation—screenplays. Where Tim Bronco found the wherewithal to write it will always be a mystery to rate with the pyramids for me. It's a wonderful idea: the last cowboy, one who never knew of silver spurs, choosing to live with his former natural enemies, the last of the Indians, rather than giving in and going to the city.

"But it's a film, Max, that you'll never make. Not at Great Western, not with our Uncle Joe at the helm. It is a film that will make—and this is bottom line—maybe twenty-eight cents and that is contingent on the size of Tim Bronco's family. It's a great script, Max. But it will never play."

"Oh yes it will, Townie. *Cowboy* is one movie I *want* to make."

They sat for a few moments as the sun set and a slight chill went through the air. One of the servants in the house was going from room to room, switching on lights. Max stood up and began to walk toward his wife's mansion, Townie following. As they entered the central hall, Townie handed him the newspaper.

"I don't think this"—he pointed to the article that had so engrossed him—"is going to make your day."

Araby arrived at Ram-A-Dies late that night, close to eleven. Officially, of course, she didn't live there. Officially she and Ram Page were "very, very good friends." *Photoplay* carried an interview with Araby that ended with the writer's editorial comment: "Something delicious is going on between Paramount's exotic Egyptian vamp and Great Western's All-American Cowboy but both insist, so far, that it's nothing very serious. Serious or not, you can take it from this reporter, Araby Moore fans, that you will be kept Hollywood Posted."

"Egyptian tramps," Araby said, whenever she discussed her refusal to make their marriage public, "ain't married." She and Uncle Joe came from the same school of public relations.

That evening she left her navy blue Rolls convertible with the two cheetahs in the back seat in front of the house. Carleton LeMay had insisted that wherever she went, the cheetahs were to follow. "You're fabulous and exotic and dangerous," he told her. "And don't ever let your public forget it."

"Get those goddamned walking fur coats out of the

car," she told Robinson, the butler, handing him
their gold chain leashes. "And spray them with
Chanel Number Five, for God's sake. All over."

The butler waited for Araby to divest herself of the
purple fox furs LeMay had decreed she wear that season before attending to the cheetahs and the car. Araby stepped down into the main drawing room which
featured a griffin motif. There were griffins on the tile
floor and griffins woven into the Oriental carpets and
griffins painted in high bas-relief on the ceiling. Only
Araby took the room seriously. "It's a decorating
scheme representative of the best in haute European
style," she said. As she walked down the three tiled
steps that led into it, she smiled, pleased with its effect. She went to the sideboard and poured herself a
Scotch.

Max was standing next to the mantel which was
slightly taller than he, marble griffins supporting it.
He had a copy of the *Los Angeles Times* rolled up in
his fist.

"How's my little cowboy?" Araby asked, taking her
drink and sitting down on the sofa. "Shoot up any
bad men today?"

Max tossed the newspaper onto the sofa. She
picked it up, unfurled it, and read the banner headline. "Jesus, this wasn't supposed to break until next
week. I'd better get Carleton on the blower and find
out what he thinks he's doing."

Max moved quicker than she. He pushed her back
so she fell onto the sofa.

"Keep those big, *galumptah* hands off me, Mr.
Meyer," Araby said, attempting to get up again. "The
only time I want you to touch me is in bed." He

pushed her back down on the sofa and stood over
her.

"Where the hell do you get the nerve to manhan-
dle me, you two-bit cowboy? I single-handedly gave
you your career. What's gotten into you?"

"I didn't mind your using me," Max said, pushing
her down once more, waiting until she sat perfectly
still. "But Anna? Anna's your daughter, in case you
forgot. Using her to . . ."

"Do you think they're paying three dollars and fifty
cents at the Rivoli Theater on Broadway in New
York City to see some mother's tits?" She tried to
stand up again and this time he let her. "Those goddamned reporters were all set to print the fact that
Araby Moore, Serpent of the Nile, had a three-year-
old baby girl by the man who only drinks homoge-
nized milk. Something had to be done and Carleton
came up with that. You don't like it, have yourself a
press conference."

"You're denying your kid. You're sacrificing Anna."

"Goddamn it," she said, swallowing the last of the
Scotch, pouring herself another. "I'd sacrifice anything or anyone that got in my way. And if you don't
know that by this time, then you don't know anything. Jesus, how I've regretted letting you talk me
out of getting an abortion. I'm not going to need a
kid in my publicity shots for another twenty years
and then I can always rent one."

He slammed her across the face with his open
hand. She fell back against the sofa and tried to kick
him in the groin. He stepped back as she bounced up
and clawed his face, breaking one of her nails. He
put his arms around hers and swung her up and over

his shoulder like a bag of flour. Holding her wrists and her ankles, he carried her out to the central hall where Robinson, Townie, and the entire staff was standing.

"Madam Moore ain't going to be living here anymore," Max said as Robinson opened the outside front door. Max carried Araby down the stairs and dumped her in the back seat of the open Rolls.

"You cocksucker," Araby shouted at the top of her voice as he went back inside the house. "When I get through with you, you won't be able to pay them to let you into the movies."

Max kept walking, up the central staircase and up to the third floor where Anna and Mitsuko slept, under the replicated Taj Mahal dome.

Robinson, after a few moments, came out of the house and stood at the top of the front steps. "Will you be wanting the cheetahs, madam?" he asked, in perfectly even, enunciated tones.

"You can take those goddamned cheetahs, Robinson, and stuff them up your ass," Araby said, getting out of the back seat of the car.

"Very good, madam." It was the first time any of the under servants had seen Robinson smile.

Townie came out of the house with Araby's purple foxes and got into the passenger seat of the car. "Carleton says you mustn't be seen without these."

"Get out of my car, you slimy little faggot," she said, not giving him the chance, starting the Rolls, and driving, erratically, to the front gates of Ram-A-Dies where she turned the ignition to off, put her head against the white leather steering wheel, and refused to cry.

"You've seen the story?" she asked.

He had. The headline, "I Am Ram Page's Other Wife," ran across the page. Under it was a photograph of Araby in a gold-plated bra and a green and gold metal skirt with several slits. On her copper-colored hair—which read black in the photograph—was a coiled, gold serpent with large jeweled eyes. The story, written by Carleton LeMay and Paramount's increasingly inventive publicity department, had been contrived to deal with rumors that Araby Moore's private life wasn't what it might have been, that she was having affairs.

It was time, Carleton and Araby decided, that Araby Moore's essential purity be established. They were going to announce to the world that Araby Moore was a Wife. But they knew it would be suicide—careerwise—to let anyone think Araby Moore was a Mother.

The story, which eventually was released to *Photoplay* and then to the other fan magazines and finally to the two-penny tabloids, began with Ram Page's early beginnings. According to the release, his parents died when he was a child, leaving him alone on the prairie to wrestle bears and brand cattle for the Double X Ranch. He had come to Los Angeles when he was a teenager. He met an older women, wise in the ways of the world, who seduced him into marriage. They had a child, the Older Woman dying during a difficult if not impossible birth. To forget her, Ram took his beautiful child and went to the Middle East. There, he heard the legend of a mysterious white woman, little more than a girl, being kept captive by a wicked desert sheik. Ram saddled his horse and set out from Shepherd's Hotel . . .

"He's such a goddamned dope," Araby said, hitting her hand against the padded dashboard. "How can I get it through his thick head that Araby Moore cannot publicly have a child."

"Let me talk to him," Townie said. "I'm his agent. I'm your agent. Let me talk to him."

"The next time anyone talks to Max Meyer for me, it will be in a divorce court."

"Now you're being the dope, my pet. Think. There were a dozen servants watching your little scene, all of them—at this very moment—resisting the itch to run for the telephone. When I go back, I will grease a few palms. But imagine how Ram Page throwing Araby Moore out of their modest honeymoon cottage will look in tomorrow's press? Think of how the fact that you denied your own child, in print, will play in the centerfold of Sunday's rotogravure. Think of Fatty Arbuckle and Mary Miles Minter. Think of your own new, wholesome offscreen image. And think of the enemies you and dear Carleton have made. And not only at Paramount. Uncle Joe Goldstein will stand by Max through almost anything. And Max will come out the winner, the father who loved his child enough to sacrifice his own career.

"Who's going to back *you* up, Araby? You start this and I guarantee you'll be deader than last year's Queen of the Nile in a month. Let me talk to him, Araby."

"I'm working on my last Egyptian epic anyway," Araby said, taking a mirror from the glove compartment, examining the bruise forming under her left eye. "That'll cover," she decided. "You drive, Townie. I'm too nervous. Take me to LeMay's. Then go and talk some sense into that big dumb lummox."

They traded seats and Townie proceeded down Hollywood Boulevard. "What're you going to be now that you're not going to be Egyptian?" he asked. "Just for your agent's records."

"A flapper, darling. Every college boy's girl. Maybe a little fast but still a virgin in the last reel no matter what everyone thinks."

She left the car and Townie spun it around and headed back to Ram-A-Dies. He now knew the real reason why she had gone to such lengths to deny she had a child. No college boy's girl could ever be a mother.

Townie didn't turn right when he reached the gates of Ram-A-Dies. He kept going until he reached Goldstein-Ville and, after a certain amount of trouble, managed to get Uncle Joe Goldstein out of his palatial bed, said to have belonged to William of Orange.

Townie explained the situation as he drove. They found Max, alone, in the Griffin Salon, a bottle of whiskey in one hand, a beer in the other.

"Always have an alcoholic chaser," Uncle Joe said, sitting next to him on the sofa. "You never know what you're drinking out of the whiskey bottles these days; but the beer, I'm told, is usually nonpoisonous."

"She ain't coming back," Max said.

It took them half the night to convince Max that if he wanted a career, that if he wanted to continue to make films, he'd have to take Araby back, at least on a public level.

"It's *mishugah*," Uncle Joe said to him. "One day you're in the papers happily married, the next day you're tossing her out on her *tuchas*? She'll ruin you, Max. I can tell you right now, she's too tough for us."

He agreed, finally, but only on the condition that they didn't live together, that a nice quiet divorce would be in the offing.

Townie called Araby, told her he'd pick her up in a few minutes, but she said she didn't want to be picked up until she knew all the terms. When he told her about the separate suites, she stopped talking.

"What the hell?" she said after a long moment. "He hasn't touched me in months, anyway, except to knock me down."

He told her about the divorce clause. "It'll be a cold day in hell before I ever give that son of a bitch a divorce."

"But we won't tell him that, will we?" Townie asked, anxious for peace at any price.

"No, we won't, Townie. Not until he asks for one."

In mid-July Max announced he was taking Anna to New York for Bessie's birthday party.

"She saw her last year," Araby objected.

"And she's going to see her this year."

Mitsuko was going, too, "to take care of Anna." In addition, an English woman, tall and blond and stiff, named Cora Dobbs, had been employed as Anna's nanny. Townie was asked to accompany them.

He said he'd be delighted. He had taken a small office on Wilshire and had two young men working for him and felt he had no real encumbrances to keep him from going. His only genuine properties were Max and Araby and surprisingly Max had asked Araby to go, too.

"We have to wait until she finishes *Nile Death*," Max said as if he and Araby were a happy American couple. Araby had convinced Max to use the trip for publicity.

"I thought you didn't do guest appearances," Townie said to Max.

"I'm making an exception."

"What about your famous accent?"

"Take it easy, Townie. I'm only going to appear once or twice. I'm not making any speeches." He explained he wanted *Texas Glory* to be his biggest success.

They had a private car on the train, courtesy of Carleton LeMay and Paramount. Wherever the train stopped, Max and Araby were to step out on the small balcony attached to their car and wave and smile. A spate of publicity stories had been released and representatives from Paramount and Great Western had gone ahead, fanning up interest.

"This should be a lot of fun," Araby said, surveying everyone getting into the car. "Taking the train to New York in our big picture hats for dear sister Bessie's birthday." Cora Dobbs got on the train, carrying her own modest suitcase. "I didn't know the new nanny was coming, too," Araby said to Townie. "Now all we need is a priest and a dwarf." She looked down at him. "Well, I don't suppose we need a dwarf."

The cross-country appearances were a success, the crowds achieving the right degree of uncontrolled ardor. At Grand Central the advance publicity man came to tell them that the crowd was virtually all women, three had fainted, and the others—"thousands"—were jammed into the central waiting room tying up train traffic, chanting for Araby and Ram.

"They're a little rambunctious," the advance man said. "Perhaps we fanned them up too much."

"No such thing," Araby said. She had changed into her *Nile Death* costume and was kissing Anna goodbye.

"You do love her, don't you?" Townie said.

"Up to a point," Araby said, kissing the child again and handing her over to Cora Dobbs.

Max came out to say good-bye, too. He had changed into his white cowboy outfit with no persuasion.

"I thought you hated this sort of thing," Townie said as he watched him clip on his tooled leather holster with the sterling silver guns.

"Maybe I'm getting to like it in my old age. Maybe I'm trying to prove a point."

"What's the point?"

"That I'm one of the most popular stars in America, western or otherwise." He adjusted his neckerchief. "Popularity is power, Townie."

"And Beauty is Truth, Max. What the hell are you talking about?"

He kissed Anna and then she and Cora Dobbs and Mitsuko and Townie went into the adjoining car from which they could disembark without being trampled.

They could hear the women chanting above them in the station: "We want Araby. We want Ram." The noise was frightening, deafening. Anna began to cry as they started up the stairs. Cora Dobbs shook her and she stopped crying. No one had ever shaken Anna before. They followed Townie up into the station and for a minute caught sight of that sea of screaming middle-class womanhood.

A policeman at the head of the stairs had been alerted to watch for them and he escorted them to a side door on the other side of which waited Bessie. She wrapped her arms around her niece and broke into tears.

At the same time a double row of policemen were forming an aisle from the top of the stairs and through the station, out to Forty-second Street where the white limousine waited.

Max and Araby suddenly appeared at the top of the steps and the crowd began to scream as if they were witnessing a biblical miracle. Max and Araby moved on down the aisle like a couple in some godly wedding ceremony, both looking untouchably real, the policeman's arms holding the hysterical crowd back.

When they reached the center of the station, it was clear that the crowd was going to break through, that the police weren't going to be able to hold them back. Max jumped up on the information booth and held out his arms, his palms upward.

The vast room suddenly became absolutely and totally silent.

"I want to thank you all," Max shouted in his best cowboy accent, "for coming here to see me and my wife, Araby Moore. I can't tell you how much I appreciate it . . . how much we both do. We jus' never expected this kind of welcome to the greatest city in our country. But I would like to ask you all a favor. If you could jus' make way for us to get to our car, it sure would be a kindness. We're both tired from sitting up all night on the train and I don't know about Araby but I sure as heck would like to get to my hotel room and take a bath."

He jumped down to the floor, took Araby's hand, and the crowd parted, allowing them to get to their car.

It was a potent demonstration, not lost on Paramount because Carleton LeMay had a movie camera filming the occasion. The heads of the studio gave Araby full marks for not saying a word, for playing Ram Page's little wife. She was the perfect little woman. Demonstrating it before the public and the cameras in Grand Central Station a day before the sizzling *Nile Death* opened on Broadway was LeMay's way of reassuring Hollywood's new and first censor, the Hays Office.

Dubious after his initial screening, Will Hays himself sent Araby a telegram after her Grand Central Station performance, telling her how much he enjoyed *Nile Death*.

It opened on August 1, 1922, at New York's Palace Theater with speculators hawking tickets at five dollars apiece. It was the Palace's first five-reel film and ran one hour, ten minutes, cutting two of the usual nine vaudeville acts off the bill. It accounted for a thirty-thousand-dollar gross in its first week.

Opening a night after *Nile Death* was Ram Page's *Texas Glory*. It played at the Rivoli, up the block from the Palace, and the house was packed from early morning to late evening.

The private screening of *Texas Glory*, and the party afterward, which Max had given for the fifteen men on Wall Street most likely to invest half a million dollars in a film, resulted in a great many warm expressions of admiration and little else. They had all read the screenplay for *Cowboy* and they had all liked it, but.

"Sorry, Mr. Meyer," Paul duPont, the last of his guests to depart, said. "You're a very electric screen personality and I'd fully back any future film in the same vein as *Texas Glory*. But *Cowboy* would be a great film to show in university and college auditoriums. It won't earn a dime and I'm not in the charity business, yet."

Ryan was still sitting in the last row of the rented screening room. "Goldstein won't touch it?"

"Not with his money," Max said, loosening his tie.

"Why don't you use your own?"

"I'd need Araby to cosign. My money is all tied up with hers and Araby isn't interested in *Cowboy*."

"What about a loan as opposed to an investment?"

"The banks won't . . ."

"I'm not talking about banks," Ryan said. "You have a few thousand shares of Great Western, don't you?"

"You're willing to lend me the money for a collateral of ten thousand shares of Great Western?" Max asked.

"You *are* slightly more than a business acquaintance, dear boy. And besides, even if *Cowboy* doesn't turn out to be such a valuable property, Great Western might."

Ryan put out his hand and Max, after a moment's hesitation, took it. "What if I default?" he asked.

"Then I'll own ten thousand shares of Great Western and Uncle Joe will have a new minority stockholder to deal with. It might not be the worst thing that ever happened to him or his company."

In the morning Max had a bank draft for five hundred thousand dollars and a very good piece of news for Tim Bronco. The kid from Poland and the kid from West Texas were going to make their movie.

CHAPTER 2

Bessie turned over in the big bed she still hadn't gotten used to, reaching for Ryan, finding he wasn't there. What am I complaining about? she asked herself, instantly awake. Half the time he's not here when he's here.

She left the bed and reached for her dressing gown. At the same time she caught sight of herself in the huge three-way mirror which took up a prominent part of her new dressing room in the triplex penthouse Ryan had rented for her on Central Park West. Eighteenth Street had become, Ryan decided, too déclassé.

Bessie dropped the gown and studied herself in the mirror. She was still slim but her breasts had grown, and, as she turned, she realized she had also put on a bit more hip. It was the morning after her thirty-second birthday party, a time to take stock, she decided.

Thank God for Miss Wald and her exercise classes, Bessie thought. And thank God for Zuckerman and the hundreds of hours he had made her put in, making her dancing acceptable. She had regained her muscle tone since she had started singing and dancing in the club again and it made her feel good to look good.

"And no one who's ever going to know me inti-mately is going to deny that I'm a redhead," she said out loud. "Not that anyone besides Ryan is going to know me intimately, I have a feeling."

She had thought about taking a lover just once, when Edward Lewis was still a junior senator, before he married his plain-faced, big-hearted Alma. He had wanted her, Bessie, so badly. She was glad she hadn't let herself seduce him. They were still good friends and they might not have been had they gone to bed.

Minnie knocked and came in. "Oh, Miss Bessie," she said.

"Don't Miss Bessie me, you've seen me in the raw before." Bessie reached for her dressing gown and put it on.

"You still look as good as the day I first met you, Miss Bessie," Minnie said, staring in admiration at her employer. "Even after staying up most of the night. You have a good birthday party?"

She had. Ryan always gave her good birthday par-ties. Jolson had sung and Eva Tanguay had done something and there had been champagne and the boys. Best of all, there had been the boys. Jake had come by himself, but she knew all about the little house and the mulatto girl who lived there. He looked happier than he had since he had come to this country. Funny how he too was doing business with Ryan now. Bootlegging. Well, she didn't believe in Prohibition and as long as no one was getting killed, or hurt, she wasn't fighting it.

She had more important things to fight for. Money

for the Henry Street Settlement. They always needed
money. That's because there were always poor
people. She had even tried, foolishly, to get Ryan to
stop his numbers games down there.

"You're taking money out of those people's pockets."

"You don't know what you're talking about," he
had answered. "I give them more hope with my numbers than all the churches and synagogues combined.
And when someone wins big, Bessie, they get out."

"I'm not working for them to get out. What I want
is for the Lower East Side to be a better place for
them to stay."

"I sometimes wonder how it is that I fell in love
with such an ardent social reformer," Ryan said, kissing her, putting an end to the argument.

Nick was as involved with the numbers as he was
with the bootlegging. He wouldn't talk about it. And
she wasn't asking. He, too, seemed happier than he
had, now that he had his Kay.

And Max. At her party, he had positively glowed.

Everyone, she thought, is happy.

"Miss Meyer," Minnie interrupted. "You got a visitor."

"Who is it?" Bessie asked, trying to brush some
sense into her curls.

"She says her name is Mrs. Ryan. Mrs. Grace Ryan.
And there's a big limousine downstairs. . . ."

Grace Ryan was sitting on the edge of the only
piece of furniture Ryan had insisted on bringing
from the Eighteenth Street house, his green leather
wing-back chair. Everything else in that room which

was some forty feet square, which featured views of
Central Park and New Jersey and downtown and The
Bronx from its wraparound windows and terrace, was
new. As new as Kay could make it.

Kay liked shopping for furniture and Bessie, who
had never had the time to develop an interest in interior decoration, liked shopping with Kay and
trusted her taste. Though she wasn't at all certain
about the blue-mirrored fireplace mantel or the low-
slung chrome and leather sofas imported from Germany. Ryan, amused, said, "It looks as if we're living
in the Bauhaus as well as in the penthouse."

Like his green leather wing chair, Grace Ryan
clearly did not belong in that room. She belonged to
another age with her gray-brown hair cut in no particular style, with her dark dress and serviceable shoes,
holding a shapeless straw bag and white gloves in her
pale hands. She wore no makeup and only one piece
of jewelry, her wedding band. She reeked of old
money, Bessie thought. Bessie had met many women
like her, sitting on committees, occasionally coming
up with surprisingly bright and practical ideas for im-
plementing social change. Sometimes she was a politician's wife; usually she was a rich man's daughter,
brought up to serve no useful purpose other than to
raise children and once a week help the poor.

Bessie suffered what amounted to the worst case of
stage fright she had ever had after Minnie had made
her announcement. But as she entered that large, airy
room, so clear and clean and bright, so unlike the
fussy Eighteenth Street drawing room, she became
more sure of herself, as she always did once she was
on stage.

"Mrs. Ryan," Bessie said, walking across the room, her hand held out with certain poise. She had put on a pale blue dress and taken off her diamonds, her bracelets. Still she knew that she was as visible, as eye-catching, as a candle in the dark.

The older woman stood and was taller than Bessie, taller than she had appeared sitting down. Heavier, too. Not at all attractive, Bessie thought. She took Bessie's hand awkwardly.

"May I have coffee brought?" Bessie asked, feeling sorry for Ryan's wife.

"No, please." She didn't sit down. Instead she walked to the French doors that led out onto the terrace and stared out at Central Park which was especially green on that sunny August morning. "You're very kind, seeing me, Miss Meyer," she said after a moment. "I can't think what I'm doing here. I mean I've known about you, of course, for years. I can't remember a time when you weren't a part of my life." She turned and smiled.

"Won't you sit down?" Bessie asked.

"No, thank you. I'd better keep talking before I lose my nerve. My dear, you're so much more beautiful up close. So radiant. That hair! You know, there was a time—I think it was immediately after I saw you at Mayor Kingsley's victory party and knew, as soon as Ryan asked you to dance, knew everything— that I decided to have my hair colored. There was a little woman off the Gramercy Park that specialized in such things and I spent a long morning with her, feeling dreadfully wicked, while she hennaed my hair, thinned out my eyebrows, taught me to use lipstick and rouge.

"I went home and I went right up to the bedroom without anyone, servants or the children, seeing me. I put on what I considered a sinfully frivolous peignoir and waited for him to come home. It was quite late when he finally came into the bedroom and all he did, when he saw me, was laugh. He sat down on the edge of the bed and laughed.

"I expect I was a fool for trying. It took forever for the henna to wash out of my hair and I spent half the month walking around with turbans and odd hats on my head. My family thought I had gone dotty, like poor Aunt Elizabeth." She looked around her. "Perhaps I will sit down." She sat in Ryan's wing chair and Bessie sat across from her in a brown leather and chrome chair.

"Perhaps I am going dotty, finally, like Elizabeth. I know how strange it is, my coming in like this. But I read in the newspaper that you had moved here and I was consumed with envy. How marvelous it must be to live in all this modernity. The past is so heavy, it always seems to weigh me down.

"And how wonderful it must be to have your picture in the paper and the reporters mentioning each time you dine out. I've always wanted to be a celebrity but father, and Ryan, would never allow it. Not done.

"Coming here isn't done either, of course. I've always had to keep a stiff upper lip, pretend I didn't know who you were, pretend that Ryan's one dance with you at those interminable banquets was merely a courtesy extended to someone whose political favor he was counting."

"Mrs. Ryan . . ."

"It never occurred to me to arrange a meeting between the two of us. I didn't want to appear foolish, the Outraged Wife. The truth of the matter is, my dear, I'm not outraged. I envy your life but I don't envy you Ryan. He hasn't been in my bed for fifteen years. It was a relief for me. I never much enjoyed it. Dear Lord, do you know I've never told anyone, not another soul? I can't think what's come over me today." She took a handkerchief from her purse and patted her forehead.

"Mrs. Ryan, do let me get you a cup of tea."

The older woman suddenly smiled and Bessie saw, for a moment, the charm, the spirit she must have possessed as a young girl. "Yes, I think I would like that, Miss Meyer."

Bessie rang for Minnie who brought tea in a china pot on a lacquered tray. "You know, my dear," Mrs. Ryan said, "I would have never come here today had I not been having breakfast with Bishop Potter. He was speaking of a church we're trying to save on Grand Street which led him to a general discussion of the Lower East Side and of the wonderful work the Henry Street Settlement does there. And then a young woman, someone who married into the Roosevelts, talked about you and the tremendous amount of money you've raised for the Settlement."

She put her teacup down and leaned forward. "It never occurred to me, my dear, in all these years, that you were a good person. I think that's the real reason I'm here. I've done you such a disservice for such a long time." She stood. "I probably won't see you again except across crowded banquet halls. It would be too bizarre if we were to become friends. But I do feel so much better now, having met you." Bessie went with her to the elevator in the foyer.

Just before the elevator doors closed, Ryan's wife looked at her and said, "You are lovely, my dear. So very lovely."

Ryan met her as she was coming in, late that night, after B's had closed. "I've heard Grace was here," he said, sitting in the chair she had used.

"She was."

"Do you care to tell me what transpired?"

"No." She was wearing a red evening dress and it shimmered as she stood there in the dim light, looking at him. "I'm going to leave you, Ryan."

He smiled. "Don't you think you should take some time to think that statement through, carefully?"

"Ryan, I've made up my mind. I'm going. . . ."

The elevator door opened at that moment and they both turned to the foyer. Nick stood there, in his dinner jacket, a once white towel wrapped around his arm. The towel was red with blood.

Bessie ran to him as he sat down in the gray suede banquette, letting his head rest against the wall.

"My God, Nicky, what's happened?"

"Call Dr. Deehl," Ryan said, pulling her away. "He'll be all right. Go ahead."

She ran to the phone as Nick told Ryan what had happened. Bumps Bogan had hijacked a shipment of Ryan's booze. Bumps and two other men who had worked for Ryan had walked into the Tenth Avenue warehouse, killed the driver, shot Nick, and beat up, fairly badly, the two boys who were loading the truck.

"We gotta kill that bastard," Nick said before he

passed out, drops of his blood creating a design on the banquette.

It wasn't until six in the morning that Ryan came up to her bedroom. Nick had been seen to by Dr. Deehl who had allowed as how Nick could be taken without harm to the apartment he and Kay shared two blocks away. As Ryan had predicted, it had been a surface wound.

Then Ryan had gotten Bumps Bogan on the telephone and they had had a long and careful conversation while Bessie went upstairs and lay down on the bed, still in her red evening dress.

Of course she couldn't leave Ryan. Jake worked for Ryan. Ryan was backing Max's film. Ryan was protecting her brother Nick. Just because I suddenly feel guilty after fifteen years, I'm going to go and leave a man who's so good to me and my family? Where would any of us be without him? But still the vision of the woman with the brown-gray hair standing in the elevator continued to haunt her; long after Ryan had come to bed; long after they had made love, which was as exciting, as disturbing as ever; long after she had agreed that she wasn't going anywhere.

CHAPTER 3

In the beginning Jake visited the Pinder Lane house four or five times a week. He'd come at night and he'd leave in the morning. He liked to watch Nancy in the early light. She had a remarkable ability to sleep through almost anything. He could caress her and kiss her and still she wouldn't awaken. It was only when he began to make love to her that her sleepy young eyes would open and her arms would steal around his neck.

One evening he arrived early to find the three women—Nancy, Frances, and Blondell—seated at the pine table on the rear porch, eating fried fish and gossiping.

"Maybe I'll come back later," he said, embarrassed. His white shirt stuck to his body from the heat. He didn't know who to look at. He never thought of Nancy except in bed. She, too, didn't know how to react. She giggled and turned her head away.

Frances took charge. "Blondell, get a plate of that fish for Mr. Meyer, would you? Jake, sit down. You haven't eaten yet, have you?"

"Well, I . . ."

"Just as I thought. Better put some of those collard

greens on the plate while you're at it," Frances told Blondell.

They sat across from each other, neither Jake nor Nancy knowing what to say. She put her hands to her mouth and laughed again, softly, and he looked up and suddenly he was laughing, too.

"I think you'd better come around to dinner more often, Jake Meyer," Frances said, getting up, preparing to leave. "It might be nice if you and Nancy got to know each other."

Everyone, even Blondell, laughed at this and Jake found himself coming up the lane more often, having his dinner with Nancy and sometimes Frances but mostly just with Nancy.

They didn't talk very much. She didn't know what to say. She was more comfortable with women, having been brought up by Madam Sucre among the ladies of her house. With men she knew she was supposed to smile but she didn't know what she was supposed to talk about.

Jake liked her smile but he wanted to know more about her—what she thought and what she liked. After a while, when she grew comfortable with him, when they indeed got to know one another, she became freer with him and shyly began to confide in him.

He was surprised to find that he loved her. He often thought of her when he was on his way to Havana, remembering the way she laughed, with her nose wrinkled and her eyes shining. When he was away from her, he missed her warm, vanilla scent. He wanted to be with her all of the time.

Nancy felt the same about Jake. She would talk to

her two friends, Blondell and Frances, about him all of the time, far more easy with them than she was with him.

One evening, while Jake was in Havana, Nancy was missing from the back porch. "I don't know where she got herself to, Miss Frances, but I ain't seen her all afternoon." Blondell's eyes were big and round and mournful. "Not like her not to come down and pass the time of day. Not like her at all."

Frances went upstairs and knocked on the door of the bedroom. She went in and immediately opened the louvered door that led to the upstairs porch. "It's like an oven in here," she said to the girl who was lying facedown on the bed. "Are you ill, Nancy?"

Nancy turned her face to Frances, and it was clear she had spent the afternoon crying. Her nose was red and there were still tears in her eyes.

"Nancy," Frances said, alarmed, going to her, taking her in her arms. "What is it? Tell me."

"I can't."

"Don't be ridiculous. There's nothing you can't tell me."

She began crying again. "Oh, Frances, I don't know what I'm going to do. He'll send me away. You have to help me."

"I'll do anything you want," Frances said, trying for a pragmatic, nonsensical tone of voice. "Within reason. Believe me, Jake is not going to send you away. He can barely attend to business he's so besotted with you. Now I want to know," she said, stroking Nancy's fresh, straight hair, "what is the matter?" There was no answer. "And I want to know now."

"A baby," Nancy said.

"What about a baby?"

"I'm going to have a baby," the crying girl said. "And Jake is going to send me back to *ma mère*."

Frances breathed a sigh of relief. "Darling," she said, pulling Nancy close to her. "If there was any certain way you could have found to keep Jake Meyer, it was to have his child."

Nancy insisted that Frances be at dinner the following night when she told him. "But, Nancy, this should be . . ."

"You must be there so he will not send me away. You will talk to him."

When Nancy finally did tell him, after Blondell had cooked ribs which were his favorite, Jake didn't even see Frances, or the ribs. He stood up and moved around the table, took Nancy up in his arms, kissed her and carried her up to the bedroom.

"That child has to eat sometime," Blondell shouted after them. "You tell him, Miss Frances."

"Not tonight, Blondell."

He spent as much time as he could at Pinder Lane and when he had to leave, he insisted that both Frances and Blondell stay with Nancy. He had both doctors, Cassell and Thompson, check her over at least once a week. He had Leon Shuster supply ice on a daily basis.

"You are not the first man to ever be a father," Frances reminded him. "This is not even the first time you are a father."

"She's such a thin thing," Jake said, worried. "She's going to be all right, isn't she, Frances?"

"As long as you don't smother her with your particular brand of heavy-handed kindness. Jake, do relax, I beg you."

The baby was born on a June night and her birth was as easy as Jake had hoped for. "That's it?" he asked Dr. Cassell not even an hour after Nancy went into labor. "You're telling me everything?"

Blondell brought out the child, a tiny, coffee-colored replica of Nancy and unceremoniously put her in Jake's arms. "I'm afraid," he said. "She's too light. She doesn't weigh anything."

"Go give her to her mother then," Frances, standing on the porch, told him. "But do be careful, Jake."

He went into the room with the child in his arms and put it next to Nancy who looked up at him with half-closed eyes.

"You think we can make love again soon, Jake?" she asked, kissing her child.

"I sure hope so, Nancy."

"You like our little girl, Jake?"

"I love her, Nancy. Nearly as much as I love you." He lay down next to the mother and the child on the bed and held them both. "What are we going to call her?"

"Coffee," she said. "She looks just like a cup of coffee, the way I like it, with a lot of milk. You don't mind, Jake, if we call her Coffee?"

He told her he didn't mind.

CHAPTER 4

Nick was being sent to Paris to line up, or straighten out, one of Ryan's recalcitrant wine merchants. Kay went with him.

"I like to travel," she told him, though she wasn't at all certain that was true. She had missed him when he had gone to Cuba to set Jake up. His wound had healed but he seemed angrier, more edgy since the shooting. Bogan still hadn't been dealt with.

"Ryan likes to keep me out of New York," he said. "In case I settle with Bogan in my own way. In case I get my own ideas."

"And do you?"

"Oh, yeah. I got a ton of ideas. But I'm keeping them under my hat. Until the time is right. I'm a patient man."

She laughed. "Nicky, you're the least patient man I know."

"Only when it comes to some things," he said, grinning, blowing a smoke ring, putting his cigar in the ashtray the S.S. *Amsterdam* provided in their luxury-class stateroom, putting his arms around her.

In Paris he was busy during the days and occasionally at night, meeting with Fournier and his distillers, winegrowers, bottlers. "Just like a regular little businessman," Nick said.

Kay went to the fashion shows and waved at old friends, bought a few dresses and gowns. She had a drink with Fatty Freeman who disconcerted her by saying she was the only woman he would ever love in a matter-of-fact voice.

"You'd better be careful, Fatty," she told him, withdrawing her hand from his. "You're going to end up being one of those pale, wasted men who wake up at sixty to find they've thrown their life away for a woman who never existed. You should marry the very next girl who's free."

That night Nick strode into their suite at the Crillion and told her to get their bags packed. "We're getting out of here in the morning."

"What's the matter, Nicky?"

"Something's not kosher. That bastard, Fournier, he's dealing in something else besides wine."

"What? Drugs?"

"I don't know. Why send dope to Cuba? It'd be easier to ship it right to New York." He lit one of the cigars Jake kept him supplied with. "Fuckin' Ryan. I'd like to know what I'm playing patsy for this time."

She liked being back in New York. It was spring and it was warm again and Central Park had suddenly bloomed while she was away.

Nick was more irritable than usual, staying out all night on two occasions which he refused to account for other than by saying, "It was business. You want an affidavit from Arnold Rothstein?" Not that she doubted him. Whatever pose he liked to assume, he was most definitely a one-woman man.

But since their return from Europe, he didn't seem able to contain his anger toward Ryan. While they were in Paris, Ryan and Bumps had come to an understanding. Bogan was now in charge of all the numbers everywhere save Manhattan. He was going to leave the bootlegging to Ryan and Nick.

"If you can't beat him, join him, right?" Nick said over Sunday brunch in Bessie's triplex apartment, the one weekly meal the family traditionally shared.

"Be logical, Nick. Certainly we could have taken care of Mr. Bogan. Nothing easier. But if we had, we would have had a war on our hands, more violence than either you or I could possibly handle, and the sort of publicity that demands federal intervention."

"Ryan," Bessie said, "we don't talk business at my table. At my table we eat and we observe the social niceties."

"Listen, you . . ." Nick began, pointing his finger at Ryan.

Bessie slapped his finger. "The same goes for you, fat boy. Now eat, while Kay tells us about Paris."

"Watch," Nick told Kay later. "In a couple of weeks we'll be back on the road. Ryan likes me out of this town."

Six weeks after they had returned from Paris, they sailed for Cuba to meet Jake, to check on the shipment Nick had arranged with Fournier. The ship's staterooms were paneled in bamboo and tiny Filipino waiters fell over themselves waiting on them.

"You like being catered to, don't you?" Nick asked as he watched her eat breakfast in bed.

"About as much as you like me being catered to."

"Can the smart talk, will you? Can't you ever give me a straight yes or no?"

"Yes."

"To what?"

"Everything."

They had three days to themselves in Havana before Jake was due to meet them. They spent them in bed at the Ambos Mundos Hotel on Obispo Street, eating huge breakfasts of Cuban bread, avocados, smoked fish, followed by syrup-thick, burnt sugared coffee.

Afterward they would walk down to the café across the *prado* from the Capitol Building and drink more Cuban coffee, Kay's laced with aguardiente, a liquor somewhat like Cuban rum but over one hundred proof and very powerful.

In the afternoon Nick would leave her for a few minutes to see if the boat from Marseilles had docked yet, to check on Armando Galvez, his "connection." "They're all crazy down here," he told Kay. "All they want to do is blow up the capitol. I've been approached by half a dozen kids, wanting to know if I have any soup on me."

"Soup?"

"Nitroglycerin, you dumb Dora," he laughed, hugging her.

They ate their dinners across from the hotel at El Pacifico, an eight-story building with four floors above ground and four floors below. Below ground hashish was smoked; one could become drugged by simply dining on the first floor. Nick insisted that they eat on the top floor. The idea of getting drugged, of losing control, was one that especially frightened him.

On their third day in Havana they were sitting at the café across from the *prado,* watching the young, beautiful Cuban men get drunk and talk revolution when Jake suddenly appeared, holding Nancy's hand.

"We're starving," Jake said, after kissing and embracing Nick and Kay, introducing Nancy. Nick refused to go back to El Pacifico so, waving away the beggars they had attracted, they went to the hotel dining room.

"You like this food?" Nick asked his brother. The fans slowly revolved above them. The tablecloths and the waiters' jackets were the only patches of white in the room. Tropical flowers were in bloom on every table, in each doorway.

Jake looked up from his plate as if the question had never occurred to him, as if the answer were obvious. "Certainly I like it. You don't?"

"It's not exactly the kind of stuff Mama used to cook," Nick said, forking a plantain, studying it, and putting it in his mouth.

Kay enjoyed seeing the two brothers together. Though they were only a year apart in age, they were light-years apart in outlook. Nick had taken on the protective coloring of New York's streets. Even in the tropics he wore a tightly fitted suit. He was like New York, Kay thought. Granite hard, wonderfully giving under that steely surface.

Jake was taller by half a head and wider by half a yard. He was quiet and gentle and it was clear that he had been permanently bruised, that there were areas in his life one could never touch.

Nancy was extremely pretty, a colored version of Kay. Jake noticed the resemblance and Kay agreed. Neither Nick nor Nancy enjoyed the comparison.

"We look a great deal more like sisters than you look like brothers," Kay said. Nancy turned her eyes away, toward the gardens. Nick gave Kay what she called his "put-a-sock-in-it" scowl. But Jake smiled at her. His eyes were a lighter blue than his brother's but the questions in them seemed to be the same.

The band, all wearing starched white and pleated *guayabera* shirts, marched through the dining room and out into the garden. They set up and immediately began to play. An earnest boy soprano attempted the popular song of that year, "Who's Sorry Now?" in English. Nick and Kay danced.

"You dance beautifully," Nancy told them when they returned to the table. It was the first time she had spoken directly to either of them.

"Why don't you and Jake dance?" Kay asked her.

"I only know the shimmy," she answered.

"I'll teach you how to fox-trot in no time," Kay promised her. Taking Nancy's hand, she led her out to the patio where they spent the following half hour practicing the fox-trot while Jake continued to tip the maestro so that he would stay with, "Who's Sorry Now?" instead of going into more comfortable Latin rhythms.

"She's all ready," Kay said, handing Nancy over to him.

"Now who's going to teach Jake?" Nick asked.

"We all will," Kay said. They spent the rest of the

evening practicing the fox-trot in the garden of the Ambos Mundos Hotel.

Later, when they were in bed under the mosquito netting, Kay asked Nick if he had had a good time. "Yeah. It was okay."

"It was more than okay, you bastard, and you know it."

"All right. I had the time of my life. Get back under the net before them gnats eat you alive." She got back into the bed and he put his arms around her. "You have to turn every occasion into a social event?" he asked, kissing her.

"Not every," she said, moving up against him.

Two days later Nick woke her at six to announce that the boat from Marseilles was in and had been for four days. "Goddamn cocksuckers never said a word. Get ready," he told her.

"For what?" she said, getting out of the bed, heading for the tiled bathroom.

"We're going to El Cacique."

"What's El Cacique?" Kay asked.

"How the hell do I know? Fournier, that dumb frog, wants us to meet him there."

The boat that took them to El Cacique was long and white and had two motors which only Jake and the Cuban boy knew how to operate. They had picked up the boy, by arrangement, in front of a bar called La Flordita. He sat in the corner by the rear engine during the entire trip, chewing on a cigarette.

The hotel's cook had packed a huge lunch in a wicker hamper and there was Cuban beer in a cooler filled with ice. They passed an armed patrol boat and Nick began fiddling with the hamper, pulling out a sandwich. "These sandwiches got ham in them," he said disgustedly.

"So what?" Jake was doing something to the starboard engine. "You ain't kosher."

Nancy hiked up her skirts and got out on the prow so that the fine spray from the turquoise waters showered over her. "My mama used to say that this was the best beauty treatment in the world," she said in her precise, musical English.

The Cuban boy watched her. She looked like a mythic figurehead, her straight hair pushed back, her skin glowing.

Nick lay in one cramped position in the back of the boat, watching Jake work the engine. He wasn't happy. He kept his suit jacket on and Kay could see the butt of his pistol pressing against the thin material. She went over and sat next to him.

"Reminds me of the boat we came to America on, doesn't it, Jake?" Nick asked.

"Don't remind me," Jake said, laughing. "That one," he pointed to Nick, "was a little runt then, throwing his guts up in the cabin ten of us had to share. The others wanted to heave him out but he held onto the bedposts so tight they couldn't budge him. He was as white as a sheet for the entire trip. Max and I had to force him to eat. Moishe Katz was certain he was going to die."

"Nothing could kill him," Kay said. He took hold of her hand and held it tightly. It occurred to her that Nick was frightened.

She turned and stared back, just able to make out Havana's harbor with the sun behind, Morro Castle at its edge, looking as if it were waiting for a returning pirate and his crew.

El Cacique proved to be an inlet a couple of hours out of Havana. A rotting dock and a group of broken-down cottages attested to the fact that it was once a port, of sorts. Men from Cojimar occasionally fished there but for the most part it was a deserted place, surrounded by purple waters.

Jake cut the motors as they approached and let the boat drift on the Gulf Stream. Kay looked down and saw long yellow fish swimming around the hull. Sea grapes gave off their mysterious, slightly acrid odor and the bleached yellow sargasso weed floated by in small clumps. It was very quiet.

"What time we supposed to meet the frog?" Nick wanted to know.

"He should be here now but I don't see his boat."

"I don't like it," Nick said. "It's too quiet."

There were half a dozen palm trees up on the beach, their fronds absolutely still despite the light breeze. Suddenly a group of gulls, disturbed, flew over their heads and out over the water. A lone pelican watched them from his perch on what remained of the rotted dock, as still as a garden ornament.

They were all, suddenly, very still.

Kay stood up and said, too loudly, "It's a beautiful day. Why are we all acting as if we're at a wake? Let's land and . . ."

"Sit down," Nick told her, grabbing her wrist, pulling her next to him. It wasn't the boat or the water, she realized, that was scaring him. "I told you," he said to Jake, "we shouldn't have taken them along."

"Shut up," Jake said and then Kay knew that he was scared, too. "Nothing's happened yet. What're you so nervous about? Nancy, get back in the boat. We're pulling out."

"Sí, sí, señor. Por supuesto, señor." Of all of them, she was the only one not affected by the place. Laughing, she stood up on the prow, gathered her skirt, and began coming toward them. Jake reached up, his arms stretched out to catch her.

There was a flat, terrible sound as Jake pulled Nancy down into the boat. Then they all lay down, their hands over their heads. Whoever was shooting was aiming for the port engine but Jake managed to start the starboard and was moving them out. From behind the palm trees, they could see white flashes as they were shot at. Nick took out his gun and rolled to the port side. He looked back, fired once, and then fired at something on the shore. There was no way to tell whether or not his second shot had hit anything; anyone.

It took hours to find the right officials to bribe before they were allowed to take her body, to give her a burial in the old Catholic cemetery. "None of you are her relatives," the uniformly fat men said. "You can see, señor, my hands are tied." Then the hands would come out.

Nancy had been hit by the first bullet. She had died as Jake pulled her down into the boat. The only other victim, as far as they knew, was the Cuban boy. He had pulled out a pistol from under his shirt and was aiming at Jake as Nick shot him through the head.

Nick left Kay and Jake and Madam Sucre with Nancy's body in the funeral home and came back an hour later. "Fournier, that goddamned frog, and Galvez are dead, too. A new man's taking over. His boys got a little enthusiastic. They didn't know they weren't supposed to kill the customers. We're getting a big discount on the first load."

Jake didn't say anything. He sat in the straight-backed chair, his eyes looking at nothing.

The next day, after the funeral, they left a stoic Madam Sucre and moved out of the Ambos Mundos to San Francisco de Paula, a village in the Pinar del Río province, some twenty minutes from Havana. They had a big house near a private white beach. "The new man," Nick said, "thought it would be safer for us. Some of his boys aren't too happy about the kid."

"Nick," Kay told him, "I want to leave."

"Okay. I'll put you on the first P&O steamer heading north. I got to stay a few more days. Get things straightened out."

She stayed.

Jake played gin rummy with his brother, smiling as he always had. The third night, over an interminable Cuban meal none of them wanted, he put his arms on the table and his head on his arms and began to cry. Kay went over and touched him but Nick told her she had better get out and shut the doors. She did so. For a long time she could hear the sound of Jake sobbing and Nick talking in a low, steady voice.

Later, when Nick came to bed, he said, "Jake feels responsible." He blew out the candle and got under the netting and into the bed. "I told him he wasn't."

"Then who the hell is?"

"Ryan."

"What?"

"Ryan's expanding. Fournier was bringing in more than booze; a quarter of that ship was carrying arms, rifles, pistols, soup. The other guys heard about it and moved in. There must be fifty different groups plotting to take over this island. Far as I'm concerned, they can have it." He turned over.

"Did you tell him?"

"What? That Nancy was killed because our sister's lover boy got greedy, that Ryan put us all in a spot where there was pretty good odds we might be killed for a couple of hundred thousand dollars? No, I didn't tell him. I'm going to let him think it was a terrible but unfortunate accident. Otherwise he's going to go tearing up to New York and he'll be dead fifteen minutes before he ever gets his hands around Ryan's throat. I'm not telling him."

Kay never met Fournier's and Galvez's replacement. Jake and Max had several conferences with him on the far side of the house while she lay on the perfectly tranquil beach, watching the pelicans. A young boy in a white jacket stood behind the thickest palm a few yards away, his hand always in his pocket, holding his revolver, his eyes continually moving across the horizon.

At the end of the week Jake's ferry arrived and Jake took her a couple of miles up the coast, out of the oil-tanker lanes, to a place called Bacuranao and loaded his consignment of wine from France. Then he took the ferry back to the Trumbo Street docks in Key West, made the necessary arrangements to clear customs (white envelopes were handed all around), and had his consignment transferred to freight cars bearing the Florida East Coast (FEC) logo.

Kay stood with him on the deck of his ferry as the cargo was transferred. "If there was only someone whose face I could go and bash in," Jake said. "If there was only someone I could take apart . . . but there ain't. I have to live with it." He allowed her to hug him and then she went to meet Nick who had gotten them the largest stateroom on the *Baron Cordoba.*

It was a full day before she learned that the ship was not going to stop in New York, that they were traveling straight through to Montreal.

"I suppose we're going there to arrange for another consignment."

"You got it."

"Will we be shot at there, too?"

He lit a Cuban cigar Jake had given him. "I doubt it. They're not running guns to Canada, last I heard. This is strictly a bootleg operation."

"My God," she said, "how much booze does New York need?"

"New York? Ryan's not just supplying New York, you dumb Dora. He makes sure the whole country gets what they want."

"You hate him too much, Nicky."

"Yeah. Nancy's just one more reason."

"You're not going to shoot him?"

"Me? Ryan? Bessie's lover boy? My boss? There's

other ways to do a man in besides shooting him. Now come here and do your stuff."

"You're such a tough guy, Nicky."

"Ain't I?" he said as he pulled her to him and held her tight.

CHAPTER 5

After seeing Nick and Kay off on the *Baron Cordoba*, after ascertaining that the booze was on its way north, Jake went to the café on the first floor of the old Jefferson Hotel. Luis San Obispo brought him a soda-pop bottle filled with beer. Jake put it to one side of the small, round table and told Luis to bring him a whiskey.

He had ten whiskeys and then finished off the beer. Luis San Obispo offered to help him up to his rooms. Jake politely refused. He went upstairs, locked the door, and drank half a bottle of bourbon and fell asleep in his clothes.

Frances stopped at his door the next afternoon but he wouldn't allow her in. The only person who got past the door for the next week was Luis, with bottles of whiskey and plates of yellow rice and black beans which usually came away untouched.

"Jake," Frances shouted on the eighth day of his self-imposed isolation. "Will you please let me in?"

"Go away, Frances," Jake said.

She went to the post office and sent a telegram and then she went to the house on Pinder Lane where Blondell was sitting in a darkened room, quietly mourning Nancy. The too fat black woman and the too thin white woman embraced. "I don't know what I'm going to do without that smiling face," Blondell said. "I didn't know her but a short time though she sure worked her way into my heart. I jus' don't know what I'm going to do, Miss Frances."

"I know. I know."

Three days after Frances Ellington sent her telegram, eleven days after Jake had retreated into his rooms, the louvered doors were opened but instead of Luis San Obispo standing at the foot of his bed, he saw what he decided was either a vision or an hallucination: a woman in red.

She stared at him for some time and then she started to give orders and suddenly the room was filled with a variety of people and sounds and just before he allowed himself to fall back into his stupor, he found himself being picked up and moved through the air as if by magic.

Luis San Obispo and Juan the waiter carried him to the car Bessie had hired and Frances drove it to the house on Pinder Lane where she and Bessie and Blondell bathed him in the tub fed by the cistern out back. Then he was carted up to the room he had so often shared with Nancy. He couldn't stop sweating.

"Should I call the doctor?" Frances asked.

"You've never seen alcohol poisoning before? When he stops sweating," Bessie told her, "that's when we have to worry."

When he fell asleep, a genuine sleep, they left him and went down the stairs to the tiny living room. Blondell brought them coffee and Frances asked if Bessie wouldn't like to rest.

"I'm too nervous to rest. Tell me about her. Everything."

"He was very much in love with her," Frances said. "In almost a paternal way. She was such a child. A dear, impossibly spoiled child, as sweet and as kind as she could be. I never could imagine her as a woman in her thirties or forties. She was far too . . ."

"What's that?" Bessie asked, standing up.

"What's what?"

"I thought I heard a baby crying."

"Blondell will see to her."

"See to who?"

"Coffee." And then it finally occurred to Frances. "You mean you don't know about the baby?"

Bessie brushed past Frances and went into the downstairs bedroom where Blondell was holding a very young child in her arms. Bessie took the baby from her and cradled her, examining her. "Is she as pretty as I think?" Bessie asked.

"Most beautiful I've ever seen," Blondell said.

At that moment Coffee began to cry and Bessie, rocking her back and forth, began to sing *"Rozhinkes Mit Mandlen,"* soothing her. A child was the one blessing she felt she had been unfairly denied. She had had such an ache in her body, in her loins; such a need to have a child. And here was this wonderfully coffee-colored Coffee, listening to Bessie's mother's favorite song as if she understood every word. She kissed the child on her forehead and was glad that Frances and Blondell had left the room. She didn't want them to see her crying.

Bessie stayed a month, while Jake convalesced.

Moishe Katz had been dispatched from Miami to
handle the Havana-Key West ferry runs but there had
been slipups, neither the Cubans nor the Conchs able
to perceive Moishe as a serious threat or a leader of
men.

"Wake up," Bessie said, coming into Jake's room,
standing over him. The platter with black coffee and
Cuban bread Blondell had brought him was standing,
untouched, on the bedside table.

"I'm awake."

"Then open those eyes."

"They're open."

"All the way."

He looked up at his sister and tears immediately
filled his eyes.

"And stop that crying. The time for crying is past.
Or it's in the future. Right now you've got to pull
yourself together. You know how much weight you've
lost on your self-pitying binge?"

"Bessie," Jake said, closing his eyes, "I don't want
to live."

She slapped him across the face as hard as she
could. He was crying again. She took his head in her
hands and forced him to look at her. "Who are you
crying for, Jakey?"

"Nancy. Who else?"

"If you believe that's true, Jake, then you're a bigger fool than I thought you were. You're crying for
yourself, Jake. You're acting like a kid whose favorite
toy's been broke. Nancy died. It's not nice or kind
but that's life, fat boy. People die. Young people.
People we love. In terrible ways."

She stood up and moved away. "I'm leaving Key

West this afternoon. I got a business to run. I got obligations. You want another bottle of whiskey, that's up to you. I'm taking Coffee with me."

"Sister . . ."

"You haven't asked for her once, not in four weeks. What kind of a father are you? What kind of a father could you be? A drunk, dependent upon his sister to keep him going? Because if you don't get back to those ferries, that's where it will end. Ryan will find someone else to run his booze.

"I won't be able to give her what you can—a father's love—but I'll give her something else: a person she can respect." She went to the door. "I'm going to pack. I'm tired of you, Jake. If you want to see your daughter, you'll have to come to New York. In the meanwhile I'll make sure there's a monthly check for you. You just might end up being my most expensive charity."

He lay in his bed and listened to the sounds of the cicadas in the back garden and the sound of Bessie's trunk being carried out front and just faintly he could hear Coffee, his daughter, laughing.

Slowly he got out of the bed, surprised to find how little strength he had. He tried to call out but no sound came. He went down the stairs and through the open door, he could see Bessie, holding Coffee, kissing Blondell good-bye, the car with her luggage at the end of the lane.

He ran out the door, barefooted, in his pajama bottoms, and went up to Bessie, and took Coffee from her and held her to him. The child's arms crept around his neck.

"You can't have her, Bessie. I want my daughter."

Bessie threw her arms around the two of them. "Thank God," she said. "Thank God."

By August, 1923, when Key West had reached a new low economically, Jake Meyer was the richest man on the island. Not that there was much evidence of his wealth. Claude Wheeler had the largest car, the biggest house, the use of his father-in-law's opulent yacht. Jake had two rooms on the second floor of the old Jefferson, the house on Pinder Lane, and an early Oldsmobile.

"What're you going to do with all your money?" Frances Ellington wanted to know.

"One problem Coffee's not going to have is where her next meal is coming from."

"Or her next limousine. I heard you bought the café downstairs."

"I don't always want to be Ryan's Key West boot-legger, Frances. Someday I may want to be the proud owner of Key West's tenth Bucket of Blood." He looked at her. "You need money, Frances?"

She told him no, but thanks for asking and he lifted his beer and gave her his shy, lopsided smile. He was twenty-three years old and, on rare occasions, looked it. Most of the time he passed for thirty.

Except for Coffee and Frances he saw few people. He knew a great many men because of his work but not many women. He wasn't the sort of bachelor invited to dinner as an extra man. He had openly kept a mulatto mistress in a town where the color bars were low but firmly in place. He had fathered a child by her, and worse, he acknowledged the child which was enough to keep him in permanent social exile.

As soon as Coffee was old enough, he began taking her by the hand and walking her up and down Duval Street. The vision of the two of them, both so proud of one another, never failed to startle, amuse, enchant. The big dark blond man in his white suit, carefully taking small steps; and the tiny, perfectly featured, coffee-colored baby in her elaborate pink dress, always laughing, always looking as if she were about to break into a dance from sheer excess of high spirits.

If the drawing rooms of Key West had been closed to Jake Meyer because he was a Jew and a rumrunner, they were locked and sealed because he was so publicly Coffee's father.

But suddenly, during that summer of 1923, when it seemed as if Jake were able to forget that Nancy had been killed—when there were rumors that Warren Gamaliel Harding had also been killed, in San Francisco—Claude paid a rare visit to the Jefferson Hotel.

He entered Jake's sitting room, nervously accepted a beer, and issued an invitation to a dinner to be held at Devon House.

"I doubt if your wife . . ."

"She asked me to invite you, Jake. I swear it. She was most insistent. You know Virginia when she wants something."

"Actually I only know her when she doesn't want something. Have another beer."

Later that evening, after Claude had left, while Jake and Frances were enjoying a *picadillo* made by Luis San Obispo in the hotel's kitchen, the senator himself stopped by the open doors of Jake's sitting room. He bowed.

"Mr. Meyer, sir," he said. "My daughter, Mrs. Claude Devon Wheeler, cordially requests that you honor her table this forthcoming Saturday night. You will be previously acquainted with several of her guests."

"Afraid I can't make it, Senator. Regrets to your daughter. I have an engagement with Frances, here."

"Of course the invitation includes Mrs. Ellington. Perhaps you and she can change your plans?"

"We could. But we ain't. I don't know about Frances but I never go places where I haven't been invited by the person giving the party."

"Fat chance," Frances said as the senator bowed himself out of the doorway.

"I wouldn't take odds on her not showing up, Mrs. Ellington. Now, if you don't mind exerting your lovely self, could you do me the honor of passing that beer?"

Jake and Frances were in his sitting room again on the following afternoon. It was a week when the ferries weren't running—the federal agents were making a periodic check of reputed bootlegging boats—and it was too hot and humid to move. A dark Packard pulled up in front of the Jefferson. Poor Willy ran around and opened the rear door.

Virginia Devon Wheeler stepped out, wearing an ankle-length silk gown of the palest mauve. Her shoes, her purse, and her gloves were a shade darker. It was a dated, matronly costume, deliberately chosen.

It doesn't suit her, Frances thought as she watched the girl hesitate for a moment at the steps. She should be coming out of a horse-drawn carriage, wearing thirty-eight crinolines and a low-cut white gown.

Virginia still refused to bob her silver-blond hair. That afternoon she hid it under a satin hat which featured a crepe de chine rose on its brim. "There's something indefinably vulgar about her," Frances said, retreating from the balcony into Jake's sitting room.

"About who?"

"Put your shirt on, Jake. My cousin's about to pay a visit."

He lay back on the rattan fainting couch, a beer in his hand, a well-bitten cheroot in his mouth. With his free hand he took a Hotel Jefferson towel and wiped the sweat from his torso.

"If you're not going to put on your shirt, Jake, don't expect me to stay here. This is going to be difficult enough for her."

"I'm not aiming to make it easy."

Frances went into the bedroom, shutting the doors behind her as Virginia knocked.

"Door's open," Jake said.

"Mr. Meyer," Virginia said in an even voice, coming into the room a few steps. "I'm here to invite you . . ."

"If you're going to be doing any inviting, you'd better come in and shut the doors behind you."

Virginia stepped into the sitting room, though she didn't shut the doors. She made it clear that the smells of the room—beer, cigar smoke, Jake's clean, animal odor—repelled her. "Mr. Meyer," she began again, "I'd . . ."

"Take off your hat and gloves, Mrs. Wheeler; sit down."

"You're not attempting to seduce me, Mr. Meyer, are you?" She remained hatted, gloved, and standing.

"If I wanted to, Mrs. Wheeler, I'd get off this couch and come over there and take your clothes off myself."

"Mr. Meyer," she said, "please come to dinner on Saturday night. Please. It's terribly important to my father and to Claude and I promised them both I wouldn't fail. Do say you'll come."

Jake studied his cheroot, found it was out, relit it, and clamped it back in his mouth. "I'd be delighted, Mrs. Wheeler."

"Thank you," she said, relieved. "And please ask my cousin Frances if . . ."

"You can ask her yourself. Frances, come out here."

Frances Ellington looked at the aging stranger in the patterned kimono in Jake's bedroom mirror and wished she were someone else. She opened the door to the sitting room, one hand jabbing at her hair, the other holding the kimono closed.

"I can't come to your party, Virginia."

"Oh, please, Frances. I can't go back to that house. . . ."

"Then I will," Frances heard herself saying. She wondered what threat the senator had used to make Virginia so desperate, to weaken her confidence so. Frances imagined it had to do with money and with the future; but even so the senator must have been badly frightened to have forced his beloved daughter into such a position.

"Thank you, Frances. Saturday, then. Eight P.M." She started to leave but before she closed the door behind her, she took a final look at Jake's bare torso and then at his hands which lay poised on his thighs.

"You want to turn up that overhead fan, Frances?" Jake asked. "It's stifling in here."

"I don't like what you did to that girl, Jake. And I don't like what you did to me."

She went to her room and lay down on her bed and closed her eyes. Occasionally, when Jake felt the need, they would make love, but she knew they weren't lovers. They knew each other too well for that. She had comforted him after Nancy died. She thought that perhaps she shouldn't have always been so very there for Jake.

An hour later, an iced bottle of Moët et Chandon was delivered by Luis San Obispo to her room. It was Jake's way of saying he was sorry. Frances drank most of it. It was her way of forgiving him.

"It suits you," Frances said. "It fits the way evening clothes are meant to fit a gentleman: loose in the right places. Though you've got far too much sex appeal to be a gentleman."

He had taken Coffee to Miami during the week, ostensibly to visit her half brother, David. While there, he had the English tailor make him up a set of evening clothes. And he had come back with a new, open Cadillac. It was cream-colored with oversized whitewall tires, wire-spoked wheels, and huge chromed door handles.

"I wanted us to go to this party in style," he said, helping Frances into the back of the car. Luis San Obispo sat behind the wheel, proud as he could be and doing his best to hide the fact.

THE WINE AND THE MUSIC   301

"You're looking very beautiful tonight, Frances."

"No, I'm not. I look like an overpriced bottle of aging French perfume. Let's stop the small talk and get on with the torture. Why do people go to parties, anyway?"

Devon House was set back a hundred feet from Whitehead Street on an acre of land the senator had had planted with a variety of Key West flora. Sago, date palms, palmettos, and banyan trees gave the gardens the appearance of a manicured jungle. The porches and verandas of Devon House were lit by Chinese lanterns, gleaming dull red in the tropical darkness.

Claude came down from one of the verandas to greet them, to take their arms, to escort them into the octagonal ballroom with its Georgia pine floors, its Venetian chandeliers. Cocktails were being openly served. To her surprise Frances knew none of the forty people assembled in that room and she wondered what it was that had brought them to Key West in the middle of the steamy summer.

Jake went to get her a martini. He was stopped by half a dozen men as he made his way to the bar. Claude ended up getting her her drink and she sipped it as she studied the women. They weren't members of the Key West aristocracy, as she had expected. These women were New Money, most of it northern. She could hear it in their crisp, energetic voices, in the alert way they held themselves in their flapper dresses and dancing shoes.

It must be very confusing for Virginia, Frances thought. She's always been taught to look backward for models of behavior and suddenly she was surrounded by a very current, very fast crowd indeed.

Frances allowed Claude to introduce her around the room, flattered that a story of hers which had appeared in a recent issue of *Vanity Fair* had been read by several of the guests. She hadn't expected anything even remotely literary and suddenly she found herself discussing Aldous Huxley. Undercutting the conversation and the old-plantation-home atmosphere of Devon House was the money these people had and something more, a new kind of sexual directness that Frances found exhilarating. But again she wondered what Virginia must be making of it.

"Evening, Cousin Frances," Virginia said, coming up to her. "I'm so very glad you could come."

Frances decided she was sincere. Virginia didn't seem at ease with her guests. She greeted Jake in much the same way as she had greeted Frances, with almost a sense of relief. At the least they had frames of reference for one another. Virginia didn't know where she stood with these others.

Eventually Senator Devon came out of his study, greeted several people, and then escorted Jake into that room, several men following.

A half hour later dinner was announced and Frances found herself on the arm of the senator who was all unrestrained charm, searching for a common topic which proved to be New Orleans.

Jake escorted a tall, redheaded woman who didn't seem to be able to stop talking while Virginia went into the dining room with the pale, sandy-haired man, the guest of honor, whom everyone seemed to know and respect.

At first sight he appeared not to have eyebrows or lashes and this gave him, Frances thought, a slightly sinister appearance, like a tortured doll. They were introduced across the dinner table. He was Bessie's Ryan. Throughout dinner he occasionally glanced at Jake at the far end of the enormous table, in a calculating way, as if he were a critic assessing a performance.

Afterward the guests went back into the ballroom where a band played waltzes and occasional fox-trots. Frances danced with the senator who held her too closely and then with Claude who smelled as if he had been dipped in a bottle of Beefeater. "I am a bit ginny," he admitted.

She was surprised when Ryan cut in. "Jake's sister, Bessie, was very impressed by you, Mrs. Ellington," he said in an accent she recognized as pristine Yale. There didn't seem much to say to that except that she had been very impressed by Bessie.

"Are you and Jake good friends, Mrs. Ellington?"

"We're slightly more than ships that pass in the night but we're not bumping into each other. Not any more."

"His sister worries about him."

He whirled her around so that she had a view of Jake dancing with Virginia. He was holding her no closer than he had held any woman while dancing. Yet there was a curious intimacy about the way they moved. Virginia seemed less nervous than she had earlier. Her hand rested against Jake's new dinner jacket in a way that signified, for Frances, at any rate, that Virginia was no longer dismissing Jake as Claude's old corrupt chum.

After that evening it would have been difficult to continue to do so. The men in the room, rich and middle-aged, had paid a special deference to the young man and Virginia couldn't have helped but notice.

They didn't dance again.

Jake had a fox-trot with Frances and suggested they leave. He had some last words with Ryan and the senator, said good-bye to Virginia and Claude, and then joined Frances in the back of his lavish new car.

"Do you want to buy me a beer, Jake, and tell me what was going on tonight?" Frances asked him when they pulled up in front of the Jefferson.

"Can you keep a secret?" he asked when they were seated on the balcony on the second floor, looking out at the Atlantic, at the unfamiliar yachts that had so suddenly filled the empty submarine cribs on the naval base. "Oh, I know you can. You're the one person I know who's able to."

He took a long pull at his beer. "The single document every two-bit *gonif* is trying to get his hands on right now is called a Permit for Withdrawal. With such a permit you can get into any government warehouse."

"Why would anyone want to get into a government warehouse?" Frances asked, visions of khaki trousers in her mind.

"That's where the feds stash the liquor they've been confiscating since Prohibition went into effect and the booze the government takes from bootleggers who get caught. *And* the one hundred and thirty million gallons of whiskey distilled for supposedly medicinal purposes until early this year when someone in

Washington wised up and realized what those medicinal purposes were and that all ended. Following me, Frances?"

"Like a dear but dead mother. How much booze does the government have in those warehouses?"

"No one knows but Ryan estimates over a hundred and fifty million gallons, most of it genuine pre-1920 McCoy."

Frances whistled.

"Now, when Senator Devon was serving his four terms in Congress, he made a few friends. Coolidge appointed one of them commissioner of Internal Revenue. He's a teetotaler from Alabama named Lear. While Congress is taking its sweet time ratifying Lear, guess who Coolidge has been persuaded to name as Acting Commissioner."

"Senator Devon."

"Exactly. That party tonight was Ryan's way of showing everyone he holds all the cards. He holds the senator who doesn't need much persuading—only money—to issue permits wherever and however Ryan tells him. He holds the politicians who made the senator possible; most of them were there tonight. And he holds the guys who have the ways and means to distribute the hootch."

"What happens next?"

"Tomorrow morning the senator is giving Ryan permits to withdraw thirty thousand cases of whiskey. Ryan intends to sell the permits to the distributors for thirty bucks a case. They'll take the booze out on Monday morning and either get it to the frontline guys themselves which isn't too likely; or redistribute it through Ryan's organization at twenty bucks a case."

"Won't there be an investigation, sooner or later?" Frances asked.

"Ryan figures there won't be one for a good while and by the time there is, all the evidence will be long destroyed. No one's going to remember who withdrew what by then."

"But they'll remember," Frances said, standing up, preparing to say good night, "the man who signed the original permits."

"I don't think the senator has thought that far ahead."

It was later that night, as he lay in his bed, sweating from the heat and the alcohol he had consumed, that he heard a knock on his door. "Come in," he said, "door's open." He didn't bother to put the sheet over him though he guessed who it was.

"I just thought," Virginia said, stepping into the room as if she were stepping into a new world, "that I'd thank you for coming to the party, Mr. Meyer."

He knew she had had a lot to drink but that she wasn't too drunk not to know what she was doing.

"Come here," he said.

"Mr. Meyer," she whispered, her voice barely audible. "I merely came to say . . ."

"Come over here."

She went to him and stood over him. She had left the door half opened. In the dim moonlight she could see his body but not his face. He reached up for her.

"Mr. Meyer . . ."

He pulled her down onto the bed, damp with his sweat, and got on top of her, kneeling at her feet. He took the hem of her dress in his two hands and ripped the dress from the bottom to the top. She wore nothing underneath.

"Mr. Meyer," she said again in that social whisper. He bent his head down and put his mouth around her nipple as he forced her legs up against her chest and went into her.

"No," she said, trying to push him away. "No."

He stopped and lay on top of her. The room was suddenly silent. They could hear the sounds of Saturday night Duval Street outside. "Say yes," he told her, starting to withdraw. "Say yes."

She pulled him back so that he was fully into her, her hands grasping his sweaty thighs. "Yes," she said and she was no longer whispering. "Yes."

CHAPTER 6

"I didn't know Ryan had business interests in California," Max said.

Bessie shook her red curls and sat down in the one chair in Max's dressing room that she considered possible. It was her first trip to California and she wasn't happy. "Ryan," she said, looking out the small window in the direction he and his guide, Townie, had taken, "has business interests everywhere. Especially here. You gave him the ten thousand shares, didn't you?"

"That was collateral," Max said, not looking at his sister.

"I'd love to know," Bessie said, standing up, going to the window, "how you could be such a *schlemiel* when it comes to money and Ryan. Why didn't you come to me, fat boy? I would've given you the money in a second. You had to go to him?"

"I didn't want to be dependent upon you. I wanted it to be strictly business."

"You had as much chance coming out of that deal in one piece as a lamb in spring. You never paid back the loan. You had two years and then Ryan got to keep the collateral. Didn't it occur to you, fat boy, that you'd never be able to pay back the loan? That you couldn't even finish the film in two years? My God, you haven't changed a bit since I found you wasting your time in the nickelodeon. No head for money. Listen: Ryan now owns fifty thousand shares of Great Western because he happened to pick up an extra forty thousand in the market for next to nothing. He is now the majority shareholder which says something, not much, about Joe Goldstein's business acumen. Ryan can close this place tomorrow and you and Joe will be walking up and down Hollywood Boulevard, looking for jobs."

"Is that what he plans?"

"Not now. There's no reason. When he comes up with a reason, watch out."

Max looked at his sister for a long moment. "Why are you still with him, Bessie?"

She stood up, put her cheek against his forehead, kissed him, and walked to the window. "I used to tell myself," she said, "that it was love. And it is. But it's not love pure and simple. Long ago Lillian Wald set me straight. I had left Ryan but I had decided to go back to him because I thought I was having a child. Miss Wald said I wasn't going back to him because of the baby but because I was a coward.

"She was right. She said I was holding onto an old dream, an immigrant's dream of America and that I was afraid to let go. I'm still afraid to let go, Max. I'm afraid my Yankee dream is really a nightmare. So I cling to Ryan. He gives me everything I want. He genuinely and truly loves me. I know that. I just make certain I never look under the rock."

She turned away from the window and looked at

Max. "I'm talking too much and it's all your fault. Let's get going. You promised me a commissary lunch and that's what I want."

Max went to Bessie and put his arms around her. "You may be a lot of things, Sister, but take it from me, you're no coward. You're the bravest lady I know."

She held onto him for a moment. "I think I needed to hear that, Max. Thank you."

Later, after Bessie had her commissary lunch, and Ryan had completed his tour of the studio, after he and Bessie had left Los Angeles for the inland town where Ryan's West Coast bootlegging operation was run, Max went to the screening room where he and Tim Bronco were to view the final, edited edition of *Cowboy*.

Though he loved his sister, he was relieved that she and Ryan were leaving California. He didn't want to think about collateral or majority stockholders. He wanted to get on with his film.

Because of his double studio obligations—producer-star—because Uncle Joe was against the project from the beginning, because Bronco had given up acting for drinking, it had taken him until 1927 to finish *Cowboy*.

When he wasn't working on his Ram Page films, he was doing everything he could to wind up *Cowboy*, shooting night for day, spending fifteen hours or more in the editing room. He had shot too much, and it was all too good. He didn't know what to keep and what to throw away.

It wasn't a great year for westerns. Hoofbeats and

scheming cattle rustlers were no longer the thrills they had been at the beginning of the decade.

Great Western was surviving on Ram Page's sex appeal as he continued to haul in villains on his unsaddled white horse, his white satin shirt invariably ripped from his body in the last reel.

Will Hays, the Moral Code Czar of Hollywood, didn't object to the shirt ripping. It was only a male Indian brave who tore the shirt from Max's body, not some seductive, amoral woman. But he told Uncle Joe to do something about the bulge in Max's trousers.

"What can I do, Will?" Uncle Joe asked, holding out his hands, palms upward. "The boy happens to be built that way."

"Tape it or I'll cut every single below-waist shot in the film." That afternoon Uncle Joe had his new chauffeur take him to Yock's Sporting Goods on Doheny where he personally bought Max an athletic supporter.

Max didn't need one for *Cowboy*. "*Mishugah*," Uncle Joe said during his first screening of that film. "You think Hays is going to let you get away with *that*?" "That" was a scene in which a nude Max, his sex organ partially hidden in shadows, got into the bed of a very young Indian woman.

"That's not even an implication," Uncle Joe shouted. "That's the unmentionable, unshowable genuine article."

"I've been a piece of beefcake long enough," Max said, switching on the lights. "I'm making a good movie. One good movie, Uncle Joe, and then I go back to Ram Page."

"If that ain't beefcake, Maxela, I'll eat it," Uncle Joe said, getting out of the plush chair with some trouble, going toward the door, shaking his head. He turned and looked at Max before he left. "And don't be so sure Ram Page is going to live forever. Even his box office is falling off."

"We're in trouble, Uncle Joe?"

"Trouble? I wouldn't say trouble. Hot water, maybe." He smiled. "But that's not your worry. I'm the business, you're the creative. Let's see what happens in the next few months."

Max turned out the lights, Tim Bronco made a sound halfway between a hiccough and a snort in his back-row seat, and the boy in the projection room began *Cowboy* from the beginning again.

When he arrived home at Ram-A-Dies, late that evening, it seemed as if everyone had gone to bed.

"Shall you be wanting dinner, Mr. Meyer?" Robinson asked.

"No, thanks. I had sandwiches and coffee at the studio."

He went up the stairs and tiptoed into Anna's room and watched her for a moment and then went to the bedroom he and Mitsuko shared. She wasn't there.

He knew where to find her. She was in her studio, wearing the old kimono she liked to work in, studying a half-finished painting of an oversized golden rose.

"Am I disturbing you?" Max asked.

"No," she said, putting down her brush, turning

and going to him. "It's not much good anyway." She held onto him for what seemed a long time.

"You all right?" he asked.

"Yes."

"No, you're not," he said, holding her away, looking at her. "You've got a funny, sad expression on your face. You always do when you come back from seeing your father."

She had been up the coast to the farm her father was working on, one he planned to buy. He wouldn't let Mitsuko help him. He wanted to do it himself. He had saved a certain amount of money while he was working for Uncle Joe and he was making more now as part of a farm cooperative. When he bought the farm, it would be in Mitsuko's name.

"It looks as if he'll be able to buy the farm any day."

"He must be happy."

"He's not. He can't be happy while his daughter is living as a concubine."

"Is that what he said?"

"No. Of course not. He doesn't say anything. He never mentions your name and if he does, he calls you Mr. Meyer. He never recognizes the fact that we live together, unmarried. Once, when I backed him into the corner and told him, he called me his American daughter. I said I was Japanese as well. And he said, 'Oh, no. You are no longer Japanese.' Implicit was the belief that no Japanese girl would live the way I do." She turned away, back to the half-finished golden rose.

"He doesn't look at me anymore, Max. I make him

uncomfortable. It makes me so lonesome to visit him. I feel so all alone when I come back."

He went to her and kissed her. "You have me," he said. "You have me."

"And I wouldn't give you up for anything, Max. But sometimes I wish I had my father, too."

The only moments when Araby and Max met were on occasional Sundays when one of the fan magazines—more often than not, *Photoplay*—would send a team of photographer-reporters up to Ram-A-Dies to interview that "happiest of Hollywood couples." Araby would arrive via the kitchen door a few minutes before the press was to appear, a dressing gown under her fur coat. Mitsuko and Anna would take their watercolors and go off for the morning while Ram and Araby would illustrate the depth of their love by asking one another to "please pass the orange marmalade, dear."

Max continually objected to the charade but both Townie and Uncle Joe insisted and he knew enough about publicity to realize how important it was to keep in the public eye. Araby enjoyed it and said so.

She was under contract to Paramount, fighting for first place with Clara Bow, making jazz films about young girls heading for damnation on a steady diet of Charlestons, fast cars, and even faster men.

She was just then finishing a film with Charles "Buddy" Rogers and managing to look a decade younger than she was.

It had been a *Photoplay* Sunday, the press had finally left, and she was sitting at the far end of the dining table which ran some twenty feet across the breakfast room.

"What are you going to do about sound?" she asked him, taking her coffee and her croissant and moving to the seat next to his.

"Sound? No one wants sound," Max said, watching her eat the roll with her usual gusto.

"In case you didn't know, honey boy, Hollywood's in bad shape this year. The movies need a new way to make money and the people who know say it's sound. Everyone in this town—from Harold Lloyd to Gloria Swanson—has engaged a vocal coach and is spending hours in the john, gargling and practicing *Gunga Din*.

"And if you think 'Ram Page Talks' is a remotely possible headline, you'd better have your head examined. You'd be laughed off the screen in the time it took you to say, 'Howdy, ma'am.' " She selected another croissant and began picking at it. "There's a part for you at Paramount. It's a chance to change your image. LeMay's producing. *The Prince and the Flapper*. You know the sort of thing: a gorgeous hunk of European prince comes to New York disguised as a bellhop and meets a young thing disguised as a flapper and they . . ."

"Forget it, Araby. I only know how to make one kind of film and that's a western."

"Silent westerns," Araby said, popping the last of the croissant into her mouth.

A month after that conversation was held, in October of that year, Max drove down to the apartment house where Tim Bronco had taken two rooms, on Fountain, and found a nude, fifteen-year-old girl

standing in the corner of the bedroom, crying. On the
far side of the mattress was Tim Bronco's body. He
had died of a heart attack. Max took the fifteen-year-
old girl to her home and then picked up Uncle Joe at
Goldstein-Ville.

The funeral was held a few days later, limited to
Max, Uncle Joe, and a dozen members of the Hollywood Posse. Max, who hadn't said much since he
found Tim's body, went out to Great Western after
the funeral. Mitsuko found him there several hours
later, alone in the dark screening room, the jacket of
his dark suit crumpled up into a ball and tossed in an
empty seat. One of the last of Tim Bronco's films was
on the screen.

Mitsuko put her arms around Max and held him to
her. "He was a lousy actor," Max said, pulling her
down into the seat next to him, kissing her. "But he
was an honest one." There were tears in his eyes
when the last reel was shown and the lights finally
came up.

Tim Bronco got two columns in *Variety* on the second page, his "historic contribution to the art of
film" duly mentioned. The first page of that issue was
devoted to the opening of *The Jazz Singer*.

"Silence is officially dead," Townie said to Max after they had both been present at a screening of *The
Jazz Singer*. "Tim Bronco always did have marvelous
timing." *Variety* agreed with Townie that Jolson's
songs and bits of dialogue portended the end of silent
movies.

So did many of the studios. Paramount quickly
grafted a sound track onto Araby's film with Buddy
Rogers. Whenever they danced, a distant version of

"Everybody's Charleston Crazy Now" could be heard in those few movie theaters equipped for sound. The dancers' feet didn't move to the music but audiences didn't seem to care. The film made money and convinced the few holdouts that talkies were no longer a future threat.

Uncle Joe resolutely refused to allow Max to show *Cowboy* at the screenings for producers. "Darling boy, at the best of times you'd have trouble unloading that piece of art. With talkies, you can't give it away." '

Max spent a thousand dollars having the titles translated and reshot in French and then, with Mitsuko and Anna, he went to France where Gaumont put the film into immediate distribution. It did well in Paris and lost money everywhere else.

By the time Max returned, Fox had come up with Movietone while Vitaphone and *The Jazz Singer* had made three million dollars for Warner's. Theaters all over America were being wired for sound.

Still, only the top studios could convince Wall Street to lend them the necessary money needed for expensive sound equipment. As a result the smaller studios continued to make silents and pray for miracles. Great Western was in the latter category.

By January, 1928, only one film was being made on the huge Great Western lot where once twenty had been shot simultaneously. It was Ram Page's last film, the only one Max ever made without Bronco at his side, *Posse from Laredo*.

Most other sets in Hollywood had huge microphones and dozens of strange new machines fighting for space, but Great Western's Western Street looked exactly as it had when Max and Araby had run the tourists' buckboard. Now the tourist bleachers were empty and the cowboys eating their box lunches seemed grim and too old for the work.

Townie arrived at noon, after the early lunch, to watch the filming of the last scene in the movie, a chase sequence. He had asked Uncle Joe to accompany him but that gentleman had said, "Tell you the truth, Townie, I don't have the heart for it." Townie left him sitting in his papal throne, playing solitaire.

Western Street was being cleaned up in preparation for the Dead Man's Fall, a must in every western and a trick Tim Bronco had been especially adept at. It was a dangerous stunt, size being a definite liability in its execution.

"Who's doing the Dead Man?" Townie asked, wishing everything didn't look so ineffably seedy.

"I am," Max answered.

"You? You're a foot and a half too tall. And you've never done it before. Max . . ."

"I've watched Tim do it one hundred and fifty-three times."

"That's a lot different than doing it yourself."

"You know something, Townie? You and my sister, Bessie, sometimes sound an awful lot alike."

"I wish she were here now to keep you from killing yourself."

"I'm not going to kill myself," Max said, getting up, walking off to inspect the old stunt bay that was always used for the Dead Man's Fall.

Townie followed him. "That poor dumb horse," he said. She was nervous and whiny and Townie couldn't blame her. She had been through it too many times. He could see the scars in her forehead where the hair had grown back in an odd way.

"It's her last time out," Max said.

"Tell it to the horse," Townie answered. "And make sure it's not *your* last time out."

One of the boys attached a leather hobble to each of the horse's hooves. Two ends of long piano wire the camera wouldn't see ran up her front legs from the hobbles to form a single wire that went under her cinch and then back to the post. She moved about nervously, missing the calming hand of Tim Bronco.

Max measured off as many feet of ground as there were of wire and marked the spot on the dirt street with a piece of yellow chalk. For a big man, Townie thought, he's very economical with his movements, very precise. Max patted the horse, calmed her, and took her down to the end of Western Street. Gingerly he mounted her. She gave a loud whinny. She knows, Townie thought, taking a seat in the tourist bleacher.

The Great Western Orchestra was missing, a sign of new economies, but the big black stationary camera at the far end of the street was still there and, at a signal from Max, began to grind, loudly.

Max touched his spurs to the bay's flanks and the horse began moving toward the camera. She took four strides and was suddenly wide open, fear forcing her to show more speed than she had in years.

When she reached the chalked X, Max hit the end of the wire. The bay had both of her front feet pulled out from under her and let out a terrifying, almost human sound. As the bay's feet were pulled up by the piano wire, Max kicked both stirrups free.

Rolling himself into a tight ball, he fell to the ground, his eyes shut tight.

"Great," the assistant producer shouted but the extras and the grips turned away as the bay managed to lunge to all fours and gave out another terrible sound.

"That wraps you," the assistant said.

Max stood up and smiled as Townie ran up Western Street.

"You okay?" he asked.

"Right as shit, as Tim Bronco used to say."

"You still mourning that little guy?"

His face covered with the dust of Western Street, Max looked at Townie and then away from him. "Him. And this." He pointed up Western Street. "Take a good, long look, Townie. It's all over." He put his arm around the shorter man and together they walked to the only dressing room still in use on the lot.

Max took off his chaps and his trousers and Uncle Joe's athletic supporter and stepped into the tub with a barely conscious grace. "I got two things to tell you, Townie," he said, lathering himself with the square bar of white soap.

"Give them to me slowly."

"I want a divorce."

"You can't have one. Araby likes the status quo. If you forced her into one—and I suppose you could— think of what you'd be doing to Mitsuko and Anna. 'Ram Page and His Oriental Mistress Have Taken My Child from Me' would be the sort of headline she'd concoct. She'd get Anna. She'd leave you without a penny or a career."

"I don't have much of a career, anyway. Townie, I want to live with Mitsuko."

"You already do."

"As my wife. In our own house."

"You see, Townie," Mitsuko said, coming in from the small room that had once served as a kitchen, "I'm going to have a baby."

"Nice reading, Mitsuko, but that line's never going to make it past the Hays Office."

"Talk to Araby," Max said, getting out of the tub, rinsing himself off with a metal scooper, getting into the terry-cloth robe Mitsuko was holding for him.

"She won't listen. She likes being married." Townie watched Max take Mitsuko's hand and bring it to his lips. He kissed it as if it were some fragile, invaluable piece of porcelain. She had grown quieter, calmer, more Oriental as she had become a woman. "Wait a year," Townie said. "This town's going nuts with talkies. In a year, Max, Araby may not have a career to worry about. Or maybe she'll be the hottest voice since Galli-Curci. And then she won't want to be married to the All-American Yiddle Cowboy. Wait."

"And the baby?" he asked.

"Oh, the baby won't mind," Mitsuko said, touching Max's face. They looked at one another in their own, intimate way and Townie felt, for a moment, uncomfortable.

"What's the second thing you have to tell me, Max?" he asked. "And should I sit down?"

"Nothing you don't already know. Ram Page is dead. I've finished acting in my last western for Great Western and Uncle Joe Goldstein. From now on,

Townie, I'm a one hundred percent producer-director."

"And where, may I ask, is Uncle Joe going to get the capital to enable you to produce and direct?"

"From Ryan, Great Western's new majority shareholder."

"How many pounds of flesh is this going to cost?"

"No flesh, Townie. All Ryan is interested in is the property."

"Ah," Townie said, sitting down, "the property."

Great Western had dozens of unused and unusable cavernous stages out in the Valley. "You want to set up distilleries," Uncle Joe accused Ryan at the meeting in which contracts were signed. "You want Great Western to be a cover-up for bootleggers."

"We believe," Ryan said, facing Uncle Joe, "that Great Western can make a profit if properly managed. Two, perhaps three films per year, Max as executive producer, you as executive-in-charge. We will close down all unnecessary buildings," he said, blinking his lashless eyes, "and use them for our own purposes, whatever they may be. They will not concern you, Mr. Goldstein."

Ryan nodded and left the room, left Uncle Joe to sign the papers which would formally give Ryan Industries control over Great Western Moving Pictures, Inc. and Uncle Joe one hundred thousand dollars per year for a two-year period at which time contract and duties would be renegotiated.

It was stressed by the lawyers for Ryan Industries that there was to be no public disclosure of the transaction. "You think I want anyone should know?"

Uncle Joe said, taking a proffered pen, scrawling his signature across the bottom of the contract.

Bessie came to stay for a month, a few weeks before Mitsuko was due to give birth. Bessie wanted, she said, to see at least one of her nephews born.

"It may be a girl, Aunt Bessie," Anna said, executing a perfect dive into Ram-A-Dies's Olympic-sized swimming pool.

"You're girl enough," Bessie said. "This one's going to be a boy." She looked at Mitsuko, sitting at her side. The doctor had said that it might be a difficult birth but Mitsuko looked radiant and healthy, shifting her canvas, putting the wooden end of the brush she was holding in her mouth.

"They have never invented a color yet, Bessie," she said, "that comes anywhere close to your hair. I'm afraid you're going to be disappointed."

Bessie stood up and looked at her portrait which was almost finished. It didn't look like her at all and yet it was exactly like her. She thought she would hang it next to the Kotuk painting Ryan had commissioned so many years ago, to refute those who insisted she hadn't changed. She hadn't aged but there was a certain maturity, a subtle hardening of the lines where enthusiasm had given way to sorrow, that Mitsuko had caught almost too well.

"Max told me that before you came West, you were invited to the White House to have luncheon with President Coolidge."

"Parsimonious man. As New England as he could be. It was lucky Edward Lewis was there or we would have had to call in a translator. I came away with promises, but he doesn't really understand city problems. His wife, though, was interesting. She was once a teacher in a school for the deaf and dumb . . . Mitsuko, what is it?"

"I think," Mitsuko said, half standing, "that you had better call Max. I'm feeling terrible cramps."

"Anna," Bessie screamed. "Get your father. Get the doctor. Hurry."

There was no time to get her to the hospital. She broke water before Max was able to pick her up. He carried her to the Falcon Suite which Araby had had designed and in which he and Mitsuko lived.

The doctor, a good-natured, stolid man named Meiselman, had ordered nurses and equipment. After the second hour of labor, when Mitsuko's cries had taken on a shrill life all their own, he had taken Bessie outside the suite. "I don't suppose there's any way we can get your brother out of there," Dr. Meiselman asked Bessie. "He's not helping."

"How long do you think this is going to go on?" There was another prolonged, terrified scream from the bedroom.

"Hours."

"Will she be all right?"

"I don't know."

Bessie went down the stairs and found Townie in the Griffin Room, looking ghost white. "Where's her father?" she asked. "We should tell him. She may not get through this."

"Mitsuko sees him once a month when she drives up the coast to the farm he bought recently and put under Mitsuko's name. He's a Japanese gentleman of the old school, Bessie: he doesn't approve of Mitsuko living with Max and he most certainly won't approve of a child born out of wedlock. As large as Mitsuko grew, he never once mentioned the fact that she was pregnant."

"Call him up. Tell him she's . . ."

"He doesn't have a telephone."

"Then get one of those cars out of the garage. The fastest. He's not going to forgive himself if she dies."

"She's not going to die," Townie said, for the first time contradicting Bessie.

"Get the car, Townie."

She called the police captain, a friend of Ryan's on his payroll, and arranged for a motorcycle escort to meet them on the Pacific Coast Highway. It took them two hours to reach Mr. Tanaka's farm.

"Won't you have a cup of tea, Miss Meyer," that lean gentleman said, standing in the center of his perfectly balanced living room.

"We don't have time for tea. Your daughter is having my brother's child. It's true, they're not married legally but they are, if there's any justice in God's eyes, and there's a chance she may die. She may be dead at this moment. She has been wonderfully loyal to you, Mr. Tanaka. She has never said a word against you. Though she might have. You have been hard and cruel and rigid, sticking to the old ways. I'm an immigrant to this country, too, and I want to share with you a lesson I learned long ago: we'll never assimilate. Their rules aren't for us. You and I, Mr. Tanaka—and Max and Mitsuko—have to make the rules to fit our needs.

"Mr. Tanaka, if we leave right now, we may be in time for the birth of your daughter's child. Or we may be in time to see Mitsuko once more before she dies. Your daughter, Mr. Tanaka, and your grandchild."

Bessie stared into his deep brown eyes and turned and went to the car. After a moment Mr. Tanaka came from the house and walked to the driver's side of the car, motioning Townie to slide over. "I'm a very excellent chauffeur, if you remember, Mr. Townsend."

Ram-A-Dies seemed too quiet when they drove up the circular driveway and stopped at the crested front door. Bessie led the way. There were muted sounds from above. Robinson, ordinarily a paragon among butlers, was asleep in the visitor's chair in the entrance hallway.

Dr. Meiselman was waiting for them at the head of the stairs. He looked tired and much older than he had when Bessie had left him. She stopped and he took her hand. Mr. Tanaka walked into the Falcon Suite and into the bedroom, past an objecting nurse. Max was asleep on the chaise longue. Mitsuko, her small hands clasped together, lay in the bed. Her father opened her hands and took one of them and kissed it. It was warm and alive and though she was too weak to speak, she opened her eyes and managed a smile which her father sensed more than saw because his own eyes were filled with tears.

And then Bessie came in, two nurses flanking her, holding the baby. He couldn't have weighed more than six pounds. He had Max's blond hair and Mitsuko's almond-shaped eyes.

"Why don't you have a child?" Mitsuko asked

several days later, as Bessie was preparing to leave Ram-A-Dies.

"I had a miscarriage a long time ago," Bessie said. "Now I can't have children."

"I'm sorry, Bessie. You could adopt one."

"I support several children at Henry Street but Ryan would never allow me to actually adopt a child even if I could get a judge to allow a single woman to go through the procedures. He thinks my life is too complicated as it is. He wants me home. He said so on the telephone this morning. After all these years I consider that a compliment. So I'm going."

"I'll miss you terribly, Bessie."

"And I you." Bessie bent down and kissed her. "But you've got Max. You've got your baby. And unless I'm very much mistaken, you've got your father."

Not very long after Bessie left that day, Mr. Tanaka drove back down the coast in his Oldsmobile, and, after shaking Max's hand and inquiring after his health, he went up to Mitsuko's room.

He bowed low to Townie who proceeded to leave and then he moved to the bed and looked down at his daughter and her son. All the sorrow and joy of his difficult life were reflected in his face as he bent over and ceremoniously, lovingly, kissed them both.

"I am grandpop now," Mr. Tanaka said, and Mitsuko, her eyes filling with tears, put her arms around him and brought him close.

"Thank you, *papasan*," she said and then she said no more because she was crying too hard.

*   *   *

A year later the confusion in Hollywood reached new heights. All of the surviving movie companies were scurrying around, sending ambassadors to Wall Street, trying to locate the enormous amount of capital needed to "go sound." Over three hundred million dollars were pumped into the studios and that still wasn't enough. Companies were merging, splitting, and remerging while actors and actresses were hiring voice coaches, desperately trying to learn how to talk.

Great Western's first sound feature was a musical western called *He Went Thataway*. It was an instant hit. Directed and produced by Max Meyer, it starred a newcomer named Rick West, "singing and riding and fighting his way into the hearts of millions."

Araby had finally agreed to a legal separation. Max had begun turning up at select Hollywood screenings for children with Anna and another child, a son, one who couldn't by any stretch of the imagination belong to anyone but Mitsuko and Max.

"Ram is having career problems," Araby told the press in the Severe Suite at Paramount reserved for solemn press conferences. She was dressed in a sedate black and white dress and wore a plain gold cross as her one piece of jewelry. "We both feel it's best that we part, if only for a little while . . ." She was about to take the plunge into genuine sound with a dramatic musical produced by Carleton LeMay called *Broadway Nights*.

It was completed in January, 1929, and had cost a quarter of a million dollars to make. LeMay had backed Araby with an all-star cast including a leading man imported at great expense from the Broadway musical stage.

Araby was, Townie thought, understandably nervous. The first one-hundred-percent talkie, *Lights of New York* with Helene Costello, had earned two million dollars. But two or three similar films that had followed had taken nose dives, their stars going down with them.

"It doesn't matter what my voice sounds like, you little dope," she told Townie when he tried to reassure her. "*I* know I have a perfectly adequate voice. It all depends on whether my fans think so. And the torture is that nobody's going to know until the film opens and the goddamned audience reacts."

Paramount scheduled its sneak preview of *Broadway Nights* on a wet Thursday evening. LeMay had hired Big Red, the interurban trolley that rode the tracks of the Pacific Electric System, to carry VIPs out to San Bernardino's sole movie theater. Only the conductor and LeMay knew the trolley's destination.

"If I could find out where that goddamned trolley is headed, I'd buy up every seat in the audience and fill it with extras," Araby said.

"But LeMay's not telling," Townie informed her.

"No shit." She closed her eyes. "I'm scared, Townie. I'm so goddamned scared."

"I know, Araby."

"No, you don't. You've only got your ten percent to lose. I've got my whole life." She opened her eyes and walked across the room to her dressing table. "Will Max come?"

"If you call him."

She reached for the white telephone. "Jesus, why is

everything so hard?" She asked the operator to get her Max's office and when she got through to him, she asked him, "as a special favor to me, to come tonight, Max. I need you there. You and Townie are the only friends I have in this town. That film flops, LeMay will drop me like a hot potato. I'm going to need someone to hold my hand, Max."

Max said he would come.

"What the hell are you smiling about?" she asked when she put down the receiver.

"You, Araby, darling. For one single second there I thought you were going to break down. There were tears in your voice but your eyes were as dry as Palm Springs in August."

"I don't cry," Araby said.

She was picked up in a limousine but Max and Townie rode the Big Red, sitting up front on the sofas, playing pinochle with LeMay and one of his flunkies. It took two hours to get to San Bernardino and they played cards and ate caviar every inch of the way.

"I saw *Cowboy*," LeMay said as they pulled up at the last stop, a few blocks from the theater where the orange beacon was revolving, indicating a special event. "It's a great film, Max."

"Where'd you see it?"

"Paris. It hasn't stopped playing there since it opened."

The short had begun by the time they got into the theater. Araby was pacing up and down the lobby, wearing a blond wig, smoking a cigarette in a jade holder, putting on and taking off her sunglasses. "I'm a nervous wreck," she said, kissing Townie, kissing Max. "I'm going crazy, Max."

"No, you're not," he said, putting his arm around her.

LeMay came out of the auditorium and told her to calm down. "It's time to go in," he said.

She turned dead white under her makeup. "You all go in. I'll wait it out in the lobby."

"Don't be ridiculous, Araby," LeMay said, catching hold of her arm.

She shrugged him off. "I can't stand it. If they laugh, I'll die."

"You'll be all right?" Max asked her.

"No. But there's nothing anyone can do. I have this terrible feeling. Go in. And keep your fingers crossed, for God's sake. Dear God," she said, closing her eyes behind her sunglasses, "if You let this happen for me, I'll do anything You want. I swear it."

LeMay, Max, and Townie left her and took their seats in the rows roped off for Paramount and its guests as the credits came up. It was clear to Townie that the sound track was off as soon as the music came on. "It sounds as if it's been recorded in a tuna-fish can with the lid on," he whispered to Max.

Broadway Nights had its quota of hilarious moments, of actors talking into vases or birdcages where the mikes were hidden, of absurd Hollywood dialogue. It was the story of a flapper lured to Broadway, getting a part in the second chorus, seduced and abandoned by the callous director. In the last reel, the seventh, she goes home to the all-American town where she grew up, asking for and receiving forgiveness from the farmer who remained faithful to her.

LeMay knew Araby was always at her best when she didn't have to feign an emotion she had never felt and devoted most of the film to her Broadway debut in which the central emotion was ambition.

Ambition she knows, Townie thought. As he watched, he thought she sang well enough, and even managed to get through the dance numbers with a surprising grace.

The last scene revealed a contented Araby washing dishes after the evening meal in the kitchen of the farmhouse. She absently turns on the radio, the sight of which drew gasps from the Paramount clique. Radios were considered movies' greatest competitor and were, for a time, verboten in most films lest the public be influenced to go out and buy one and stay home and listen to it.

LeMay showed a certain amount of bravery in using one. As Araby tunes it in, a song from some faraway station comes across the airwave and into her home. It is the song she sang when, as a half-nude chorine, she paraded up and down the Broadway stage.

Her voice, despite the faulty sound equipment, held a note of pathos that Townie, personally, found extremely effective.

> *"Broadway nights are calling me.*
> *Broadway lights reminding me.*
> *Champagne and bubbles*
> *dissolve your troubles*
> *all on a Broadway night."*

The farmer came into the kitchen at that moment, Araby turned off the radio and put her arms around him for the final dissolve.

The lights took a moment or two to go up and, for one split second, there was silence. Then a kid in a tennis sweater stood up on his chair, stuck out his tongue, and gave out with an enormously loud raspberry, followed by a series of boos.

Townie turned and saw Araby grasping for the door. Max began to get up, to go to her, when the booer was pulled down into his seat. The rest of the audience was standing, cheering, screaming for Araby Moore.

LeMay ran out and found her, and a few minutes later she appeared on the stage, without her wig. She thanked everyone in a pretty, calm, and unemotional speech. She left the stage as the audience worked itself into a crowd frenzy, calling her name over and over again.

Afterward Araby was nowhere to be found. LeMay looked at his watch and smiled. "I'll give you any kind of odds that she's on her way to a rendezvous with her latest Mexican gardener and his lover. Araby usually celebrates major victories with a low-keyed sandwich fuck."

Max led the way to the trolley but sat toward the rear, by himself, on the way back to Hollywood. Everyone else was toasting the absent Araby. As the trolley neared the Paramount lot, Townie went and sat next to Max.

"What's the matter?" he asked.

"I've been thinking."

"About what?"

"About whether we can get LeMay to put up the money for an all-talkie version of *Cowboy*."

"LeMay? What about Ryan?"

"Ryan's already turned me down. He said he was only interested in making money, not losing it. He wants me to keep making oaters. He told me to leave the art to the artists."

BOOK FOUR

AFTERNOON

CHAPTER 1

After they had been married for ten years, Nick and Kay gave up hope. The doctors, the medical experts, had said it was no one's fault. They simply could not have children. Nick reacted in much the same way Ryan had when Bessie suggested adoption. He didn't want, he said, someone else's mistake. He was bitter. He wanted a son.

Kay was bored with her life but she wasn't bored with Nick.

After Cuba, after Nancy had been killed, he stopped taking her with him on his "cementing relationship" trips. When he was away, Kay found herself spending her evenings at B's Other Place with Bessie.

"So we can't have kids," Bessie told her, hugging her. "We've got other comforts. Our men. Our family. One another." And that was true. The two women had grown fond of one another despite their differences in age, background, style. They both had a need for female affection.

Bessie also had, Kay thought, her career, her continuing interest in the Henry Street Settlement, her friends in high places whom she continually pressured into doing something for the poor.

All I have, Kay thought, is Nick.

For a time Bumps Bogan thought that she should also have him.

He had gotten his name at an early age from the state in which his victims were found. He had graduated from the blackjack to the knife to a snub-nosed revolver. He thought it was time he graduated to a better class of woman.

"Nick leaves you alone a lot," he said to Kay one afternoon while she was waiting for Bessie to appear at the club.

"Absence makes the heart grow fonder," she said, not liking the way he was looking at her.

"Out of sight, out of mind," Bumps countered but then Bessie came out from her office and Bumps moved away.

"I told Ryan that that bum was not allowed in here," Bessie said, taking Kay's arm. "I don't trust that character."

Bumps was a full captain in the Ryan hierarchy now, still in charge of the numbers, in keeping the competition from encroaching on Ryan's territory. Of all Ryan's interests the numbers—or the combinations, as he occasionally called them—was the one of which Ryan was the most protective, most ready to go to war over.

"My mother liked the numbers," he enjoyed telling Bessie. "They couldn't be all bad."

"They're bad enough. There's too many gangsters involved. Too many little men like Bumps Bogan. And the money comes from the pockets of the poor. Let it go, Ryan."

"No, the combinations give Bumps something to gnaw on. Without them, he might get dangerous."

It was when Nick was in Canada, arranging for a large shipment of French and English liquor, that Bumps Bogan again approached Kay at B's Other Place. He asked her to dance. She didn't have time to say no. He took her wrist and pulled her out onto the dance floor, holding her too close, pushing himself up against her as he moved her around the room.

"Is that a pencil in your pocket?" she asked him, trying to put some distance between them. He smelled mean, like a bottle of cheap whiskey.

"No," Bumps said, his hand slipping down her back, "it's a quill pen. When you going to let me dip it in?"

Ryan was at his usual table on the third tier. He blinked his seemingly lashless eyes. A big man came and cut in on Kay and Bumps; and then another big man was talking earnestly to Bumps as he walked him to the rear door.

From that moment on Bumps politely nodded when he saw Kay, keeping his distance. But there was a look in his eyes that said, wait.

Ryan, of course, had other interests besides numbers and bootlegging. In 1931, while people Kay had once known were jumping off tall buildings, Ryan was opening offices in them. Occasionally, because he liked the way she looked, he would take Kay around, to his offices, to lunch at one of his clubs.

She knew Nick hated him but she found Ryan interesting, if not altogether likable. On the surface he appeared to be a polished, well-educated product of Old New York, not dissimilar to her father. But under the cultivated veneer was something far less civilized, more basic and dangerous. Kay knew what kept Bessie so enthralled.

Besides being the kingpin of the bootlegging industry in America and head of the numbers in New York and chairman of the corporation which owned the controlling interest in Great Western films, Ryan had bought into dozens of other businesses. He owned two hotels in Atlantic City, a score of speakeasys, the largest brewery in New York State, two gambling casinos in Miami plus racetracks in New Jersey, Illinois, and Montreal. He also owned pieces of the Brooklyn Dodgers Baseball Club and the New York and the American hockey clubs which last numbered New York's mayor, James J. Walker, among its board of directors.

Jimmy Walker and Ryan were friends, that dapper man appearing at B's four and sometimes five nights a week. He was invariably invited to sit at Bessie's table. He was never, however, invited to Grace Ryan's home in Oyster Bay.

Ryan liked to turn up at her afternoon parties with Nick and Kay in tow. Grace Ryan was aging badly. She was growing stouter and grayer and more forgetful though she always made it a point to ask Kay after her sister-in-law, Miss Meyer. When she stood next to Ryan, they seemed at least a generation apart. She deferred to him in the way a poor, discarded mother acts toward her rich and successful son.

Kay usually knew at least one of the women who stood around the drawing room in Oyster Bay, drinking grape juice and tea, attempting sedate chic, achieving a flat, even dullness. A few of the guests would talk to her; others would smile and look away, at the Burne-Jones's and Alma Tadema's with which Grace Ryan covered her massive, dun-colored walls.

Kay was clearly a bad hat in Grace Ryan's guests' eyes, a jazz baby who had gone too far and too fast, quite possibly Ryan's young mistress. "That man," said Father Heart, Grace Ryan's confessor, "would go to any lengths to embarrass his wife. And she, she's a saint, the Lord bless her."

Nick would stand at the arched entrance to the vast room, sipping his grape juice, looking nervous and unhappy.

"Why do we bother?" Kay asked him.

"I thought you got a kick out of seeing the kind of people you grew up with. You're not meeting such classy types at the joints we . . ."

Kay laughed.

"What's so goddamned funny?" he wanted to know.

"If you had any idea how much I hate them. They're all so boring, so smug and insular. Why do you think I married you?" She kissed him. "So I could get away from all that."

"Thanks," Nick said, putting his arms around her, holding her close. "I thought for a minute that you married me because you loved me."

She looked into those steely blue eyes. "If you only knew how much."

When he wasn't traveling, they'd spend the night moving from speak to speak, ending up at five in the morning in the apartment on Central Park West. They'd make love, sleep half the day, and then walk to Bessie's for a meal, for her all-embracing family love.

"It's not much fun when you're off on some caper," Kay told him.

"I wish the hell you wouldn't talk like that," Nick said. "You sound like someone's moll."

"Aren't I?"

"No. You're my wife, you dumb Dora."

Some of her old friends had drifted back to New York from Paris. After the Crash the remittance men were no longer receiving their remittances. But their idea of spending an afternoon was to drink it away in speaks in the West Fifties. However lonesome she was, Kay knew she didn't want to turn into a drunk again.

Frances Ellington took a small apartment on lower Fifth Avenue during the summer of 1931. She told Kay she had had to get away from Key West before her brain atrophied, that she had just been paid more money than she would have thought possible from Scribner's for her new novel.

Nick liked Frances in the same way Kay did. She had a wonderfully free, no-nonsense way with a beer bottle which instantly endeared her to him. She reminded Kay of Colette and she wished she had her bravery.

Bessie instantly made Frances one of the family, inviting her to the daily meal, conferring with her over Jake and Jake's children.

Occasionally, when Nick was out of town, Frances would take Kay with her to the Algonquin, where Frances liked to trade literary wisecracks with Kaufman and Dorothy Parker. One afternoon Fatty Freeman turned up, looking distinguished and not nearly as thin as he had when Kay knew him in Paris; but still, thin enough.

"The beautiful Madam Hull," he said, his face breaking into an engaging smile. "I thought I'd never see you again."

"Madam Meyer now, if you please."

"You married that gangster?"

"Careful: he'll rub you out."

"And what else do you do besides sitting by the fire at night, polishing his pistol?"

"Polishing Nick's pistol is a full-time job, Fatty."

Frances liked him and the three of them began lunching together. The Crash had diminished his fortune, he allowed when he picked up the check for all of them; but he still had a few million to go before he was broke.

Toward the end of the summer, on a hot Tuesday afternoon, when the New York air was as thick and as still as polluted water, while Frances was attempting to decide whether or not to return to Key West, Fatty asked Frances if she knew of anyone who wanted a job as an editorial assistant on a new fashion magazine.

"What's an editorial assistant do?" Kay asked, watching Robert Benchley act out an elaborate charade in the center of the Algonquin lobby.

"Not much," Fatty answered. "A lot of everything. The job's at *Vanity*, a new magazine I'm trying to get off the ground."

"And you immediately thought of me," Frances said, laughing.

"Actually I immediately thought of Kay. And you can take the red out of your violet eyes, my dear. I simply thought you might need something to keep your mind busy. Have a drink with the editor and talk about it. What have you got to lose?"

"A pistol."

Nick returned from the Canadian side of Niagara Falls late that night after delivering a caravan of trucks carrying a hundred cases of whiskey. As usual he and Kay spent the morning in bed, making love, and the afternoon eating. "The food in Canada," Nick said, "is almost as bad as the food in France."

As they were on their way to the eleven P.M. show at B's, the telephone rang. It was Red Schenk. He had somehow attached himself to Nick. Red Schenk was a six foot four escapee from the New Jersey State Penitentiary in Rahway, New Jersey (armed robbery, ten years to life) and if he adored Nick, he worshiped Kay.

"You want to talk to Nick, Red?" Kay asked, after she had inquired, formally, about his health and he had reciprocated.

"Naw. Just tell him we're all set. I got the box man."

She gave him Red's message as Nick carefully locked the door of their apartment. "What's a box man?" she asked as they stepped into the elevator.

"None of your business." He looked nervous and happy at the same time and Kay decided to put off telling him about her job until she found out what was going on.

"This is it," Nick said as they walked into B's Other Place which was crowded with people waiting for tables.

"This is what?" she asked as the headwaiter led them around the waiting line.

"This is the night when I make my own personal declaration of independence."

"Nicky . . ."

"Sit down and watch the show. I'm going to have a little talk with your friend, Ryan."

She went with the headwaiter to the family table. Bessie smiled, kissed her, and turned her attention back to the stage. The headliner was Legs Diamond's girl friend of the moment, Nerida, a nobley built woman who danced with a ten-foot python to Ravel's *Bolero.*

Kay tried to watch as the python slid around Nerida's magnificent breasts and down around her rump and then, in time to the sinuous music, in between her thick, firm legs. Nerida seemed to be in genuine ecstasy.

Kay could see Bumps Bogan standing at the far right on the stage wing. Legs Diamond was sitting at a front row table. Both were watching Nerida with a certain pride of ownership in their eyes. The bouncers and the waiters were looking at one another, waiting for trouble. Kay said something to Bessie about Bumps and Legs and Nerida but Bessie took her hand and patted it. "Not in my club," she said. "They wouldn't dare."

Kay tried to feel comforted but she wasn't really worried about Bumps and Legs shooting it out over the tourists' heads. Her mind was occupied with Red Schenk's box man, with Nick's declaration of independence, with his meeting with Ryan.

* * *

"You wanted to see me, Nick?" Ryan was sitting in a leather chair behind Bessie's desk. "Sit down, Nick. Sit down."

"I like to keep on my feet." Nick propped himself up against the mirrored wall. The two men were reflected in it as in a nineteenth-century period drawing. Both wore dinner suits, stiff white collars, patent leather shoes. Ryan, with his sandy blondness, seemed especially at ease, a native son. Nick, sleek and black haired and smooth featured, looked indefinably alien, non-American.

"How can I help you?" Ryan asked.

"I'm resigning, Ryan. Quitting."

Ryan blinked but showed no other sign of surprise.

"I'm going out on my own, Ryan. I'm going to be my own boss."

"How is that, Nick?"

Nick thought for a moment and then he told Ryan. He knew Ryan wouldn't stop him.

"I don't like it, Nick. You're going into territory that's already charted. I don't want a war with Capone or anyone else."

"I told you: I'm doing this on my own. You don't have to worry. There won't be any war."

"If you go ahead, Nick, you'll never be able to come back to work for me. You realize that? There won't be any job for you in New York or anywhere around here."

"I'll find a job when I get back. I'll have the capital to invent one."

"I'm warning you, Nick," Ryan said, his eyes blinking a little faster, "I don't care if you are Bessie's brother. Don't plan on playing my turf."

"Sure," Nick said and turned to go.

"Why do you hate me so much?" Ryan asked.

Nick turned back and looked at his sister's lover. "You use everything," he said. "You take a person and you bleed them dry and then you get rid of them."

"I've never used Bessie."

"Bullshit. You used her from the day you met her. She's your lifeline. She's your strength. You can do anything with Bessie behind you. Look at what you've done to us, her brothers. Jake's a third-rate rumrunner in Key West. Max is running a movie studio fronting for your hootch operation on the Coast.

"And me? I'm still a punk hoodlum, taking orders from bloodsuckers like you and Bogan. Until tonight, that is. Tonight I'm breaking with you, Ryan. I've been waiting for the past ten years to do it and now I've got the right opportunity.

"Remember, Ryan: this works both ways. I don't care if you are Bessie's lover. Fuck this up for me and I'll cement this relationship right into the East River."

He left, carefully shutting the door behind him. Ryan sat in the leather chair for a few moments, his eyes looking at his reflection in the blue mirror, but not seeing it.

Nick sat down at the family table as Bessie, in a dark red gown, diamonds in her hair, came on stage and began to sing. Of late she had given up the novelty songs and begun to sing torchers.

"Where's Legs and Bogan?" Nick asked Kay.

"They both disappeared after Nerida's act. To everyone's relief. What happened to you? You're sweating. You never sweat. Are you ill?"

"Shut up and listen to Bessie." He took her hand and held it tight as his sister began to sing.

> "Unrequited love
> That's what it's all about
> Unrequited love.
> My man is always out.
> He's got a wife and kids and family
> ... and I'm up a tree with
> Unrequited love.

> "Lord knows I shouldn't have fallen
> I should have run as fast as I could.
> Lord know I would send him packing.
> If only I could.

> "Unrequited love.
> That's why I wait here in this dreary little room.
> Telling myself I've sealed my own doom.
> Because he's gone again
> and I'm alone again
> with unrequited love ... unrequited love ...
>   unrequited love."

"Let's go," Nick said, standing up as everyone else was clapping.

"What's the matter with you?" Kay asked when they were standing under the marquee.

"We'll talk about it later. I want to celebrate."

"You don't look as if you want to celebrate. You look as if you want to kill someone."

They went to the Stork Club on Fifty-eighth Street and had a drink with Billingsley and then they walked down to Fifty-fourth Street to watch Helen Morgan sit on a white piano and listen to her sob out, "He's Just My Bill."

Bumps Bogan was there, his eyes, like round pennies, on Kay, one arm around Nerida's voluptuous white shoulders. She wondered what had happened to Legs Diamond, what drug Bumps was on, and how dangerous he was. She told Nick she wanted to go, she wanted to talk, and they left. As they walked by his table, she realized Bumps Bogan's doped eyes weren't on her, they were following Nick.

"Let's go see the Killer at the Five O'Clock Club," he said when they were on the street.

"You go see the Killer," she said. "I want to go home."

"Calm down, will you?" He held her in the taxi and she cried all over his dinner jacket.

"What's the matter with you?" he asked when they were in the apartment.

"I got a job today on a magazine called *Vanity*. I'm an assistant editor." She sat down on the bed in her long black satin gown and waited.

"You got it or you just think you got it?"

"I got it."

"What do you want it for?" he asked, undoing his tie, taking off his dress shirt, carefully storing his platinum studs in his jewelry case.

"I'm bored when you're not here, Nicky. I need something."

"So what're you asking me for? Go ahead. Try it. See how you like being a member of the working class." He went to her and took her in his arms. "I know you haven't been all that happy, lately."

She looked at him. Nothing about that hard face or that tough body would give anyone a clue he might be sensitive to a woman's unhappiness. She told him so.

"Yeah, I'm a shrinking violet. Anyway, you're going to need something to keep you busy."

"How so?"

"I resigned from Ryan's employ tonight. I'm going out on my own with Red Schenk. We're going on our first business trip together."

"For how long?"

"Six months and you can't come because you'd stick out like a sore thumb in Kansas City, Kansas, and I don't want you telling anyone, not even Bessie."

Nick left on the morning she began work. She expected to miss him but she didn't except at night. During her days *Vanity* expected and got a great deal of work for its twenty dollars.

On weekends she went to Bessie's apartment for late brunches. But she kept away from the club, from the chicken farmers, from Bumps Bogan. Neither Bessie nor Ryan mentioned Nick's absence.

In September, 1932, Nick Meyer, Red Schenk, Kimmel Smith—the box man—and an electrician named Fish Dinelli rendezvoused in Chicago at the Colosimo Café.

Capone sat down at their table and made it known

in that shorthand language gangsters employed that he wasn't happy one of Ryan's lieutenants was in Capone country.

"Ain't you heard, Al?" Red asked. "Nick doesn't work for Ryan no more."

Nick made it clear that he was working for himself, that he was not acting as one of Ryan's relation cementers, that he had no intention of doing business in Capone's territory.

The next morning the four of them left Chicago in a La Salle touring car, driving to the outskirts of Kansas City where they split up. Nick and Red took rooms in a Southside boardinghouse, the others finding beds around the city in cheap hotels.

Nick didn't like the boardinghouse, having to share the bathroom, having to pass the cabbage at the long, linoleum cloth-covered table in the narrow dining room. Red didn't seem to mind.

They had several frustrating meetings with a Spanish fence, El Jefe, who billed himself as a Midwestern Ryan. "I ever tell you about the time Ryan came to my place for dinner?" he asked Nick several times.

He owned a chili parlor with a speak in the back and would insist that Nick and Red—both strictly meat and potato men—eat his chili with him. Nick picked all the green peppers out of it and even then suffered during the night.

Finally, after a half dozen of those meals, El Jefe agreed to take all the whiskey they could get their hands on at forty-five percent of the market. "But it has to be the real stuff," El Jefe cautioned. "None of your bathtub preparations."

Nick assured him that it would be the real stuff.

After shaking hands with El Jefe, Nick began to work. He spent a month studying the target, a government whiskey warehouse that covered fifteen acres and that had withstood three documented assaults by various hijackers.

"None of them had the organization," Nick told Red. "That's one secret Ryan taught me: organization."

He spent three hundred dollars convincing a man who unloaded barrels at the warehouse to develop a chronic and disabling illness and to pass his job on to Nick.

"You must hate it," Red said each night when he came back to the Southside boardinghouse.

"Wrong. This is the part I like. It's hard work, unloading those goddamned barrels. I'm getting rid of all the flab and I'm learning a few things in the meanwhile." Ryan had also taught him to be thorough.

One of the things Nick learned was that the elevators—which took the barrels confiscated by the government from bootleggers and illegal distillers to the basement storage rooms—were run by electricity. Each night the guards would disconnect the elevators, turning off the electricity, as a security precaution.

The government, Nick found, employed a full-time staff as another security precaution. The nighttime security staff consisted of three armed guards, two watchmen, a maintenance man, and a checker.

Red Schenk was daunted. "We should've taken it over in '28 when they couldn't afford so many men. You know, Nick, this ain't a game for some gentleman *gonif*. It's going to be like moving against Fort Knox."

"No, it's not."

"Why not?"

"Because you can't buy the guards at Fort Knox."

"Oh." Red helped himself to one of the few luxuries Nick allowed himself in his boardinghouse room: a Cuban cigar. "How much?"

"Fifty grand each."

"You got that kind of money?"

"Yeah, I got that kind of money."

The guards could only allow policemen in uniform into the warehouse after six P.M. The director was explicit about that rule when he hired them. "I don't care if my mother's here after six. You don't let her in unless she's a policeman *in uniform*."

By the time Nick felt they were ready to strike, it was late February but the uniforms Nick had gotten were summer issue.

"I'm freezing my ass off," Red Schenk complained. It was a Friday night with a quarter moon and a slim possibility of snow. One of the guards called in sick. He had "developed" a bad cold over the week and had gotten a doctor to say he had to be in bed. The other two guards opened the gates. Red "bashed them up a little" to make it look authentic, tied and gagged them, and left them in the main office, sitting upright in the director's visitors' chairs.

At the same time fifty men Nick had hired for the job were coming in the four gates they had managed to open. Kimmel Smith had arranged for the trucks, fifteen of them, each costing three thousand dollars plus one thousand each for the drivers.

Red handed each of them a map of the area and instructions for reaching their loading zone. He and Nick then went to the main entrance to meet with the four mobsters they had imported from New York.

The mobsters, big men, were to walk the night watchmen through their rounds, making certain each one went through his usual routine, punching his clock at the right times. Nick gave each of the mobsters a list and watched them move off, their guns in the watchmen's backs.

"And don't kill anybody unless you absolutely have to," he shouted after them. They all had, he knew, trigger fingers.

As the trucks began rolling into the main loading area, Kimmel Smith took the keys he had taken off the head watchman and walked down the emergency staircase to the basement with Fish Dinelli. While Fish reconnected the electricity and got the elevators working, Kimmel blew the steel vault door into a great many pieces with the "soup" he was never without.

Nick got the men into the elevators and they went down to the basement and through the doorway Fish had blasted into the warehouse. It was a bootleggers' dream: fifty-gallon barrels of imported whiskey in rows as far as the eye could see.

It took them three hours and twenty minutes to load up the trucks. Nick figured that he could have used another fleet and fifty more men.

They ended up with twenty thousand barrels, all of which were in El Jefe's warehouses before the weak winter sun was up and the first snowflakes began to fall.

* * *

"Congratulations," Ryan said the first time they met over supper at Bessie's apartment. "You've pulled off quite a coup."

"Thanks," Nick said, looking away.

"What're you planning on doing now, Nick?"

"I'm going to study my options," he said, and there was a silence around the table even Bessie found difficult to break.

"And you," Nick told Kay that night. "You quit your job. It was terrific while I was away but now I want you around. Tell them what they can do with their twenty bucks a week."

She was making forty and she had gotten her first by-line over an interview with Marlene Dietrich that Frances had arranged. She had sat with Dietrich for four hours in a friend's apartment on Park Avenue and she had spent almost a month writing the article and then rewriting it. She only handed it in because Frances said if she waited any longer, if she made it any more perfect, they would have to engrave it on her tombstone.

The powers that be at *Vanity* were pleased. Dietrich didn't give many interviews. It was well written with exactly the right balance of hard reporting and slightly acid supposition that made *Vanity* such a popular magazine among women with money. Kay not only got her raise, she was promoted to associate editor.

She managed to talk Nick into letting her keep her job. They continued to go to Bessie's for meals and to B's Other Place for entertainment. Ryan was rarely without Bumps Bogan at his side. And now that Nick was a millionaire bootlegger in his own right, considering his options, he never went anywhere without Red Schenk at *his* side.

CHAPTER 2

Early in 1933, Carleton LeMay wrote to an agent named Nan Orshevsky, inquiring if a novel one of her writers had written were available. The novel was called *Neon Lights* and its author was Frances Ellington.

"Available for what?" Nan Orshevsky cabled back.

Therein began a complicated cross-country correspondence ending in mutual disappointment and some despair, one year later.

During that year, however, hopes were raised, excitement was generated, and for one glorious moment, Frances Ellington thought she was going to allow herself to "sell out to Hollywood."

"This is much too complex," Frances told Nan over luncheon at B's Other Place. "If this LeMay character wants to meet with me, why don't you tell him to come to New York?"

"He says he can't come to New York," Nan said, spearing a black olive with her fork and popping it into her mouth.

"Why? Is he wanted here?"

"He has a counteroffer," Nan said, sucking the olive pit with gusto. "He has to be in Miami Beach and he thought you might like to rendezvous there. He's offered to pay all your expenses which I think is damned generous of him, Frances. Do you want that other black olive?"

"It's all yours."

Frances thought about LeMay's Miami Beach offer for a day and then called Nan and said she would "rendzevous" with LeMay in Key West at the Casa Marina Hotel, all expenses to be paid by him.

To her surprise he agreed. She wondered if she hadn't made a mistake. "I don't really want to see my heroine twelve feet high on a movie screen," she told Kay Meyer. "Carmela belongs between the very attractive covers of Scribner's book."

"What does your agent think?" Kay asked.

"That peroxide-blond Bronx bagel baby? She doesn't think. She only reacts when she sees or smells money. Nan Orshevsky has as much right being a literary agent as I have being an aviatrix."

"LeMay really wants that property, Frances," Nan said a few days later. "He really and truly wants it, I can taste how bad he wants it."

By that time Frances had learned something of his reputation, had heard that those who knew called Carleton LeMay Carleton DisMay. But the idea of "Hollywood" was, she admitted, attractive, like a torrid night in hell; and, though she didn't admit it, she did want an excuse to visit Key West.

In mid-February Frances Ellington checked into the Casa Marina, another endearing Flagler folly finished in the early twenties, which looked as if it had been transplanted, intact, from Beverly Hills. It featured a miniature golf course and offered skeet shooting for its guests who skeeted. After eight P.M. a live orchestra played rumbas for indoor-outdoor dancing.

A great many Hollywood, Broadway, and literary people stayed there. It was comfortable as well as luxurious and a nice, out-of-the-way place to rest after a face-lift or a blast of the wrong sort of publicity. No self-respecting Conch would go near the place which was the reason Frances had chosen it. She was now, she told herself, a hard and handsome New York lady, a successful novelist, wooed by the Movies, dressed by France.

She arrived a few days early and immediately hired one of the few cars left on the island. Poor Willy was driving it and she asked him to take her around, to start with the house on Pinder Lane. She wanted to see Blondell.

The black woman came running out of the house pulling off her apron and hugging and kissing Frances with great gusto. She told Frances Coffee was up in Miami, visiting her stepbrother. They went inside and shared a Coke but Blondell wouldn't say much about Jake without prompting; Frances wasn't prompting.

"That Coffee's just going to be sick that she missed you, Miss Frances."

"How is she?"

"Too pretty and spoiled for her own good, you ask me." Then Blondell's face broke into a huge smile. "But she's a nice child *when* she wants to be."

Poor Willy opened the back door of the De Soto and Frances told him to take her over to Duval Street, to drive around. She wanted to see what had

happened to the island town she had left five years
before.

For Frances Ellington the Depression was a curious, selective phenomenon. In New York she knew
there were men selling apples on Fifth Avenue for
nickels but somehow she never really saw one. And
she knew or had heard of people who had committed
suicide but their deaths somehow seemed unreal to
her. She never actually saw a bread line or a soup
kitchen though the papers were full of them. Bessie
would tell her stories of the poor's terrible depriva-
tion and she gave what she could to a score of causes.
But everyone she knew personally had some money
and she had some money and Hard Times was an intellectual idea she never quite grasped.

Until she reached Key West. She had expected to
find the sleepy town she had left. She hadn't expected
to find it had died. Half the shops on Duval were
boarded up and the other half wore yellowed "To
Let" signs. The only work in town, Poor Willy told
her, was at the pineapple canning factory down at
the foot of James Street and that was only when the
pineapples came in from Cuba.

"Jus' about everyone else," Poor Willy said in the
longest sentence of his life, "is on the dole." The
Civil Works Administration hadn't gotten off the
ground then and even the most loyal Conchs were
thinking of going North.

Of the eighteen thousand people who had lived in
Key West when Frances had left it, only twelve thousand remained. The look of defeat on the tired faces
of the men sitting on the dock at the end of Simonton
Street, fishing poles held loosely in their hands, was

the most visual, most personal expression of the times she had seen.

She told Poor Willy to take her by Devon House and asked him why he wasn't driving for the Wheelers and the senator. He didn't say anything; he only shook his lean, elongated head and turned up White-head. The house looked as it always had, its fine garden a tribute to the series of cisterns the senator had designed to keep the grounds eternally verdant; like some far-seeing cemetery director, Frances thought.

She sat in the back of the De Soto for some minutes, looking at the house, thinking of other times. Then she told Poor Willy to take her to the Jefferson. She had seen Jake four times in the past five years, always at Bessie's birthday parties. They had danced but they hadn't really talked and at Bessie's last yearly event he had been absent.

"His son," Ryan explained, "has a touch of the flu. Jake thought he had best go to Miami and stay with him."

The Jefferson, she was relieved to see, hadn't changed except for the sign above its café which now read "Bucket of Blood Saloon." Luis San Obispo was sweeping up the sidewalk in front of it when the De Soto pulled up. He greeted her as if they had seen each other the day before. *"Sí,"* he said in what he liked to think of as his pure, Castilian accent, *"el señor es aquí."*

She climbed the familiar steps and found *el señor* reclining on the fainting couch, uncharacteristically reading, a cheroot between his lips, a Cuban beer on the table at his side.

"You haven't changed, Jake," she said, going into the room, thinking that he was thinner, that the smell of that room was different: lacier, more perfumed.

"Want a beer, Frances?"

"Don't mind if I do, Jake." He banged his foot on the floor and a moment later Luis San Obispo appeared with a beer.

"Nice to see the *señora*," Luis said, acknowledging her half-decade absence, bowing himself out.

Frances took a long swallow from the beer bottle. "Thank God I never have to drink out of one of those bloody pop bottles again." Three-point-two beer had recently been legalized.

Jake laughed.

"How do I look, Jake?"

"Damned good, Frances."

"I thought you'd never tell me."

They studied each other for a while, drinking their beers. "You broke?" she asked.

"I wouldn't say broke."

It took three more beers and a good half hour to pry it out of him and even then she had to fill in the gaps. All his bootlegging money had been in the Florida State National which had the distinction of being the fifth bank in the country to fail. Bootlegging was, Jake said, making a joke, on its last legs because no one had the money to drink and repeal was right around the corner, anyway.

"Besides," he said, "I got a little tired of being Ryan's boy in Key West." He banged his foot on the floor, signaling Luis to bring another beer. "Anyway, I'm land rich."

"Yeah?"

"Yeah. I own a helluva lot of Key West."

Ryan, who had, at the end, owned the ferries, sold them. "He wants me to come up to New York. So does Nick. They both been down here, trying to get me to move. What the hell am I going to do in New York? Ride shotgun for one of them?

"Max has been here, too. Half a dozen times. 'I hate to see you like this,' he told me. 'Like what?' I said. He wants me to come to California, to work 'with' him. They don't understand: I don't need charity. I don't want to leave Key West. I got my son up in Miami and Coffee's here and"—he looked at the louvered door that led to his bedroom—"other ties that bind."

The door opened at that moment and Virginia came out of the bedroom. "We like it here, Cousin Frances. It suits us, doesn't it, Jake?"

Her hair had finally been bobbed. She looked thin and pale in her flowered shorts and halter. She was wearing high-heeled mules, too little rouge, too much pink lipstick, and a cheap metal bangle bracelet. It had been her perfume that Frances had smelled. It was a fake floral scent and it fought the frangipani crawling up the veranda.

Virginia crossed the room, took a bottle of Canadian Club from its shelf, and poured herself half a tumbler. She sat down next to Jake on the fainting couch, taking his hand, looking at it, letting it go. She crossed her long and perfect legs and stared at Frances.

"You think I'm a twenty-eight-cent whore, don't you, Frances?" She drank a quarter of the whiskey. "I

probably would be if it weren't for Jake." She closed
her haunted eyes. "Sometimes I hate myself so much,
I want to die. I sent my two daughters away, Frances.
Up to my sister in Tavernier. Claude comes here on
Sundays and I get all dressed up and put on a hat
and we go visit them, take them to church. Then we
come back to KW and Claude goes off to get drunk
and I come on up here to Jake's rooms and he comforts me. It's some goddamned life, isn't it, Frances?"
She opened her eyes and finished her CC.

"Listen," Frances said. "Maybe you'd like to come
up to the Casa Marina for dinner one night." She
knew she was being ridiculous, retreating into her
mother's hostess pose, an everything-will-be-all-right-if-
we-only-follow-the-conventions attitude. Jake laughed
but Virginia looked up.

"Really?" she asked.

"Of course. Let's do it tomorrow night before this
man I have to deal with arrives. We'll have a little
celebration and I'll charge it all to him."

"God," Virginia said, standing up, taking the
bangle bracelet off her wrist. "I'll have to find something to wear." She opened the door to the bedroom
and went in. Frances could see her standing in front
of the mirror she herself had stood at so long ago
when their positions had been somewhat reversed.
"We can go, can't we, Jake?" she called out, furiously
combing her hair with her fingers. "Can't we?"

"Sure," Jake said. "Sure we can, honey."

Frances said good-bye but she wasn't certain that
Virginia had heard her. Jake pulled an undershirt
over his head and walked out onto the balcony with
Frances. "Where you going, Jake?"

"I'll be right back, honey."

He went with Frances down the stairs, the book he had been reading in his right hand, his left hand on her arm. Though she was in a state she thought of as very much like shock—"Jesus, what has happened to that girl?"—the electricity of Jake's touch, of his nearness, still held a few high-voltage amps in it for her.

He got into the back seat of the De Soto with her. "Remember that cream-colored Cadillac, Frances?" he asked, laying his head back against the worn upholstery. "That was some car."

"What's happened to Virginia, Jake?"

He took a deep breath. "A month before the Crash, she came to the Jefferson to collect her father, to take him home to Devon House for dinner. We were sleeping together by then but she was still treating me like the clerk in Leon Shuster's Store. Claude was already drunk most of the time by then.

"The senator was in his rooms next to mine. He had been spending most of the past week there. He hadn't told anyone but he had received a letter from an old pal of his. The writer said that he wanted to give the senator fair warning, that he was only out to protect the senator's interests. That the senator was about to be arrested and put on trial. That there was going to be a hell of a lot of publicity, general unpleasantness for everyone. The writer said that maybe it would be for the best if the senator went away for a while. Disappeared for a time. Like forever. If they couldn't serve him with the subpoena, there wouldn't be a scandal and his daughter and granddaughters and his good name wouldn't have to suffer.

"The feds had finally gotten around to investigating the old Belle Distillery business, that time when the senator was acting director of Internal Revenue and had signed all those Permits of Withdrawal. The permits had turned up and there was only the one name on them, the senator's. It was pretty damned certain, the letter writer said, that the senator was going to go to jail. Someone had to take the rap and the other boys had been too smart.

"Senator Devon was almost seventy years old and too fat and too used to the good life. He knew jail would kill him and he didn't want to die in jail.

"He spent the afternoon with his little Cuban girl, the mortician's daughter, who by now isn't such a little girl, and then he sent her home with a thousand dollars in her purse. Whatever else might be said about him, he was a generous old bastard.

"Then he had a couple of shots of bourbon, took a rope, and swung it around a beam and hanged himself.

"But maybe he had too many shots or maybe he was tired from his last session with his little Cuban girl because he messed up. He didn't die right away. When Virginia found him, he was still gasping and fighting, dancing in midair.

"By the time I got him down, he was finally dead but he wasn't pretty. His face was all blue and his tongue was sticking out and his little eyes were wide open." Jake looked up toward the senator's rooms and took another deep breath. "I got the coroner, Old Goody, and the doc, Jimmy Clark, to issue heart-attack certificates and between us, we got him buried the next day. Most of the Conchs know what happened but they ain't talking and naturally we're not either.

"Your cousin Virginia got a lot of nice telegrams. One from the President. One from his old pal, Ryan."

"He wrote the letter, of course," Frances said.

"Ryan didn't sign it but he sure as hell wrote it. He wasn't taking any chances on the senator getting up in front of a congressional jury and telling all. If he hadn't committed suicide, Ryan would have had him shot."

Jake looked out of the DeSoto window at the faultless blue sky but Frances wasn't finished. She wanted to know everything. "He didn't leave any money," Jake told her. "He'd been in debt for years and Claude hasn't helped. They got a little money when your aunt died and they sold Rokeby but that wasn't nearly enough. They had to sell Devon House, too, and what they got for that just about took care of the bills. Claude went over to Havana for a two-month toot and by the time he got back, Virginia had taken the girls up to her sister's and had moved in with me at the Jefferson."

"And what about you?"

"I manage. Moishe's doing all right, working at one of Ryan's casinos in Miami and he's paying for my son's military-academy education. I don't like the academy and I don't like Moishe paying but David's Esther's kid, too.

"Anyway I got Coffee. She's the one pure joy in my life, Frances. I'd do anything for that kid. Shame you're going to miss her. She's the spittin' image of her mother. I keep her and Blondell and the Pinder

Lane house going thanks to the Bucket of Blood." He pointed to the Jefferson's saloon.

"That's what I do now, Frances. I'm a speakeasy owner. Mr. Hemingway comes in every now and then with his mob and there's gambling in the back room, but no girls, and . . ." The woman's-tongue tree over on United Street began to make that fearful racket it does when the seed pods get rattled by the wind and they both looked up to find Virginia on the balcony staring down at them.

"Remember when I first met the two of you, up in Savannah at your aunt's plantation? She was so beautiful. So clean and pure and American. And so goddamned stubborn. Now she's like a kid. She depends on me for everything."

"Jake, I . . ."

"Don't pity me, Frances. I got what I wanted, didn't I?" He opened the door and left the De Soto.

"You will come tomorrow night?"

"Don't count on it, Frances. I'll have to see what kind of shape she's in."

It was later on, when she was in her room, that Frances realized the book Jake had been holding was *Neon Lights*.

Frances didn't really expect them to show up and she wasn't at all certain that she wanted them to. She went down to the hotel's sprawling lobby and wandered about, amused by the Deco-Spanish-Moorish fantasy the designer had invented, impressed, despite herself, by the ballroom. Its polished wood floors and ceiling of black cypress were the sort of sumptuous simplicity Frances enjoyed.

Except for essential staff there wasn't a soul around. She knew why. It was seven P.M. and between seven and seven fifteen, every weekday night, anyone who wasn't hopelessly deaf or senile tuned in to hear what was going on between the Kingfish and Madam Queen. I'm the only person in America, Frances decided, who is immune to the charms of *Amos 'n' Andy.*

She left the ballroom, stepping out through an arched doorway onto the loggia which led to a piazza which led to a tropical garden of coconut palms, Bermuda grass, bougainvillea, hibiscus, and purple orchid plants. The beach was just beyond the garden, a crescent-shaped half acre of white sand and arched palm trees. Half a dozen white yachts were moored a little ways out, the moon was obligingly full and she felt painfully, awkwardly lonely.

She told herself she had had enough of full moons and perfect beaches and turned to go inside when she noticed, sitting in one of the private little places the Casa Marina's architect had created for lovers, two people, a man and a woman, who also didn't suffer from *Amos 'n' Andy* addiction.

She couldn't see the man's face because it was buried in the woman's neck. The woman, however, was looking straight up into the sky, as if she were alone, as if her lover were not sitting next to her but was some more mythic being in the heavens.

It didn't strike Frances as particularly odd that *she* was at the Casa Marina. After all, it was known as a place to get relief from the rigors of Hollywood. Odd, no, she said to herself as she stepped into the lobby. Ironic, yes. It was just as well that Jake wasn't going to turn up.

But there he was, coming through the main entrance doors, wearing one of his old white suits, looking more devastatingly manly than ever, Virginia at his side.

Frances decided Virginia had become more beautiful, if anything. It was a new kind of beauty, thinner and more highly strung, more suited to the times. She wore a pale crepe dress which clung to her body and Blondell had done something to her hair so that it fitted her head like a sleek, blond cap. It seemed a kind of minor miracle to Frances that the distraught woman she had seen the day before, furiously combing her hair in a chipped mirror, was the one she was seeing with Jake, walking across the tiled floor, one arm in his, her free hand grasping a clutch bag.

"Too early?" Virginia asked with something of her old assurance.

"If you hadn't appeared now, I was going to jump into the pool. You look marvelous, Virginia."

"I told Jake all I needed was an evening out, didn't I, Jake?" Her voice gave her away on that line. It wasn't that it broke, but there was the suggestion, the possibility that it might, without the necessary support.

Jake gave it to her. "You sure did, honey. You do look marvelous. So do you, Frances."

"I'm trying for a serene-older-woman appeal. Is there any place we can get a drink in this tomb? I'm feeling as serene as an electric eel in mating season."

Constance Bennett was sitting in a banquette in the lounge, drinking whiskey from a teacup. The three of them looked at her and she smiled at them and then the people at her table turned and smiled and they were all smiling and listening to the rumba band playing in the courtyard and drinking gin from the fancy restaurant china except for Virginia who was drinking ginger ale and Jake who was drinking three-point-two beer.

Frances suddenly remembered Claude Wheeler when he was courting Virginia up in Savannah and how he would shout, "Let's all get ginny."

The three of them talked about the people they all had known in Key West: who had died and who had moved away and what unlikely alliances had been made and how difficult it was and how happy they were that Roosevelt was in and that perhaps the sponge industry the Civil Works Administration was planning would help Key West and Frances kept ordering "tea."

By the time they went in to dinner, Frances was more than a touch tight and she resolved to order coffee but then the waiter brought her another cup filled with gin and she drank it.

Constance Bennett and what Frances thought of as the Hollywood Set were seated at a table facing theirs in the huge dining room with its cypress ceiling and its French doors opening out onto yet another loggia where the rumba band played its sinuous music.

They had gotten through the first course when the woman and the man she had seen making love in the moonlight appeared on the dance floor just beyond the French doors. They began to dance, all eyes in the dining room on them.

"My dear," Frances said, "they're going to sizzle the steaks on our plates if they're not careful."

The Hollywood Set applauded loudly as Araby

Moore and her partner—a blond boy with a hairline moustache—ended their dance and entered the dining room.

She was wearing black silk evening pajamas, nearly transparent; it was clear she wore nothing underneath. She wasn't pretty, Frances thought; not at all beautiful as one tended to think of her. Not nearly as classy as Constance Bennett, or as riveting as Virginia in her new, neurotic incarnation. But she managed to give the impression that she would be the best one-night stand a man would ever have. She was thirty-six years old but, as Frances admitted, it was a very good thirty-six years.

The rumba band broke into the title song from her then current film, *Seventeen Miles with You,* and she crossed the dining room floor, with that peppy, jazzy music choreographing her every step, with her young and moustachioed blond boy next to her, radiating as much conscious glamour as anyone Frances had ever seen.

To get to her table, she had to pass theirs. "Jake," Araby said, coming over to him. "Jake!" He stood up, she put her arms around him and kissed him on the lips. Everyone was watching, intently. "Jake," she said, linking her arm in his. "I had no idea you were still in Key West. You know, Max and I . . ."

In half a dozen lines of dialogue she managed to give more information than Frances thought she could get into three pages of tightly written expository writing. She and Max were having an amiable separation. No divorce. Her new religion wouldn't permit it. Of course she'd always adore Anna and "think of her as my very own child." And wasn't it sad all the trouble Great Western was having but Max would never have any difficulty getting a job because he was really a very, very good producer and not a bad director and all he needed was one decent property.

At that moment a tall, handsome man left the Hollywood table and joined them. Araby introduced them both.

Frances immediately forgot the boy's name but the tall, handsome man was Carleton LeMay. "Isn't this a perfectly marvelous way to meet?" Frances said, wondering how drunk she was.

He said that wasn't it fortunate he allowed Araby to carry him off a day early from his meeting with Winchell in Miami Beach.

"What were you meeting with Winchell about?" Frances asked, curious.

"None of your business," Carleton LeMay said and for a moment she almost liked him. "What is your business is that Araby wants to play Carmela in the film version of *Neon Lights,* and we're both here to persuade you to let us do it."

This was said sometime later, after the Hollywood table and their table had joined and Virginia had been convinced by the young blond man with the hairline moustache to have one little drink and Araby had cornered Jake to try to work her art on him.

"This much irony in my life I don't need," Frances said, watching them.

Carleton LeMay laughed and told her, "Of course we'd have to make Carmela a couple of years older."

"Like fifteen."

"And of course you'd write the first draft screenplay."

"You'd best talk to my agent."

At that point someone—Frances thought later that it must have been the blond boy feeding Virginia gin—suggested everyone should go on to the Havana-Madrid Club.

The Havana-Madrid Club was a huge, open-air structure on Front Street which featured a nightclub, a casino, and a variety of tiny cubicles for its patrons' use. It was said that if you couldn't get what you wanted at the Havana-Madrid Club, it didn't exist.

In a short time they were all there, seated in the ceilingless nightclub at the front table, more full teacups in front of them. A group of young and beautiful Cubans, the Comparsa Dancers, dressed in ruffled shirts and skirts that opened all the way up the front, were performing to yet more rumbas.

After their first performance everyone at the table got up to dance. LeMay with Araby, Virginia with the blond boy with the hairline moustache. Frances sat back down again. "I'm too old and too drunk to rumba, Jake." He didn't answer. Virginia and the blond boy were over at the far edge of the dance floor, by the door which led to the cubicles; they weren't moving in time to the music. LeMay and Araby were dancing automatically, having a long and what looked like a serious conversation.

"What're you thinking about, Jake?" she asked him.

"I'm thinking," Jake said, "about how I'm always getting myself hooked up with weak women." Over the years his voice had taken on a soft, Southern inflection. She liked listening to it. "And I'm thinking about Max out in California and Nick and Bessie up in New York and whether or not they're happy. And I'm thinking about my son, David, up in that fancy school in Miami and my little girl, Coffee, and how she's growing and looks the spittin' image of Nancy and what's going to happen to her.

"And I'm thinking about you, Frances. You're the best woman I've ever known, Frances. No, hear me out. I want to say this. You're the only one I didn't have to take care of. I didn't have to watch over you; I didn't have to worry about you. You're your own person, Frances. A man gets to appreciate that."

"Be quiet," she told him, looking for a handkerchief, having to make do with a napkin. "You're making me cry, you dope." He took her hand and held it.

Virginia and the blond boy disappeared for half an hour and when they came back, Jake stood up and said he would be going if Mr. LeMay would give Frances a ride back to the Casa Marina and Mr. LeMay said of course he would.

Jake kissed Frances good-bye and good night and Araby said she would come to see Jake because she was going to be in Key West for a few days but Jake said that was too bad because he was going on a fishing trip for the rest of the week, one he couldn't put off.

He reached over and kissed Frances once again and she hugged him. "It's a damned fine book," he said, which was enough for her to know that she wasn't going to let Araby Moore and Carleton LeMay make a damned bad movie of it.

Later, in the car going back to the hotel, she passed

the Jefferson. She could see Jake sitting up on the balcony, a cheroot clenched between his teeth, his feet propped up on the balustrade. Virginia was in the bedroom, standing just inside the doors behind him, furiously combing her hair with her hands.

CHAPTER 3

By the end of 1933 Mitsuko's and Max's first child, Douglas, was beginning to talk and their second child, Jane, had just been born.

"Who's minding the baby?" Bessie wanted to know when she called the house from New York. She had planned to be in Los Angeles for the birth but Jane had arrived two weeks early.

"Douglas and the nurse and Townie and my father." Anna continued to live with Max and Mitsuko, Araby still maintaining that an actress of her fame and sex appeal could not have a child.

"And your father doesn't mind?"

"He was on the doorstep with a tiny silk kimono fifteen minutes after Jane was born. He's decided I'm a fallen woman, beyond redemption, but Janie offers him a fresh start. He's smiling from ear to ear and looking tall and proud. For a man who's famous for never touching anyone, he can't keep his hands off her."

There weren't many in Hollywood at the end of 1933 who were smiling and looking tall and proud. No one was surprised when Uncle Joe Goldstein's Great Western films went under, just in time for

Christmas. Every major studio—with the possible exception of Warner's—was in the middle of either bankruptcy or receivership and the only question was how Great Western had managed to survive as long as it did.

Few people knew that Ryan's money had been behind it, that he had been using its huge and antiquated stages and storehouses to stock bootlegged whiskey, to house the largest distilleries on the West Coast. But by the end of that year repeal was a fact and Ryan owned a string of legal distilleries in the Midwest. He sold off Great Western's properties for whatever he could get, receiving less than ten cents on the dollar for the expensive sound equipment he had had installed.

Uncle Joe sold Goldstein-Ville to a Mexican millionaire, kissed Max, cursed Ryan, and took his wife, daughter, and son-in-law to London where he had a Mayfair town house done up by Lady Mendel and two million American dollars in the vault. "You'll come and see me, Max?" he asked, putting his arms around him. "You won't be a stranger?"

"I'll come see you, Uncle Joe," Max promised, embracing that short, fat man, wondering how he was going to survive a Hollywood without Uncle Joe.

Townie managed to get Max a young actor known as the Mexicali Kid (Rick West) a contract at Paramount where they made one film, *Pecos Posse*, universally admitted to be a "stinker." Nevertheless it crawled into the black thanks to the fact that people were beginning to drink in the open again and people were beginning to come up and out of the

speakeasies and people, finally, were going to the
movies again.

Townie didn't feel that Paramount was "in love
with Max or the Kid" and after a few months he
managed to switch them to Metro. Araby and Carleton had been there a year and though the competition was fierce (Shearer, Crawford, and Harlow were
under contract), Araby had managed to stay in the
top ten with a series of bedroom farces LeMay produced.

Metro didn't seem to be any happier with Max
than Paramount had been. Not too long after Max
had gone there, Townie paid an afternoon visit to
the house Max had bought after he had given Ram-
A-Dies to Araby, following their separation agreement.

It was a Sunday afternoon and Max was sitting by
the pool, a glass in his hand, his eyes seemingly concentrating on the diving board. Funny thing was,
Townie thought, during Prohibition Max hardly
touched the stuff but the moment the Volstead Act
was repealed, Max couldn't get enough. He had a
trick of placing half tumblers filled with Scotch in the
freezer and then taking them out to the pool and sipping his liquor through a glass straw.

He offered Townie one and Townie said he wasn't
in a drinking mood. "This way you don't need ice,"
Max said, forcing one of the frozen tumblers into
Townie's hands. "It's the most creative idea I've had
in months."

"Where's Anna?" Townie asked. Usually she kept
her father company during the long afternoons, practicing her diving.

"Araby picked her up early this morning."

"And Mitsuko?"

"In her studio, painting. Janie and Douglas are with Miss Dobbs, Robinson is in his room, sleeping off a bout of croup, the upstairs maid is . . ."

"Max . . ."

"Don't say it, Townie. Don't tell me and don't lecture me. Sure I should lay off the sauce but we both know that's not the trouble. I'm no alky. The trouble is me. I bombed at Paramount and I'm bombing at Metro. Get that look off your face. I'm not giving up. I'm going to hold on. But it's no fun sitting on my keister day after day in that prison they call the producers' building, sending scripts up to the front office and never hearing one goddamned word about them. Good, bad, or indifferent.

"Listen, Townie: I'm collecting fifteen hundred a week and my contract has a year and some odd months to run and I know you can always get me something at RKO or Universal and maybe someday it will come to that but meanwhile I'm riding it out. The sauce just makes the trip a little smoother, that's all."

"Sooner or later," Townie told him, "they're going to have to give you a picture if only because you're on payroll."

Max took a long pull on his glass straw and closed his eyes. "There are too many old men of forty sitting in those little rooms in the producers' building, Townie, waiting for Mayer or Thalberg to remember them because they're on the payroll. And then there are the ones who don't want to be remembered." He opened his eyes and put his drink down. "Maybe you should see if you can get me out of the contract, Townie?"

"And what'll you do for money if I can't get you something at RKO?"

"I got a little here and there."

"Horse manure. You took a beating like the rest of the world, Max. I know that fifteen hundred just about keeps you going. I know how much this house and the kids' schools costs." He stood up. "You sit still. I'm going to try and see Thalberg."

Townie left Max sitting by the pool with his frozen Scotch beginning to melt. He met Anna, coming up the front staircase, returning from a breakfast Araby had given visiting royalty.

"How was the Duke of Kent?" Townie asked her. She was nearly as tall as he and had, he thought, more social presence. There was no doubt in anyone's mind that she was going to be a beautiful woman.

"Nice. But you should have seen Buggsy Siegel, Townie. He has the most incredible eyes. When he looked at me, I thought I was absolutely going to melt." She went on for several minutes about Buggsy Siegel and then Townie kissed her and moved on.

Araby was at the foot of the stairs, her famous hips resting on the blue Cord she allowed her gardeners to drive. Her current gardener sat behind the wheel, smoking a short, brown cigarette.

"What am I going to do about those tits?" Araby asked Townie, looking up at her daughter who had stopped on her way upstairs to wave from a second-floor window.

"Maybe she'll grow into them."

"How is he?" Araby wanted to know.

"Not good. Suddenly he's a drinker."

"It's the goddamned studio. *And* him. Max hasn't a clue how to work those guys."

The gardener put his thick brown hand outside the car window, flashing a thin gold and silver watch at Araby. He tapped the face of it twice, with his highly manicured index finger. "You'd better be careful, buster," Araby said, leaning down for a moment, addressing the gardener. "Or I'll take that watch back and I'll send you to Mex Town to that greasy chili parlor where I found you. When I want you to be seen or heard, I'll let you know." She stood up, parked herself back on the car, and looked up at the house Max had bought for Mitsuko. "I still miss the bastard, you know that, Townie? He may be the last honest man in Hollywood."

"Why don't you give him a divorce, anyway, Araby?"

"And wake up some morning married to that?" she asked, pointing to the man in the driver's seat.

On Wednesday of that week, while he was still attempting to get an appointment with Thalberg to plead Max's case, Townie was having breakfast at Schwab's when Carleton LeMay turned up and sat next to him.

LeMay looked around, ordered a bagel and lox and coffee, and said to Townie, "Where would everyone go to be seen on a weekday morning if there were no Schwab's? It's a frightening thought, isn't it?"

It was a sunny morning in May, 1934, and half of Hollywood was moving in and out of Schwab's, reading newspapers and magazines, eating bagels, and looking as if all were right with the world. Townie knew that LeMay sitting next to him at the counter meant all was not right, with his world, at any rate.

"They want the Mexicali Kid to do a film with Janet Gaynor," LeMay said, putting cream cheese on his bagel.

"The Kid won't work without Max."

"The Kid would work without pants if Thalberg asked him to."

"And Thalberg's asking?"

"It's his idea."

Townie broke the news to Max later that day. Max shrugged and reached for another frozen Scotch.

Araby Moore's dressing room was in one of the more opulent shacks on MGM's back lot. "The trouble with Max," she told Townie, "is that he never goes to parties." She was trying on a black wig for a twin-sister comedy she was making with herself as the twins and Ronald Colman as the love interest. She looked at herself critically in the three-paneled mirror. "And don't hand me the Mitsuko story. He hides behind her."

"You know what they think of Orientals in this town."

"And you know what they think of Jews on Park Avenue," Araby said. "You still see them on it." She began to remove her eye makeup, no easy task. "I'll tell you what, Townie. I'll give a party. You get Max and Yum Yum to come and I'll try to get the Thalbergs. Norma owes me a favor or two."

Townie studied Araby's reflection in the mirror almost as intently as she. "Why?" he asked after a moment.

She turned and looked up at him. "I need a big picture. A big, big picture. What they don't hand to Shearer on this lot, they give to Crawford and what they don't give to Crawford they give to Harlow. I need a little something to push me on up ahead of those, uhm, ladies. I thought I was going to get it when LeMay was trying to option *Neon Lights* but Jake Meyer's girl friend was too highfalutin to stoop to selling her novel to Hollywood.

"Thalberg decided *Speakeasy* won't do for Gaynor but it might do for me. And Max could handle it in a minute, if Thalberg let him. It's not as if Max doesn't know from gangsters and he may be the only guy in this town who could get that wad of muscle known as Rick West to read a line as if it weren't a Fanny Farmer recipe."

She stood up and walked across the dressing room to the door. "It's time I gave my fans more depth, Townie. I want to make a film full of social realism and moral betterment. I want to sing in a roadhouse. I want to shed real tears as my man walks down that last mile to the hot seat. If I get this picture for Max, he'll have to keep the camera on me every inch of the way." She flung open the door. "You go work on Max."

He didn't. Instead Townie went to work on Mitsuko. The house she and Max lived in and which he put in her name was high in the Hollywood Hills, a large, clean-lined, open house, built of glass and stone. Inside it was cool and white and furnished with a minimum of furniture: low, dark sofas, lacquered tables, two or three paintings by Mitsuko. It was as unlike Ram-A-Dies, which Araby now occupied, as it could be.

Mitsuko had just then begun working with large and sometimes silk canvases. With what appeared to be a half-dozen strokes of the brush, she managed to suggest vast and highly refined landscapes, innumerable ancient worlds filled with exquisite ladies, polished by centuries of civilization.

He found her working on an enclosed patio which overlooked the pool where the children, Douglas and Janie, were swimming.

"I've been waiting for you, Townie," she said, kissing him, beginning the laborious job of cleaning up. "I knew you would eventually come to me." He watched her as she put her brushes in a solvent-filled bottle, thinking how much more lovely she was than Araby or any of the other ladies of the screen.

She moved beautifully; with her marvelous shoulders and her surprisingly long legs, she might have been one of the women she painted. When she was at home, working, she wore her jet black hair long and free. It, too, looked as if it had been painted with a few, sure strokes.

"He won't tell me what the trouble is though of course I know it has to do with the studio, with the fact he's not making films." She turned to look through the floor-to-ceiling glass window at the pool where Anna was poised on the diving board. The girl looked like an Art Moderne goddess, a Packard hood ornament, Townie thought. Anna looked up, saw Mitsuko and Townie, and gave them her version of her mother's infectious smile and then performed a perfectly executed dive.

Douglas, who looked exactly as his father looked at his age, but with Mitsuko's eyes, came next and his dive was as nearly as perfect as his stepsister's. He was just five, with a serious, determined expression. Janie, a year younger and the image of Mitsuko, but with Max's fair coloring, applauded from the side of the pool where that quintessential English nanny, Cora Dobbs, was holding her.

"Anna knows everything about Hollywood. She tells me they won't give Max any films to make. 'It's his image,' she said. Townie, you'd better tell me what's wrong with Max's image and why it interferes with his doing what he loves to do best."

Townie spent the next hour giving Mitsuko a short course in political science, Hollywood-Metro style. She asked pertinent and correct questions. He gave appropriate answers.

"I'm so naïve," she said. "I thought all the studios were run exactly the way Uncle Joe ran Great Western. What can we do?"

He told her about Araby's offer of a party at Ram-A-Dies to relaunch Max, to introduce Mitsuko to Hollywood.

"Is that a good idea?" she asked. "We're not married and we have two children."

"As long as that's not public knowledge, it's not going to stop anyone in this town."

"And then, of course, I'm Japanese. Most of the time I forget and then I see myself in the mirror and I wonder who that exotic lady is. But you know what they think of the Japanese in this state. My father, as successful as he is, as rich as he's become in that farming commune he and his friends have up the coast, is still not allowed to own property in California, simply because he wasn't born in this country. As a result I'm an important property owner, Townie. I not only own this house but I also own my father's farmlands."

She stopped talking and turned to him. "I'm sorry. I've been rattling on to cover my thinking. I have another idea, Townie. Instead of being guests at Araby's, what if Max and I gave a party? Would Mr. Thalberg, Mr. Mayer, and Mr. Mannix come to a West Coast birthday party for Bessie?"

Townie reached up and kissed Mitsuko on the cheek. "How can anyone be so beautiful and so smart at the same time? An actor going to New York and not being seen at B's is like a cardinal going to Rome and not breaking bread at the Vatican. Bessie knows everyone in this town on a first-name basis. They love her because she's got something they ain't: integrity."

"There's one problem: you and I both know how adamant Max has been about letting Bessie know his career is in trouble. You've heard those phone calls between them: 'Everything's great, Bessie. Starting a big new feature with Harlow next week.' He'll be very upset, Townie, if he thinks we told her."

"He'll get over it. *After* we tell her."

"Then it's decided," Mitsuko said, reaching for the white telephone. "Max and I are going to give Bessie her birthday party this year. The first person I'd better call is Bessie. And the first person I'd better invite is Araby Moore, don't you agree, Townie?"

* * *

Townie had warned them from the beginning that the party was a gamble. Everyone had accepted, but who, he asked, is going to show up? Max's career depended upon the arrival of three people: Thalberg, Mayer, and Mannix. "All the rest," Townie said, "are window dressing."

Guards in black suits had been hired to stand duty at the gates, to check invitations, to lend the event a celluloid gangster quality with gun butts causing bulges in their jackets.

Gary Cooper and George Raft, the first genuine luminaries to arrive, were photographed being frisked. Robert Montgomery wanted Bessie to come and dance with him but she told him she'd take a rain check, that she had to stand at the door to greet people.

Mary Pickford was driven through the back gates to a private entrance where no one was being frisked or photographed. With Pickford there, Bessie and Townie breathed easier, her arrival signaling the approval of Hollywood aristocracy.

By midnight everyone had arrived except the Thalbergs, Eddie Mannix, and Louie B. Mayer. "It's after twelve," Townie told Bessie, who stood in the long, cool marble hall, welcoming guests to her birthday party.

"Bring Mitsuko down," she told him, not looking happy. "It doesn't look as if they're going to show."

Bessie, who had insisted on choreographing the event, had been holding Mitsuko back, attempting to time her descent down the starkly modern but still monumental staircase at exactly the moment Irving and Norma Thalberg were to enter from the rear doors opening onto the entrance hall.

Townie made his way up the stairs as fast as he could. All of the rooms on the first and second stories of the house had been opened and were filled with guests, squads of waiters circulating food and drink and plainclothesmen in dinner jackets watching the exist and entrances and everything in between.

Ramon Novarro was in the music room, at the piano, playing Beethoven and staring into the eyes of a very young man named Bobby Carr. Marion Davies's crowd had had a great deal to drink and were blocking the stairs, playing musical chairs on the steps. Paul Lukas, Clark Gable, Jean Harlow, and Nick were at the poker table in the library. As Townie made his way past, he saw Eddie Mannix sit down and take over Paul Lukas's hand. Kay, who was watching over Nick's shoulder, told Townie that Mannix had arrived through a side entrance a few moments before.

"That's good," he said and thought that it wasn't good enough. He found Mitsuko reading to Douglas, Janie, and their exquisite cousin, Coffee, in the third-floor nursery. Predictably they all made a fuss when she stood up to leave.

"Now, children," Cora Dobbs said in her inimitable nanny voice. "You've stayed up far too late as it is. Into bed and not one more word out of you."

"Pish," said Coffee audibly, but she allowed herself to be tucked in.

Mitsuko kissed them and began to descend the stairs. She was wearing a jade-green gown that tied around her neck but left her shoulders and most of her back exposed. Her long, lustrous black hair had been cut into a severe pageboy. She wore no jewelry, her beautiful arms deliberately bare.

In a place where lovely women outnumbered the plain, one had to be extraordinary to create a sensation. Everyone, even Ramon Novarro, stopped what he was doing to watch Mitsuko as she descended the marble staircase.

At the first landing Townie was separated from her when Tallulah Bankhead grabbed his arm and demanded to know "who that stunning creature is, darling?"

As Mitsuko made her descent into the entrance hall, three new guests were being brought in through the rear doors to greet Bessie. Irving Thalberg looked up at the moment Mitsuko reached the last step and held his breath for a moment. He knew and appreciated great beauty when he saw it. Norma Shearer, his wife, kept her well-practiced smile on display and the boy genius of Hollywood's mother, Henrietta, for once kept quiet.

Thalberg and Mitsuko met in the center of that huge, marbled space. Bessie, her arm through Mitsuko's, introduced her as "my brother's companion."

Mitsuko took Thalberg and his wife off to the buffet where Max was waiting while Bessie tackled Henrietta.

Louis B. Mayer was announced shortly after that and Kay appeared to escort him into the drawing room where one of three bands were playing executive two-steps. Soon Louis B. Mayer could be seen dancing with Kay, his little head all smiles.

Townie, Jake, and Frances Ellington were just

making their way down to the entrance hall when Araby Moore and the former Mexicali Kid, Rick West, marched in.

Townie felt a terrible apprehension about the outcome of Araby and Bessie meeting face-to-face. They had carried on a silent but still potent coast-to-coast enmity for many years.

The two antagonists stared at one another from opposite ends of the sixty-foot room for a full fifteen seconds. Then Araby gave her chinchilla wrap to Robinson and walked across the marble expanse in that patentable slither she affected and threw both her arms around her sister-in-law.

"Darling," Araby said, as half of Hollywood waited and watched. "Darling!"

Bessie put her own arms around Araby and said, in the very same voice—she was marvelous at mimicry—"Darling. Darling!"

They strode off, arm in arm, to the bar while Townie went elsewhere to find a drink.

"We were working," Bessie told him later, "for a very worthy cause."

On the Monday morning following the party Max was summoned to Thalberg's innermost sanctum, his screening room. He was sitting in the first row and motioned Max to sit next to him. Not a word was said until the final credits appeared and the film, Frank Capra's *It Happened One Night*, came to an end.

They discussed it for several moments and then Thalberg said, "That was a marvelous party you gave your sister the other night."

"Thank you. Bessie certainly had a good time."

"I've never seen a woman who seemed to have a better one. Your companion is extraordinarily charming. My wife and I would like you both to come out to the house on Sunday."

Max said that they would. Thalberg's inner circle congregated there each Sunday for sumptuous meals and entertainment provided by the guests.

Then Thalberg stood up. "Araby Moore, as well as a good many others on this lot, are lobbying for you to direct *Speakeasy*, Max. I've thought about it and I'm sorry, neither she nor you are right for it."

Max said he was sorry, too, and, thinking he was dismissed, began to leave. Thalberg stopped him. "I want you to know I've read everything you've sent over, Max. Some very exciting ideas, none especially commercial. There is a project I'd like you to try, however. It's from a novel and you'll have to work with the author of the screenplay. I've just put her under contract. I expect you know her and the book. Frances Ellington's *Neon Lights*. I met her at your party and she said *Neon Lights* wasn't available unless she wrote the first draft, you directed it, and Araby Moore did not star in it. I agreed on the spot."

In its first year of release *Neon Lights* grossed over six million dollars for Metro and won every conceivable award, including Best Actress and Best Director from the Academy of Motion Picture Arts and Sciences. Araby Moore did star in it, Max having his loyalties, too, getting Frances Ellington to finally agree that Araby did look fifteen years younger on screen.

It established Max as both an artistic and commercial director, gave Araby Moore an entire new image as a dramatic star, and confirmed Frances Ellington's dearly held belief that she must never go near Hollywood again. In her considered opinion she and Max had made a great film of *Neon Lights* but Araby Moore had made a lousy Carmela.

CHAPTER 4

Kay was later to call those dark months in 1935 the Winter of Death. They had begun well enough, though she had been annoyed with Nick's numbers.

"Why can't ex-bootleggers ever let go of the numbers?" she wanted to know.

"Don't start making up some love story," Nick told her. "The numbers bring in the money; they're keeping us rich."

"I thought Ryan had them all sewed up in New York. I thought . . ."

He took her by the shoulders and said, "Look: you keep out of my business and I'll keep out of yours. For the last time: I took Long Island. It was there and I got it. If Ryan was going to do anything about it, he would've done it a long time ago. I'm his girl friend's baby brother. We're like family. What's he going to do, bump me off?"

She didn't push it. There was too much hate in his eyes when he spoke of Ryan; it scared her. She had a hope, a dim one, that the taxicab company he had bought would turn out to be a legitimate enterprise.

It had belonged to Larry Fay but Larry was killed

by the doorman at the nightclub he and Texas
Guinan co-owned, the El Fey Club.

"Larry shouldn't have gotten hit by a lousy doorman," Nick said, as if it mattered, as if there were a
rigid code of chivalry among the racketeers. He re-
named the taxies Nick's Fleet, Kay designed a logo
which featured a Mercury looking like a cherubic
Nick riding atop a chrome yellow taxi, and Nick was
in business, with the largest taxicab company on
Long Island. The drivers made the collections,
handed out the payoffs for the numbers.

At the same time Kay had been promoted. Fatty
Freeman's magazine, *Vanity*, was off the ground, and
Kay had stepped into the fashion editor's position.
Nick didn't like it but he didn't hate it enough to
stop it and she made certain that it didn't take up
enough time to aggravate him.

They were arguing on and off all through that fall
and into the winter about moving out of the city.
Nick wanted to move to Long Island. It was where
his taxi fleet operated, where his numbers were run.
"You can get a goddamned mansion out there for
what we pay here a month."

"I like the city," Kay said. "It keeps me young."

"You ain't so young," he told her. Then he reached
for her hand. "All right. We can keep the apartment,
too."

"Nicky, I don't want a house on Long Island. I
don't want . . ."

"That's your trouble, Kay. You don't want anything.
You don't want a house, you don't want a kid . . ."

"That's not exactly all my problem, is it, Nick?"

"So it's mine?"

396   DAVID A. KAUFELT

"Nick, let's not let his degenerate . . ."

" 'Degenerate.' Now she's throwing the fifty-cent words at me." He walked to the window that looked out on Central Park. "You ever see anything so filthy? I want to wake up in the morning and see something clean, for crying out loud."

She threw the comforter back and went to him, putting her arms around him, kissing his cheek. "You're such a sulky, spoiled baby, Nick. That's beautiful and you know it."

Central Park was covered with new snow. It looked wonderfully unnatural, Kay thought, like a Ziegfeld stage set, icicles on the trees, the frozen lake in the background with its goldfish-bowl bridge. All it needed was a troupe of six-foot-high chorus girls dressed in ermine pasties. But it was Sunday morning and the only occupants were the kids, just getting to their favorite slides, pulling their sleds behind them.

"It'd be nicer in the country," Nick insisted.

Kay was tempted to ask where this new concern for "nicer" had come from but decided, instead, to give in. "All right. Let's go to the country and buy baby a house. You have any particular country in mind?"

"You mean it, Kay?"

"Why not? Just as long as you don't expect me to be at home every evening with a stew in the oven, an apple pie cooling on the rack, waiting for you to come home from a tough day with the Fleet."

"It'll be our weekend house," Nick promised, hugging her.

He's such a child, Kay thought, hugging him back.

As always, on Sundays, they had late brunch at Bessie's triplex. Ryan was as polite, as distantly civil, as he had been toward Nick since their break. Nick gave him the minimum hello and little else.

Kay wondered, not for the first time, if Bessie genuinely didn't know how much they hated and feared one another; or if Bessie had an authentic blind spot when it came to her lover and her brother. There had to be an effort of will on her part, Kay decided, for Bessie not to see how much anger lay between the two men, how difficult it was for them to be in the same room together.

Nick told Bessie about the proposed country house. "Good," she said, looking as radiant as ever in her scarlet peignoir, her red curls seeming to have a life of their own as she directed Minnie, who was moving around the table with a large platter of cold meats. "You both need a place to run to when New York becomes too much."

"Does it ever become too much for you, my dear?" Ryan asked.

Bessie considered for a moment and then shook her head. "No, I think New York and I are just about right for each other. Now I want you to drive carefully, fat boy," she said to Nick.

"I don't drive anymore," Nick said. He had bought a long, black Packard limousine which was chauffered by Red Schenk. Nick went to the telephone and called Red but his wife said he was ill. "Laryngitis. A cold. The works."

"Red never gets sick," Nick complained.

"But when he does," Red's wife said, "watch out."

"So we'll go next week," Nick told Kay, but he was clearly disappointed. "I ain't driving that truck. They'll think we're the butler and the maid."

There was a moment of silence while Bessie poured tea. And then she looked up and said, "So get another driver." She hated to see Nick disappointed.

"Or use ours," Ryan said casually. "We're staying home today."

"Sunday?" Kay asked, surprised.

"I told Grace," Ryan said, "that the weather would necessitate my remaining in the city." He smiled.

"Go ahead," Bessie said. "Take Smitty. We're not leaving the house all day." She looked across the table at Ryan. Kay intercepted the look and almost found herself blushing. Here again was evidence of how alive and strong Bessie's and Ryan's intimacy was after so many years.

It seemed pointless and rude not to "take Smitty" though Kay knew Nick didn't like the idea. "That's very kind of you," Kay said. "I accept. If we're going to buy the little prince a castle, we might as well get to it."

"Take our car, if you like," Ryan offered.

"No, thanks," Nick told him. "We got our own car."

"Very smart neighborhood," Kay said, pulling the fur rug over her, arranging Nick's arm around her shoulder. "If a little familiar." Grace Ryan's house was in the vicinity.

"We'll just look around," Nick said, closing the glass window between the passenger and the driver compartments. "If it's good enough for Ryan's wife . . ."

"It might do for us."

It had taken them over an hour, the roads being what they were, to get to Oyster Bay. By that time they had a half hour before it became too dark to see. They passed half a dozen estates, all of them with "For Sale/For Rent" signs on their gates.

Nick had Smitty drive into each driveway that seemed promising. "They're not going to mind," he told a protesting Kay. "They want to unload these dumps." There was one he was especially taken with, a mock French chateau.

"It looks as if it'd be awfully dark inside," Kay said, not liking it.

"We'll put in electric lights. How old do you think she is?"

"Oh, a good fifteen years."

He took a pencil from Smitty and wrote the real estate agent's name and telephone number on the back of an envelope.

"You hungry, Mr. Meyer?" Smitty asked through the speaking tube.

"Mrs. Meyer is," Kay replied.

"There's an old roadhouse the fellows used to eat at up ahead. Great steaks."

Kay looked at Nick, and he said into the tube, "Let's go."

It was all so beautifully choreographed, Kay thought later. So well thought out.

The roadhouse, obviously once a speak, was called The Road House. It was designed in Ye Olde Tavern style. There were a few people in the room called The Bar and a few couples in the back, fox-trotting to a three-piece band known as The Trio. Kay felt as if she had stepped into a primary reader for slightly corrupt adults.

They sat at the bar and Kay ordered a martini,

Nick a ginger ale, and Smitty excused himself to wash his hands. "He's very polite, that Smitty," Kay said. "He could have said he was going to take a piss."

Nick pretended to cuff her under the chin. "You got a terrible mouth on you, you know that, Kay?"

She felt a sudden chill and pulled her fur coat around her. The place was badly lit and damp. She shivered. "Someone's walking across my grave."

Nick laughed. He was happy, in a good mood. "Try not to be so goddamned sensitive, will you?" He pulled her to him and kissed her on the lips, not something he usually did in public. She held onto him for a moment. His body was taut, even in his most relaxed moments.

A man in a greasy dinner jacket showed them to a table in an alcove at the far end of the roadhouse, near the dance floor. "I wonder what's become of Smitty?" Kay asked, picking up the menu.

"Maybe he's car sick."

Kay saw him first, standing at the entrance to the alcove, over them.

"Hey, Nick," Bumps Bogan said, a short, ugly gun in his right hand. "I hear you like numbers. Here's two of them for you." He shot Nick twice, in the chest. Then he disappeared.

It was all too simple, Kay thought. Like The Road House, The Bar, The Trio: The Hoodlum Shot My Hero.

Smitty tried to get her out of the alcove but she refused, holding onto the table, screaming. "You fucker. You set us up for this." She slipped down to the floor and put her arms around Nick, her white mink coat sponging up his blood.

Two other men tried to pull her out of the alcove but there wasn't enough room what with the table and Nick's body and Kay screaming and kicking at them. Finally they had to call the police. That or shoot Kay and no one had orders to kill her.

That hour after Nick was murdered was to remain perfectly clear for Kay for the rest of her life, as crystalline, as lucid and unnatural as Central Park had been that morning. She knew she would always remember every detail. The terrible gray suit Bumps had worn; Smitty's sad, knowing face; a woman at the bar giggling hysterically.

But her clearest memory, her worst punishment, was the terrible odor that permeated that alcove and continued to haunt her: the smell of bad booze, cheap perfume, and death.

Bessie insisted she stay in the guest room in the triplex. She was all right, in control most of the time except when she thought of Nick crumpling down under the table and then she would break. Bessie kissed her, forced her to eat, held her in her arms.

"If I didn't have you to take care of," Bessie said, putting her hand on Kay's forehead, "I'd go out of my mind."

It was dark gray and the snow had melted into a filthy mess on the day of the funeral. "It's more than I can bear," Kay said, but Bessie had taken her arm, adjusted the black veil, and led her down to the lobby, through the crowd of photographers and reporters and into the waiting limousine.

"We're both going to bear it," Bessie said.

At the cemetery, when they lowered his coffin with the carved Star of David on its lid into the ground,

Kay fainted but Bessie stood there, grimly watching the coffin's progress. And then she gave the one sign that showed the terrible pain she was suffering. It was a harsh cry that reverberated around that gray, cold place, a cry that seemed to settle in the hearts of all the mourners gathered in that bleak cemetery. "Nick," she screamed but once.

Her two brothers put their arms around her but she didn't respond. She stood there as the rabbi began to chant the Mourner's Kaddish, that most final of prayers, dry-eyed and defiant.

Kay stayed with Bessie during the week of mourning while Max, Mitsuko, and Jake stayed at the apartment she had lived in with Nick. After, both Bessie and Ryan pressed her to stay on. She refused.

Frances Ellington wanted to take her south, to Key West. "Jake's invited us," she said.

But Kay said no. She moved back into the apartment. All she wanted to do was lie on the bed and remember. No one was going to allow her to do that. Fatty Freeman said he wouldn't let her work for a month. Bessie came to her and said, "I think you should get out of New York, Kay. You'll heal better far away."

"And you?"

"I'm never going to heal," Bessie said, looking at Kay. There were no tears in her blue eyes. There hadn't been since she heard that Nick had been killed.

The following morning Kay called Frances and said yes, she would go with her to Key West if the offer were still good.

Two days before they were to leave, the doorman

rang and said there was a delivery man on his way up. Food from Bessie, Kay thought, telling her maid to stay where she was, going through the apartment to the service door, opening it.

Red Schenk stood there, wearing a stiff white butcher's coat, his face looking as if it had been gone over with a meat ax. "Come in, Red," she said, suddenly feeling weak.

"Can't. I just wanted you to know, Kay, that I didn't run out on Nick. They worked me over pretty bad, got my wife so scared she told him I was sick. They left me for dead, Kay. I ain't dead. I just wanted you to know that."

"Red, come in!"

"Can't." He set the delivery box down on the counter. "Nick told Ryan to get rid of that bastard years ago. Ryan should have taken his advice." He touched her shoulder and was gone.

A week later, after Kay was safely ensconced in Jake's house in Key West, she received a letter from Bessie which contained an Associated Press clipping. Four men had been found in a burning car in the Astoria section of Queens. They had been gagged and bound before the car had been set on fire. All four were dead by the time the police ambulance got them to the hospital. Identification was difficult but one was thought to be Joseph "Bumps" Bogan, the racketeer. Another, a man tentatively identified as Jack "Smitty" Smith, a reputed gangland hit man.

Bessie didn't comment on the clipping; she sent her love to Kay and to Coffee, Frances, and Jake, and hoped they would all be together soon.

In a postscript she said that Grace Ryan had died

of cancer. She had been ill for years but had told no one. Ryan was very broken up though he pretended he wasn't. Bessie was attempting to console him.

It was three weeks after his wife's death that Ryan found Bessie in her bedroom, getting ready for a luncheon appointment with Mrs. August Belmont. They were planning an opera benefit with the proceeds to go to the Henry Street Settlement which needed funds more than ever.

He sat down in his green leather chair, crossed his legs, and watched Bessie apply makeup, fuss with her red curls, and give orders to Minnie as to which articles of clothing should be brought out.

"Do you mind if we dispense with Minnie for a moment?" Ryan asked.

"I'm late as it is, Ryan . . ."

"I have something important to say to you. It won't take a moment." She told Minnie to leave and she swiveled round to face him.

"No," he said, "go back to your mirror. Continue what you're doing. I can see you perfectly well."

"Ryan," she said, still facing him, "what it is?"

"I suddenly find myself at a loss for words. I think I'm feeling shy."

"Ryan, do tell me what it is you want. I must get down to the Metropolitan . . ."

"I want you to marry me, my dear."

"Why?" she asked, before she could think.

"I love you."

"And I love you, fat boy. But we've been perfectly comfortable like this for years. Why change now?"

"Grace, the one obstacle to our marriage, has died.

I'm selling the Long Island house. What would I do with it now? I have no place to live."

"You have this place, *our* home."

"But don't you see, Bessie, that now there's no reason not to marry you. I couldn't simply live with you. It wouldn't be right. I would lose face."

"But Ryan . . ."

"And there's the money. If I die tomorrow, you'd get nothing."

"Oh, don't worry, fat boy. I'll probably go first."

"Bessie, why don't you want to marry me?"

"I don't know. I don't see any reason to. There were times when I would have done anything to marry you but now it seems so unnecessary."

He uncrossed his legs, reached over, and took her hand. He looked suddenly old and dry, as if he might be ill. "It's very necessary to me, my dear. I need you so badly."

And then she saw a sight she had thought she would never see. There were tears in Ryan's eyes. Tears of self-pity. She stood up and put her arms around him. "Of course I want to marry you, fat boy," she said. "We'll do it next week, very quietly. Bessie Ryan. My grandparents will be spinning in their graves. Oh, my God," she said, letting go of him, catching sight of the silver clock on her dressing table. "Eleanor Belmont thinks lateness is the number one cardinal sin. I'll have to run."

"Bessie," he said, holding onto her for another moment.

"Yes, fat boy?"

"Thank you, Bessie."

They were married on the following Tuesday in

the mayor's chambers. She sent notes to her brothers, formal announcements to her friends, and allowed a half column to appear in the *Times*. Ryan gave her a very large diamond ring which she found herself making excuses for not wearing. Finally she had it put in the vault. Ryan didn't seem to mind. As always he had gotten what he wanted.

The one piece of jewelry she never seemed to be without was a gold locket Kay had given her. Very often, when she was alone, she would open it. In one compartment was a picture of Ryan taken when he was a young man. In the other was a photograph of Nick.

CHAPTER 5

It was obvious to Frances Ellington that behind the witty patter and the fashionable makeup, Kay was feeling a terrible sense of loss, terrible pain, all of the time.

She had only spoken of it once and that was during their first night in Key West. They had arrived late, the Overseas Railway predictably several hours behind schedule. Jake met them and drove them to William Street where they had to get out and walk up Pinder Lane, his old De Soto too wide for that narrow street.

The house was both larger and more charming than Frances had remembered it. Blondell and Coffee were sitting on the front steps of the small porch, waiting for them. They had a light supper in the kitchen, made and served by Blondell. Coffee, a long and thin thirteen, and more beautiful if possible than her mother, sat and watched, unable to take her huge eyes off Kay.

Jake, too, seemed to suffer an unspoken but terrible pain due to the loss of his brother. He sat at the head of the kitchen table, his face smiling but his eyes a cold and lonely blue. He had bought the two ad-

jacent houses and had them moved up against the
original Pinder Lane house, the upstairs rooms
redesigned with bathrooms and balconies.

"Oh, I'm beginning to make a living," he said
when Frances asked him, point-blank, where he had
gotten the money. "The gambling now takes up two
floors and in the winter all the artists come into the
saloon for local color. Then the local color shows up
to see the Northern artists. I'm no millionaire, but
I'm doing all right, Frances."

Blondell unpacked for Frances and Kay and after
supper they sat on the second-floor veranda, overlooking the garden, Kay answering Coffee's questions
about New York and fashion until Blondell took her
away. And then the three of them, Kay, Jake, and
Frances, sat quietly, breathing in the perfumed air. It
was a perfect Key West night.

"That fucker," Kay said suddenly, breaking the
peace. She stood up and went through the louvered
doors into her bedroom and they could hear her crying. After she had stopped, Jake left and Frances remained alone on the veranda, smoking and thinking.
She wondered which fucker Kay had meant: Bumps
or Nick?

Kay didn't leave Key West after the thirty days she
had given herself were up. She found, she said, that
she was mending more slowly than she thought she
would. "At first," she said to Frances, "when Nicky
was killed, I wanted to die, too. Now, I don't care one
way or the other."

They avoided the Casa Marina and only very occasionally would see someone from New York, some va-

cationing writer trying to work his way in with Hemingway's "mob" or an actress with intellectual pretensions "soaking up the atmosphere" in Jake's Bucket of Blood Saloon. Then they'd be very polite but distant, finish their beers, and get themselves up off the red leatherette barstools and make their way home to that sleepy, unlocatable house on Pinder Lane.

Not that there were too many visitors in that winter of 1935. Not that there was too much to visit. Key West was in even worse shape than it had been the last time Frances had visited. Of the eleven thousand remaining residents, over eight thousand were on the dole. People got their food by fishing for it. The naval station, long a source of revenue, was shut down. The pineapple and sugar had stopped coming from Cuba and the North and Gulf steamship lines had declared themselves bankrupt.

"One of those Roosevelt acronyms has been called in," Frances wrote to her editor, "but all the little men in their rimless glasses can come up with is a mass evacuation. They've proposed moving everyone to Tampa. God knows what Tampa is supposed to do with eleven thousand hungry Conchs.

"Their other idea is to turn Key West into an 'island resort.' Two tons, net, of fancy booklets have been printed up and the men are helping to put in sewerage and a central water system and eventually, they promise, streetlights. Meanwhile we're all waiting for the tourists."

Jake came every night to eat with them. "You don't have to, Jake," Kay told him. "You don't have to take care of me."

"Look, Kay: I been taking my supper in this house every night for the past ten years. Just 'cause you're here don't mean I intend to stop now."

Frances wasn't at all certain that she was supposed to hear that. One, she knew it was a lie and two, it was said in an oddly intimate way. She was in her room, writing letters, while Kay and Jake were on the veranda. Frances stood up and looked out and saw Kay reach over and put her young, fresh hand on Jake's tanned, used one and then and only then was she prepared to allow herself to think about "the lay of the land."

On two occasions Jake brought Virginia Wheeler with him. She was restrained and absurdly proper, her hands folded on her lap, her flowered skirts and halters clean and neat and somehow unwholesome.

"Virginia Wheeler," Frances said to Kay after the second such visit, "is the only woman I have ever met who manages to give the impression of being scrupulously sanitary and, at the same time, overwhelmingly sexy."

Before, she had never allowed her skin to tan but then, in 1935, she didn't seem to care. Frances thought again that her sun-darkened skin and her blond hair and her new and taut cheekbones made her much more striking than she had been in her "plantation belle" days.

"She should be on the cover of *Vanity*," Kay said. "She's the quintessential Depression beauty."

The scent of the gardenia perfume Virginia wore did nothing to disguise the medicinal odor of the gin she had had to drink to fortify herself for the Pinder Lane dinners.

"She'll sleep with anyone," Jake told Frances one afternoon when they were out on the Gulf in a borrowed fishing boat. Kay was aft, dozing under a straw hat. All Frances could see was the metallic glint of the sunshine on the surface of the Gulf Stream. Portuguese man-of-wars, like partially inflated pink balloons, rode on the hard blue surface while occasional white gulls flew overhead.

"Does it bother you, Jake?"

"Nope. Virginia stopped bothering me a while back."

"Do you feel guilty?"

He smoked his cigar for a while and then said, "Responsible. If it hadn't been for me, she and Claude might have made a new start somewhere, after the senator died. But I wouldn't let them be. I wanted her so bad, Frances. Well, now I got her."

Jake made certain that Claude ate and had just enough money to keep himself in a six-day stupor. He wasn't allowed in Jake's Bucket of Blood. Not since the day he strode in with a cocked rifle, looking for "that no good slut of a wife of mine." Jake had had to take the rifle, carefully, out of Claude's hands only to find it hadn't been loaded. "Story of Claude's life," Virginia had said, watching Claude collapse like a child into Jake's arms.

By the end of April, after Frances and Kay had been there four months, when the frangipani were in full bloom, filling the Pinder Lane garden with red, pink, yellow, and white blossoms, Fatty Freeman turned up.

"What are *you* doing here?" Kay asked him, lighting one of her rare cigarettes, making drinks. It was late afternoon, the sky turning its customary red and blue.

"That's what I wanted to ask you."

"I'm convalescing, Fatty." She handed him a glass filled with bourbon.

"Oh?"

"I'm still in mourning, Fatty."

"I came down here to find out one thing, Kay: you want your job or not?"

"Not."

It seemed to Frances that Fatty had come to Key West to find out if he had a chance. Kay was telling him he didn't, but all the same she was relieved to see him.

They let him talk them into going to the Casa Marina for dinner. For the first time since she had arrived in Key West, Kay put on a real dress, earrings, what she called her "fighting woman" makeup. She studied herself in a full-length mirror while Coffee stood behind her like a sepia shadow, nearly faint from the glamour Kay seemed able to turn on at will.

"That's the most beautiful dress, Aunt Kay."

"No, it's not, Coffee. But it's not a bad dress." It was black and one piece and edged in bright crimson around the short, furled sleeves. She kissed the child and went out to join Frances.

They had dinner with Fatty in the Casa Marina dining room, so redolent for Frances of Araby Moore and Carleton LeMay and the blond boy with the hairline moustache. She wondered what had become of him.

They had said hello to half a dozen people one or the other knew and they all danced a bit and drank a great deal and by the end of the evening, when Fatty put them into a taxi, Frances knew that Kay was ready to go back.

"You want to come with me on the train tomorrow?" he asked her, his handsome, earnest face staring at her.

"I don't know, Fatty. Give me a few more days."

"I'm leaving tomorrow, Kay."

The driver pulled away and headed down Duval. Kay told him not to turn, to keep on going. "I want to see Jake," she explained.

It was just before midnight when Kay and Frances entered the saloon, causing a minor stir. Two women in New York dresses were not an accustomed sight in Jake's Bucket of Blood that late at night. But they were soon ignored. The defeated men, in their undershirts and suspenders, with their cigar stumps, nursing their glasses of nickel beer, categorized them as just two more tourists from the hotel.

A boy was singing the song of the year, "Isle of Capri," up on the stage over the bar where Luis San Obispo sat, one hand on a sandbag, the other on a pistol. Violence at Jake's Bucket of Blood was sporadic but devastating. Luis signaled Jake who came out of the casino, looking concerned.

"Jake," Kay said to him. "I wanted to talk to you."

"I'll take you home."

They drove through the tree-lined, drowsy streets, the old houses needing paint and something more. Jake pulled up at the start of Pinder Lane and Frances, feeling, she said, like someone's third arm, gave them a generous good night and went up the lane and into the house.

Kay didn't appear until the following morning, in a frenzy to pack, to get to the station to meet Fatty. Frances helped her while Coffee ran out and got the taxi, tears in her sloe eyes.

Kay gave her the black dress and told her how to shorten it and what to do to make it attractive for her. "When you're seventeen," she said, "I'm going to get your father to send you to New York to spend some time with me."

"You mean that, Aunt Kay?"

"Absolutely. You belong in New York. In the meantime I'll send you magazines and keep you posted on what everyone is wearing. That way you'll be prepared when you arrive."

Kay kissed and hugged Coffee and gave Blondell an envelope. Blondell began to cry and Kay kissed and hugged her, too. Frances rode with her to the station.

"Of course I slept with him," Kay admitted. "What did you think we were doing all night?"

"And?"

"Oh, it was everything it was supposed to be. Possibly more. But what's the use? There's no future, it's too soon, and he's a gent of the old school. He'd never leave her. You heard him. He's responsible. I'm getting out now before I can't. You'll be happy to know my cure is complete. I only think about Nick eighty percent of the time and I hardly feel guilty at all about sleeping with his brother and enjoying it. I'm quite ready to face anything again, Frances. Well, almost anything."

Fatty Freeman arrived and the train made noises and Fatty got her luggage aboard and Kay and Frances kissed and suddenly Frances felt that terrible vacancy, that awful loss, of not having a family. Suddenly she was wishing that Kay were her sister or her daughter, that she had some sort of blood tie on her.

"Take care of him," Kay shouted as the train got underway.

Frances stood back and waved. She saw, in the last car, Virginia and Claude Wheeler, looking as respectable as any Sunday Baptist couple, sober and neat, traveling up to Tavernier to visit their daughters.

It's a wonder, Frances thought as she walked back to Pinder Lane and her typewriter, how they manage to get themselves together every Sunday morning, a minor miracle for the Christians.

She kept her mind busy with these and other thoughts because she didn't want to think about Kay and she didn't want to think about Jake and she especially didn't want to think about the two of them making love on Boca Chica's beach in the early morning hours while Virginia had paced nervously behind the louvered doors of the Jefferson and Frances had chain-smoked on the veranda of the house on Pinder Lane.

Though she hadn't planned to, Frances found herself spending the summer in Key West, writing a melancholy novel in the mornings, taking melancholy walks in the late afternoon.

She usually wound up her afternoon walks at the Jefferson, sitting with Jake on the balcony, drinking Cuban beers, just as they had in another time. Occasionally Virginia would join them; but for the most part she sat in the room behind the louvered doors, doing things to her hair, reading magazines.

Jake and Frances talked as if she weren't there, as

if she were a child too young to understand their adult conversation.

Below them the town looked as poor, as stricken, as the men who walked up and down Duval Street, hawking melons, coconuts, bananas, whatever they could get their hands on. Frances discovered that the reason behind Jake's improvements to the Pinder Lane house was that they gave him an excuse to provide employment. The Conchs had a difficult enough time accepting public monies; private charity was unthinkable. Whenever Jake amassed some money, he'd buy a house and renovate it, giving the Conchs much needed work and salaries. "You've got to get out of here, Jake," Frances told him several times as the long, infinite summer wore on. "It's not doing you any good staying here." Implicit in her statement was that it wasn't doing Virginia any good, either.

At first he wouldn't answer. Then he said he was "marking time."

"Or serving it," Frances told him. "Paying for real and imagined crimes against Mr. and Mrs. Claude Wheeler."

"My biggest problem," Jake said, going into another, more palatable subject, "is finding dice changers. Either they're so quick I can't catch them and then they're sure to cheat me. Or they're so bad, any dumb Conch can figure it out and there's a fight and I have to get that damned crooked sheriff in to haul ass."

"I thought the sheriff found religion."

"He did. That's when we found a new sheriff."

"Well," Frances said, bored with the subject, order-

ing a new beer, "perhaps you should hire honest
croupiers."

"Nobody wants that. Where would the fun be?"

It was August and she was beginning to suffer from
what she self-diagnosed as Mental Acid Indigestion.
"Too much turtle meat," she told Jake. "Too little
intellectual exercise. I'll be finished with my first
draft in a few weeks and then I'm going to take my
own advice and head for New York. I've been here
too long. Key West is taking over."

"I'll be sorry to see you go, Frances."

She finished the manuscript a week before Labor
Day. She packed her papers that morning, annoyed
that they had already begun to mildew, threw her
clothes in her suitcase, left notes and presents for
Blondell and Coffee, a letter for Jake, and caught the
train north.

In her letter to Jake Frances wrote, "Enough with
good-byes already, as Bessie might say."

It was a beautiful Labor Day weekend. The Gulf
was a deep turquoise and exceedingly calm. Key West
was quiet. There was no traffic because there weren't
many cars left in the town and there wasn't any place
to go with the possible exception of Boca Chica, the
small key to the north where Key Westers liked to
picnic and swim.

A few big houses were being kept up but most of
the houses in the town were gray and unpainted. Key
West was still, at heart, a Cuban town. At night only
the streetlights the government had succeeded in in-
stalling on Duval Street showed any life.

Labor Day Monday was even quieter than the ordinary Mondays. Virginia and Claude had decided to take advantage of the railroad's special excursion fare, going up to Tavernier on Labor Day instead of Sunday.

Early that morning Jake lay in his bed in the Jefferson, watching Virginia turn herself into a proper matron once again. The night before, sitting at the blackjack table in the Bucket of Blood's casino, she had looked like a sporting lady with no present, little future, a great deal of past.

But on Labor Day morning she wore a white dress that reminded Jake of a dress she had worn when she first came to Key West. It was designed to imitate a naval uniform with a sailor's collar, blue and red stars on its pockets. When she was satisfied with her hair and her lipstick, she put on a straw hat and gloves and low-heeled white shoes.

She looked a little like the girl Jake had fallen in love with, except maybe around the eyes and the brim of the hat hid them fairly well.

"You look great," he told her.

"Yeah?"

She was being efficient that morning, all cut-and-dry. She walked across the room and kissed him good-bye. She hadn't bothered with that for a long time. She stood looking down at him. With the sunlight behind her and the wide brim of the hat, he couldn't see her all that well.

"I've come to a momentous conclusion, Jake," she said, putting a white straw bag she had saved from better days under her arm.

"What's that?"

"It's not your fault."

"What's not?"

"None of it. My father. Claude. Me. It's not your fault, Jake. You can stop feeling so goddamned guilty."

She stepped out onto the balcony and stood there for a moment, one hand holding the purse, the other grasping the balustrade. And then the louvered door slammed itself shut and she was gone.

He shaved and dressed, lit a cigar, and walked to the Cuban café on Petronia and had his morning coffee. No one was on the streets but every house had its radio on, most of them tuned in to the same Havana station.

You could walk from one end of this town to the other and not miss a program, he told himself, adding, if you happen to *habla* the *español*.

He strolled along Duval for a while. Coffee had gone to a picnic with friends and he had nothing to do but think and he thought about what Virginia had said.

After a while the Cuban boys began to come out, dressed up, waiting for the girls. It was a holiday. Couples were walking up and down Duval Street. Jake went back to the Jefferson and sat on the balcony, drinking the Cuban beer Luis had brought him, listening to the rumba music coming from the rooms above his and the sound of the woman's-tongue tree over on United Street rattling in the wind.

Later he went down to his saloon. Luis San Obispo had opened it but there wasn't much business. They agreed to keep the casino closed. It was a family day.

Luis gave him another beer and turned on the radio. It was five o'clock in the afternoon. Reports of

the hurricane were first coming in. Jake looked at
Luis who gave him his *qué pasa* shrug and Jake went
outside and walked to the docks.

The sky was as clear as it could be. He thought,
something's got to be wrong. He went back to his
saloon and had Luis turn the radio back to an American station. The announcer was talking about a hurricane off the Florida keys.

I must be crazy, Jake thought. There's no hurricane out there.

The announcer said it was the worst hurricane in
history. But there was hardly a breeze in Key West.

He got into the old De Soto and made it as far as
Boca Chica before a young Coast Guard lieutenant
with bad skin and a high-pitched voice turned him
around.

He asked if he could get a boat out. He told them
he had friends who had gone up on the train. "What
am I supposed to do?" he asked the lieutenant.

"Nothing, mister. There's nothing to do."

He drove back to Key West, to the comfort his
daughter and the house on Pinder Lane were able to
give him. The people in the cafés looked worried
now. The rumba music was gone with the holiday
spirit. A radio announcer up in Miami was describing
the two-hundred-mile-an-hour winds and the twenty-
foot-high wall of water that had washed the train out
to sea.

The eye of the 1935 Labor Day hurricane, which
wrecked Flagler's Overseas Railway once and for all
and left five hundred dead, had a barometric pressure
of twenty-six point thirty-five, the lowest ever record-

ed in the Western hemisphere. For no reason at all it missed Key West.

It hit Tavernier with its full force.

Virginia and Claude and the two girls, in their white summer dresses, were walking to the white clap-board church when the first rains and winds came. The girls cried out and Virginia and Claude looked at one another with apprehension. They all knew what the sudden downpour meant. Virginia's hat went sailing off her head and down the church steps onto the dirt road. Claude made as if to go after it but Virginia stopped him.

"It's just a hat, Claude. No reason to get soaked to the skin for it."

She led the way into the church where the minister, a good-looking white-haired man named Wilfred Mercer, was beginning to preach a sermon on the in-equalities of life on earth to the half-dozen churchgoers who had turned up for the special late afternoon Labor Day services.

The rain and the wind became progressively louder, drowning his voice out, and the girls huddled against their parents. Virginia found herself touching Claude for the first time in a very long time.

Suddenly the church doors flew open and a dozen men, women, and children came running into the church, their clothes wet, many of them crying. The men closed the doors, forcing them shut against the terrible winds.

"Perhaps," Reverend Mercer shouted, "you should all come down front. Ruth," he asked his wife, a tall handsome woman, "are there any blankets in the back, the ones from the work camp?"

Mrs. Mercer opened the door which led to the back room of the church and several feet of water came pouring out of it. Her husband helped her to get the door closed but water kept seeping through over the sill.

And again the church doors were flung open and a huge wave of water was coming up the steps and into the church. One of the men tried to swim toward his wife and child, standing on the benches, horrified, and was instantly sucked up by the water and drowned.

Claude pulled Virginia and the girls up to the pulpit. "Get Chrissie up," he shouted. Virginia followed Claude's example, taking her eldest daughter, holding her above her head as the relentless wave of water grew higher and higher and in no time at all, engulfed everyone and everything around it. The noise, Virginia thought. That awful noise.

Virginia's last sight of Claude, with their youngest daughter held over his head, was of him as a young man with yellow-blond hair and a boundless, endless enthusiasm for life. Her last feeling was one of overwhelming regret.

Jake managed to get halfway up the keys on Thursday as a member of the Key West rescue team. Everyone seemed to need rescuing. There were one hundred and forty-three passengers from the stranded liner, *Dixie*, no one knew what to do with. Ten boats, carrying medical supplies from No Name Key to Matecumbe, where the worst trouble had been, dumped the supplies and took on the stranded passengers.

At Tavernier, the twenty-foot wall of water had caused virtually every structure to completely disappear. Bodies were impossible to identify and the authorities were anxious to burn them as soon as possible because of the heat, because there was no fresh water, no sanitation.

Jake couldn't find any trace of the Wheelers or of Virginia's sister's family. It was as if none of them had ever existed.

The heat made everything twice as difficult. Bodies were being found faster than they could be buried. Toward the end of the week, the governor, Dave Sholtz, gave the order to start burning the bodies that couldn't be buried.

Jake watched as national guardsmen made a funeral pyre for the dead. One guardsman fired a rifle while another unfurled an American flag and within minutes a cloud of black smoke was wafting out into the clear blue skies over the Florida keys.

Jake stayed with the rescue team throughout the following week, until it became apparent that they weren't needed any longer. He went back to Key West, moved out of the Hotel Jefferson and into the house on Pinder Lane with his daughter, Coffee.

BOOK FIVE

NIGHT

CHAPTER 1

In the early spring of 1938, as Kay was preparing for her annual trip to Paris to cover the fashion show, Fatty Freeman walked into her office, unannounced.

"You can take your debonair rump and park it on someone else's desk," she told him, without looking up from the design book she was studying. "I have no time for chitchat."

"Neither do I, darling. And lest you forget, I am still your boss."

"I haven't forgotten, Fatty," she said, making an elaborate business of closing the design book, folding her hands and looking up at him. "Shoot."

"As long as you're going to be in Europe anyway, I want you to hop over to Berlin and cover the German spring fashions."

"I don't have to 'hop over to Berlin' to tell you what every good German hausfrau will be wearing next year: Fuller brush moustaches, wraparound raincoats, and sterling silver swastikas in their ears. Listen, Fatty, I have no intention of going to a country where . . ."

She went on while Fatty, with his narrow, friendly eyes, waited until she ran out of breath. Then he told

her he wasn't sending her to Berlin to heil Hitler or
to swear eternal allegiance to the German military
machine. "All I want you to do is report on German
fashions."

"There is no such animal. And even if there were,
no one would be even remotely interested."

"You're wrong, Kay. The Nazis may be monsters
but every female in America wants to know what
their women are wearing."

She pushed herself away from her free-form desk
and went to the windows which looked south on Fifth
Avenue. "The truth of the matter is I'm a coward,
Fatty," She turned and looked at him. "My husband
wasn't exactly a pristine Aryan, you know."

He went to her and put his arm around her shoulder. "Kay, do you honestly think I'd send you there if
there was the remotest chance of danger? I've already
spoken to Germany, to their Fashion Institute.
They're very excited: New York's premier fashion
writer has deigned to take in their collections. You'll
get the full VIP treatment, I promise you." He
paused. "And I'll give you the front cover with a big,
fat by-line."

She removed his arm and went back to her desk.
"All right, Fatty Freeman. You win. But if you never
hear from me again after I've stepped foot in Berlin,
don't say I didn't give you advance warning."

"If I know you, darling, you'll end up by captivat-
ing Hitler, becoming Mrs. Führer, and turning Germany into a free state for Jews."

She was still living in the apartment on Central
Park West, still living with Nick's ghost. Occasionally

she slept with Fatty Freeman who still proposed to her once or twice a month.

She saw as much of Bessie as their complicated lives permitted. Bessie was often in Washington, playing sophisticated political-economic games with senators. Her old friend, Edward Lewis, had been Roosevelt's defense secretary but had resigned to become chairman of the presidential advisory board on European immigrants. It was a job that entailed a great deal more than its title implied.

Ryan complained she saw more of Lewis and the Roosevelts than she saw of him. "Irony is so delicious," Ryan said to her. "Now *I* spend three or four nights of the week wondering if you're going to turn up in my bed." Since Grace's death he had become querulous and less likely to retreat into his cool-handed manner when offended. As Settlement work and politics kept Bessie going, the numbers kept Ryan going. "Everything else runs itself. But the numbers, they still have to be looked after, the runners still have to be vetted every now and then."

Bessie didn't say that it was too bad he hadn't vetted Bumps Bogan before he killed her brother, that he hadn't cemented that relationship before it took the joy out of her life. She treated him more carefully than she once had. He seemed more fragile. But she still put in eighteen-hour days, working with Edward Lewis and his wife, Alma, on a project she refused to discuss even with Ryan.

And while Bessie was in Washington, Kay was on the Coast interviewing Carole Lombard or in Seattle interviewing Eugene O'Neill or in Brazil, writing about South American culture. They managed to talk to each other at least once a day. They had established a very necessary, very mutual emotional dependency.

"And you're not going to Germany," Bessie non-sequitured on the Sunday before Kay was to leave, after her afternoon guests—an amalgam of politicians, humanitarians, and private-interest lobbyists—had departed. She was wearing a gray tailored gown and a string of white pearls. The only color in the drawing room came from her red curls, her blue eyes. She looked, Kay thought, as if she had gone to boarding school with the women who filled the boxes in the Diamond Horseshoe at the opera house.

"What were you and Mrs. Roosevelt talking about?" Kay asked. Bessie and Eleanor Roosevelt had spent half an hour tête-à-tête in a corner, holding teacups, totally involved in their conversation.

"Domestic problems," Bessie said, pouring herself yet another cup of tea.

"FDR doesn't have time to cheat."

"You'd be surprised how little time it takes to cheat. And what makes you so certain that we were talking about Franklin's cheating?"

"Eleanor Roosevelt committing adultery? Now that would be . . ."

"Listen to me, Kay: you're not going to Germany."

"Bessie, it's all been arranged and I . . ."

Bessie interrupted with a knowledgeable and detailed summary of the rise of the Nazi party, their attitude toward women who married Jews, and the general tenor of Berlin in 1938.

"Do you have any idea of what they're doing to Jews in Austria?" Earlier that month Germany had invaded and annexed Austria, paving the way for future expansion into the Danube valley.

"Bessie, I'm only going to be in Berlin for four or five days at most."

"Talking to you, Kay, is like talking to a wall. Or like talking to Mitsuko. Do you know she plans to go back to Japan again this year? To study painting. I told her she paints well enough, that it's dangerous to hobnob with Japanese war lords. She laughed. She told me that 'art, dear Bessie, has nothing to do with politics.' I told her that in times like these, everything has to do with politics. I can't bear the thought of her going back to Tokyo. And now you're going to Germany, which is far worse."

"Bessie: a lovely, asexual, apolitical man is going to meet me upon my arrival, escort me to half a dozen fashion shows, and then he's going to put me on a train and send me back to Paris. It's all been arranged. I'm going."

Bessie looked out at Central Park, just beginning to show signs of life, the trees going green. She turned back to Kay. "Then if there's nothing I can say to stop you, I'm going to ask you a favor. I won't lie to you, Kay. It's dangerous. You have any qualms, you tell me now and we'll forget it. I won't love you any the less. But you must believe me, Kay: what I'm asking you is important."

She stood up and Kay followed her to the bedroom on the top floor where a safe had been installed in the fifteen foot square closet. Bessie worked the combination and removed what looked like a cartridge belt, handing it to Kay.

"What's this?" Kay asked, not liking the feel of the thing.

Bessie smiled for the first time since her guests had left. "It's what we used to call a money belt. I made Moishe Katz buy one a thousand years ago when I sent him to Poland to get the boys."

Kay began to unzip the pocket but Bessie's hand came over hers, stopping her. "It's money. And other items of worth. They'll help certain people get out of that madhouse. And they'll help certain people get in. If you get caught, Kay, you say you were planning to sell the money on the black market. They won't believe you but after Austria they're being more careful and we could always kick up a fuss. But you must remember, Kay, that this is dangerous. You don't have to do this. If it scares you one iota . . ."

"How the hell do I get it into the country?"

"You wear it."

"Wear it? It weighs a ton."

"You'll put on something nice and loose that day."

The Paris shows were especially elegant that year, the gowns sad and sophisticated. The parties were the same as the fashions, people drinking more but getting less drunk. Coco Chanel gave a dinner and Kay sat next to a man in a heliotrope silk dinner jacket. He bemoaned the fact that "there is no frivolity in Europe."

Kay couldn't stop thinking of the package she had left in Cesar Ritz's safe. She wondered, as she tried to pay attention to what he said, if she were not the last of the frivolous Americans.

It was a relief to leave Paris, to leave that special

European melancholy that pervaded everything: the mannequins who glided up and down the runway in their long, fragile dresses; the much decorated doorman at Chez Emile's; the journalists and the modistes and the rich young men with their blue suits and black ties and airs of doomed fatality. They all seemed to be waiting for the lion. I'm taking the overnight train into his mouth, Kay thought.

She had two martinis before her train crossed the border. She was shocked to see how pale she looked in the mirrored wall of the compartment. It was a wonderfully luxurious train but that didn't help. She had to sit down and hold her hands in her lap when the immigration official came in. But he merely poked around a bit in her suitcase, gave her a grim smile, and left, closing the door after him. She put her passport away and had another drink.

When the train pulled into Berlin's Charlottenberg station, there was a hard rap of knuckles on her compartment door. She opened it, forcing herself not to think of the heavy weight around her waist under the blue camisole dress she was wearing.

A young soldier in full Nazi regalia stood before her, clicking his heels, bowing from the neck and then allowing his level blue eyes to stare at a point somewhere above her head. "Frau Katherine Meyer?"

"Yes?"

"Please to accompany me." He about-faced and strode off.

She draped the light spring coat she had bought in Paris over her shoulders and took one last look at herself in the mirrored wall. Her inclination was to faint, to go into the bathroom, rip off the belt, flush it down the toilet. She wanted to start running, fast. Instead she walked as purposefully as she could to the end of the car.

The soldier was waiting for her on the platform. He had perfect skin with a touch of pink on his cheeks, symmetrical blond eyebrows, pale lips. Kay wondered if he were human or some wondrous machine the German scientists had developed. "Where are we going?" she asked.

"Please to accompany me."

She refused to do double time through the station. He was forced to walk at her pace which was as leisurely as she could make it. She was being childish, she knew; but she didn't want to appear cowed so early in the game.

He opened the door of a large, ominous black Daimler, closing it after her, taking his own place in the front with the chauffeur. Her trunk and luggage, she was informed, had already been placed in the boot of the car. She was driven out and along the Unter der Linden.

Everyone seems so prosperous, she thought. Much more so than they had in Paris. She had to remind herself that this was a country that had been bankrupt in 1931. Yet the cafés were full and the people on the streets walked with style, with purpose.

The Daimler pulled up in front of the Kaiserhof, a grand hotel festooned with the sort of half-circle balconies Kay imagined Hitler delivering speeches from. Canopies overhung several entrances and there were three large restaurants with glass walls, filled with diners looking as if they were rehearsing for a modern-day version of a Rudolph Friml operetta.

The hotel's manager and his assistants sailed out of the main entrance, like a shark surrounded by several pale pilot fish. The soldier waved them away.

"Shouldn't I register?" Kay asked, attempting to act as if the trip from the station had been expected, routine; trying to act as if she didn't expect to be taken upstairs to a room where she would be interrogated, tortured, unthinkably debased. She didn't want to disappear without a trace. She wanted to register.

"Not necessary," the soldier said.

They rode to the top floor in the gilded cage of the elevator while a small army of bellhops ran up the stairs encircling the elevator shaft, each carrying a piece of Kay's luggage.

The soldier led her to a door at the end of a carpeted, heavily furnished corridor. He threw the door open and allowed Kay to step in.

It was a lavish, fully draped, fully sofaed, fully radiator-covered nineteenth-century deluxe German hotel suite. Standing on the balcony and coming in through the doors was a man in a chocolate-brown suit with eyes to match; he had dark hair, combed straight back, wide shoulders, narrow hips. He moves nicely, Kay thought.

"Frau Meyer?" he asked, somewhat unnecessarily, in fairly unaccented Anglo-English. "I am Peter Heslin and I have the delightful assignment of being your guide for the next few days. I thought we might start off with a bottle of Piper-Heidsieck, though you must promise never to tell the tourist bureau that I endorse French champagne."

Her luggage was being opened in the bedroom, her clothes being neatly put away, and her uniformed escort had taken himself elsewhere. Kay found herself gladly accepting the glass from the manicured hand of the beautiful man facing her.

After he left, she went into the bedroom and removed the money belt. Its elastic underside had left red marks on her waist, like an animal's tracks in the snow.

She bathed and tried to read but the money belt sitting in the top drawer of the ornate bureau was all she could think of. Ten minutes before she was due to meet Peter Heslin in the lobby, there was a knock on the door. A young unhealthy-looking woman in a maid's uniform stepped into the suite and asked if she could arrange the bed, "for the sleeping."

She went into the bedroom while Kay sat in the living room, petrified. She came out a few moments later, a rumpled towel over her arm. "Good night, Frau Meyer. My regards to Fraulein Bessie."

She closed the door. Kay forced herself to go into the bedroom and open the drawer. The money belt was not there. She should have felt relieved but somehow didn't. She went downstairs to thank Peter Heslin for the flowers, to allow him to show her a bit of Berlin, *via noche*.

He was a perfect gentleman during the four days they spent together. Too perfect, Kay thought. He occasionally kissed her hand, he often took her arm, but that was all the physical contact between them.

They went to half a dozen fashion shows which featured slightly militaristic parodies of what she had seen in Paris. But the elegance, the sadness, had been left out. And the handsome German women were wrong, she thought, for the fragile dresses their designers tried to put them into. The models were too solid, too proud, for that sort of ephemera.

At a show of furs she bought a blue fox jacket. Peter Heslin was amused. "You must be very rich to indulge such whims," he said.

"It's been rather cool at night," she said, dismissing the subject. It was exactly the sort of fur Nick would have bought for her.

As Fatty had suggested, she engaged a local photographer to take photographs at the shows. Herr Hillman was a small man of fifty, with garlic breath and a constant tear in his right eye. He had a very direct photographic approach. Each morning Kay would find an envelope slipped under her door, filled with ten to fifteen shots of the models she had seen the day before. They were all head on, monochromatic, and oddly effective. They would be a nice change, Kay thought, from *Vanity*'s usually preferred overhead angles.

Herr Hillman had become something of a joke between Peter and herself, Peter referring to him as "your phantom lover. Oh, I know you American women. Each night, when I take you home, Herr Hillman is waiting in your bed, another exotic night of reckless passion ahead of you."

When it occurred to her to wonder why she was getting what she privately called the Duchess of Windsor treatment, she put it down to the importance the Germans placed on public relations, to the position *Vanity* held among the world's fashion publications.

On their last evening they dined in a restaurant

called the Blue Danube. It was filled with men in a variety of glossy uniforms, their women in full and low-cut gowns. Several men half stood, nodding and smiling at Peter as they came in. He abruptly nodded back. Though everyone else in the restaurant mingled freely, going from table to table, no one approached theirs. By the time they left, they had gone through two bottles of clear Moselle wine and Kay was feeling, she admitted, "no pain."

"Are you a Nazi?" she asked Peter Heslin as they stood under the blue canopy of the Blue Danube, waiting for the Daimler to pull up.

"That is a word we never use," he said, smiling, helping her into the back of the cavernous car.

"Are you?" she asked, pulling the blue fox jacket around her, looking up at him.

"My dear Kay, do you know of what you are speaking? Do you have any idea of what it means to be a member of the National Socialist German Workers' Party? I think I should like to explain it to you. May I come with you for what you call a nightcap, to your suite?"

She said that he might.

He ordered a bottle of brandy and handed her a full snifter after the waiter had left them. "To progress," he said, half emptying his glass. Then he took her glass, set it down on a table, and, putting his arms around her, kissed her.

"I thought you were going to tell me about the National Socialist German Workers' Party," she said.

"First, you must learn how a German male makes love. That is the basis of everything."

She knew she was drunk. She also knew she hadn't

been in bed with a man for months and that when she had, it had been an underwhelming experience. She was in a strange place, she told herself, frightened and lonesome. I have a great many excuses but the fact of the matter is, she told herself, that I have wanted to go to bed with Peter Heslin from the moment I saw him.

They went into the bedroom. He took off his clothes without looking at her. He had the kind of long, overdeveloped muscles one sees at professional sporting events. He was tan all over. He turned off the overhead light and went to her. His body was warm and hard.

There was no preliminary action other than that first embrace. He pulled her legs up against his shoulders and went into her with a brutal thrust. She cried out. He looked down at her and carefully spat in her face. When she protested, when she tried to break away, he slapped her. Then Peter Heslin proceeded to go to work.

He was painstaking, slow, very thorough. After he was finished—and it took him some time—she finally knew what the phrase that often popped up in the woman's magazines meant: "he used me." Peter Heslin used her in ways she had never been used before. He had forced himself into her front and into her back and into her mouth. He had debased her in ways she had never thought possible and if she had, she would have been disgusted.

But she had to face the fact, she told herself, that a part of her responded to him and enjoyed what he was about.

Afterward, as he lay smoking a cigarette, as Kay lay

against the wall, despising herself, he began to talk in
his low, pleasant voice. He spoke for well over an
hour. He spoke about Germany before Hitler, he told
her how Germany and German men had been cas-
trated, made impotent by the Allies.

"Yes, Frau Meyer, Hitler demands obedience. But
it's a small price to pay for the strength, the self-suffi-
ciency, the respect he's giving the German people. We
are becoming an Aryan nation once more, returning
to our Teutonic heritage, purifying ourselves of the
Jewish taint which has polluted us for so long."

Peter Heslin, she realized, as he spoke, was another
one of the hopeless unemployed men whom Hitler
had put into uniform (she had no doubt he usually
wore a uniform), whom Hitler had given an identity.

But he was also a monster, she thought. One she
had had sex with.

In the morning, while he slept, she packed. She put
on her makeup. She forced herself not to think. As
she picked up the telephone to call for the porter, he
came out of the bedroom, still nude. "Oh, no, dear
Frau Meyer. I am not finished with you yet. There
are now some questions I must ask of you. For example, there is the little night maid who came to your
room on your first day here." He took the receiver
out of her hand and placed it back on the cradle.
"She was found with an empty money belt soon after.
We would like to know what was in . . ."

There was a knock on the door; a shy, hesitant
knock. "Who is it?" Peter asked in German.

"Herr Hillman. I have the photographs for Frau
Meyer."

Peter laughed and went to the door. Herr Hillman

entered with an envelope in his hand. He didn't appear to think that the situation was odd, to ask why Frau Meyer was standing by the telephone wearing her blue fox jacket and Herr Heslin was standing in the middle of the room without clothes.

"Put them on the table," Peter said, turning his back, reaching for a towel.

Little Herr Hillman took a pistol from the pocket of his seedy suit jacket and, standing on his toes, hit Peter Heslin on the head with the butt. Peter started to turn but Herr Hillman hit him again, harder, in the same spot. Then he hit him once again.

"Come," Herr Hillman said to Kay. "We have need to get you on an aeroplane. Immediately."

"A plane?"

"The train might be a trifle slow," he said, looking down at Peter Heslin's body.

She was met at the private airport in Paris by a young American with brilliant teeth and an ambassadorial suit. He said he was going to drive her to Le Havre. She said she wanted to rest, to stay overnight in Paris but he insisted, saying, with his incredibly young voice, that it would be better if she went directly to Le Havre.

She was the last passenger to board the U.S.S. *Atlantic*.

She spent the voyage taking showers—"neurotic showers," she called them—having her meals in her stateroom, disliking herself.

She couldn't sleep. She thought about Nick and she thought about Jake and though she desperately didn't want to, she found herself thinking about Peter Heslin.

In the middle of the night, on the third day of the voyage, she went up to the top deck and tossed the silver blue fox jacket overboard.

Bessie met her at the pier and fussed over her, taking her back to the triplex, forcing her to eat a light meal, surrounding her with that peculiar, all-embracing, all-forgiving Bessie Meyer warmth.

After the meal she took Kay up to the guest room and closed the door. "Tell me everything," she said.

"I'm surprised you're not crying," Kay said after she indeed told Bessie everything.

"I don't cry anymore," Bessie said. "And there's nothing to cry about. We all do what we have to do." She kissed her. "You're a heroine. You proved yourself to be a brave woman, Kay. I'm proud of you, darling."

She tucked Kay into an enormous bed, kissed her again, and went off to a meeting with John L. Lewis at the Waldorf.

Kay wondered, just before she fell asleep, if anything was ever going to be right again in the world.

CHAPTER 2

The last half of the 1930s were an idyll for Max and Mitsuko. Nothing, it seemed, could go wrong for them. *Neon Lights,* with its instant artistic success, became a film that was always being shown somewhere, a film that was eventually used to teach college students the art of movie making.

Max ended up directing *Speakeasy* and went on to produce and direct a series of realistic gangster films which, besides accounting for a large percentage of MGM's income, won critical acclaim at the same time.

And just when it seemed that the gangster film's vogue was over, Thomas E. Dewey went gang busting in New York and the public clamored for more.

At the same time Mitsuko's painting had been "discovered" when she allowed Townie to convince her to show at a small Beverly Hills gallery. Word spread among art collectors of her sophisticated techniques and in a short time she found that her works were being hung in museums, that they were selling for ten and twenty thousand dollars.

She took Anna, Douglas, Janie, and her father, Mr. Tanaka, to Japan in 1937. It was the summer, Max was on location in New York, and she wanted, she said, to find out about the country from which her family came.

"I'm as American as you are," she told Bessie when the woman objected. "But I have a need to know what came before me."

"You're more American than I am," Bessie told her, "and I have a need to know you're on safe territory."

She studied for a month with a teacher at the Imperial University of Tokyo and learned that traditional Japanese art had a great deal to teach her. On the whole, however, she rejected its techniques, liking her own seek-and-find art. The children learned to use chopsticks, to sit on the floor, to eat raw fish as they followed Mr. Tanaka around each day while he visited friends and relatives.

When they returned, Townie asked Mr. Tanaka if he had wanted to stay in Japan. "Oh, no, Townie," he replied. "I am American now." His "little patch" of three hundred acres up the coast, just below Selvane, held one of the richest, most productive produce farms in California.

Townie said he would have liked to have seen the Japanese reaction to Anna. "There was a great deal of staring," Mitsuko said. "They thought she was a blond goddess."

Anna had become, predictably, the sort of girl who couldn't walk into a room without causing comment, without making people wonder. After the trip to Japan she took the train to New York to meet her father who was scouting locations for a film based on Dewey's life. She spent one glorious week with him at

Bessie's triplex, Bessie insisting they visit every night-club and every clothing store in Manhattan. Then Max drove her to Philadelphia's proper Main Line where she enrolled in Bryn Mawr College.

"You miss California already?" Townie asked when she had called him, collect, "just to say hello."

"No, I don't. Though everyone here is very different. The boys in the neighboring schools call us Bryn Martyrs and think we're stuck-up which we are. Anyway, it's not California, I miss. It's you, Townie."

"Oh, George," he said, doing Gracie Allen, "I bet you say that to all the girls."

She laughed and said that her cousin, David, Jake's son, was a sophomore at the University of Pennsylvania and would take her under his wing.

"Who's taking whom under who's wing?"

"Townie, he's introduced me to the most marvelous fellow. A communist."

"I'm sure that will gratify everyone in your immediate family."

Araby, while still not claiming ownership, was proud of Anna, and not ill pleased with herself. According to the 1938 *Photoplay* poll, Araby ranked number twelve behind Gable, Mickey Rooney, Bette Davis, Garbo, Deanna Durbin, Errol Flynn, and a few other notables.

"Not bad," Townie said, congratulating her. "You certainly survived the twenties."

"Listen, you little numb nut, I have every intention of surviving the thirties, the forties, and probably the fifties."

"What if you don't?"

"I've got my real estate to keep me warm. Not to

mention my art collection. Did you know I bought a Mitsuko? Well, why not? I've always liked her. She's been marvelous to Anna as well as to Max."

"Still no divorce?"

"I'll never divorce him. Not now. I'm too rich. Do you suppose I want to give Max half my property?"

Townie never came away from Ram-A-Dies without a faintly acrid taste in his mouth, as if he had swallowed brimstone.

In the summer of 1939, when Ryan had learned about television and was putting money into developing it, Bessie called Mitsuko, begging her not to go to Tokyo for what was becoming an annual visit. "Two years ago," Bessie said, "it was only an idea I had. This year I know. Mitsuko, please don't go."

She said she would think about it but in the end she went. She had promised her teacher she would be back. But she left the children and her father home. Perhaps it was Bessie's warning, perhaps it was the atmosphere in Tokyo, but she found herself not enjoying her visit, shortening it by several weeks.

Later when she remembered the opening years of that new decade, the forties, she would immediately think of the huge mahogany radio Bessie had sent them, a double-decker affair with a cabinet covered with carved cupids.

It wasn't the sort of furniture Mitsuko would have chosen but she liked it nonetheless, mostly because it was so reminiscent of Bessie. She had it placed in the far corner of the family room and that's where they would sit each evening, listening to England's early battles with Germany as if they were happening outside their door.

Mitsuko and Max would hold hands while sitting on a low sofa covered in gray silk. Douglas and Janie sat on huge pillows on either side of the radio as if they, too, were carved cupids. Townie, and his young friend, Charlie, sat on another silk-covered divan, looking tense and unhappy. Charlie was about to be drafted and Townie didn't want him to go.

It seemed that each time they would gather, they would hear the details of another historic battle, another further encroachment by the Germans. In silence they listened to the collapse of Holland followed by Belgium and, unthinkably, France. They followed Neville Chamberlain's defeat, Winston Churchill's rise.

During the broadcast of the air battle over the Strait of Dover, with bombs bursting in the background, Robinson appeared to announce that Miss Moore was in the central hall.

Mitsuko went out and brought Araby into the family room. Max moved to an easy chair, the two women sat side by side as the announcer began to describe the slaughter he was witnessing.

Afterward Araby refused coffee. "No, thank you, Mitsuko. I just felt terribly lonesome and I knew I couldn't sit through that by myself. I must leave, I'm hours late for drinks." She embraced Mitsuko and the children and left.

Later Townie learned that she had donated an ambulance to the London war-relief effort. The drivers, in gratitude, named it the Araby Moore, painting her name and her most prominent features on its fenders.

The morning after the broadcast Max was called to Washington. There he met with Edward Lewis and the man in charge of FDR's propaganda machine. Max was put in charge of producing films to aid the war effort, to act as liaison between the Pentagon and Washington.

In the following months he spent as much time in Washington as he did in Los Angeles, preparing scripts, lining up stars to make them.

On December 7, Max was in Washington and Townie and his friend, Charlie, were having Sunday luncheon with Mitsuko, the children, and Miss Dobbs.

As a special concession to the children the radio had been left on during the meal. Halfway through the musical program they were listening to, the announcer broke in with the news that the Japanese had attacked Hawaii and the Philippines. He then launched into a prepared diatribe against the Japanese race. "Each and every one of them," he said, "is a potential spy for Japan."

Mitsuko called her father after the broadcast and asked him to come and stay with her and the children. He arrived the following day, tall and spare and just in time to hear FDR declare war on Japan.

Max returned to California for further discussions with the studios, determined to get the studio heads to be more generous. He arranged for the initial group of actors the studios were willing to loan him to be flown to Washington with him. Dick Powell, Joan Crawford, and Alice Faye were the first to appear in the shorts, selling war bonds.

Max was to be gone for a two-month incommunicado stay. "They're all nuts, Townie," he told his friend over the last gin rummy game they were to play for some time. "Secrecy nuts. For Christ's sake, we're only making fifteen-minute trailers to sell war bonds. Those guys at the Pentagon are acting as if we're putting all our submarine-attack planes on film in living Technicolor and dubbing them for German distribution."

Max didn't think the war in the Pacific could affect the Japanese in the United States just as the war in Germany wasn't affecting German Americans. As he watched Max's plane take off from the supposedly top secret army airport in Encino, Townie wondered if any of the generals visiting Max's set (located in Virginia, some twenty minutes from the Pentagon), hobnobbing with the stars, had any idea that Max's "companion" was of Japanese descent.

The day after Max left, as FDR was launching into one of his fireside chats, a Japanese I-17 appeared a couple of thousand yards off the California coast and lobbed a dozen rounds of five and one half inch shells at an oil-tank complex located not far from Mr. Tanaka's farm.

The Japanese submarine didn't do any actual damage but there were rumors, inflamed by the Hearst papers, suggesting collusion between the Japanese farm cooperative and the submarine.

Townie wanted Mitsuko to leave California. "Have you read what the papers are saying? Have you listened to the radio? They're building up a mountain of sentiment against *all* Japanese."

"Townie, I am an American. I was born in this country. I am Nisei, second generation. My father is Isei but still, he's been an American citizen for years.

We are—I am, at any rate—large property holders. And this isn't Nazi Germany. It's Mr. Roosevelt's America."

In early March, with Hearst's papers galvanizing the already hard core of California's anti-Japanese feelings, Mitsuko put in a call to her father. She was told by the operator that she couldn't get through, that the lines were down. It was a Saturday morning, a beautiful California spring day.

She decided to run up to the farm, pick up her father, and bring him down to the house for a short vacation. She missed Max, her painting wouldn't go right, and Townie was off in Baja with his Charlie. She refused to read the newspapers or listen to the radio. She wondered how they were allowed to print and broadcast the things they did.

Douglas and Janie had been taunted at school for their "yellow taint" and she kept them home that morning, thinking that a long ride in an open car might make them all feel better. "We need airing," she said.

She collected them and their nanny, Miss Dobbs, and the dog, a collie named Shakey, and they drove up the coastal highway. Miss Dobbs sat in the back with Douglas and the dog. Douglas insisted on wearing his baseball cap, an authentic Brooklyn Dodgers cap that Bessie had sent him. Janie, angry over some slight, sat in the front with her mother, not saying a word, clutching an old Shirley Temple doll. She had taken the taunts at school more to heart than her brother. Mitsuko drove the old Rolls convertible with one hand on the wheel, one hand holding her daughter's free and sticky hand.

They hit the first roadblock ten miles south of the farm. A scrupulously polite army officer looked at Mitsuko for a few careful moments, read her driver's license and the car's registration carefully, and asked where she and her passengers were headed. Mitsuko gave her father's name and address. The officer consulted a harmless-looking sheaf of papers, flicked a check off against something listed there, and told Mitsuko to continue.

In the rearview mirror she could see him handing the papers to a soldier and striding off to a tiny building made of concrete blocks.

She had always been good in emergencies but that day, that morning in early March, she could feel the sweat coming out all over her body. Douglas would not shut up about the Dodgers and Jane began asking questions, the kind that even normally were irritating.

Cora Dobbs knew what was going to happen before Mitsuko did. She tried to quiet the children while Mitsuko tried to drive. A few miles after the checkpoint she pulled over to the shoulder, turned the ignition off, and rested her head against the wheel, closing her eyes. The children became very still. They could all hear the sound of the surf and the traffic passing by.

"Perhaps," Miss Dobbs said after a few moments, in her cool, precise voice, "if we turned back?"

"I doubt if that would help," Mitsuko said.

"Then don't you think it might be a good idea if we switched places?"

Mitsuko looked at Miss Dobbs's encouraging face, got out of the car, and gladly gave her the wheel. Miss Dobbs immediately put up the canvas top. Mitsuko sat in the back, hugging Douglas, attempting not to communicate her fear to him.

Miss Dobbs drove the Rolls through the heavy wooden gates which marked the beginning of the farm cooperative. A short ways up the road, a Jeep blocked their way. Two men, one in uniform, one in a dark suit, came toward them.

They asked the same questions as those that had been asked earlier. Mitsuko, her mouth dry, found herself unable to speak. Miss Dobbs became the spokesperson, efficiently economizing her words, answering each question with a terse directness. "We are visiting," she told the civilian, implying it was none of his business and that it had been an impertinence to ask, "Miss Tanaka's father who owns a farm here."

"Miss Tanaka owns the farm," the civilian corrected her. "Whose kids are these?"

"Mine," Cora Dobbs said without hesitation. "Whose did you think they were?" she asked in an invincible British accent. Jane with her blond hair, Douglas with his blue eyes and baseball cap stared forthrightly up at the man leaning in the car's window, his lean American face attempting a reassuring smile.

"I'm afraid," he said after a moment, "that we're going to have to detain Miss Tanaka."

"That's absurd," Cora Dobbs said. "Miss Tanaka is a world renowned artist . . ."

"Please get out of the car, Miss Tanaka."

Mitsuko did so, trying not to look at Douglas or

Janie, willing them not to say anything. She wanted to cry, to shout, to beg them to let her go. She didn't. Instead she said, very clearly, "Cora, I will be in touch. Please remember me to Mr. Townsend." And then Mitsuko remembered Townie wasn't at home, that he was somewhere in Baja with Charlie. "And, of course, to Mrs. Meyer." Bessie, she was confident, would fix everything. "Good-bye, Cora. Children."

It was the first time that she had ever addressed Cora Dobbs by her first name in all the years that she had known her and her voice broke on the word "children." Still she managed to walk with what she hoped was dignity to her father's house. He was in the huge, old kitchen, sitting at a handsome, pine table, drinking tea.

"Go home," he told her, standing up. "Go home, quickly, Mitsuko."

She put her arms around him and kissed him for the first time in a long time. "I am home, *papasan*." There wasn't much use in telling him that they wouldn't let her go.

Two hours later the man in the blue suit came and told them that they were not under arrest: they were under "detainment" by virtue of Executive Order 9066, which he cited. "For your own safety," he said, "you are going to be held in protective custody, then relocated out of Area One."

She had no idea what he was talking about. What was Area One? He didn't answer. He told them they had three days in which to sell any personal property, that they would not be allowed to leave the farm, that they might bring two suitcases with them when they were evacuated. He told them what the suitcases might contain.

She was allowed to make one telephone call. She called their lawyer who was on vacation, his butler said, for several weeks.

The man in the blue suit brought in another lawyer from Selvane who had forms already printed up. He said he represented a group of local Americans— Californians for Democracy—who were willing to give her a dollar an acre for the farm.

"That's very kind, Mr. Carter," Mitsuko said. "However, I am selling all of my property to a Mr. Charles Harrison Townsend, Jr., of Hollywood, California, for one hundred dollars, payment of which is to be made in one year's time. If you could please draw up the necessary papers?"

The lawyer, Carter, began to protest but the man in the blue suit asked him to step outside for a moment. Mitsuko could hear their conversation through the open kitchen window and she wasn't at all certain that she wasn't meant to. The man in the blue suit said that she wasn't a "dumb Jap," that she had rich connections, that she had arrived in a Rolls-Royce, that they had better let her have her way if they didn't want trouble later.

The lawyer reluctantly agreed. On the following day he appeared with a young woman whom he said was the notary and several papers which Mitsuko read carefully and signed, selling her father's farm and her house in Beverly Hills to Townie for one hundred dollars.

The following day—two, not the three promised— Mitsuko and her father were marched with fifty other

Japanese-American men and women to a bus which took them to Santa Anita racetrack.

As soon as they were inside the gates, they were searched for knives and straight-edged razors. Then officials went through their suitcases while a team of medics examined their arms for vaccination marks.

A man with a bright bald head and an ill-fitting khaki uniform assigned each of them to quarters. "Stable numble twelve," he told Mitsuko and her father. "Stall thirty-three."

It was only when they entered that stall that she broke down. It wasn't the indignity of being housed where horses had once been. It was the fact that the floor hadn't been cleaned. Her fifty-dollar shoes were covered with manure.

Mr. Tanaka, never a demonstrative man, took her in his lean, tough arms and repeated over and over again: *"Shikata ga nai."* Mitsuko knew that it translated, roughly, into English as, "It can't be helped." But it could be helped, she thought.

It was Mr. Tanaka who insisted on going to stand in the mess line. He brought back boiled potatoes and four slices of stale white bread. "No more canned sausages," he told her, trying to smile. "They ran out."

The authorities weren't ready for them. They were the very first. The other detainees in that early group were mostly older people. They were worried about what they would do when they got out. Most of them had sold their possessions to Californians for Democracy for virtually nothing.

The lines at the two public phones never seemed to

get any smaller and one was allowed only a single call. To make another, one had to go back to the end of the line, whether the first went through or not.

She gave up after a single try. No one answered at the house in Beverly Hills and she had no idea how to reach Max or Townie or Bessie. She felt, suddenly, very tired.

They had been issued bed ticking bags which they had to stuff with the straw that had been left in the stalls. When Mitsuko returned from the telephone line, she found that her father had already stuffed the bags. They slept, holding hands. They had always been close but now they were developing a physical intimacy. They had a need to touch one another, to reassure each other that they weren't alone.

The man in the next stall talked to himself all through the night. The cash he had brought with him was already low. "What is going to be?" he asked Mitsuko in the morning. "What will happen when there is peace and I am left with no money? This problem, Miss Tanaka, worries me night and day."

"The authorities will take care of us," Mitsuko answered and was surprised to find that this gave him some solace.

She felt desolate and deserted, as if everyone—friends, family, even Max and Townie—had deserted her because she wasn't Caucasian, because she was Japanese.

In her more rational moments she knew someone was going to arrive to get her and her father out, sooner or later.

That is until the early morning when the soldiers

came and marched them out onto the racetrack where there were more buses. The buses, they were told, were taking them out of Area One, to the Ownes Valley, to Manzanar.

"Such an ugly name," someone said.

"It means apple orchard in Spanish," a soldier told them.

The bus was filled with rumors. Manzanar, one of her father's friends said, was crawling with snakes, a hideout for addicts and thieves.

They arrived in the middle of a not unusual dust storm. None of them could keep their eyes open. Dust covered everything: the people, the bus, the camp. They realized that the real enemy at Manzanar wasn't going to be the snakes or the thieves; it was the dust.

There weren't many in that first contingent: sixty-one men, twenty women walked through the gates of Manzanar on the first day of spring, March 21, 1942. Manzanar was, in effect, the United States' first concentration camp for its own citizens.

There was little furniture in the barracks, a couple of chairs left over from the days when it was a WPA camp. Again they slept on straw-filled mattresses. The old barracks had been divided into one-room apartments, twenty by twenty-five feet. Mitsuko and her father were to live in one of them with another family consisting of two polite brothers and their frightened, angry wives.

There were fourteen other barracks. Only two had a shower and flush toilets. Everywhere one went was the dust and the nauseating chemical smell of Chic Sale outhouses.

They were put to work immediately, readying the barracks for the others who would be coming. If it hadn't been for her father's determined smile and his *shikata ga nai*—which became something of a camp slogan—Mitsuko didn't know how she would have survived.

Townie once described Cora Dobbs as "a saint. She's all English, tight, a girl who's obviously never been kissed, much less laid. A saint." He was later to reflect that she was exactly the sort of woman they all needed in those early days of 1942.

She had driven the children straight to the house, packed their clothes as she explained, in measured words, exactly what was happening. There was to be no panic. Tears were unthinkable. Mummy was perfectly all right and would continue to be so if they acted like the brave little soldiers she knew they were.

Miss Dobbs sent the children down to the kitchen to have cookies with Robinson and then she went to the telephone. She tried calling Townie intermittently but he had left word with his service that no one, not even L. B. Mayer, was to be told where he was staying. It was to be his last time with Charlie before that young man went into the service.

When she wasn't trying Townie's number, she was attempting to get in touch with Bessie. Finally Minnie answered and she put Ryan on the line but all Ryan could tell her was that Bessie was in Hyde Park, that she hadn't left a number, and that she would be back in a day or two and could he help?

At last she remembered that Mitsuko had told her

to get in touch with Mrs. Meyer. Though Mitsuko had meant Bessie, to Cora's logical mind there was only one Mrs. Meyer and that was Araby Moore.

Araby didn't hesitate. She told Cora to bring the children to Ram-A-Dies where no one would find them, and she installed them in the Pegasus Suite along with Miss Dobbs.

She called Robinson and told him to close the house, not to take any calls. She thought there was a real chance that the authorities would try to find Mitsuko's children, to put them in a concentration camp, too.

She tried to locate Max. The three people she called in Washington weren't any help and she didn't call the fourth on her list because she knew if she did, she would eventually have to sleep with him.

There were a great many people in Hollywood who were determinedly and genuinely patriotic. Max, for example. But, as Araby knew, there were also a great many people in her town who were determinedly and genuinely scared.

Carleton LeMay, for example. He hung up when he found what she wanted.

Martin Dies, who had shouted to the world that Hollywood was communist dominated in 1940, had not been forgotten. No one wanted to be accused of being a Fascist, a Japanese sympathizer, in 1942.

Araby tried a few other people but their reaction was the same as Carleton LeMay's. She finally reached Townie, who had come back from Baja with Charlie. She told him in short, graphic sentences what the situation was. He tried Washington but was informed by half a dozen different voices that Mr. Meyer could not be reached for at least a week, if then.

Araby finally broke down and called her general. "He's sixty-two going on a hundred with a cock just like you'd expect a general to have," she told Townie as they drove out to the army's secret airport near Encino. "Long and straight and narrow, a little flat on the top, and always knife hard. Your standard-issue bayonet. It takes him forty-five minutes to reach orgasm and then neither of us are very positive he has. You know that this means I'm going to have to do it with him at least once more, don't you? And probably soon."

The general had located Max and Max had gotten through to Townie. He got off the plane looking pale, anxious, and thin. They wasted two frustrating days at Tanforan which was another racetrack assembly center someone had marked down as Mitsuko's point of detainment.

"These goddamned papers are all screwed up," Max said, holding out the report he had managed to get hold of.

"You have to forgive them," Townie said. "They're new to the concentration-camp business."

By the time they got to Santa Anita and worked their way through the eighteen thousand Japanese Americans "assembling" there, it was the beginning of the following week and Max, in Townie's estimation, was treading a thin line.

Finally someone in Washington who wanted Max to hurry up and return to finish the bond drive shorts called and told him Mitsuko and her father were already at Manzanar.

Max and Townie got into the Rolls and began the long drive a few minutes after Max received the call. It was early in the morning and there was a low fog hanging over Los Angeles. They passed the drugstore on Santa Monica Boulevard that they had all patronized. It had been owned by a Nisei Japanese family called Suzuki. Across its door was a big, proud sign in red, white, and blue letters: "I Am An American." The sign hadn't helped. Directly above it was another piece of cardboard that read: "Sold. Harpoon Realty."

On every telephone pole were posted "Instructions to All Persons of Japanese Ancestry," telling them where and how to report, how to divest themselves of a lifetime in three days.

The Manzanar project director, a thin, gray-haired man, was waiting for them at the gates. Miss Tanaka was in her room. Nervous, he said that he had asked her to meet them in the town which was, with a sure sense of wrongness, called Independence. Miss Tanaka had refused. The project director said that she felt it was bad for morale, that if the others saw her leave, they might complain.

"Christ," Townie said. "I hope to God they're at least complaining."

Looking put out, the project director led them to the room in the barracks where Mitsuko and her father lived with six other people. The dust and the smell of chemicals was pervasive.

Mitsuko was sitting on a cot, her hands playing with a thin army blanket. Her father was standing, as tall and straight as ever, looking out a small window.

She was crying. She went to Max who took her in his arms and held her.

"He won't leave," she said, her voice muffled by the material of Max's jacket. "He won't leave."

"Mr. Tanaka," Max said. "You must come with us."

"No. I will not leave this place. Not while my friends are kept here. I could not live with myself, Mr. Meyer." He turned and looked at them. "I cannot go."

"Then how can I?" Mitsuko whispered, breaking out of Max's arms, turning to her father. "How can I?" she shouted.

"You have children. You have a man," he said, for the first time admitting that Max and Mitsuko had something more than an employer-employee relationship. "Your duty is to them."

"I have a father," Mitsuko said. "I won't leave you here."

"Please," he said, walking across the room, putting his hand on Max's arm. "Please, Max. Take her from this. You understand, I know. I must stay here."

"Mitsuko," Max said, taking her in his arms again. "You have to come with me. Douglas and Janie are all right for the time being but we have to get them—and you—far away from California as soon as possible. If your father changes his mind, we can always come for him."

"Did you hear that, *papasan?*" Mitsuko asked. "Will you promise to think about leaving and if you change your mind, will you let us know?"

"Yes," the old man lied. "Yes, my daughter."

Max put a roll of money into the old man's Levi's jacket, Mitsuko kissed him and they left him there, in that bare room filled with dust, smelling of chemicals, in his farmer's clothing, looking like a member of an ancient, imperial court.

Above his bed, carefully hung, were his framed American citizenship papers.

They all stayed the night at Ram-A-Dies. "It's just like Araby," Townie told Cora Dobbs. "It's gone through half a dozen cosmetic transformations but at heart it's still the same funny, vulgar, endearing piece of work it's always been."

Townie had received the legal papers deeding him all of Mitsuko's property for one hundred dollars. He signed it over to Max while Mitsuko and Cora Dobbs were getting the children ready. As soon as the lawyers were gone, Townie called the number he had been given and arranged "transport. I'm becoming a whiz with army lingo," he told Cora as he waited with one hand over the telephone's mouthpiece.

Max had found and purchased a small house in Georgetown for a large sum of money and what couldn't be moved there would be put in storage. Robinson was to arrange for the moving and then follow Max and Mitsuko to Washington. The house as well as the farm was to be let.

Araby and Max were sitting in the drawing room having a drink, remarkably comfortable with one another, when Townie came in to say that the transport was on its way.

"Even if we wanted to stay," Max told Araby, "we

couldn't. Mitsuko is plain Miss Tanaka, a first-generation Japanese American, a Nisei. There'd always be the possibility of her being put in a camp."

"Of course if they were married," Townie said, "she'd be safe."

Araby stood up and mixed herself another cocktail and launched into movie talk. She told them who was sleeping with whom, who was joining the army air force and who was coming up 4F. "There's an awful lot of flat feet in this town," she said.

Mitsuko, looking as if she had come from a month at a spa instead of a week of internment, came into the room with Douglas and Janie. Everyone stood up and kissed, formally. Then they went out to the khaki limousine, the transport that was waiting. Townie had specified khaki; he wasn't taking any chances on them being stopped in a civilian car. "Not in this police state," he said.

Araby's general was just pulling up behind the transport in a twin limousine. "My heart is sinking," Araby said as she put a hail-the-conquering-hero smile on her face and turned toward the aging soldier.

Max was the last person to get into the car. As he did so, Araby called to him from the steps where she was standing with the general, the general's hand on her shoulder.

"Darling," she called, "stay in touch. I shan't be around for the next few weeks, however. I'm going down to Mexico. I'll let you know as soon as the divorce is final. Not to mention what it's going to cost you."

They left her as they had left Mr. Tanaka. Only Araby, in her purple and gold dress, seemed more like an imperial courtesan than a member of the court.

And unlike Mitsuko's father, there were tears in her eyes. It was the first time anyone had ever seen Araby Moore cry, off-screen.

CHAPTER 3

On a bright, hot day in early August, 1942, Ryan told Bessie that he wanted to give her a fiftieth birthday party. "The world's going up in flames and he wants to give parties," she said, sitting down at her dressing table. "And even if it weren't, I don't want a party, Ryan. You know I don't celebrate birthdays anymore."

"And you don't cry anymore and you don't laugh anymore and you don't make love anymore. Isn't it time, my dear, that you gave up mourning Nick?"

"If I could, Ryan, I would."

"You're becoming hard, Bessie."

"It's the company I keep."

She examined herself in the vanity mirror and thought that he might be right. She had always thought she would get plump with age, gradually turning into a red-cheeked motherly sort of person like the grandmothers she remembered on the shtetl in Poland.

But at fifty she had the same figure she had had when she appeared on Second Avenue as the Statue of Liberty. Her curls were as unmanageable as they had always been, only a few white hairs among the red.

But there was, she had to admit, a haggard, disappointed look around her blue eyes, an almost imperceptible tightening of the mouth. She wondered if she was turning into one of those querulous, never satisfied women—the sort who always looked middle-aged—the kind who spent their later lives trying to milk what satisfaction they could from sitting on civic committees.

She looked at Ryan who was watching her from the green leather wing chair he had insisted be brought up into the bedroom. He was holding a copy of the *Times,* but not reading it. He wasn't interested in the news.

Like herself, he was aging well. His sandy-colored hair was lighter now, his seemingly lashless eyes a bit duller. But that dangerous excitement he used to carry with him was gone, revoked with Prohibition.

The war meant nothing to him. In a way he admired Hitler and Mussolini and their contempt for the law. But the small wars, the ones in the city's streets, were the ones he cared for. He had thrived on the tiny battles that took place in the back corridors of City Hall, in the closed sessions in Albany. He wasn't having a good time with this war. He was being left out and he felt it.

Increasingly Ryan's conversation consisted of references to the past, of reminiscences of bootlegging coups, of memorable scams. His legitimate business effectively ran themselves. His only real interest still lay with the numbers. There he could be as ruthless as he had once been, replacing the chiselers and the

gonifs and the police informants he constantly ferret-
ed out with new chiselers, new *gonifs,* new canaries.

Bessie supposed that he mourned Bogan in much
the same way as she mourned Nick. Bogan had been
another side of Ryan, representative of his free summers as a boy, running with the Hudson Dusters. Not
that there had been any question of allowing Bogan
to live, Bessie knew. Once he had taken Ryan's law
into his own hands, once he had murdered Nick and
gone too far, he had to be killed. After Nick there
would always be the possibility he would go after
Ryan. But it was one relationship, Bessie knew, Ryan
regretted having cemented.

It hadn't helped Bessie that Bumps Bogan had
been killed. It hadn't helped when she had finally become Ryan's legal wife. She continued to think of
Grace in that role, anyway. Nothing had really
helped after Nick died.

Ryan put his newspaper aside and came to her,
putting his arms around her. But the electricity of his
touch—once she would have gladly died for it—was
gone now, as if it had never been.

"I'd like to give you that party, my dear."

She kissed him because, after all, it wasn't his fault.
If she had believed that he could keep Nick safe,
well, it wasn't his responsibility that he hadn't been
able to. He had always acted in good faith. He had
always been honest with her even when she hadn't
wanted him to. She, too, had a certain responsibility.

"Listen, fat boy," she told him, "I'm just about going to get through the ceremony this morning."

After all these years a dream shared by a great
many people on the Lower East Side was about to

come true. The mayor, the governor, and representatives from half a dozen federal, state, and city authorities were to gather together as Edward Lewis introduced Eleanor Roosevelt and Eleanor Roosevelt introduced Bessie Meyer. And then Bessie would open the door to the public housing she had worked so hard for, the public housing which had been named, despite her protests, after her.

"You're absolutely certain you don't want me there?" Ryan asked as Minnie helped her on with the blue linen dress and fussed over her curls.

"Positive. It's going to be hot and long and boring and for some reason I'm suddenly nervous. I wish I didn't have to speak."

"You could sing," Ryan said, whistling a few bars of "Hey There, Fat Boy." He embraced her again. He had become increasingly affectionate of late. "I'll see you at dinner then?" he asked, standing up. "I have an appointment later on with an old acquaintance. I'm curious to see what he wants."

For a moment there was the old fire in his eyes. "Go on, then," she told him, knowing better than to ask who the old friend was and not, after all, caring very much.

After he had gone, she went out onto the terrace which was shaded by a huge striped awning. She went to the balustrade and looked down at the street where Ryan was getting into that enduring affectation of his, a black Ford. She wondered where he had gotten the gas coupons for it and decided she didn't want to know that, either.

She finished dressing and went down to her own car, telling her driver—a man too old for the army

and really too old to be driving—to take her down
Second Avenue.

She asked him to stop in front of the house on
Eighteenth Street and she remembered the morning
when Moishe Katz had brought her three brothers to
her in their striped suits. She could almost hear Nicky
clattering up and down the steps; she could almost
see Max sneaking out the servants' door to go to the
nickelodeon.

She had visited with Max and Mitsuko when she
had been in Washington the previous month. Mitsuko had seemed sad but still lovely, almost ephem-
eral. Earlier in the year her father had been taken
from Manzanar and flown to New York where he
died in a suite in the Flower Fifth Avenue Hospital.
The doctors had said it was cancer. Max said it was
disappointment.

"With what?" Bessie wanted to know.

"America."

"Manzanar isn't America, Max. America is all our
boys going to fight Hitler and Mussolini and the other
monsters. If it weren't for America, Max, where
would the world be now? The German concentration
camps . . ."

"Put down the flag, Sister. I saw the concentration
camp Mr. Tanaka was shoved into."

There hadn't been much to say to that. Still Max
continued to make propaganda films and Mitsuko
was painting again and Janie and Douglas gave the
narrow house in Georgetown a spirit and life all its
own.

The driver took her down the Bowery and across
Grand Street, past Mookie Goldstein's restaurant. She

remembered her closet bedroom and Mookie's terrible wife and the night Zuckerman gave her tickets to the theater. And she thought of Jake and once more she felt a sudden rush of guilt for forcing him to marry Mookie's unpalatable daughter.

But suddenly Jake was rich, richer than any of them. What Key West land the navy wasn't renting from him, they were buying from him at exorbitant prices. And he was in the navy, commissioned with the rank of captain, continually requesting overseas duty. Bessie prayed no one would listen, that the powers in charge would keep him at the naval base in Key West.

His son, her nephew, David, was already in England, on loan to the RAF, the youngest, handsomest pilot she had ever seen. When he came to New York to say good-bye, she thought her heart would break. He was too innocent, too brave.

When Jake went into the navy, he finally allowed Coffee to come to New York. Bessie wanted her to stay with her but she chose to live with Kay in that apartment on Central Park West. And then Frances Ellington's apartment house was requisitioned by some government branch no one had ever heard of and Frances moved in. The three women got on famously, creating their own manless family, establishing their own mini-USO in their living room. Bessie was never there when a couple of stray soldiers or sailors weren't sleeping on the sofas.

Coffee, with her looks and Kay's direction, was becoming the highest-paid model in New York, living a nightclub life, reputedly mistress to half a dozen famous men.

Bessie discounted those rumors. Kay was too motherly and Frances too wise to let that happen. Bessie
found herself visiting the three women as often as she
could, enjoying the feminine atmosphere of the apartment. Even Anna would occasionally turn up, with
her communist on her arm, wearing determinedly
dowdy suits, low and serviceable heels.

She was studying political science at Columbia
Graduate School, living with her communist. It
would pass, Bessie was confident. Hard as she might
try, Anna could never quite manage to hide that in-
cipient glamour she had inherited from her mother,
that quiet grace she had learned from Mitsuko.

The car finally pulled up in front of 264 Henry
Street, a new red brick building with casement windows and wide entrances which would eventually
house one hundred needy families in apartments that
had been destined to be both attractive and practical.

A group of neighborhood people had already
formed along with phrotographers and junior senators
and mayorial aides. She found herself saying hello to a
dozen people she had known when she was a girl,
people she had continued to see and to care for during her long years with the Henry Street Settlement.

Edward Lewis eventually pushed himself through
the crowd surrounding her and took her arm and led
her up to the new building. "I thought today," he
said, kissing her cheek, *"I'd* give *you* the A Tour."

Eleanor Roosevelt was found, the dignitaries assembled, and the newsreel cameras began to roll. After a
number of speeches Bessie was handed a large gold
key with which she formally opened **the doors to**

Bessie Meyer Houses. She found her hand trembling. It had taken so long.

After the first needy family was shown to their new quarters, she and the Lewises and Eleanor Roosevelt went across the street into the Settlement House where tea was served and poured by Miss Wald's successor, a handsome woman with a sure sense of who she was, Helen Hall. Bessie found herself telling the story of how Lillian Wald found her in the street after being hit by the red ice van.

Later, when everyone had left, she found herself staying on in the second-floor sitting room, wanting not to move, to remain at the Settlement, to savor its threadbare but very genuine comfort. Even with Miss Wald gone, it still worked for her.

People helping people, she thought as she finally said good-bye to Helen Hall and members of the staff. Not such a terrible idea to build a life upon.

She took a last look at the Bessie Meyer Houses. Someone had suggested calling them Bessie Meyer Ryan Houses but she had objected, vehemently for her. She thought that the government should build hundreds more like it, that the government should wipe out the blight of tenements which still hung over the Lower East Side and give people a chance to live a decent life. Perhaps she was a socialist, after all. And perhaps, after the war, the government would do something more. She would certainly try to nudge them a little.

Sighing, she got into the back of her car. Someone was there, waiting for her. A man with white hair and terrible scars on his face. A man who had once been big and now was shrunken. It was only after he said, "Hello, Bessie," that she recognized him.

"Red Schenk."

He said that he had seen her picture in the paper and that was how he had known where to find her.

She said she thought that he was in prison and he said that he had been, that he would still be serving his armed robbery term in Rahway but that he had broken out with five other guys.

"If you need money, Red . . ."

"No, Bessie. I don't need money."

They sat quietly for a moment in the back of the car while the driver slept in front of the glass window that separated them.

"You didn't have to kill Bogan," Bessie said after a moment. "There were other ways. The police could have . . ."

"That's what I want to tell you, Bessie: I didn't kill the bastard. Smitty—the finger—knocked him off."

"I thought Smitty was in the burnt-out-car. . . ."

"They made it look that way. The cops weren't too fussy. They found a wallet with a name in it and they bought it. So did I. Until a couple of weeks ago when this little guy who looks familiar gets put away up at Rahway. I managed to get him alone for an hour after I recognized him. He told me the whole story. Just before he died."

"How did he die?"

"He fell on a spoon, sharpened into a knife." Red Schenk looked away. "The guy had nothing to lose, Bessie. He knew I was going to kill him. He told me the truth."

"Tell me," Bessie said, although she already knew. She supposed she had known all along.

"We all should've known Ryan never was going to stand for it. Not Ryan. No one was going to cut up a piece of his pie—not even your kid brother—and not get sliced. He had Bogan kill Nick and then he had Smitty kill Bogan. Bogan had too much on Ryan to live. So Ryan got everything. Nick dead, his numbers back, and you, Bessie."

He reached for the door handle. "I just wanted to tell you, Bessie."

"Where you going, Red?"

"I loved that Nick like nobody else in the world. He was the only guy I ever met who was straight with me all the way. He shouldn't have died like that, Bessie. Not in the back of a gin mill, knocked off by Bumps Bogan. Not in front of Kay." Red opened the door. "I got nothing to lose, Bessie. I'm going to keep my appointment with my old pal Ryan." He smiled a terrible smile and then he was gone.

Bessie reached for the door. She would use the Settlement's phone, call Ryan, warn him. But suddenly she felt weak as the enormity of what she had heard penetrated and she put her hand to her chest. She touched the locket she wore. She opened it. And there he was, Nick, in one of his rare photographs, wearing a too tight suit, his sly eyes, so heavily lashed, not quite smiling. "The numbers," she told his ghost. "You had to have the numbers."

And there was Ryan's picture in the opposite compartment. I'll be his murderer, she thought, as sure as if I were standing with Red Schenk in that office in the AT&T Building, pulling the trigger. I have to call Ryan.

But she didn't. She sat there with one hand on the door, her eyes closed, and she thought of Nick. Nick dancing with her around the polished floor of B's Other Place while the band played "Hot Mustard." Nick walking away from her with that Jimmy Cagney strut of his as he took Kay to find a house in the country.

"Nick," she said aloud.

The driver, awake, lowered the window between them. "Are you all right, Mrs. Ryan?"

"Fine," she said. "You can take me home now."

The telephone was ringing when she let herself into the triplex. Minnie answered it and then held out the receiver. Bessie walked across the marble foyer floor and took it from her.

As she listened to the hoarse, official voice, in her mind's eye she saw Ryan as he had looked when she had first seen him. He was smiling. That direct, American smile of his. Do I trust it even now? she asked herself. That ghost's smile.

She said the appropriate words to the man on the other end of the wire, agreed that it was a terrible tragedy, and handed the receiver back to Minnie. Then she went up to the room they had shared. She sat in his green leather wing chair and, for the first time in seven years, for the first time since Nick died, Bessie began to cry.

By the bestselling author
of the *Wagons West series*

YANKEE

by Dana Fuller Ross

A rich and historical saga that will
carry you back to Revolutionary
America. From the shores of a
young nation to the fabled Ottoman
empire, a young man sailed in
search of honor, adventure and
love.

A Dell Book $3.50   (19841-0)